THE FRONTIERS SAGA

PART 2: ROGUE CASTES

EPISODE 5

BALANCE

RYK BROWN

The Frontiers Saga Part 2: Rogue Castes
Episode #5: Balance

CHAPTER ONE

Nathan sat patiently in the transaction office next to Jessica and Deliza. It was the sixth financial institution they had visited on just as many worlds, in their effort to move Ranni Enterprise's wealth further away from the Pentaurus cluster. It was tedious work, but critical to the future of the new Karuzari rebellion. Without the funds, the rebellion against the Dusahn Empire would die before it gained any momentum.

Jessica and General Telles had assured Nathan that there were better things for him to do with his time than chauffeur Deliza from place to place as she traded large sums of currency from one world's denomination to another. Nathan, however, had felt otherwise. Although Jessica had accompanied Deliza to provide security while on the surface, the Seiiki was still *his* ship, and he felt the need to be on her whenever she flew.

Although the Seiiki was still wanted by the Dusahn, she was the least likely ship to draw undue attention at civilian spaceports. It was not uncommon for ships of her ilk to be chartered by corporate types for multi-system hops. And Connor Tuplo *was* the Seiiki's captain of record, throughout the Pentaurus sector and all the sectors surrounding it. More than a few eyebrows would be raised if the ship arrived without her captain, and there was no time to go through the complex process of changing the ship's registration in dozens of ports.

At least, that had been Nathan's argument. The truth was, Nathan had little interest in the logistics of creating the Karuzari fleet. The recent addition of three more cargo ships, two propellant tankers, and the luxury liner, Mystic Empress, brought their numbers up to eight ships; plus four of the cargo pod haulers commonly referred to as boxcars. The coordination of communications, propellant conservation, jump plotting, and the distribution of consumables among all the ships was currently in disarray, but it was a task at which both Cameron and her executive officer, Commander Kaplan, not only excelled, but thoroughly enjoyed. Nathan was just relieved that no one had asked *him* to do the job.

As captain of the Seiiki, Connor Tuplo had left such tasks to Marcus and Neli, which they had managed nicely. In fact, once Captain Taylor and Commander Kaplan completed their list, Marcus and Neli would be called upon to help them acquire what they needed. It seemed an unlikely priority, considering the circumstances, but they needed to stock up on the essentials of life now, before the Dusahn's influence spread beyond the Pentaurus cluster and made acquisition of the basics even more difficult. The further out they needed to go, the more time and resources the act of acquisition required. They needed a buffer to protect themselves against future difficulties, and all of that required funding.

That had been a strong enough argument to convince General Telles that Nathan should be in charge of this mission. Not that the general would have stopped him from coming, but it was preferable that it did not come to that.

So, here they sat, waiting while yet another functionary in a well-tailored suit, basking in his own self-importance, came up with reasons to delay their transaction, hoping to keep Ranni Enterprises' funds in their little institution for just a few minutes longer. It was all Nathan could do to resist grabbing the little man by the collar and giving him a good shake as he told him the truth about what they were doing and what was at stake.

Of course, the man would likely only ponder the many ways that his institution might profit from all the doom and gloom which his world, and the rest of the Pentaurus sector, was facing. That alone was enough to keep Nathan's impulses at bay.

Nathan sighed as he leaned closer to Jessica. "This guy is taking longer than the rest," he whispered.

"I know," Jessica whispered back. "Good thing we aren't armed. I would've shot him by now."

Nathan caught the disapproving glance from Deliza, who was supposed to be his employer in the eyes of the silver-haired financial officer sitting across the table from them, and sat up straighter.

"I trust there are no problems with the requested transaction?" Deliza asked the man.

"None that I can see," he assured her. "However, it is a rather sizable transfer, and it must pass through several interstellar exchange intermediaries, all of which require the use of jump comm-drones to verify the details of the transaction prior to final execution."

"Of course."

"If you'd prefer, I can have verification sent to your hotel, and we can complete the transaction later if it's more convenient."

"That will not be necessary," Deliza insisted in a businesslike manner. "However, I should remind you we are pressed for time, as we have one more stop to make today."

"Of course. I'm sure it will not be much longer," the man promised.

Jessica's eyes darted to her left, looking through the clear partitions separating the transaction office from the institution's main floor. A new guard came and joined the one already on duty at the west door, as if to relieve him. However, the original guard did not leave. Instead, he began to look about the room, his eyes finally fixating on the very office in which they sat. Although the guard could not see through the one-way glass, Jessica felt as if he were staring right at her.

Nathan also noticed the addition of the second guard and turned his head casually to his right as another guard joined the one at the east door. A shared glance between him and Jessica confirmed that she, too, was aware of the additional guards.

"Perhaps it would be best if we were to continue on to our next destination," Jessica suggested to Deliza. "Assuming you can forward confirmation of the transaction details to Miss Ta'Akar *there*?" she asked the transaction agent.

"Uh, yes, but I'm afraid Miss Ta'Akar needs to be present at the moment of execution," the transaction agent replied.

"How much longer do you expect it to take?" Jessica asked, appearing slightly annoyed at the delay.

"These things are often hard to estimate..."

"It takes a dedicated jump comm-drone one and a half hours to complete a full cycle, system to system," Nathan commented. "We have been here nearly two hours, and an institution *this* size surely has its own personal jump comm-drone at its disposal for such transactions, does it not?"

"Of course, we have several of them, in fact," the transaction agent replied defensively. "But there is no way of knowing what delays are taking place at each of the institutions involved, and the final destination *is* outside of the Pentaurus sector..."

"Who did you notify about our presence here?" Jessica asked.

"Pardon?" The agent's hands moved from the desk to his lap.

"It was an easy question," Nathan added.

The agent began to move his right hand forward under the desktop.

"Move that hand another millimeter, and I'll make you wish you hadn't," Jessica warned.

The agent looked at her, unsure if she was serious. He then looked at Nathan.

"No, she's not kidding," Nathan assured him.

The agent looked at Deliza. "Miss Ta'Akar, I'm not sure what..."

"Do you really think the Dusahn will honor whatever agreement they made with you?" Deliza asked.

"Withdraw your right hand...now," Jessica instructed with just the slightest hint of malice. "Slowly."

"I assure you all... I am only following company policies..."

"How many guards and where are they located?" Jessica asked.

There was a determination in her voice, a confidence, and it made the transaction agent quite nervous. "Please..."

"I will not ask again," Jessica assured him.

"Two at the main doors; two at the back," the transaction agent confessed. "Palee security is undoubtedly on their way, as well." He tried to muster confidence of his own. “It would be best if you simply surrendered.”

A menacing smile came across Jessica’s face. “Well, at least there’s finally a reason for us to be riding shotgun on this trip,” she said as she rose from her seat and moved toward the transaction agent.

“What are you doing?” the agent asked, his eyes widening as he rolled back from his desk in a vain attempt to keep his distance from Jessica.

“I’m checking to see if these partitions are really one-way only,” she replied as she moved quickly around the desk toward the agent. “Get up!”

A guard from each of the doors began moving hastily toward the transaction office.

“They can see us,” Nathan reported, also rising to his feet. “Time to go.”

“Please don’t hurt me,” the agent begged as Jessica grabbed him by the collar.

“Just a little something to remember us by,” she said, after which she punched him in the nose and dropped him to the floor.

“Guns are out!” Nathan warned, grabbing Deliza and pushing her around the desk toward Jessica.

Jessica picked up the agent’s chair and tossed it through the clear partition, shattering it. A look of surprise came over her. “I didn’t actually expect that to work,” she said.

Customers on the main floor of the institution screamed as the clear partition shattered, and began running toward the exits.

“I’ll take care of the guards!” Jessica shouted. “Get Deliza back to the ship!”

“What about you?” Nathan asked.

"Pick me up on the run!" Jessica yelled back as she ran out across the main floor.

"Let's move!" Nathan urged Deliza.

Jessica stepped quickly, the assistive bodysuit under her business attire aiding in her movements. She dodged from side to side as she charged toward the nearest approaching guard in case he tried to open fire, which was unlikely since the room was full of panicking customers. Within a few steps, she launched herself in a diving tackle toward the approaching guard, taking him down and disarming him in one fluid motion. In the blink of an eye, she was back on her feet, standing over him and firing at the other three guards. First, the second guard coming toward her, then the two at the doors; her shots timed perfectly to pass between fleeing customers without hitting them. She then spun to her left, dropping down and driving her right knee into the throat of the guard she had just disarmed, removing him as an immediate threat as she took aim on the two guards approaching rapidly from the back of the main floor.

Nathan and Deliza mixed in with the fleeing customers and headed out the east door. As they passed through the exit and onto the concourse, Nathan pulled his comm-unit from his pocket and activated it.

"*Nathan?*" Vladimir's voice inquired over his comm-unit. "*What's all that noise?*"

"Get ready for immediate launch," Nathan ordered into his comm-unit.

"*What's wrong?*"

"No time to explain, just get ready to go!"

"*Shall I file a departure request now, then?*"

"Screw procedure!" Nathan insisted. "Josh knows what to do!"

"*Will you be coming here?*"

"I'll let you know," Nathan replied.

Jessica picked up one of the downed guard's weapons as she exited, meeting Nathan and Deliza outside. "Here," she said, handing Nathan one of the weapons. "They're only short-term stunners, but they're better than nothing."

"I've got the Seiiki on standby," Nathan told her.

Jessica quickly scanned the area, noting that the overhead trams were not moving. "Transit is locked down, which means local security is in on this."

"How are we going to get back to the ship?" Deliza wondered.

"Since security will be the only ones with working transports, we'll have to borrow one of theirs," Jessica replied. "Keep that gun under wraps and follow the crowds. Try to blend in, and keep moving in the direction of the spaceport."

"What are you going to do?" Nathan asked.

"I'll draw them away," she replied. "If I'm lucky, I can pick up transpo in the process."

"The spaceport is at least ten clicks, Jess," Nathan reminded her. "We'll never make it before security catches us."

"Then tell the Seiiki to liftoff now and pick us up on the fly, before they send fighters!" Jessica insisted, turning to run the opposite direction.

"Shit," Nathan muttered.

"Where is she going?" Deliza wondered.

"Don't worry about her," Nathan urged. "Just run!"

Jessica charged down the pedestrian boulevard

between the tall buildings of the Palean financial district. In the distance, she could hear warning sirens blaring as security forces approached.

Paleans stepped aside as she ran past, not wanting to get involved in whatever was going on.

Jessica ran around the corner and into one of the many transit plazas where overhead trams met to allow transfers between lines. She came to a stop, looking around as the sirens neared. She turned in the direction of the sirens and spotted several small dots in the distant sky, coming toward her between the rows of buildings.

Jessica charged up the escalator to the nearest tram platform. Once at the top, she turned toward the crowds below and opened fire with her stunner, felling innocent people left and right. Two men on the platform charged toward her, but she turned quickly and paralyzed them with her stunner. She continued down the platform, firing in all directions, making sure to draw the attention of everyone around her and, in turn, the approaching security forces.

Nathan pulled Deliza along by the hand, weaving through the surging crowds now running away from the repeated stunner fire in the distance behind them. He could only imagine what Jessica was doing back there.

"I thought we were supposed to blend in!" Deliza reminded him.

"You're right," Nathan admitted, slowing his pace to only slightly exceed those around them. He looked around as they moved, pausing occasionally to peer over the heads of others. "We need to find a place where the Seiiki can pick us up. Someplace open."

"We're in the middle of the financial district," Deliza reminded him. "There *are* no open spaces."

"Then we need to get the hell out of this district," Nathan decided. He pulled out his comm-unit as they made their way through the crowds of people. By now, they were clear of the panicked customers who had fled the financial institution and were among those merely making their way around the district as they went about their day. Sirens were not uncommon and drew little attention.

Nathan and Deliza glanced skyward as several security officers on small personal flying platforms streaked over them at high speed.

"They're going after Jessica." Deliza realized.

"Jessica can take care of herself," Nathan assured her. "We just have to keep moving."

"To where?"

"There's a park around here somewhere. I remember seeing it on the terrain-following sensors on the way in. Somewhere over there," Nathan said, pointing to his right.

Jessica finished dealing with the last of the would-be good samaritans on the transit platform, then spun around to face the approaching security forces. Four uniformed officers, riding small flying platforms controlled by tiny handlebars sprouting from their centers, were speeding toward her, descending between the rows of buildings. They swooped in low over the promenade, dividing into pairs, approaching on both sides and a few meters above the transit platform on which she stood. Jessica fired at them, intentionally missing. One officer from each pair began to decelerate, falling slightly behind the others while their partners continued to charge forward. The two leading officers returned fire, the pale-blue beams from their stunners streaking toward her. Jessica dodged from side to side as she turned and started running toward the far stairs. She felt one of the stunner beams graze and numb her left shoulder as she dodged right. She returned fire over her shoulder, looking back to gauge their rate of approach. Finally, just as they neared the platform, she leapt up onto the railing and launched herself several meters into the air just as the lead officer on her right caught up to her. She collided with the officer, sending him and his hover scooter tumbling toward the promenade below.

Jessica landed on both feet, her assistive bodysuit tensing to protect her joints from the kinetic energy of the impact. She rolled several times on the ground, avoiding multiple stunner shots from the trailing security officer as he too streaked overhead.

The officer she had collided with had not landed as gracefully and was lying dazed in a nearby flowerbed. As the other three security officers decelerated and began to turn around, Jessica leapt to her feet and sprinted to the downed officer.

The downed officer began to regain his senses and raised his weapon to fire at the approaching woman, but was too late. A stunner blast caught him in the head and chest, rendering him paralyzed. The officer lay there, staring helplessly as the perpetrator stripped both his weapon and his hover scooter.

"Sorry about that," Jessica said sarcastically, "but you should've seen that move coming. I'm gonna need to borrow your flying thingy." Jessica stuck his weapon in her belt, stepped over and picked up the officer's hover scooter, turning it upright. She glanced at the controls for a moment, pressing buttons to get it to start. Unfortunately, every attempt resulted in the same prompt on the tiny control screen. "Crap!" she cursed, trying to remember what the Palean words on the screen meant. She stepped off the scooter and moved back over to the downed officer, ripping his ID badge from his uniform. "I'm gonna need this, too."

She stepped back onto the scooter as she affixed the downed officer's ID badge to her shirt. The scooter's control screen lit up, and a green 'ready' indicator appeared. "Now, how the hell does this thing work?" she wondered.

Several stunner blasts whizzed past her. She glanced upward, realizing two of the three remaining security officers had turned around and were heading for her again. She instinctively grabbed the handle on the scooter and pushed the thumb lever on the left grip all the way forward. A restraint ring came out from the scooter's handlebars, encircling her, as two clamps came down over her feet. A split second later, the scooter's thrusters fired, sending her straight up in the air like a missile. "Holy shit!" she exclaimed, her stunner falling from her right hand as she grabbed for the other handlebar.

The scooter continued its rapid ascent, spiraling around as Jessica fought to keep her balance. A stunner beam glanced off the bottom of the scooter, and one of the thrusters quit for a second, causing the scooter to lean to one side. The scooter accelerated in the direction of the lean, trading its rate of ascent for horizontal speed. The thruster kicked back on, and Jessica finally got control of the scooter. She pulled back on the thumb lever, decreasing the thrust and transitioning into a hover at least one hundred meters above the promenade below.

Two more stunner beams streaked past her, one from below and behind and the other from her left. She leaned, bringing the scooter into an accelerating left turn in the direction of the stunner fire. As she guided the scooter into the turn, she pulled the stunner she had taken from the paralyzed officer out of her belt and fired several times. Her second and third shots both found their target, and the now-paralyzed officer slumped forward, his body barely supported by his scooter's restraint ring as the scooter's autopilot took over and started a smooth descent to land.

"Sweet!" Jessica exclaimed, leaning forward to increase her speed. Two more stunner beams streaked past above and on both sides of her. She glanced back as the other two officers fell in behind her to pursue.

And the chase is on, she thought as she leaned forward and increased her scooter's thruster power.

"*All public transit is locked down,*" Nathan told them over Vlad's comm-unit. "*It'll take us forever to reach the spaceport by foot, and I doubt Jess can keep them away from us for that long. I need you to dust off now and pick us up at that park northwest of the financial district.*"

"What park?" Vlad asked no one in particular.

"I know the one he's talking about," Loki assured him.

"If they locked down public transit, I doubt they'll release our controls for liftoff," Josh warned.

"Not a problem," Marcus insisted.

Everyone in the Seiiki's galley turned to look at him.

"When we had the ship's transponder hacked to

change her name to the Seiiki, I had them build in a manual override for her remote auto-flight systems," Marcus explained.

"Wouldn't they be able to tell?" Loki wondered.

"*Did you copy?*" Nathan asked over the comm-unit.

"Yes, I copied," Vlad replied.

"If we engage the override, the status signal doesn't change," Marcus added. "So, they'll still think they have control of us."

"We'll dust off immediately," Vlad promised Nathan over his comm-unit. "Right?" he questioned, casting an uncertain look toward Josh and Loki.

"They could move security ships in our way," Loki warned, "blocking our exit."

"Not if we liftoff quickly," Josh said. "I can quick-start the engines...get us off the deck in less than a minute."

"Not with full power, you can't," Loki argued.

"We don't need full power," Josh countered. "Not for a few minutes, at least. Not until we break atmo." Josh and Loki both looked at Vladimir.

"What are you looking at me for?" Vladimir asked. "Get us in the air." Vladimir looked at Marcus and Dalen as Josh and Loki charged out of the galley toward the flight deck. "Get to the guns, but don't spin them up until we're airborne. We don't want the power surge to tip off the port controllers."

"You got it," Dalen replied, rising from his seat.

Vladimir grabbed Marcus by the arm as he, too, rose to exit. "Are you sure the override will work?"

"It'll work," he assured him.

"What about me?" Neli asked.

"Cargo hold," Vladimir told her. "I suspect we'll be picking them up on the run, so we'll be flying with the ramp down. Be sure you stay hooked up."

"What about the door gun?" she asked as Vladimir headed for the exit.

"As soon as we dust off, fire it up. I suspect you'll need it."

Jessica leaned forward as far as she could, pushing her scooter's thrusters to full power, enabling it to achieve maximum forward speed without losing altitude. It was a delicate balancing act, since the scooter's thrusters were designed to point straight down the unit's vertical axis. Leaning too far forward traded altitude for forward speed, while not enough lean resulted in the opposite unless you throttled back... And there was no way Jessica was doing *that*. Her pursuers were already too close for comfort. Were it not for the buildings she kept weaving between, she would be an easy target for their stunners, and the chase would be over.

It had taken her a few minutes to get the hang of it, but she was already piloting the hover scooter like a pro. It reminded Jessica of the time she had tried skyboarding at the behest of her brothers, only a few years before enlisting in the Earth Defense Force. The big difference was that, although this required similar balance and body movements, the scooter had power.

Jessica leaned to her right, pulling the scooter's handlebars in the same direction and pushing them slightly forward to shave off a few meters of altitude as she picked up speed in the turn. As she rounded the corner, two blue stunner bolts streaked past her left shoulder. She ducked, squatting as she shifted her weight hard left, and pulled back on the handlebars. The scooter responded by coming around to the left, slowing, and quickly ascending.

She pulled back even harder, bringing the scooter's forward speed down to almost nothing and causing it to shoot skyward like a rocket, barely avoiding a collision with the much taller building that had appeared in front of her after her last turn.

Only one of her pursuers was able to pull off the same maneuver. The other had tried to steer around the building instead of climbing up over it and failed to make the turn in time. He glanced off the side of the building, taking a chunk out of its masonry exterior. His scooter spun out of control, flipping over twice before its autopilot systems kicked in and brought the dazed officer to a clumsy, but survivable, landing.

"*Attention, attention. This is a security directive,*" the public-address system blared across the promenade. "*All citizens are directed to evacuate the area. Please report to the nearest transit platform checkpoints and be prepared to show identification before boarding.*"

"Great," Nathan said as the message repeated. "We have to find a way off the main boulevard."

"Someone will notice," Deliza warned as they followed the mass of people slowly making their way toward the nearest transit platform.

"Probably," Nathan agreed, "but they'll definitely be on to us when we show our IDs." Nathan looked around as he started making his way to the left toward the edge of the crowd. "That park can't be more than two clicks away. If we make a break for it, we might make it." He looked at Deliza, noting her dress and shoes. "Can you run in that?"

Deliza kicked off her dress shoes, leaving them where they fell. "Not in those."

"Are you sure you want to do that?" Nathan wondered, coming to a stop. "Not all the pathways are going to be as smooth as this one, you know."

"I grew up on Haven, remember?" Deliza replied as she reached down and grabbed the hem of her business skirt and ripped the right side of it open at the seam, all the way up to her hips.

Nathan watched as Deliza tore open the left side of her skirt as well, then continued toward the side of the moving mass of people. "There's a service path coming up on the left," he told her. "Be ready."

Josh bounded up the ladder into the Seiiki's cockpit, with Loki hot on his heels. "Port control will start hailing us as soon as we start spinning up our reactors," Josh warned as he climbed into his seat on the left, "so be ready to bluff."

"What about the ground power umbilical?" Loki asked as he slid into the right seat.

"If we unlock it remotely, it'll fall off when we liftoff," Josh replied.

"It'll damage their umbilical connector," Loki stressed.

"They can bill us," Josh said as he started activating systems.

"Primaries are set, power is on internal batteries."

"How are we lookin' outside?" Josh called over his comm-set as he put it on.

"*Clear to port!*" Dalen reported over comms.

"*Clear to starboard!*" Marcus added.

"Everyone get in position for takeoff," Vladimir ordered as he topped the ladder and took up his position standing behind Josh and Loki.

"We're ready for quick-start," Josh announced.

"Spin us up," Vladimir confirmed.

"Spinning up port reactor," Loki announced.

"Spin them both up at the same time," Josh insisted.

"Batteries aren't powerful enough to start both reactors simultaneously," Loki warned.

"Then switch back to shore power," Josh instructed.

"That's not in the procedures, Josh," Loki objected.

"Neither is dusting off before the reactors are at full power, Loki."

"If there's a limiter on the umbilical..."

"The extra power will fry it," Josh said, cutting Loki off mid-sentence. "I know. They can bill us for that, too."

Loki looked back over his shoulder at Vladimir. "There might be phase problems, as well."

"I can compensate from here if there are," Vladimir assured him, moving to take a seat at the auxiliary console. "Start them both."

"Yes, sir," Loki replied, turning back to his console. "Starting port *and* starboard reactors."

A distant whine began to emanate from the Seiiki's port engine nacelle, followed a few seconds later by a similar whine from starboard.

"*Seiiki, Port Control. We show your reactors are cycling for start-up. You are not cleared for start-up. Confirm your reactors are cold and safed.*"

"Well, that didn't take long," Josh mumbled as he continued to prep for takeoff.

"What do I say?" Loki wondered.

"Just make something up," Josh told him.

"Like what?"

"Jesus, Loki!" Josh patched his comm-set into the control channel. "Port Control, Seiiki. We're showing both reactors cold and safed here. Maybe you have a malfunction on your end?"

"Josh, they can hear our reactors spinning up, you know," Loki reminded him.

"Ground crews can, but the *controllers* can't."

"But the ground crews will tell them."

"The controllers will call the ground crew foreman, and the foreman will check with the crew for our bay, who will report back to him, and then back up to port control. By that time, we'll have nearly enough power to dust off!"

"Jesus, what kind of mind works that way?"

"Works what way?" Josh demanded.

"Comes up with lies so easily," Loki replied, "and well-thought-out ones at that."

"One that gets us in the air," Josh replied.

"*Seiiki, Seiiki. This is Port Control. Your reactors are spinning up. Shut them down immediately, or we will be forced to lock down and impound your vessel.*"

"Marcus, are you sure the override will work?" Vladimir called over his comm-set.

"*It'll work!*"

"Port Control, Seiiki. We have a malfunction in our reactor control systems," Josh lied over comms. "Our reactors are starting up all by themselves."

"*Seiiki! Port Control! You are ordered to initiate a full reactor scram, or your ship will be subjected to a directed EMP blast to force your reactors to go cold! You have ten seconds to comply!*"

"Can they do that?" Vladimir wondered.

"Uh, yes, they can," Josh admitted.

"Why didn't you say that before?" Vladimir wondered.

"I forgot."

"You forgot?" Loki exclaimed in disbelief. "Do you know what an EMP will do to our systems?"

"Where are the EMP emitters?" Vladimir barked.

"In the edges of the bays!" Josh replied. "All along the rim!"

"Marcus! Dalen!" Vladimir called over his comm-set. "Do you have weapons power?"

"*About ten percent,*" Marcus replied.

"Take out the EMP emitters along the top edges of the bay! Start with the ones nearest the nacelles! Quickly!"

"Gladly," Marcus replied, powering up his turret and swinging it aft. He quickly opened fire, blasting away indiscriminately at the top edge of the bay roof that encircled the Seiiki. Chunks of permacrete flew in all directions as red-orange streaks of plasma energy leapt from both barrels in rapid succession.

"*Seiiki! Have you lost your mind?*" the controller's voice declared over comms.

"That's for all the times these fuckers overcharged us to land here!"

"I said to shoot out the emitters, Marcus!" Vladimir objected over his comm-set. "Not the whole damned building!"

"*I wanted to be sure I didn't miss any of them!*" Marcus laughed.

"I've got four security shuttles launching from the far side of the port!" Loki warned.

"How long until we have enough power to lift off?" Vladimir asked.

"At least thirty seconds," Josh insisted.

"They'll be here in twenty," Loki warned.

"Guess we can't wait, then," Josh replied, pushing the lift throttles forward.

"Josh! We won't even clear the bay!" Loki warned.

"We'll clear it," Josh argued confidently.

"Not with twenty percent power, we won't!"

"We're light, we'll clear it!" Josh insisted, pushing the throttles all the way forward.

"The book says she won't produce enough thrust at that..."

"Fuck the book!" Josh insisted as the Seiiki's engines began to scream.

"Josh!"

"*Four shuttles coming fast from starboard!*" Dalen warned over comms.

"I've been flying this bucket for five years, now!" Josh exclaimed as the ship struggled to get off the ground. "She'll make it!"

"They're coming right at us!" Loki declared. "They're going to block our takeoff!"

"*Fire between the shuttles!*" Marcus instructed Dalen. "*Make'em spread apart!*"

"*Vlad?*" Dalen called, unsure of what to do.

The ship began to rise slightly, the scream of her engines intensifying.

"Do it!" Vladimir ordered.

"*Oh, fuck!*" Dalen replied as he opened fire.

The Seiiki began to rise more quickly.

"They're still coming!" Loki warned as the walls of the bay outside slid downward.

"Fire again!" Vladimir ordered.

More red-orange bolts of plasma leapt from behind the cockpit to their right as Dalen opened fire again.

"We're rising!" Josh declared. "Come on, baby!"

"Again! Fire again!" Loki declared.

Dalen didn't wait for Vladimir to confirm the

order, firing three more blasts toward the incoming security shuttles.

"It's going to be close!" Loki declared as the Seiiki continued to rise.

Vladimir turned and looked out the forward cockpit windows as the ship rose above the damaged bay roof that had surrounded the ship only moments ago. As they cleared the top, four onrushing Palean security shuttles peeled right and left, barely avoiding a direct collision with them.

"We gotta move!" Josh declared.

"Not yet!" Loki warned. "Get more altitude first!"

"*I've got enough power to take those shuttles out, if you'd like,*" Marcus declared.

"Not yet!" Vladimir replied.

"Gimme power to the docking thrusters!" Josh insisted.

"What?"

"Trust me!"

"You got it," Loki replied.

Josh grabbed the docking controller and fired the forward docking translation thrusters at full power, holding them there long enough to get the ship moving forward, albeit at a slow rate of speed.

"It's going to take more than that," Loki warned.

"Yeah, but now we're thrusting against the roof instead of the ground," Josh pointed out as the Seiiki continued to rise.

"Reactors are at twenty-three percent!" Loki declared.

"*Those shuttles are coming back around,*" Marcus warned. "*I've got two on my side.*"

"*Two on my side, as well!*" Dalen added. "*Coming fast!*"

"If those shuttles have EMP disruptors..." Loki began.

"They won't fire them while we're over the port," Vladimir insisted. "They won't risk us crashing down into other ships!"

Four screeches came from their port side as Marcus opened fire again.

"What are you doing?" Vladimir wondered. "I didn't tell you to fire!"

"*I'm just giving them something to think about!*" Marcus replied.

Dalen followed suit, opening fire. "*Me, too!*"

"Twenty-five percent!"

"I'm gonna start moving forward!" Josh decided.

"I'd give it another ten meters," Loki warned. He was not surprised when Josh ignored his advice.

Jessica leaned to her right slightly as she backed off on her hover scooter's throttle, causing her climb to angle slightly right. As her rate of climb decreased, she glanced straight down to her left and spotted her pursuer climbing after her, pulling out his stunner to take aim as he gave chase. Seeing his stunner appear in his hand, Jessica immediately straightened up and then chopped her throttle to idle. As her vertical rate of climb quickly diminished, she pulled her stunner out of her belt again. A few seconds later, her ascent stalled, and she and her scooter began to fall back toward the surface. With the gap between them now rapidly closing, the pursuing officer opened fire with two shots streaking past Jessica on either side and the third one slamming into the bottom of her hover scooter. Despite the descent, she twisted her falling scooter around to get a clear shot and landed two stunner blasts directly into the officer climbing toward her. She fell past him as he went limp, held up only by the restraint ring around his abdomen.

Jessica throttled back up to slow her descent, but nothing happened. "Oh, shit!" She pumped the throttle several times, but still nothing. The console showed the engine was shut down, and she was falling rapidly with only seconds until she would hit the ground. She shut the system down and tried to restart it several times but, again, to no avail. She scanned the surface rushing up toward her as she tried to restart a fourth time, hoping for some trees or bushes that might break her fall, but there was nothing but concrete and open ground below her. Then, just as she was resigning herself to her inevitable demise, the scooter's thrusters sputtered to life. She jammed the throttle to full and felt an immediate surge of power that would have collapsed her knees without the help of her assistive bodysuit. Regardless, the force of the thrusters caused her to half-squat to absorb the sudden force. Her descent slowed quickly, and she came to a hover only a few meters off the ground, causing the people below to scatter in all directions for safety. An overwhelming sense of relief washed over her. She took a deep breath and sighed, looking around at the stunned faces of those in the crowd around her. A little girl, clutched in the arms of her frightened mother, looked at Jessica, smiled, and waved.

It had been a bold maneuver, more so than she had originally intended, but it had worked. She had shaken her pursuers.

Jessica pulled out her comm-unit as she continued to hover a meter off the ground. "Seiiki! Nash! What's your status?"

"*Jess!*" Vladimir replied over the comm-unit. "*We*

just dusted off! We are on our way to pick you up at the park northwest of the financial district! ETA is two minutes!"

"I'll meet you there," she replied. Jessica put the comm-unit back into her pocket, smiled and waved back to the little girl, then leaned forward hard as she gunned her throttle, speeding off between the buildings as she began to climb again.

"*You! In the black coat!*" a security officer yelled at Nathan and Deliza.

"Uh-oh." Nathan grabbed Deliza's hand, dragging her behind him as he shoved his way past the last few people between them and the edge of the promenade. He glanced behind him and spotted two officers suddenly looking his way, alerted by the other officer's shouts. "We have to make a run for it," he urged as they broke through the crowd and headed down a side street at a full run.

Deliza followed him, quickly becoming accustomed to the sensation of running barefoot, as she had in her younger days on Haven.

About halfway down the side street, Nathan stopped and turned back, firing his stunner at the two officers coming around the corner. Neither officer had anticipated the stunner fire. The first officer took a stunner blast head on, dropping him paralyzed to the ground in an instant. The second officer tripped over the first and caught Nathan's third shot in the left leg, paralyzing it, as well. His arms still working, the second officer returned fire, barely missing Deliza as she scrambled to the side for cover. Nathan fired again, this time completely immobilizing the second officer, as well. "Let's go!" he ordered, grabbing Deliza's hand again and continuing to run.

"We're not gonna make it!" Loki exclaimed as the Seiiki continued to lose altitude as she accelerated forward. One of the spaceport's many control towers was directly ahead of them, rushing toward them. "Brace yourselves!" he added, closing his eyes and readying himself for impact.

Josh pushed his flight control stick slightly left, firing thrusters that were normally used in space to push the ship to port, barely missing the control tower. "What a wuss."

After a moment, Loki opened his eyes, surprised that they had not collided with the tower.

"I can't believe you've lost faith in me," Josh complained. "And after all these years."

"What makes you think I *ever* had any faith in you?" Loki replied, returning his attention to his copilot duties. "Reactors are at thirty percent." He glanced over at the sensor display in the center of the forward console. "Port security does not appear to be pursuing."

"*Damn right they aren't,*" Marcus sneered over their comm-sets. "*They don't want to get lit up!*"

"Palee has military forces, you know," Josh reminded them. "They'll be on us in minutes."

"Just keep us low and over populated areas," Vladimir instructed. "Maybe they'll be afraid of collateral damage."

"You don't know the Palee militia," Josh said.

Jessica darted between buildings as she sped along just above the highest transit lines, snaking her way between buildings, rising as much as she dared, mentally willing the scooter to keep working. Suddenly, two security officers, who had been lying in wait, darted out in front of her from behind a building, nearly colliding with her in the process. She leaned hard to her right, chopping her throttle to idle as she did so. She and the scooter rolled over within arm's length of her airborne enemies, who were visibly upset. As she rotated upright, Jessica gunned her throttle again, the sudden surge of thrust nearly knocking the scooter out from under her feet. She wrestled with the scooter for several moments as she hurtled toward an oncoming transit car, regaining control and climbing above the car at the last moment.

Jessica glanced over her shoulder, spotting two more officers falling in behind her. She leaned further forward to increase her forward speed to maximum, turning toward the rendezvous point as she accelerated.

Nathan and Deliza ran down the street, weaving through the last of the Paleans making their way out of the area as instructed. Behind them, officers shouted for Nathan and Deliza to stop, but they ignored them.

Suddenly, blue stunner bolts slammed into one of the nearby Paleans and the man fell as they sprinted past. More stunner bolts whizzed past them, barely missing. Another bolt struck a woman beside Deliza causing her to stumble and knock Deliza to the ground, pulling Nathan down with her.

Nathan jumped up, pulling Deliza back to her feet as more stunner blasts streaked over his head. He returned fire, dropping two of the four nearest security officers, but a quick scan of the surrounding area revealed that more were closing in from either side. "Come on!" he urged, pulling her to her feet again. "We're almost there!"

Deliza scrambled back to her feet and continued on Nathan's heels. The sparse number of remaining bystanders had scattered to avoid getting taken down by stray stunner fire from the Palean security officers. While the newly empty walkways made for easier going, Nathan and Deliza now had the sickening sense that they had become easier prey.

Nathan could see the park at the end of the block, but he could also hear the screech of thrusters in the distance. Unfortunately, they were not the Seiiki's thrusters, and their sounds seemed to be coming from all directions.

Twenty seconds later, they reached the park. Nathan looked around, but the Seiiki was nowhere to be found. There were, however, at least a dozen Palean security officers closing in from all sides.

"*Drop your weapon and surrender!*" one of the officers ordered.

Nathan raised his hands slowly, indicating his surrender.

"*Drop your weapon!*" the officer repeated.

"Deliza?" Nathan whispered.

"Yes?"

"Get down... NOW!"

Deliza dropped to the ground as Nathan dove to his left. He tucked and rolled, coming up firing, taking down two officers with the first three shots. He stepped from side to side as he ran, finally diving behind a park bench while blue streaks of stunner energy rained past him, sizzling as they slammed into the trees and ground around him.

Deliza tried to find cover herself, but was immediately hit in her left leg with stunner fire. Her leg instantly went numb and limp, and she fell to the ground as two more shots completely paralyzed her.

A bolt of stunner energy caught Nathan in the left hand, causing it to go numb and limp, as well. Two more shots slammed into the bench from behind him. He spun around to return fire, only to take a blast directly in the face. He collapsed, paralyzed, on his side, staring helplessly out across the park as security officers approached.

Vladimir held his comm-unit to his ear. "Why isn't he answering?" he wondered aloud. He looked forward at Josh and Loki, who were periodically glancing out the forward windows as they flew low over the outskirts of the city, headed for the taller buildings of the financial district. "How long?"

"Thirty seconds," Loki replied. "Reactors are at forty-two percent and rising."

"These are the slowest damned reactors I have ever seen," Vladimir cursed.

"This ain't a military ship," Josh pointed out.

"Remind me to take a look at them when we get back to the Aurora," Vladimir said.

Nathan and Deliza helplessly listened to the Paleans shouting in both Takaran and Angla, advising their prisoners that they were under arrest. One of the officers cried out in warning, pointing at a distant ship approaching from between the buildings and closing in fast.

"I've got them!" Loki declared, pointing out the front windows. "They've got them!"

"Not if I can help it," Josh decided, pushing the ship lower.

"What are you doing?" Loki asked.

"I'm gonna give them a haircut," Josh replied with a slight giggle. He pushed the ship down closer as they passed between the buildings and out over the park, barely passing between two tall trees on both sides of the intersection.

The security officers hit the ground, several of them covering their prisoners, protecting them from the unknown ship's thrust wash. Two officers who failed to hug the ground were tossed into the air, sending them tumbling.

"Bring us in over that open area and spin us around so our aft end is facing them!" Vladimir ordered as he climbed out of his seat. "Then put us into a hover just above the surface."

"Where are you going?" Loki wondered, noticing that Vladimir was leaving the cockpit.

"To rescue them!"

"What?" Loki replied in disbelief.

"Marcus!" Josh called over his comm-set. "Go aft to help Vlad!"

"*On my way!*" Marcus replied.

"Dalen, can you keep those fighters away from us for a few minutes by yourself?" Josh asked.

"*I can if you keep our starboard side to them!*"

Vladimir slid down the short ladder from the forward landing to the cargo bay floor as the cargo ramp lowered. He stepped quickly over to the port weapons locker and grabbed an energy rifle, checking to ensure it was charged and ready.

Neli watched as Vladimir pulled the lid off a rectangular cargo pod and headed for the ramp, which was now approaching the level position. Her eyes widened as Vladimir continued marching out onto the ramp as it came down. "What are you doing?" she shouted.

"Break out that gun and cover me!" Vladimir ordered. "I'm going after them!"

"Are you nuts?" she yelled back, but it was too late.

Vladimir ran out and jumped off the end of the ramp, dropping the last three meters to the grassy park below as the Seiiki settled into a hover and began rotating to bring its aft end around to face Nathan and Deliza in the distance.

"Shit!" Neli cursed as she scrambled to swing the overhead mounted plasma cannon down and into the ready position. "Vladimir jumped out!" she called over her comm-set. "Hurry up and swing us around!"

Vladimir rolled as he landed, coming up firing in the direction of the nearest officers who were moving in to assist with the capture of Nathan and Deliza. Within seconds, he had dropped two officers and was running toward his friends, raising the lid from the cargo pod in front of him as a shield and dodging side to side to avoid the incoming Palean stunner fire.

Blue bolts of stunner energy bounced off of Vladimir's shield as he advanced. With the shield held in front of him with his left hand and his energy rifle in his right, Vladimir fired wildly in the direction of his friends, taking care to keep his aim at least a meter off the ground to avoid hitting them. His weapon was at its lowest power setting; he had no desire to kill any of the Paleans. As far as they knew, they were only enforcing the laws of their world.

If hit, it was unlikely to kill them, but they would definitely be knocked off their feet for a short time. Finally, he got close enough for a clear shot at the officers guarding his friends. He took out two more officers but was forced to cower behind his shield as six more opened up on him with their stunners.

Vladimir's shield was not big enough to cover him, and he took a glancing hit to his left foot, causing it to tingle. He crouched down, keeping the shield only a few centimeters above the turf, careful to keep the rest of his body behind it.

When he closed to only a few meters, several of the Palean security officers surprised him, switching their stunners to higher settings. His shield began to burn his hand as it absorbed the unending fire.

Just as Vladimir was beginning to doubt his headstrong decision-making, the area around him was flooded with red-orange energy bolts coming from behind, striking three of the six Paleans, burning holes through their bodies and dropping them to the ground in smoldering heaps.

Vladimir glanced back over his shoulder, spotting Marcus charging toward him from behind, continuing to fire as he ran.

The remaining security officers turned their fire toward Marcus, just as another of them fell. Vladimir rose and lunged forward, throwing himself shield first into the remaining two officers, bowling them over. The three men crashed to the ground together and Vladimir rolled over them to get back on his feet.

One of the officers raised his weapon to fire at Vladimir but was struck by fire from Marcus's weapon, killing him instantly.

The last officer had dropped his weapon and was about to pull his stunner stick when Vladimir swung the cargo pod lid, striking the officer in the side of his head and knocking him unconscious. "I just saved your life," he mumbled as he dropped his shield and moved over beside Nathan.

Vladimir looked at Nathan, whose eyes were open but staring straight ahead. He bent down to check that his friend was still breathing, then picked him up and put him over his shoulder.

Marcus ran up to join him, firing at the Palean officers on the nearby corner, holding them at bay.

"Get Deliza!" Vladimir ordered. "Neli," he called out over his comm-set as he struggled to his feet, his captain slung over his shoulder. "Keep the officers across the street away from us! We're on our way back!"

"Put us down!" Neli urged Josh over her comm-set.

"*There's not enough room!*" Josh insisted.

"How much more room do you need?"

"*It's wide enough; I just need a few more meters to fit in!*" Josh replied.

Neli swung the gun to her left and opened fire on the statue in the middle of the nearby fountain, blowing it to pieces. She continued firing, sweeping left to right along the edge of the fountain, blowing its waist-high walls apart and sending the massive fountain's contents spilling out onto the walkway and the grass surrounding it. "I just got you an extra twenty meters!" she told him.

"*Nice,*" Josh replied over her comm-set. Neli smiled. It wasn't often that she got a compliment from him.

Deliza, draped unceremoniously over Marcus's shoulder, bounced limply as he ran across the park. She could hear the sound of his footfalls, his breathing, and the sound of the Palean stunners, as well as the Seiiki's plasma cannons. She could smell Marcus's jacket, which desperately needed to be washed. She even caught glimpses of the grass below. But she could neither move nor speak. She was there for the ride, come what may.

"*Bring her to port so I can get a shot!*" Dalen yelled over the comm-sets.

"Neli! How far away are they?" Josh demanded.

"*Fifty meters!*"

Josh pushed his flight control stick hard over, rotating the ship quickly to port as it hovered only a few meters above the ground. "How's that?"

"*A little more!*" Dalen replied.

Josh repeated the process, stopping when he heard the screech of Dalen's plasma cannons.

"Come on, you little fucker," Dalen muttered as he fired away. The inside of his turret flashed with red-orange light as his plasma cannons fired continuously. Left, right, left, right...each barrel discharging every half second. He glanced between his targeting screen and out the windows of his turret bubble, sweeping his weapon left and right as he tried to lock onto the Palean fighters diving toward them.

"*They're in firing range!*" Loki warned over Dalen's comm-set.

"*They're thirty meters out!*" Neli warned. "*If you don't put it down they'll be unable to work their way around because of our thrust wash!*"

The diving fighters opened up, sending a spray of explosive rail gun rounds toward them. As they opened up, one of the fighters suddenly erupted in a fireball, causing the other to break off his attack run to avoid debris from his doomed leader.

"I got one!" Dalen exclaimed triumphantly.

"The other fighter is breaking off!" Loki announced as he watched the sensor display in the center of the Seiiki's main console. "He's maneuvering to come around to port!"

"I got it," Josh declared, pushing his flight control stick hard right.

Neli held on tight, one hand on the side rail and the other on the plasma cannon, as the Seiiki rotated quickly back to starboard, sending the scenery outside the open cargo bay door shifting rapidly from right to left. As she held on, she felt herself become lighter as the Seiiki dropped two meters. The sound of their engines increased in volume and pitch, and the ship set down with a thud, nearly knocking her off her feet. "Jesus! When are you going to turn on the inertial dampeners?" she wondered aloud as she put both hands back on the plasma cannon and took aim at the Palean security officers who were still giving chase to Marcus.

"*We can't spare the power until the reactors are at full power!*" Loki replied over her comm-set. "*Can you see them?*"

"Yeah!" Neli replied as she opened fire on the distant officers. "Vlad is ten meters out! Marcus is twenty!"

Vladimir ran the last few meters to the Seiiki's ramp, no longer bothering to cut left and right to avoid fire. He charged up the cargo ramp, barely changing his stride, his paralyzed friend slung over his shoulder.

Neli stopped firing to help Vladimir.

"No! Keep firing!" Vladimir insisted, falling to his knees and dropping Nathan's limp body onto the cargo bay deck. He quickly checked Nathan's pulse, then scrambled back to his feet and headed down the ramp to help Marcus. As he raised his rifle to help Neli provide cover fire, something above him caught his eye: three fast-moving objects in the sky above the opposite end of the park, closing on their position. Vladimir raised his rifle to open fire on the lead element, but paused in surprise as that element fired on the two that were following it.

Jessica cut her throttle momentarily, allowing her scooter to descend quickly after passing over the trees on the outer boundary of the park. As she fell, she leaned back, then gunned her throttle again, arresting her descent and cutting her forward speed in half at the same time. Her two pursuers streaked over the top of her. She fired, dropping one of them, but the other turned left at the last second, avoiding her fire completely as he, too, descended quickly and dove between some trees.

Jessica leaned forward again, bringing her throttle back to full power, accelerating toward the Seiiki on the far side of the park. As she did so, she could see a Palean fighter circling around to the Seiiki's starboard side at least a kilometer away. Somewhere, the other airborne security officer was lurking, waiting for her, but she had no choice. If she wanted to get off this world she had to get onto the Seiiki, and quickly.

Marcus came bounding up the ramp with Deliza slung over his shoulder as stunner fire slammed into the ground behind him. Vladimir and Neli continued their barrage, staving off incoming fire as Marcus topped the ramp and laid Deliza gently onto the deck next to Nathan.

"*We gotta liftoff, now!*" Josh declared over comm-sets.

The deck surged up under them, nearly knocking Vladimir off his feet as the Seiiki's engines screamed, and the ship leapt off the ground.

"*Rotate to port! Rotate to port!*" Dalen insisted.

Vladimir tumbled to starboard as the ship suddenly shifted to port. Neli grabbed him to prevent him from tumbling down the cargo ramp, hanging onto the side rail to avoid being pulled out the door with him as the ship rotated and climbed.

"What about Jessica?" Vladimir yelled as he scrambled to his feet.

"*We'll pick her up on the fly!*" Josh declared. "*We've got incoming!*"

A split second later, rail gun rounds slammed into the ground outside where the Seiiki had been sitting only moments ago. The slugs exploded as they struck the ground, sending grassy soil spewing in all directions, including into the cargo bay itself.

"Cargo ramp, coming up!" Neli announced as she slapped the control button.

"I've got her!" Loki declared, pointing ahead slightly left of center. The repetitive screech of Dalen's plasma cannons echoed throughout the ship as the Seiiki's cockpit was illuminated in fiery light.

"I see her," Josh replied as he guided the ship off the ground. "What the hell is she doing?"

"She's in a spiraling climb."

"On purpose?"

"Marcus! Get to your turret and help out Dalen!"

"He's only got one fighter to deal with," Marcus grumbled as he rose and headed for the ladder.

"Where there's one, there are others."

"I know," Marcus replied, struggling to keep his balance as the Seiiki tipped to one side.

"Two more fighters inbound, three clicks out!" Loki announced.

"I guess they don't like ships lifting off without permission on Palee," Josh quipped. "Hang on!"

"The cargo bay door isn't closed yet, Josh," Loki warned.

"That's why I said hang on!" Josh declared as he advanced the throttles and pitched the nose up.

Again, Vladimir went flying, but this time Neli went flying with him. Both of them landed against the cargo bay ramp as it rose past forty-five degrees relative to the cargo bay deck. Neli rolled up the ramp, headed for the constantly narrowing gap at the end, but managed to put her arms out to stop her tumble before she fell out the back.

Vladimir, who now had one hand holding tightly to the grated ramp deck, grabbed Neli's sleeve with his free hand. "I've got you!"

Jessica continued her spiraling climb, avoiding both the fire from the pursuing officer on a hover scooter and that of the attacking Palean Militia fighter as rounds meant for the Seiiki missed their target and continued on toward her. As she rotated around, she fired her stunner again and again, each time the pursuing security officer came into her line of fire. Finally, her stunner found its target and the officer went limp.

There was a sudden jolt and the sound of an explosion. Jessica felt her stomach jump into her throat as her scooter's thrust suddenly vanished and her scooter stopped climbing. "Oh, shit."

For a moment, as she reached the stalling point in her climb, she felt weightless. Then she began to fall. She glanced at the scooter's flight display. She was still eight hundred meters in the air, and there was little chance that she would survive the impact, even with the Ghatazhak assistive bodysuit under her clothing.

Josh held the Seiiki's gradual climb, taking care not to pitch straight up for fear of dumping the occupants in the cargo bay out the back of the ship.

"She's hit!" Loki declared. "She lost her engine! She's falling!"

"I can see that!" Josh replied. "Neli! Cargo bay door! Emergency open!" Josh pushed his flight control stick forward, bringing the ship level as it continued to climb, shifting to port to slide the ship underneath Jessica.

"What are you doing?" Loki asked, afraid that he already knew the answer.

"Playing catch."

With the ship now level, Neli allowed herself to roll back down the cargo ramp onto the deck, then jumped to her feet and ran to the door. She glanced over her shoulder to make sure Vladimir was also clear of the ramp. She pressed two buttons, then slapped the open button with her open palm. The cargo door suddenly reversed its direction, quickly opening. "Hang on to them!" she warned Vladimir.

"The door is open!" Loki announced.

Josh pushed the nose over as he killed the throttles, putting the Seiiki into a nose-down free fall back toward the surface of Palee. He quickly scanned his flight dynamics display as well as the contact info on the sensor display that represented Jessica.

"She's closing too fast," Loki warned.

"*What the fuck are you doing?*" Marcus barked over their comm-sets.

Vladimir tried to cover both Nathan and Deliza with his body, but failed to get a hold of the deck plating before the Seiiki pitched over and began her free fall. He and the two paralyzed bodies lifted off the deck, floating in the middle of the cargo bay, slowly rotating. Vladimir floundered about, finally getting a hold of Deliza.

"*Clear the middle of the bay!*" Josh ordered over the cargo bay's loudspeakers.

Vladimir glanced to his left out the open end of the cargo bay, spotting Jessica and her hover scooter falling toward them. His eyes opened wide. "*Oh, bozhe*!"

Vladimir shoved Deliza's limp body toward Nathan, hoping to knock them both to the other side of the cargo bay and out of the way. The force sent Deliza into Nathan and both of them began drifting toward the port side of the bay as they tumbled. The force had the opposite effect on Vladimir, sending him spinning toward the starboard side, but at a much slower rate.

Jessica struggled to get free, but her damaged scooter refused to release its grip on her feet or remove the restraint ring around her abdomen. The last thing she wanted to do was hit the ground with a scooter full of propellant. That would surely seal her fate.

As she spun and tumbled, she spotted the Seiiki in a dive directly below her. *Is he nuts?* Unfortunately, it was her only hope, so she put her arms up over her head and braced herself for impact.

A second later, she passed through the open end of the cargo bay and the Palean sunlight disappeared. She felt the scooter strike something hard, jolting her and stopping her tumble. She slammed into the cargo bay's forward bulkhead, scooter-first, careening off the ladder and onto the deck. She and her scooter rolled, bounced off the port wall, and finally came to a stop. There was a sharp pain in her left ribs. She looked down and saw that the scooter's restraint ring had snapped and tore into her skin, likely breaking one of her ribs in the process.

Despite the distraction of pain, Jessica spotted Nathan and Deliza lying on the floor just two meters away, both unmoving with eyes open.

"She's in!" Loki exclaimed with delight and amazement as he watched the cargo bay camera monitor. "Holy shit! I can't believe you did it!"

"Oh, ye of little faith," Josh replied as he pulled the ship's nose level and brought the engines back up to full power to arrest their free fall. The Seiiki settled into a hover once again, only a few meters above the buildings of the financial district below.

"How the hell did you think of that?" Loki wondered.

"It's in the Aurora's logs," Josh replied with a grin. "It ain't the first time Jess has been scooped up by a spaceship."

"*Close the cargo bay door and hold the fuck on!*" Josh instructed over the loudspeakers. "*We've still got fighters inbound!*"

Neli reactivated the cargo bay door's drive motors, causing it to begin its close cycle once more.

"*Gospadee*!" Vladimir exclaimed. "Are you alright?"

"Get me the fuck out of this thing!" Jessica demanded, wincing in pain.

"Take it easy, Josh," Loki reminded. "We still don't have inertial dampeners, and the door is still open back there."

"That's why I told them to hold on!" Josh replied in frustration as he continued to maneuver the Seiiki wildly to avoid the incoming rail gun fire from the approaching Palean fighters.

"I just don't want anyone to fall out the back!"

"And I don't wanna get shot down by those fuckin' fighters!"

"Just take it easy for one more minute," Loki pleaded. "Then we'll have enough power to give them at least some stability back there."

"Fuck!" Josh exclaimed. "What the hell are you two doin' back there!" he called over his comm-set. "Shoot those fuckers down, will ya?"

"*Keep your shorts on, you little shit!*" Marcus cursed. "*I'm not even in my turret yet!*"

"What the hell is taking you so long?" Josh demanded.

"*Wasn't exactly easy getting up here from the cargo deck while you were bouncing us about, ya know! I think I broke my fucking leg in the process!*"

"Finally!" Neli declared as the inertial dampeners came on.

"*Inertial dampeners are on, but not at full strength,*" Loki's voice warned over the cargo bay's loudspeakers.

"Are they alright?" Jessica asked as Vladimir cut through the restraint ring with a laser cutter. "Why aren't they moving?"

"Stunners," Vladimir replied as he finished cutting. "This is going to hurt." He looked at her to make sure she was ready, then quickly pulled the piece of metal tubing out of her side.

Jessica winced in pain. Blood began to ooze through her suit at the puncture sight.

Vladimir looked at the piece of tubing he had just removed. "It was in there pretty deep," he told her, concerned. "You may have a punctured lung."

"My nanites will take care of it," Jessica insisted. "Get to the bridge and make sure that crazy little fucker gets us the hell out of here."

"What about Nathan and Deliza?" Vladimir asked, finding the manual release lever on the floor of the scooter and releasing her feet from their restraints.

"I'll take care of them," Jessica insisted. "Go."

Vladimir nodded, rising to his feet. He turned to Neli. "Help her."

"I'm on it," Neli replied.

"Get me the med-kit," Jessica told her, moving slowly to crawl over to Nathan. Every movement caused intense pain in her left side. On top of that, she thought her right leg was fractured or, at the very least, very badly bruised.

Marcus climbed up into his gun turret and quickly strapped himself in. He unlocked the turret and swung it around to face the incoming fighters, opening fire as soon as his gunsight spotted a target. "I never did like this fucking planet."

"Two fighters attacking from port!" Loki warned over his comm-set.

"*What the hell do you think I'm shooting at?*" Marcus grumbled.

Loki looked at Josh, wide-eyed.

"I had to grow up with that," Josh reminded him.

"That explains a lot."

"*They're coming across to ya, kid!*" Marcus barked over Dalen's comm-set.

"I've got'em!" Dalen replied, swinging his gun to port and opening fire, then swinging his turret back to starboard as the two Palean fighters passed over them. "Damn it!"

"*I thought you said you had them!*" Marcus retorted, sounding half-serious.

"If Josh could hold this ship still for two seconds I might have nailed another one!"

"*If I hold still for two seconds it'll be the last two seconds that we're all suckin' air!*" Josh defended. "*Maybe if you could shoot straight...*"

"*...I wouldn't have to evade their fire!*" Josh finished.

Jessica opened the medical kit and pulled out a multi-med, preloaded pneumo-ject. She dialed in her medication of choice, adjusted the dosage, and then pressed it against Nathan's neck. She slid it around to where she expected his carotid artery to be located until the illuminated activation button on the top of the device turned from red to green. She pressed the button and released it. The button flashed orange several times and then turned green again, ready to deliver another dose. She looked at Nathan, who blinked. "You know how to use this?" Jessica asked Neli.

"Yes."

Jessica adjusted the dosage on the device to accommodate Deliza's lesser weight and then handed it to Neli.

"Just give me two more degrees to port," Marcus insisted. The ship turned to port, as requested, as it continued to jink about to avoid incoming rail gun fire. Marcus waited until his sights turned green and then pressed his trigger. Red-orange bolts of plasma leapt from his twin barrels, again casting flashes of light into the interior of his little bubble. There was a small flash and a puff of smoke in his sights, and the Palean fighter dove to escape. "I hit him!" Marcus declared.

"*Yeah, but you didn't kill him, old man!*" Dalen teased.

"Just so long as he can't shoot at us anymore," Marcus replied. "That's all I give a fuck about."

Vladimir stumbled through the port corridor as

the Seiiki shifted side to side and up and down, occasionally rolling to one side or the other. He rounded the corner around the forward-lift turbine housing, grabbing the cockpit ladder to keep from tumbling to starboard as the ship suddenly rolled and twisted to port.

"*More fighters inbound,*" Vladimir heard Loki announce as he started up the ladder. "*Flight of six; they'll have range on us in two minutes.*"

"Jump us out of here already!" Vladimir demanded as he topped the ladder and stepped into the Seiiki's cramped cockpit.

"The reactors are only at eighty percent!" Loki replied. "We couldn't even jump to orbit, let alone out of the system!"

Vladimir slipped into the seat behind Loki, turning toward the auxiliary console. "Jess, Neli! Strap in!" he ordered over his comm-set. "I'm shutting off inertial dampeners and all gravity plating!"

"That isn't going to be enough," Josh warned.

"It will work!" Vladimir insisted as he prepared to shut down systems and channel all available power to the jump drive.

"Range in one minute!" Loki reported.

"Give me a couple of safety harnesses!" Jessica ordered Neli.

"What's going on?" Nathan mumbled as the medication finally began to take effect.

"We're being chased by Palee Militia fighters," Jessica told him as she caught the safety harness tossed to her by Neli. "Put one on her!" she instructed Neli as she slipped the harness over Nathan's left arm.

"Why don't we just jump?" Nathan mumbled, confused and still groggy from the Palean stunners.

"Josh had to liftoff before the reactors were at full power," Jessica explained as she slipped the harness over Nathan's right arm.

"You can't do that," Nathan insisted, his speech still slightly slurred. "Too much load, it will take them longer to reach full..."

The ship suddenly lurched to one side as something exploded outside.

"*Incoming fire!*" Loki warned over the loudspeakers.

"Fasten her to the deck," Jessica told Neli, noticing that she already had the harness secured to Deliza. "Yourself, too."

"What about you?" Neli asked, noticing that Jessica hadn't yet donned the harness that Neli had dropped on the floor next to her.

"Don't worry about me," Jessica insisted, tightening the waistband on Nathan's safety harness. She hooked his safety clip onto the deck grating, reaching for her harness to put it on when the gravity suddenly disappeared, and she began to float up off the deck.

With the medication taking greater effect, Nathan was able to seize hold of Jessica's jacket to keep her from drifting away. In the next second, the ship shifted to the left, and Jessica was jerked away. Nathan kept his grip, causing her to roll over violently. He refused to let go, struggling to raise his other arm, flailing about until he finally managed to grab the back of her jacket with both hands.

Again, the ship rocked, shifting to the side. Nathan pulled with everything he had, trying to bring Jessica in closer, but he lacked the strength. He could feel his hands weakening, his grip fading. Just as he was about to lose her, Jessica grit her teeth against her injuries and twisted to grab his arm. They pulled each other closer as the scooter drifted past her.

Jessica's safety harness, although not completely secured, was on well enough to be useful. She looped the free end of one of the lose belts through Nathan's harness, quickly tying it in a simple knot, tugging it tight just as the ship was hit with another series of explosive rail gun slugs, sending its aft end sliding to port and her to starboard. The strap held as she and Nathan clung to one another for safety. "This has got to be Josh's idea," Nathan mumbled, still feeling the pins and needles in his extremities.

"Eighty-five!" Loki reported.

"Jump us to orbit!" Vladimir ordered.

"It's still not enough," Josh argued.

"Throttle down to zero!" Vladimir insisted. "That will be enough to get us to orbit and away from those fighters!"

"Uh, this thing doesn't fly too well without thrust...remember?" Josh replied.

"Just point it at the sky for a few seconds and shut down!" Loki insisted.

"Do it!" Vladimir ordered. "We can't take any more hits!"

Josh pulled the nose up, holding full power for several seconds. "Chopping power!" he announced, pulling his throttles back to idle.

"Shutting down the mains," Loki reported.

"I can't believe we're doing this," Josh said.

"Plotting jump to orbit," Loki added.

"We're losing speed...fast!" Josh reported.

"Ninety percent!" Loki continued. "It's working!"

"We're slowing!"

"*Four fighters approaching fast from our six!*" Marcus barked. "*Why the fuck are we slowing?*"

"We'll be falling in ten seconds!" Josh warned.

"*They're firing!*" Marcus reported.

"Jump calc complete!" Loki announced. "Jumping!"

The Seiiki's windows turned opaque, clearing a second later, revealing the inky, star-filled blackness of space.

"Holy shit!" Josh declared. "I can't believe that worked!"

"Jump flash!" Loki reported. "New contact! Dusahn gunboat just jumped into orbit! Closing fast!"

"Reactors are up to ninety-five percent!" Vladimir reported enthusiastically.

"Uh, we had almost no forward speed when we jumped, guys," Josh chimed in.

"The gunboat is painting us!" Loki warned.

"We're nowhere near orbital velocity!" Josh pointed out.

"Ninety-six!" Vladimir exclaimed. "It's working!"

"We're falling back to Palee!" Josh reached for the throttles. "I'm throttling back up!"

"Not yet!" Vladimir insisted. "Ninety-seven!"

"We're falling!"

"They've got a target lock on us!" Loki warned.

"Ninety-eight!"

"Vlad!" Josh exclaimed.

"*Podazhdee*!"

"What?"

"Wait, wait, wait!" Vladimir replied. "Ninety-nine!"

"Missile launch! They've launched four!" Loki announced.

"We don't even have a clear jump line now!" Josh exclaimed.

"Twenty seconds to missile impact!" Loki announced, panic in his voice.

"One hundred!" Vladimir exclaimed.

"Quick-starting mains!" Loki announced.

"Fucking finally!" Josh cursed, reaching for the throttles.

"*Dalen!*" Marcus called over comms. "*I've got no shot! Can you get a lock on those missiles?*"

"*Negative!*" Dalen replied. "*Our fuselage is in the way!*"

"Mains coming up!"

"Throttling up!" Josh reported, pushing the throttles slowly forward.

"Plotting jump!" Loki added. "Ten seconds to missile impact!"

Josh stared at his flight displays, watching as the horizon of Palee slowly fell away as the Seiiki accelerated and her nose came up. "Full power!"

"Jump plotted!" Loki announced. "Five seconds!"

"Come on," Josh urged under his breath. "Come on."

"Three..." Loki counted down.

"Come on!" Josh exclaimed.

"...Two..."

"*Oh, bozhe.*"

"...One..."

The horizon line on Josh's flight display turned green. "NOW!"

The Seiiki's windows turned opaque again, then cleared a second later.

"Loading anti-pursuit algorithm," Loki announced, breathing a sigh of relief.

"Coming hard to port and pitching up," Josh added.

Vladimir sank back down into his chair, also

breathing a sigh of relief. “Nicely done, gentlemen.” He turned back to his console. “Reactivating inertial dampeners and gravity plating.”

“You see how much easier that was?” Josh said to Loki.

“What was?”

“Not saying ‘jumping’ or ‘jump complete’,” Josh said. “It’s just a waste of time.”

“*We’re clear,*” Vladimir announced over the cargo bay loudspeakers, relief obvious in his voice. “*I’m reactivating the gravity and inertial dampeners.*”

Jessica’s full weight suddenly settled upon Nathan as the Seiiki’s gravity came back on. She rolled off of him, untying her harness from his. “Are you alright?”

“No, but I suspect I will be soon,” Nathan replied. “What about you?” he added, noticing the blood.

“I’ll be okay,” she replied. “Nanites, remember?”

“I gotta get me some of those one of these days.”

“Hey!” Deliza exclaimed in slightly slurred speech.

Nathan raised his head, turning to look at Deliza. “Are you alright?”

Deliza looked at the banged up Palean hover scooter lying on the deck a meter away from her. The side of the housing around the thrusters was torn off, revealing one whole thruster engine. Her jaw dropped in indignation. “Those are my thrusters! They’re using my thruster design! Those bastards are violating my patent!”

“Be sure to file a complaint next time we’re on Palee,” Nathan joked, laying his head back onto the deck to rest.

CHAPTER TWO

Cuddy sat patiently in the corner of the small room he and Birk shared, studying the data pad Michael had issued him the day after their arrival. The room was small, but comfortable, and had a viewer connected to the planetary networks to keep him entertained when he wasn't studying.

The door opened, and Birk entered in his usual huff.

"Nothing?" Cuddy presumed by the look on his friend's face.

"Three days," Birk mumbled as he took off his jacket. "We've been stuck here for three days, doing nothing." He looked at Cuddy sitting contently in the corner, staring at his data pad as usual. "Tell me you're not getting impatient."

"Actually, I'm rather enjoying it."

Birk's mouth dropped open. "How could you possibly be enjoying this? We do nothing. We know nothing. We can't even call any of our friends or family!"

"You don't have any friends," Cuddy remarked, his eyes still fixed on his data pad. "Other than me, that is."

"I have friends," Birk protested.

"Not ones who are going to miss you."

"Well..." Birk thought for a moment. "I have family."

"That you normally go weeks at a time without contacting," Cuddy pointed out.

Birk threw up his hands in exasperation, tossing his coat on his bed on the other side of the room. "There is nothing to do around here," he protested, plopping down in a chair at the table. "We don't even know where *here* is."

"We know it's somewhere in the Dannon valley," Cuddy said. "We can see Mount Wellesly to the east."

"Unless that's what they *want* us to think," he countered.

"Right." Cuddy put down his data pad and looked at Birk. "They've surrounded us with a giant hologram to make us *think* we're in the Dannon valley. Or better yet, they've built a massive underground dome and made it look like we're outside, just like they do in the shopping malls of Paradar." Cuddy rolled his eyes and returned his attention to his data pad.

Birk sighed in resignation. "What happened? I'm supposed to be the calm one, and you're supposed to be the crazy one."

"I'm on vacation," Cuddy replied.

"What are you talking about?"

"Vacation."

"How is *this* a vacation?" Birk argued.

"What do you do on a vacation?"

"Have fun! Party! Meet girls!"

"Or...you sit around and relax, doing nothing."

"Doesn't sound like much of a vacation to me," Birk protested.

"Compared to the previous three days, I'd say it is. At least, there are no Dusahn around here. *And* I don't have any guns buried in my backyard."

"Oh, I'm pretty sure they've got plenty of guns around here," Birk insisted. "And I'm pretty sure the Dusahn are not far away. Doesn't it worry you that they could show up at any moment?"

"We tell them we were kidnapped and interrogated by the resistance because someone saw us talking to the Dusahn in Aitkenna, for no reason, just like Michael told us."

"Like they're really going to buy that."

A knock came at the door, interrupting their conversation. Birk looked at Cuddy, then went to the door to open it. Standing on the other side was Michael Willard, the man who had greeted them when they had first arrived three days earlier.

"Am I interrupting?" Michael asked politely.

"Michael," Birk replied in surprise.

"You are surprised to see me?"

"Uh, yes."

"I did say that I would return in a few days."

"Yes, but..." Birk stumbled on his words. "I didn't even hear you drive up."

"That's because I walked."

"From where?" Birk wondered. "There's nothing around for kilometers. I mean...*nothing*. Nothing and no one."

"I apologize for that," Michael replied. "You must have felt quite abandoned." He looked around. "May I?"

"Of course." Birk stepped aside, allowing Michael to enter the small room.

"Why did you leave us here?" Cuddy wondered, doing his best not to sound like he was complaining.

"We had to be sure you were not being tracked by the Dusahn."

"By leaving us alone in the wilderness for three days?" Birk wondered. "We could have been attacked by wild animals or something."

"You were never really alone," Michael corrected. "You have been under surveillance the entire time. If your safety had been threatened, we would have responded quite promptly."

"From where?" Cuddy wondered.

"We are nearby."

Birk's eyes grew wide. "Where? I've walked all over this area and there is nothing but trees, rocks, and bushes as far as the eye can see."

Michael smiled. "We are...well hidden."

"How? By a cloaking device or something?" Birk accused.

"Nothing quite so *high tech*. If you'll gather your things, I will show you," Michael offered, stepping to the side and gesturing back toward the door.

"What things?" Birk replied, grabbing his jacket in earnest. "I hope you've got bathing facilities. We're both a little *ripe*."

Michael smiled. "I wasn't going to say anything."

"Lead the way," Birk insisted, ready to roll.

"Very well." Michael opened the door and headed out with Birk and Cuddy trailing behind.

The three men stepped out onto the porch of the small cabin and down the steps, heading out on the only path. Birk glanced behind at the old cabin that had been their prison for the last three days. He had been quite certain that they were too far from any pockets of civilization to risk hiking out on their own, especially considering what little provisions they had on hand. And, while he had been convinced that they were alone in this vast area of wilderness, for once, he welcomed being wrong.

"Where are we, anyway?" Birk asked as they followed Michael through the woods. "I mean, I know we're in the Dannon valley, but *where*?"

"Our precise location will have to remain a mystery a bit longer, I'm afraid," Michael replied. "I have only been cleared to move you to phase two of your quarantine period."

"You can't tell us where we are?" Birk wondered.

"Quarantine period?" Cuddy asked.

"Yes. It is standard procedure for new recruits. It is necessary to protect the organization," Michael explained.

"You've been *cleared*?" Birk asked, suddenly realizing the implication. "Then you're not in charge of the resistance?"

"Me?" Michael laughed to himself. "Hardly. I am simply your handler for the induction process."

"What is the induction process?" Cuddy inquired as they continued walking.

"The resistance is only a week old," Michael replied. "Our numbers are few, and we are widely scattered. In fact, none of us really knows how many of us there are. My job is to put you through a vetting process to ensure you are not Dusahn spies or sympathizers who might turn us in."

"So, the resistance isn't really a *resistance* just yet," Birk surmised.

"If you are asking if we have committed any acts of aggression against the Dusahn, then the answer is no. The only thing we are guilty of is the collection of weapons dropped to us by Na-Tan."

"But Na-Tan is dead," Cuddy said, adding, "isn't he?"

"Yeah, we saw his body on the news," Birk added, "from the memorial service on Earth. He's even got a major spot on the Walk of Heroes. They don't do that for you unless you're dead."

"I argue none of what you say," Michael replied as he turned left at a fork in the trail.

Birk stopped. "I've been that way, Michael. It's a dead end. Just a rock face. A nice waterfall, but nothing else."

Michael stopped and looked back at Birk and Cuddy, smiling. "Indulge me." He turned to continue, picking up where he left off. "I too believed Na-tan dead, but the leaflets prove otherwise."

"Dude, they're just leaflets," Birk insisted. "Anybody could have made them."

"Did you notice the characters along the bottom edge of the leaflets?" Michael inquired.

"The ones that were barely visible?" Cuddy questioned.

"Yes."

"Just a meaningless string of characters," Birk dismissed. "I figured they were a printing error or something."

"They were not an error," Michael insisted. "It was an encrypted message. A quote, actually."

"How did you decrypt it?" Birk challenged.

"It was encrypted using an old Corinari algorithm," Michael replied. "One that we are quite familiar with."

"What did it say?" Cuddy asked.

Michael stopped again, turning back to face them. "The price of freedom is the blood of those who seek it."

"That sounds familiar," Birk admitted.

"It should," Michael said as he continued down the path. "It was Na-Tan who said it."

"In his speech," Cuddy realized. "The one he gave after defeating the Yamaro...on the Walk of Heroes!"

"Precisely."

"That still doesn't prove that he's alive," Birk countered.

"No, it does not," Michael agreed. "But it does give us hope. And hope is the most powerful weapon imaginable."

"Na-Tan said *that,* as well," Cuddy pointed out. "In that very same speech, in fact."

"Which still proves nothing," Birk argued as they walked.

"It matters not if Na-Tan is alive or dead," Michael said. "What matters is that someone out there is trying to help us take back our world. Someone is risking *their* lives on *our* behalf, and without being *asked* to do so. Whether they are trying to tell us that Na-Tan is alive, or whether they are merely using his name to inspire us to fight; what matters is that we take action."

"So, because someone dropped a bunch of leaflets saying Na-Tan is alive and dropped a few weapons along with them, you're all willing to risk your lives?" Birk asked in disbelief.

"You're here as well, are you not?"

"Well, yes, but we've hardly *risked our lives.*"

"You risked your lives by trying to contact Anji," Michael pointed out.

"It was his idea," Cuddy told him, gesturing toward Birk.

"We were desperate. We needed credits," Birk defended.

"You could have declined Anji's invitation to join."

Neither Birk nor Cuddy had any reply.

"There is an old Earth quote from many centuries ago," Michael said, speaking more loudly to be heard above the sound of the waterfall they were nearing. "'All that is necessary for the triumph of evil is that good men do nothing.' We may not yet know *what* we will do to try to drive the Dusahn from Corinair, but we *do* know that we will not stand by and do *nothing.*"

They followed the trail around a large formation

of boulders, coming to a large pool of water at the base of a tall rock face. A stream of water about five meters in width poured from the top of the rock into the pool. It was a tranquil setting, one that Birk had already witnessed during his exploration of the area.

"I told you," Birk said. "Dead end."

"This place is great," Cuddy commented. "Why didn't you tell me about it?"

"I did," Birk replied. "You were too busy with that damned data pad to care."

"We could have taken a bath here," Cuddy insisted.

"Unwise," Michael said. "There are goran lizards in these pools. Not big ones, mind you, but big enough to take a sizable chunk out of you."

"Can we go back now?" Birk asked, already turning around.

Michael reached into his pocket and pulled out his comm-unit. "It's so pretty, I believe I'll take a picture."

Birk and Cuddy watched, confused, as Michael held up his comm-unit, pointing it at the waterfall to take a picture.

"There," Michael said, putting his comm-unit back into his pocket. He turned back to look at Birk and Cuddy, smiling. "I hope you don't mind getting wet."

Before they could respond, a rusty, old, metal walkway began to slowly protrude through the waterfall toward them.

"What the hell?" Birk exclaimed, watching the walkway slowly extend across the pool of water. After nearly thirty seconds, the walkway reached their side of the pool, hovering mere centimeters above the shore in front of them.

"Follow me," Michael instructed. He stepped up onto the rusty, old walkway, taking hold of the rails on either side. His first step caused the near end of the walkway to set down onto the shore, and he walked confidently across toward the waterfall, disappearing into the water a moment later.

"Unbelievable," Cuddy said in awe, stepping up onto the walkway to follow Michael.

"You said it," Birk agreed as he followed his friend across the walkway and into the waterfall, as well.

* * *

Terig sat staring out the kitchen window into the community open space behind their new home. They had only moved in a day and a half ago, after nearly two days of interrogation by the Dusahn. These surroundings were a big change for them after living only in tenement buildings since adulthood.

"It's going to take a while to get used to the view outside," Dori said as she entered the room. She kissed her husband on the forehead as she passed, moving to the window herself. "Did you notice the playground over by the grove? There are already children playing out there, this early." She turned back to the kitchen to start preparing her breakfast. "I think I'm going to like married housing."

"I already miss Gorson's," Terig commented, sipping his beverage.

"The carefree single life," she mused. "I guess we'll just have to learn to cook our own food now."

"Cook? You mean stick a package in the oven and press start?"

"No," she replied, "I mean actually prepare our food, from scratch. You know, cleaning, chopping, cooking, seasoning...all that fun stuff."

"I hope you don't expect us to grow it, as well."

"Aren't you going to be late for work?" she asked, noticing the time.

"I'm not sure I'm ready," Terig replied.

His wife looked him over again. "You look ready to me."

Terig turned to his wife. "Dori, what if I called in sick today? Or maybe for the next few days? I'm sure they'd understand, considering what we've been through."

"They'll respect you more if you show up as planned," she insisted. "It could work in your favor. Once they see how strong you are, they may even promote you to director of communications."

"A bit of a leap, don't you think?"

"Perhaps," Dori admitted, "but we have to think of our future. We need to make more money if we want to get our first pregnancy permit."

"Our *first*?" Terig said, rising from the table. "Let's not get ahead of ourselves."

"You know what I mean," Dori insisted, placing her hands on his chest as he approached. "Now, do the right thing and go to work."

"What will you do?" he wondered, putting his arms around her.

"My new job doesn't start for two more days, so I'll probably just get to know the neighbors, do a little decorating, and get us settled into our new home." Dori kissed her husband and then pushed him away. "Now, go. You don't want to be late."

"Yes, dear," he replied. Terig kissed her one more time, then headed for the front door. He grabbed his jacket and exited their home onto the front stoop. The tram stop was just a few houses down, and he could see several people already gathered, awaiting the next automated car to take them into the center of Mahtizah.

Do the right thing. Her words echoed in his mind. He wondered if she would feel that he was doing just that, if she knew the truth.

* * *

"Not exactly the kind of shower I was hoping for," Birk commented as he toweled off.

"What is this place?" Cuddy asked, hanging up his towel.

"An abandoned terrak mine," Michael explained as he dried off his hair. "This whole range is littered with them. Terrak was Corinair's primary export when it was first settled. But all mining moved to the asteroid belt once resources allowed."

"I thought these mines were sealed off because they were unstable," Birk commented.

"Yeah, didn't a lot of people die in them?" Cuddy asked. "In cave-ins?"

"Yes, which is why the Dusahn will not be looking here," Michael replied.

"Are we safe?"

"Many of these mines were used by the Corinari during the Takaran wars. They were reinforced with permacrete, and the walls were sealed to prevent degradation. They used them to store weapons and supplies, so the Corinari might continue to resist if we were invaded."

"I don't remember anything about a Corinari resistance," Cuddy remarked.

"That's because there was none," Michael explained.

There was an obvious melancholy in his tone.

"When faced with the prospect of Ghatazhak attacks, our leaders opted to accept Caius's terms of surrender in order to better preserve our way of life. It was either that, or face extinction."

"Then these mines were never used," Cuddy surmised. "Were they still stocked?"

"Some of them, yes. Unfortunately, not this one. This one was more of a fallback facility."

"Then there are others," Cuddy said.

"I assume so, although I do not know where."

"And the Dusahn don't know about them?" Birk asked as he hung his towel up.

"Our leaders destroyed all records of the mines, especially the ones that were retrofitted. Only a handful of Corinari leaders were aware of their locations. We almost couldn't find this one."

"Have you guys thought about installing a repeller field over that walkway?" Birk suggested. "Probably save you a lot on towels."

"And create an energy field that the Dusahn could easily detect from orbit," Michael countered as he headed through the door.

Birk and Cuddy followed Michael into the next room. There were dozens of lockers on either side.

Michael pointed to the lockers on the right. "Lockers forty-one and forty-two are yours. Among other things, you'll find a change of clothes in them."

Birk and Cuddy moved to the right side of the small cavern, reading the numbers on the lockers until they found theirs.

"You both have ID chips, right?" Michael asked as he began to change out of his wet clothes.

"Got them when we started college," Birk replied. "It's a requirement."

"Before you can go out again, we'll have to reprogram them."

"You can do that?" Cuddy asked, surprised.

"I thought that was illegal," Birk commented. A moment later, he realized how stupid his remark sounded.

"I thought they were locked, so you couldn't reprogram them once they were injected," Cuddy said.

"Are you kidding?" Michael replied. "I was hacking ID chips when I was a teenager." He looked at Cuddy. "I thought you were studying computer programming."

"It's not like they teach you how to hack government systems in school," Cuddy defended.

"Cuddy's not exactly the hacker type," Birk teased.

"I can hack," Cuddy insisted. "It's just that I'm more of an algorithm guy. Efficiencies and stuff."

"I'm sure we can make use of that," Michael replied. "After all, inefficiencies are usually where you find exploitable code."

"You see?" Cuddy told Birk.

"How many people do you have down here?" Birk wondered, ignoring his friend.

"Only fifteen, including the two of you," Michael replied sheepishly.

"That's it?"

"It has only been three weeks since the Dusahn invaded," Michael defended. "Far less since Na-Tan called us to arms. These things take time. We need more than just people. We need weapons, supplies, infrastructure, communications, methodologies, intelligence... The list goes on."

"Then I take it you're not going to ask us to pick up a gun and start fighting any time soon," Birk surmised.

"It is likely that you will never be asked to do so,"

Michael said as he donned his shoes. "Putting a gun in your hands would be a waste of resources, same as putting one into mine. There are more ways to fight than with brute force and violence." Michael stood, looking over Birk and Cuddy. "Are you ready?"

"So, what's the plan?" Birk asked, also standing.

"I'm not entirely sure, to be honest. You are the first recruits without military training to come here. I guess we could start with a brief tour of the facility, such as it is."

"Michael, is there any way we could contact our families?" Cuddy wondered. "To let them know we are alright?"

"Unfortunately, we do not yet have secure communications. We can communicate safely between cells, but not through the public networks."

"I promise I won't tell them anything," Cuddy insisted. "You can even listen, if you'd like."

"It is not that of which I am concerned," Michael told him. "The public networks use location tracking in order to route calls more effectively. Even with our modified comm-units, our signal would give away our location to the Dusahn."

"Assuming they are looking for it," Cuddy pointed out.

"Yes, but the existence of a signal from such a remote location might be enough to peak their curiosity. We must first find a way to mask that signal, or send its initial routing through another location. Unfortunately, I am not up on the current communications technologies. I was hoping that you might be."

"I'm only a third-year student," Cuddy said.

"You managed to break into Troji's comm-unit," Birk reminded Cuddy.

"Not the same thing," Cuddy insisted.

"All I can ask is that you give it a try," Michael said.

"I'd be happy to," Cuddy assured him.

"Very well; perhaps we should start our tour with the mess hall?" Michael suggested.

"That depends," Birk said. "Do you have anything other than the rations that were in that shack?"

Michael smiled. "I believe we have a bit more variety, yes."

* * *

"The loss of the Mystic Empress is a minor issue," General Hesson insisted.

"She would have made a fine addition to our fleet," Lord Dusahn disagreed.

"She was poorly constructed, and poorly retrofitted," General Hesson insisted. "She would have taken far too much time and resources to make battle-worthy."

"But she would have made an excellent diplomatic vessel," Lord Dusahn added. "One that we need."

"I was not aware of any diplomats amongst our ranks."

Lord Dusahn smiled at his advisor's attempt at humor. "I was speaking of myself."

"You are a conqueror, my lord, not a diplomat. Although, I am certain that you could be, if you wished."

"Our forces are spread thin. There are many worlds in this sector that might be convinced to cooperate with us without the threat of annihilation. Palee is an example."

"Palee is a world of opportunists and businessmen who make their fortunes through investments and accounting tricks," General Hesson insisted. "Their only loyalty is to their profit margins."

"As one would expect of such men," Lord Dusahn reminded his general. "I chose to secure their support through peaceful means to ensure the stability of the Pentaurus economies. An act that also demonstrates to the citizens of these worlds that we wish to enhance their security, both physical and financial."

"You need not explain your reasoning to me, my lord," General Hesson insisted. "I know your heart is that of a warrior."

"Sometimes, I must remind myself," Lord Dusahn said with a sigh.

"Do not lose faith, my lord. Your family has gotten us across the stars, to this place. It is here that the Dusahn Empire truly begins."

Lord Dusahn turned to look out the window across the city of Answari. "The young man who works for Lord Mahtize. I trust that our people are watching him?"

"Along with the rest of the passengers who arrived in the second wave of escape pods," the general replied, "as instructed. If any of them do anything suspicious..."

"He is not to be touched," Lord Dusahn insisted. "Not without my permission. But I do want to know everything he does, and I want copies of every communication that comes and goes from that facility."

"You do not trust Lord Mahtize?"

"I trust no Takaran. Especially House Mahtize."

"There is another matter," General Hesson confessed.

Lord Dusahn turned away from the window, back toward the general.

"There has been a flurry of recon drone activity the last few days," the general explained. "Not only in this system, but in all the systems within the Pentaurus cluster. Their jump signatures are somewhat subdued and difficult to detect."

"Simply shoot them down when they are detected," Lord Dusahn said, annoyed that he had to give his top general the instruction.

"They are never around long enough for us to target," General Hesson explained further. "Their sensor images do not match any of the technologies we have encountered in this sector. I suspect they are from the Aurora."

Lord Dusahn sighed with displeasure. "That ship continues to plague us."

"She has made no overt attacks as of yet," the general reminded him.

"She will," Lord Dusahn insisted. "She is only gathering intelligence on our abilities. Soon, she will begin conducting probing attacks to test our responses."

"Which will be swift and decisive," General Hesson assured his leader.

"I have an idea," Lord Dusahn said.

* * *

"Are you going to medical?" Nathan asked Jessica as they stood in the Seiiki's cargo bay, waiting for the ramp to descend.

"After I check in with Telles," Jessica replied.

"What about your ribs?"

"They'll heal."

"And the leg?" Nathan wondered as the inside of the Aurora's main hangar deck came into view beyond the descending cargo ramp.

"Just a bruise," she replied.

Nathan looked at her. "Bruise, my ass."

"I'll be fine," Jessica insisted in no uncertain terms as she started down the ramp.

"Do it for me?" he asked, following her. "I'll feel better if you do."

"*After* I report to Telles," Jessica insisted. "He *needs* to know that the Paleans are cooperating with the Dusahn."

"You both look like hell," Cameron commented as she approached the bottom of the Seiiki's cargo ramp. She looked at Jessica's torn up clothing and the bloody bandage on her side. "Are you okay?"

"What is it with you people?" Jessica wondered, stepping off the end of the ramp just before it touched the deck.

"What's with her?" Cameron asked Nathan as Jessica passed her by.

"It's that whole tough Ghatazhak thing," Nathan explained, also stepping down off the cargo ramp. "I tried to get her to go to medical and get checked out, but she insists on reporting to Telles first."

Cameron turned around to call to Jessica. "Jess, wait!"

Jessica turned around, looking annoyed.

"If you're looking for General Telles, he's waiting for us in the command briefing room." She turned back to Nathan. "There's been a development."

"For us, too," Nathan replied, falling in beside Cameron to follow Jessica.

"What happened out there?" Cameron asked.

"We had a little trouble at the bank on Palee."

"What did you do, try to rob it?"

"That probably would have been easier," Nathan replied as they walked. He tapped his comm-set. "Marcus, Jess and I have been called to a briefing.

You and Dalen give the ship the once-over and make sure she's ready for action. And tell Vlad to double-time it to the command briefing room and join us."

* * *

Passengers moved slowly through the boarding tunnel that connected the ship to the transfer station in orbit above Takara. It had been weeks since commercial passenger vessels had regularly plied the interstellar routes. Only recently had the Dusahn begun to allow the flow of travelers between systems.

The result was a surge of people seeking transport, resulting in long lines and overcrowded facilities at every stopping point. The orbital transfer station was no different. At least six ships were now docked at the station at the same time, each ship carrying at least a few hundred passengers, all of whom were scrambling to make their connecting shuttles to various points on the surface of Takara.

To make matters worse, just as many people were arriving from the surface, hoping to board ships preparing to depart for other systems within the Pentaurus cluster. Combined with the Dusahn's enhanced security measures, the process was even slower and more chaotic. The Dusahn officers assured irate travelers that scrutiny would return to normal levels in due time, but it was not enough to ease the minds of those stuck in the endless queues. Had it not been for the ominous-looking Zen-Anor, who frequently demonstrated a lack of patience for irate travelers, the crowds may have become unruly, but instead were on their best behavior despite the numerous problems and delays.

Tensen Dalott didn't mind the crowds or the delays. If anything, they worked in his favor. It had taken him two weeks to find a way back to Takara. With all of his accounts frozen, he had been forced to sell everything he had on his person to raise enough credits to get his ID chip hacked and to buy passage back to Takara. He even had to leave his wife behind with friends, much to her objection. She had begged him not to go, but he had no choice, and she knew it. He could not stand by and watch the world on which he had been born and raised be subjugated by the Dusahn. Especially after hearing the rumor that Na-Tan had returned and was arming the people of Corinair. He did not know if the rumor was true, but he knew the Corinairans. He had spent the last seven years in the Darvano system, much of it on Corinair itself. They would fight, with or without Na-Tan. And he was bound and determined to bring the same fight to the Dusahn on Takara. He was a well-connected man, and that was exactly why he had to go. He knew people who stood to lose significant wealth if the Dusahn remained in power for too long, and now he needed to make contact with them.

The problem was, he had parted on bad terms with most of them. There was a possibility that his past transgressions might be overlooked, considering the possible gains he offered, but it was a slim one at best. Takarans would do anything to protect their own wealth, even if it meant sleeping with the enemy. He would simply have to convince them that the Dusahn were lying to them.

But first, he had to get past the incoming security checkpoint.

CHAPTER THREE

Abby's eyes darted back and forth between view screens, studying the data her assistant had just brought to her.

"You see what I mean?" Derek asked, watching over her shoulder. "T-seven and T-eight, A-four and A-five, and F-one through six; all of them show at least a four-degree increase before failure. I think the new mixture might be making a difference."

"Are you sure these aren't anomalies?" Abby wondered.

"We ran the test three times under the same conditions and got the same results each time."

"Without any variance?"

"No more than a degree, and always on the same sensors."

"But these tests were not at full power," Abby reminded him.

"We need your approval to do full-power tests," Derek said.

"Four degrees is not going to be enough, not at full power," Abby pointed out. "We're going to need at least ten before I can justify a full-power test."

"Don't you think you're being a little too cautious?"

"I'm just following protocol, and you know it," Abby pointed out.

"I doubt Beta team is sticking to protocol."

"That's Suda's problem."

"I'm just sayin'... It's *your* invention, Abby."

"It's my father's invention, not mine."

"You know what I mean. It would be a shame if it was Suda who took it to the next level."

Abby sighed. "Increase the terrenium content by another seven percent and retest."

"And *then* we can do a full-power test?" Derek urged.

"If we get a ten-percent temperature increase before failure, yes."

"Yes, ma'am," Derek replied, doing his best to hide his frustration.

Abby returned her attention to the view screens as her assistant departed. A moment later, her concentration was interrupted again.

"I'm willing to change the safety protocols, *if* it will speed things up," a female voice suggested from the doorway.

Abby knew who it was without looking. "The safety protocols are there for a reason, Admiral."

"Without risk, there is no reward," Admiral Teagle replied as she entered the room. "We all appreciate your dedication to safety, Doctor Sorenson, but these are dangerous times. We need our ships to be able to jump in and out without being detected."

"And if your ships jump in, and *then* the emitters fail?"

"We have no intention of pulling their existing systems."

"I have told you time and again, Admiral, if an emitter blows during a jump, there is no telling what the effect on the ship will be. Are you really willing to take that chance?"

"Yes, I am."

"Well, I'm not," Abby replied flatly. "And as long as I'm in charge of this research team, it's my call."

"You're not the only physicist on the planet, Doctor," Admiral Teagle reminded Abby.

Abby did not care for the admiral's tone. "No, just the most qualified."

"I would think it a matter of family pride," the admiral added, trying a different approach.

"Ego makes for poor science," Abby remarked. She finally took her eyes off her view screens and turned to the woman who was annoying her. "Did you just come here to harass me again, or was your purpose more constructive?"

"I shouldn't have to remind you that Command wants results, Doctor."

"And you don't. Trust me, Admiral, when I have results, you'll be the first to know. Meanwhile, why don't you go and harass Beta team."

"Beta team doesn't need to be pressured," the admiral replied. "They realize what's at stake."

"As do I," Abby commented. "Believe me." Abby signed off her terminal and turned off her screens. "If you'll excuse me, Admiral."

"Where are you going?" Admiral Teagle asked, surprised that Abby was leaving in the middle of their conversation.

"It's after nine, and I have been at work for more than fourteen hours now. For once, I'd like to see my family while they're still awake." Abby looked the admiral in her eyes. "Unless you plan on restricting me to my lab."

Admiral Teagle did not respond at first, looking tempted to call Abby's bluff. "Of course," she finally responded. "Why don't you take the day off tomorrow, Doctor," she said, forcing an insincere smile. "Clear your mind and start fresh the next day."

"Not a bad idea, Admiral," Abby agreed. She took off her lab coat and hung it on the coat rack, picking up her overcoat and purse. "I think I'll give the entire team the day off, as well," she added, knowing that it would irritate the admiral. "That way we can all start fresh on Thursday." Abby headed out the door, not even turning her head as she bid the admiral farewell. It wasn't the first time that Admiral Teagle had tried to play her, but it might possibly be the last; Abby was certain that Alliance Command would not tolerate her lack of progress for much longer.

* * *

"Deliza," Yanni said, delighted to see his wife again. "I wasn't expecting you back until tomorrow. Is everything okay?"

Deliza walked up and threw her arms around her husband, burying her face in his neck and hugging him with all her might.

Yanni's expression changed to one of concern. It wasn't like Deliza to greet him this way, especially in front of others. "What happened?"

"I'll tell you later," Deliza promised, pulling away.

"Tell me now."

"Later, please," Deliza insisted. She turned toward the motorized cart being directed by one of the Aurora's deckhands.

"What is that?" Yanni wondered, looking at the banged-up device lying on the cart.

"It's a flying platform of some kind. Palean security uses them to get around the surface quickly," Deliza explained.

"I've never heard of them."

"They're using our thruster designs, Yanni."

"What?" Yanni moved closer, examining the thrusters. "Are you sure? It's kind of hard to tell, all banged up like this."

"I'm sure."

"Well, why bring it here?" Yanni wondered. "It's

not like we can take them to the Pentaurus patent courts."

"*This* is our next project," Deliza told him. "Guys," she called to several technicians working on the jump sub. "Take a break from the jump sub for a bit. I want this thing taken apart and scanned, piece by piece, at replication-level resolution. Materials recognition, as well."

"What do you have in mind, Deliza?" Yanni wondered.

"No time, I've got a briefing to attend," she told him. "Make sure they get it done, okay?" she added, kissing him on the cheek, before turning to exit. "See ya later."

Yanni took in a breath, letting it out slowly. "You heard her, gentlemen. Let's tear this thing down."

* * *

Terig stood on the street, a few meters to one side of the driveway that led to the main gate into the House Mahtize compound. Over the past five years, on his way to work each day, he had walked past this spot countless times, but this time was different. His heart was racing, and only intense focus kept him from becoming lightheaded. He felt anxious, as if everyone could read his intentions on his face.

Security at House Mahtize was more relaxed than one might think upon first glance. There were guards, cameras, and sensors everywhere. But their intent was to monitor guests, not employees who were thoroughly vetted prior to employment and periodically reviewed to ensure their loyalty.

The truth was, Terig had nothing to fear. He was doing exactly as he was instructed by Lieutenant Nash during his incredibly brief training aboard the Mystic Empress. He had left the data ring she had given him at home for now, opting not to take any unnecessary risks until after he was settled back in. They couldn't read his mind, and even if they did notice something unusual about his demeanor, he could assuage their suspicions with tales of his experiences on the Mystic.

What perturbed him was the knowledge that the Dusahn would be keeping an eye on him, even though he had not yet done anything wrong. Lieutenant Nash had explained to him that all of the passengers and crew who left the Mystic Empress *after* Captain Scott's speech would be suspect and under surveillance for months, if not years. She also told him that, even if the Dusahn *knew* what Terig was up to, it was likely they would *not* arrest him but rather would leave him in play as a way to leak *false* intelligence to the rebellion.

This had not made him feel any better. If he was going to risk his life, and the life of his new bride, he at least wanted his efforts to count for something. Lieutenant Nash's assurances that even false intel had value had eased his mind at the time, but now that he was about to begin his new career as a rebel spy...not so much.

Terig took several deep breaths, trying to calm his nerves. At this point, he had little choice but to report for work as expected. To do otherwise would cause even more suspicion. But the same thought kept running through his head. *Am I doing the right thing?*

The Dusahn had invaded and conquered the Pentaurus cluster, and had done so in brutal fashion...more so than the former regime of Caius Ta'Akar. But, for all intents and purposes, life on Takara appeared unchanged, as best he could tell.

The info-nets were full of both positive and negative propaganda about the Dusahn. Many argued that the Dusahn would at least keep the noble houses from having too much control over the masses and that, as the Dusahn expanded their empire, opportunities for Takaran export would increase. All that was required was for one to ignore the Dusahn's lack of respect for basic human rights and freedoms. Was that too much to ask in return for safety and prosperity? It had been an acceptable trade for Takarans under the reign of Caius. Were the Dusahn any different?

Most of his friends felt that there was nothing *they* could do about the Dusahn. In fact, most of them blamed Suvan Navarro and the Avendahl for their plight. Had the threat of retribution not curtailed the growth of the Takaran defensive fleet, the Dusahn might never have invaded.

Terig had asked himself time and again, ever since his return, if he would have made the same decision had he heard both sides of the argument. He hoped he would have, but could not be sure. He also wondered what his wife would say. She held considerable disdain for some of the atrocities committed by the Dusahn, but she, too, seemed of the mindset that it was better to yield to their new rulers and live, rather than resist and perish. He doubted she would support his decision.

It hurt Terig to keep the truth from his wife, but he had been instructed to keep her in the dark for her own protection. If the Dusahn had the same abilities to extract information as the Jung, she could be proven to be complicit and subject to execution were he caught and convicted.

Terig convinced himself that he was only being the man she had married, and, that no matter how angry she might be at him for not telling her, she would understand and forgive him in the end.

He closed his eyes and took one last deep breath. He was doing the right thing. He had made a promise; a promise to people who were taking far greater risks for worlds not their own. He had made a promise to people of honor, to people who, like him, felt obligated to do the right thing, no matter the risk.

Terig Espan opened his eyes, put one foot in front of the other, and headed up the driveway to return to work.

* * *

Tensen Dalott tried to appear uninterested as he waited in the arrivals security checkpoint line at the transfer station. The truth was, he was eavesdropping on everyone around him, trying to determine what to expect when his turn came. He had been in line for over an hour and was finally only a few steps from the checkpoint. As best he could tell, the workers simply scanned his embedded ID chip, asked some questions, and made their decision. He had seen several people escorted away, under guard, through a door to the side, but had not seen them come out. Sometimes it was an individual, sometimes an entire family. He had not been able to determine why the Dusahn had taken those people away. Had their ID chips failed inspection? Had they answered one of the Dusahn's questions incorrectly? Those who had been escorted away had not resisted in the slightest. Was it because they knew they had done nothing wrong? Or because they knew that resistance would only worsen their situation?

Tensen wondered what he would do if he were not allowed through the checkpoint. Logic dictated that he remain calm. It was entirely possible that those people were simply searched more thoroughly and then released on the other side of the checkpoint, out of Tensen's view, and allowed to continue to their shuttle of choice to the surface of Takara.

It was also possible that they were taken directly to a holding cell to await interrogation and whatever fate followed.

Another passenger was allowed through the checkpoint, and the line moved forward three steps. Tensen stepped forward. He was now the second person in line. He tried to listen but heard nothing but mumbling. He did not think there was a sound suppression field in use; he had heard one of the inspectors call to the next inspector in the row of checkpoint stations, asking him a question.

After a few minutes, the passenger at the checkpoint, a young man, threw his hands up in obvious frustration as a Dusahn guard led him toward the infamous door to the side. He was the fourth person in the last six persons to be led off.

The person in front of Tensen stepped up to the checkpoint station, and Tensen stepped forward to the holding line on the floor. From this distance, he could almost hear the questions being asked: the purpose of his visit, if he had ever been to Takara before, why he left whatever system he had come from, and what he did for a living. The questions seemed more of a way to kill time while confirming the passenger's identity.

Another woman was escorted toward the door. His odds were getting worse. Tensen stepped forward, placing his left hand, palm down, on the counter in front of him. A beam of green light passed over his hand.

"State your name and place of birth," the guard stated in heavily accented Angla.

"Tensen Dalott, Navarro province, Takara," Tensen replied.

"Why were you off-world?"

"I was on vacation on Ursoot. I've been trying to get back for more than two weeks now."

The inspector was unmoved. "Current residence?"

"Rega Seven, Pittar and Olliwilde, number three two seven, Mahtize province."

"I thought you were born in Navarro province?" the inspector questioned, casting a suspicious glance at Tensen.

"My father's contract was sold to House Mahtize when I was young. I was raised in Mahtize province."

"What do you do in Mahtize province?"

"Speculative investments," Tensen lied.

"Unmarried?"

"Widower," Tensen replied.

The inspector raised his hand, signaling for a guard.

"Is there a problem?" Tensen asked.

"Follow the guard," the inspector instructed.

"What's wrong? What did I do?" Tensen tried not to overreact but felt a display of concern was warranted.

"Citizen," the guard stated in a strong and confident tone, as if requiring absolute compliance. "You will keep your hands visible at all times, and you will follow me."

Tensen tried his best to look confused, as well as worried, as another guard stepped over and moved behind him. "Of course," he finally complied, trying to appear as scared and subdued as the guards expected him to be.

Tensen followed the first guard toward the door to the side, the same door through which he had seen others before him enter but had seen none exit. He glanced back over his shoulder, confirming that the other guard had fallen in behind him. As they approached the door, he felt his options quickly fading away. If the door led to a holding area, it was likely far more secure than out here in the open. He contemplated overpowering the guards. He had training, but had not utilized it in many years and doubted he still had the speed and agility necessary to take out both guards. Even if he was successful, there were more nearby, all well armed and wearing cold, distant expressions. His chances of escaping uninjured were less than zero.

Seconds later, they reached the door. The guard punched in a code and then pushed the door open, stepping inside. Tensen followed him in, looking around the room as he entered.

It was unremarkable, with a desk, an ID chip scanner station, and what appeared to be some sort of medical kit. A technician was standing to one side, cleaning some device.

"Sit," the technician instructed, speaking in perfect Takaran. Tensen complied as the guards stepped back out, undoubtedly to escort some other poor passenger to their doom.

"What is going on?" Tensen asked. "Did I do something wrong? I was just trying to get back home."

"You came from a world that is not yet controlled by the Dusahn. You will need to be re-chipped," the technician stated calmly.

"What's wrong with my chip?" he wondered, feeling it was an obvious question for him to ask.

"It is not of Dusahn issue," the technician explained. "All citizens of the Dusahn Empire must carry a Dusahn ID and tracking chip."

"Is that really necessary?" Tensen wondered.

"Is there a reason you do not want to be chipped?"

Tensen sighed. "I don't really like needles very much," he admitted. "And I bleed easily. It's a bit embarrassing, to be honest."

"It only requires a small puncture on the inside of your non-dominant forearm," the technician said as he prepared the injection device. "The bleeding should be minimal."

"And you've done this to everyone on Takara?"

"We are working on it," the technician replied. He armed the device then moved toward Tensen.

"Do you have to remove my original chip?" Tensen asked.

"That will not be necessary," the technician explained. "You can still use it to access your health care system, but you will no longer be able to use it to pay for goods and services. For that, you will need to use the Dusahn chip I am implanting."

"Very well," Tensen agreed, reluctantly.

The technician placed the device against Tensen's arm and pressed the trigger. There was a sudden pinch on his arm and a sharp pain. The technician pulled the device away, revealing a small wound that was oozing a little more blood than one might expect.

"See what I mean?" Tensen grimaced.

The technician dabbed the wound with a small white pad, then sprayed it with a healing compound that stopped the flow of blood and closed up the tiny puncture site. He handed Tensen a small medical packet. "If it begins to bleed again, apply the cream and bandage within this kit and see your physician."

"And this chip contains all my information, the same as my old chip?" Tensen inquired.

"A direct copy," the technician replied. "But it is tied to the Dusahn database and tracking system, as well."

"That's it?" Tensen asked in disbelief.

"That's it. You may go."

Tensen stood, unsure of which way to go.

"The other door," the technician stated.

"Thank you." Tensen took a step toward the exit, then paused. "May I ask a question?"

The technician looked at Tensen.

"What do you think of the Dusahn? What are they like?"

"The Dusahn have only our best interests at heart," the technician stated, as if reading from a script. "They will lead us to new levels of happiness and prosperity."

"Of course," Tensen replied, heading for the exit.

"Shuttles to Mahtize province are to the left, five gates down. They depart every hour. Welcome home, Mister Dalott."

Tensen nodded. "Thank you," he replied, just before he stepped through the exit.

* * *

"We apologize for the delay," the housing officer said, leading a group of refugees down the corridor. "The Mystic Empress was not set up to accommodate families. We had to combine adjoining suites, put in additional doors, and create more storage areas. We still have to create kitchenettes in many of the suites, but we can do that while they are occupied. In the meanwhile, those of you who do not yet have kitchen facilities will have to take your meals in your assigned dining facilities, according to the dining schedules."

"A far sight better than living in the cargo pods on the Glendanon," one of the refugees commented.

"Yes, I imagine so," the housing officer agreed.

"Is it safe for children?" a woman clutching her young daughter asked.

"As long as they remain in the public areas, yes. Most non-public areas normally have secured access, but many of those have been temporarily disabled to aid in the reconfiguration process. We would recommend that children not be allowed to roam the ship unattended."

The procession reached a small central hub, from which the corridors split into four directions. The housing officer stopped, turning around and stepping backward toward the far side of the intersection to allow most of the group to enter the hub. "This is your new neighborhood: section four, level C. Odd numbers are to port, even numbers are to starboard. There are small observation decks to either side of this hub, with gangways that lead up and down. All of the cabins in this section are currently unlocked, and the door controls are in programming mode. Once you are inside your cabin, do not leave until palm scans of all members of your family have been added to the door controls for your cabin. If you have any problems programming the door controls, please contact passenger services using your cabin communications console. Loaded into your entertainment systems, you will find an information program to acquaint yourself with the ship and her rules of conduct and operations procedures. I urge you to spend some time watching that program, as it will make everyone's life a lot easier." The housing officer took a breath, raising his data pad. "I will now call out your cabin assignments. Please listen for your family name and move to your cabins as expeditiously as possible. And welcome aboard the Mystic Empress." The officer looked at his data pad. "Tarallo, family of four, C one zero three."

A man and woman, each leading a child by the hand, worked their way forward through the group. The man looked at the housing officer as they approached. "That way?" he asked, pointing forward beyond the officer.

"Second to the last door on your left," the officer replied, smiling.

"Thank you," the man said, nodding respectfully. He put his free arm around his wife's shoulder, leading her and their children past the officer toward their new home. For the first time in weeks, hope dared to show itself on their faces.

"Contois, family of three, C one zero four," the housing officer announced.

A woman standing nearby stepped forward, followed by a teenage boy and young girl. "Thank you," the woman said as she passed.

"You are most welcome," the officer replied. "Down the corridor and on your right." He looked at his data pad again. "Nash... Uh, there are a lot of you, aren't there. Let's start with Nash, Keith, family of three, cabin C one zero nine."

Keith Nash, patriarch of the Nash clan, stepped forward, followed by his wife, Laura, and their granddaughter, Ania. "Thank you, Mister Jokinen," he said, reading the officer's name tag.

"You're quite welcome, Mister Nash." The officer looked at his data pad again as the first element of the Nash clan passed by. "Nash, Alek, family of five, C one one zero."

Keith led his wife and granddaughter down the corridor, each of them lugging what little they had managed to bring with them from Burgess. Behind him, he could hear his sons' names being called as the housing officer passed out the cabin assignments to everyone in his family. He reached their door and paused, turning to look back and watch his sons and their families coming down the corridor behind him, their faces beaming with anticipation. It had been a miserable couple of weeks, but they had survived just as they always had.

Ania was not waiting. She pushed the door to her new home open, entering with a squeal of delight, followed by her grandmother.

Keith stood at the door, waiting to exchange glances with each of his sons as they, too, led their families into their new homes. His son, Tommy, who was still single, would not be housed nearby, as he had taken a position on the Mystic's crew and would be bunked in the crew areas. But his family was safe, for now. All but Robert and Jessica... But he had become accustomed to his oldest and youngest always putting themselves in harm's way for the sake of others, and he was proud of them for it.

Once satisfied that the last of his sons' families were safe, Keith stepped through the door to join his wife and granddaughter in their new home.

* * *

As the car made its way down the streets of the base housing complex, Abby stared at the perfect little houses, each a close facsimile of the others, properly manicured and evenly spaced. Trees, so young they did not yet block the moonlight, were centered in the middle of every front yard. The only differences between the homes were their colors, the cars in their driveways, and the occasional decorative items hanging on their front porches.

Despite their attempt to create a welcoming and comfortable environment for the families of the scientists and technicians working for Special Projects, they had created the equivalent of a prison. There were no bars, guards, or fences, but their communications were monitored, and their movements were tracked by a combination of security escorts, drones, and tracking devices implanted within them. They were living in a sterile, pretend world. But they were safe.

Was that really all that mattered? It was a question Abby asked herself every day. They were undoubtedly far better off than when they were living in the refugee camps on Tanna. And they were definitely better off than many on Earth who were still living in poverty, waiting for the *recovery* to include them.

The car pulled to the side of the road and stopped. Abby looked out at her home, a single vehicle in the driveway, a light on by the front door, and a few more within.

The Alliance security officer in the front passenger seat got out of the car and looked around, then stepped back to open her door just as he always did. Abby stepped out into the evening sea air, smiled politely at the young man, bidding him a pleasant evening before heading up the walk. As usual, the man waited until Abby was safely inside before returning to the car. He and his partner would wait in the car in front of her home until such time as they were relieved. In the morning, there would be another, identical car, with two different men.

Inside her home was the only place Abby felt like the eyes of Galiardi and his military were not following her every move. Their homes were constructed to block the tracking chips implanted in their forearms. After all, they needed *some* privacy, and how much time they spent in any particular room in their own home was none of the military's business.

Abby leaned against the closed door a moment, sighing. She closed her eyes and took a few slow breaths, allowing herself to relax a bit. Afterward, she removed her coat and shoes and placed them in the closet, donning her slippers before continuing into her home, such as it was.

Inside, it was a very different story. Although all the interior layouts were virtually identical, the furnishing and decorations were not. Abby's husband had managed to procure many things from their country of birth, so at least the *inside* of their home was their own.

She made her way across the living room and down the hallway; the doors to both her children's rooms were open and their beds empty. For a moment she was concerned, but then remembered that their son was away at lacrosse camp, and their daughter was sleeping over at a friend's house down the street. She felt disappointed that she would not get to see them. She had missed the first decade of their lives while working with her father on the original jump drive project. Although she had managed to reconnect with the children during their stay on Tanna, it had been short-lived, and upon their return to Earth, she had been forced to return to work.

It is for the good of Earth, she had told them. *For the good of all humanity.* She had believed it at the time. Her father had been right all along. The jump drive had changed everything. Worlds that once were years distant were now only an hour's flight. One could literally live on Earth and commute to the Tau Ceti system, eleven and a half light years away, every day for work. She could send a message to a colleague on the other side of the sector and have a response within minutes. All because of the jump drive. Her *father's* jump drive. *Her* jump drive. Goods were imported and exported; technologies, arts and culture, and philosophies and religion were all shared throughout the core worlds of earth. All the worlds of the Alliance thrived because of the increased interconnectivity provided by the jump drive.

Yes, things had changed. But had they changed for the better?

Abby entered her bedroom and plopped down on her bed. She could hear her husband in the bathroom, music playing and water running. The man made noise wherever he went, no matter what he was doing.

Just as she was about to drift off, the bathroom door opened. "When did you get home?" he asked, carrying his dirty clothing to the closet.

Abby opened her eyes, gently stretching. "Ten minutes ago, maybe."

"I wasn't sure how late you were planning on working. There are leftovers in the fridge, if you're hungry."

"I ate at work." Abby sat up. "I have tomorrow off."

"Really?" her husband replied in disbelief. "How did you manage that?"

"Long story."

"Maybe we should go somewhere," he suggested, coming over to sit next to her on the bed.

"I think I just want to sleep in and then spend the day doing nothing, for once."

"I can do nothing," he assured her. "I'm actually pretty good at that." He reached over and took her hand. "You know, this would end if you just gave them what they want."

"You know I can't do that."

"What others do with your inventions is not your responsibility, Abby," he insisted. "You know that."

"Or so we tell ourselves, to appease our guilt."

"Your guilt is self-generated."

"Perhaps, but can you honestly tell me that no one would blame me if I gave Galiardi a stealth jump drive, and he used it to completely annihilate the Jung?"

"It isn't Galiardi's decision," he reminded her. "At least not his alone."

"Are you certain of that?"

"No one can be certain of anything," he replied. "That's the way it has always been, and that is the way it will always be. Look, I know how much you worry about this, but what if the Jung get their own jump drives? If that happens, a stealth jump drive may very well be the only thing that keeps us alive."

"Until *they* develop one." Abby looked at her husband. "Don't you see? It never stops with these people. It's a constant struggle to gain an advantage over the enemy, and exploit that advantage while you still have it. Galiardi won't be satisfied until the Jung are annihilated."

"Again, you're making assumptions..."

"The man fired a slew of KKVs at them!" Abby

exclaimed, rising from the bed in frustration. "He killed hundreds of thousands of them, if not millions."

"*After* they attacked *us*!" her husband argued.

"They didn't *attack* us," she countered, "they entered Alliance space without permission."

"Given their past transgressions, do you really think you should be splitting hairs?"

"Yes, I do! I really do!"

"Abby," her husband began, lowering his voice in hopes of defusing a commonly occurring argument in their household, before it got out of control. "If you don't give it to them, Suda will."

"At least, then I could live with myself," she insisted.

"And if Suda's stealth jump drive has a fatal flaw?" he wondered. "One that isn't discovered until it is too late? What then? What if that flaw is what the Jung exploit to get their revenge? You said it yourself, Abby, it never ends. We keep one-upping one another, into eternity. That's just the way it is. It's not *your* responsibility to decide what should and should not be created, nor how what you create should be used. You are a scientist. Your job is to discover truths. Others decide what to do with those truths."

She looked at him for a moment, gazing deeply into his eyes. "Maybe that's the problem."

CHAPTER FOUR

"How many ships are we talking about?" Nathan asked Cameron as they stepped out of the elevator and onto the Aurora's command deck.

"Six, so far," Cameron replied, "two battleships, a cruiser, and three frigates. But that's not all. Two of the ships are the same ones that we engaged in the Sol sector three weeks ago."

Nathan stopped in his tracks. "Are you sure?"

"Reasonably sure," Cameron admitted. "Emission patterns, reactor signatures, hull composition; everything matches. There are a few variations in the hull profiles, and some of the comms tech is different. But one of them had damage to one of their engine fins. Damage from a plasma cannon blast."

"Didn't you take out a chunk of a Jung cruiser's engine fin?" Nathan realized.

"We did. How did you know?"

"I read your combat logs. Nice moves, by the way."

"Then it *is* a false-flag op," Jessica commented as they continued walking toward the command briefing room.

"I knew something wasn't right about all this," Cameron said.

"No insult intended, Cam, but if *you* could figure it out, then so could Galiardi," Nathan pointed out.

"You don't really think Galiardi *wants* a war with the Jung, do you?" Jessica said.

"It is kind of hard to believe," Nathan replied.

"You wouldn't say that if you'd spent the last seven years in the Alliance," Cameron insisted. "Galiardi has been beating his drum and scaring the hell out of everyone for years now. After all the suffering the

Jung caused on Earth and throughout the core, he's virtually preaching to the choir. Although many won't admit it, most would love to see the Jung destroyed."

"But you're talking trillions of lives," Nathan said.

"Galiardi is crazy, not stupid," Jessica said. "I doubt that he would target civilians."

"No, but he has no problem if they die as a result of attacks against legitimate military targets," Cameron pointed out.

"You really believe he *knows* it's a false-flag operation?" Nathan wondered as they entered the command briefing room.

"It is a reasonable assumption," General Telles said. "Welcome back. I hear you had an interesting visit to Palee."

"Indeed," Nathan replied, taking a seat at the conference table.

"It would explain why Galiardi was so quick to recommend a missile launch," General Telles said, continuing with the original topic. "He wanted to provoke a Jung response before the leaders of the Alliance worlds learned the truth. That would give him plausible deniability, and an excuse to respond to the Jung's counterattack with even greater force."

"We may not have started this war, but we are damn well going to finish it," Nathan mumbled.

Everyone in the room looked at him.

"A quote from Earth's past. I don't remember who said it exactly."

"Do you think he knew all along?" Jessica wondered.

"It is possible," General Telles admitted. "Unlikely, but possible."

"You don't think he was working *with* the Dusahn, do you?" Cameron suggested.

"We have no evidence to support such a claim, but we also cannot rule it out."

Nathan sighed. "That's a very dangerous accusation, Cameron," he warned. "I know we're just speculating, but I would strongly suggest that such statements never leave this room. We have enough problems as it is."

"Captain Scott is correct," General Telles agreed. "We need facts, not speculation."

"Are we one hundred percent certain the ships that just arrived in the Pentaurus sector *were* part of a false-flag operation in the Sol sector?" Jessica asked.

"What?" Vladimir exclaimed as he entered the room. "Did I miss something?"

"We will need further readings to be certain," Cameron admitted. "But, as of now, both my chief sensor officer and my head of security and intelligence agree on a ninety-percent probability that at least three of the six ships are the same ones we encountered in the Sol sector three weeks ago."

"*Bozhe moi*," Vladimir said under his breath, sitting down next to Nathan and Jessica.

"Furthermore," Cameron continued, "the ships in question have changed their appearance. They no longer carry Jung markings."

"Then, assuming they are the same ships, that confirms they were trying to convince the Sol Alliance that Jung ships were invading their space," Jessica said. "The Dusahn were trying to start a war between the Alliance and the Jung."

"Undoubtedly to ensure the Sol Alliance would not come to the aid of the Pentaurus cluster," General Telles added.

"We have to do something," Vladimir insisted. "We have to let the people of Earth know the truth."

"Most of the people on Earth would love to see Galiardi erase the Jung from the galactic map," Cameron said. "They're not going to believe you, not without proof."

"Then we must get proof," Vladimir replied.

"It may not be necessary," General Telles said. "At least, not yet. The Jung have yet to retaliate for the missile strike, correct?"

"As of ten days ago, no they have not," Cameron admitted. "But don't forget, they don't have jump drives. Just because they haven't retaliated *yet* doesn't mean they aren't on their way to do precisely that."

"I'm with Vlad on this one, General," Nathan agreed. "We have to tell someone back in the Sol sector."

"We could tell Robert," Jessica suggested.

Cameron looked at General Telles. "He *is* expecting an update from us in a couple days."

"*He* would believe us," Jessica insisted. "Not that he could *do* anything about it, though."

General Telles noticed that Nathan was staring at the center of the conference table, deep in thought. "What is it, Captain Scott?"

Nathan looked up at the general. "We need to tell my father. And I'm the one who should do it."

The room became quiet.

"If the Jung discover that you are alive," Cameron began.

"That's a foregone conclusion at this point," Nathan reminded her. "Hell, we announced it to all of Corinair, remember? Sooner or later, word is going to get back to the Jung. And considering that the

Alliance just attacked them, it's not like they *need* another reason to retaliate."

General Telles thought for a moment. "It will carry more impact coming from you," he agreed. "However, it would be better for you to keep a low profile. A *very* low profile."

"Understood."

"How the hell are we going to get Nathan back to Earth without being noticed?" Vladimir wondered. "The Sol system is locked up tightly these days."

"In the Mirai," Deliza suggested, speaking up for the first time since the meeting had begun.

"You mean the Seiiki," Nathan corrected.

"No, I mean the Mirai," Deliza insisted. "Change her registration back for the trip to Earth. Pretend it's still my ship and that I'm coming to Earth to make a personal plea for help."

"But the Seiiki is armed," Vladimir reminded her.

"I don't think it will surprise anyone on Earth that we added a few guns for protection," Deliza assured him, "considering what's going on here."

"She's right," Nathan agreed. "We can send a message ahead of time, via jump comm-drone, requesting an audience with the Alliance Council."

"They'll ignore her request for help," Cameron insisted. "They'll apologize and swear that if there was something they could do, that they'd do it..."

"Agreed," Nathan said, "but they *will* hear her. That's all we need."

"How will you get past Earth security?" Cameron asked.

"We'll jump," Jessica replied. "With wingsuits, just like we did on Corinair."

"No good," Cameron insisted. "You'll have a fighter escort all the way down. They'd spot you."

"What about a HALO jump?" Jessica wondered.

"They'll follow you from space, down through atmospheric interface, and down to the surface," Cameron explained.

"We can mask their exit," Vladimir suggested.

"How?" Nathan asked.

"Coat the bottom of the hull with something that will melt away in bunches, then pretend to have a thermal shield malfunction on the way down. Make a big plasma trail behind us that will force the fighters to keep their distance, and hide your exit from the Seiiki...I mean, the Mirai."

"You want us to jump out into the middle of a plasma wake?" Nathan asked in disbelief.

"Actually, our jump suits can handle the temps. They're made of the same stuff the space-jump rigs are made of," Jessica told him. She looked at Vladimir and smiled. "That just might work, big guy."

"General, is this really necessary?" Cameron asked. "I mean, you yourself said it may not even be necessary to tell the people of Earth the truth right now. And we could still try passing the information along using Captain Nash. That's got to be a lot safer than sending Nathan and Jessica back to Earth."

"All good points," the general replied. "But there are even more compelling reasons to send Lieutenant Nash and Captain Scott back to Earth."

Cameron's eyebrows rose, as did everyone else's as they looked at the general.

"We are currently looking at a significant imbalance of power in the Pentaurus sector," the general began. "The arrival of additional Dusahn ships exacerbates this problem. The longer the imbalance remains, the more emboldened the Dusahn will become. Once they are confident in their dominance over the cluster, they will expand their sphere of influence to cover the entire sector. If they control the entire Pentaurus sector, they will have the resources, infrastructure, and population needed to become an unstoppable force."

"We can't even stop them now," Jessica commented. "Not with one warship and a handful of fighters."

"No, we cannot," General Telles agreed. "But we can harass them. We can make them uncertain of their dominance, at least for a while."

"And when they realize that we can do nothing more than harass them?" Cameron wondered.

"We need an edge," Nathan realized. "That's what you're getting at, isn't it, General?"

"Indeed."

"What edge?" Jessica wondered.

"A stealth jump drive for the Aurora," Nathan replied. He looked at Vladimir, who smiled.

"Do you think you can convince her to come?" Vladimir wondered.

"I can try," Nathan replied.

"Abby?" Jessica surmised. "Why would she want to leave the safety of Earth? Especially to come here. She's got a family, remember?"

"Actually, she just might," Cameron said. "I saw Abby at the Founders' Day celebration in Winnipeg last year. She didn't look happy. Especially when Galiardi and Teagle came by to say hello. She tried to hide it, but I could see the distrust in her eyes. I tried to get her to talk about it after they moved on, but she wouldn't. The most I could get from her was that she didn't get to spend much time with her family these days. I got the impression that Special Projects is working them pretty hard."

"Are you sure about that?" Nathan asked.

"No," Cameron admitted. "Like I said, it was just an impression."

"Another reason I should return to Earth," Nathan said to General Telles.

"Even if she agrees to come back with you, and even if she knows how to make the stealth jump drive work on the Aurora, that's not going to get you a balance of power," Cameron warned. "Not for months, if ever."

"If we can steal enough Cobra gunships, we can harass the Dusahn quite a bit," Nathan told her. "That might buy us the time we need to get the Aurora her stealth jump drive."

"We don't even know if we *can* steal some gunships," Cameron reminded him.

"We don't know that we can't either," Nathan countered. "General, all of this—stealing the gunships, telling my father the truth, convincing Abby to come back with us—we're only going to get one shot at all of it, so it all needs to be done on the same trip; at the same *time*, if possible."

"Agreed," General Telles said.

"How are we going to get Abby and her family away from the Alliance?" Cameron wondered.

"We'll figure something out on the fly," Jessica insisted. "I'm good at that."

Cameron did not look pleased. "And how do you expect to get in touch with her? Are you just going to show up at the base and flash a smile at the guard?"

"It's not like I don't have some inside connections," Nathan reminded her. "I got a message to you, didn't I?"

* * *

Admiral Galiardi entered the briefing room at the

Alliance Command Center deep inside Port Terra, moving quickly to his seat at the head of the table. Per the admiral's request, there were no salutes, or other payments of respect due his rank, offered by his subordinates. This was the room where he conducted business. This was the room where his people told him what they thought, and he did not want rank and protocol to interfere with that, at least not with *these* men and women.

"Good afternoon, people," Galiardi greeted in routine fashion as he took his seat. "Admiral Marchon?" he asked, calling to the man sitting to his left.

"The number of warships that have departed the Jung primary systems, and that we no longer track, has increased to forty-seven."

"Any change in their battle platforms?" Admiral Galiardi asked.

"None. The eight platforms that we know of have not changed their positions, nor have they shown any signs of increased activity that might indicate they were preparing to depart."

"For all we know, they are *always* ready to depart without notice," Admiral Paretti commented, tapping her stylus on the table in her usual, nervous fashion.

"Battle platforms are not rapid-response ships," Admiral Marchon replied. "However, she has a point. The usual traffic we see between the Jung battle platforms and their support worlds may simply be maintaining a constant state of readiness."

"We should assume *all* Jung forces are in a constant state of readiness," Admiral Paretti insisted.

"I thought that we were," Admiral Marchon replied.

"The Jung will not move their battle platforms,"

Admiral Galiardi insisted. "They are their most valuable assets, and they will not use them offensively."

"They know we can take them out with super KKVs," Admiral Paretti interjected.

"But they also know that we would not do so unless an all-out war breaks out," Galiardi pointed out.

"If they *do* move those battle platforms, it will be because they are expecting us to attack them," another admiral added. "And, in that case, they will move them toward Earth."

"Admiral Lewell is correct," Admiral Galiardi said. "In fact, I believe that, if the Jung suspect that we are about to attack, they will send their battle platforms into FTL and attempt to have them all come out as close to Earth as possible, so that we cannot launch our super KKVs against them for fear of destroying ourselves. That is why I am recommending a full strike on those platforms."

The room became quiet for a moment.

"Scott will never approve it," Admiral Marchon commented. "Neither will the council."

"The council just might," Admiral Paretti said.

"The council follows Scott's lead," Admiral Marchon argued.

"Not always," Admiral Galiardi insisted. "Not if given enough reason."

"You're talking about attacking the Jung's greatest military assets...the pride of their fleet," Admiral Lewell said. "That will cause them to retaliate...*in force*. Hell, I'm surprised they haven't already."

"For all we know, they may be about to," Galiardi replied. "They could have been cold-coasting ships deep into our territory for years now. Even if they haven't, we've still only got a one-year buffer between them and us. If they haven't sent ships already, they will, whether we launch a preemptive strike against their battle platforms or not."

"But sir," Admiral Paretti began to argue.

"There are forty-seven Jung warships missing," Admiral Galiardi reminded them all. "And that's not including the ones we never knew about. For all we know, there are twice as many unaccounted for."

"Which is precisely why a preemptive strike against their battle platforms is a bad idea," Admiral Paretti insisted. "We still don't know why the Jung haven't launched an all-out offensive against the nearest Alliance worlds. They've got at least eight ships within twelve days' travel of Mu Cassiopeiae. And it would be a proportional response on their part."

"Except for the fact that *they* encroached on *our* space to begin with," Galiardi said. "In clear violation of the cease-fire."

"We don't know that," Admiral Paretti argued.

"They were Jung ships," Admiral Marchon snapped.

"Have you forgotten that *we* have a Jung ship?" Admiral Paretti countered. "Would you blame the Jung if Captain Roselle took the Benakh and attacked Earth?"

"Please..."

"What *reason* would the Jung have to sneak around Alliance space and risk another war?"

"They're Jung!" Admiral Marchon exclaimed. "They cannot accept defeat. In their minds, we took what was rightfully theirs!"

"How was Earth, and all the other worlds of the core, rightfully theirs?" Admiral Paretti asked.

"The Jung believe they have the right to take everything!"

"People," Admiral Galiardi interrupted. "All I care about are the facts. And the facts are that ships of Jung design, and likely belonging *to* the Jung, entered Alliance space illegally and engaged our ships. That is a clear act of aggression. I don't *care* if these actions were sanctioned by the Jung leadership, or if they were the acts of rogue elements of the Jung military castes. All I care about are *Alliance* assets and *Alliance* worlds. If we wait for the Jung to make the next move, that move may be to launch an all-out attack against Earth, using sleeper ships that have been coasting their way in and lying in wait for years."

"That would have required most of their journey be in FTL, Admiral," Admiral Lewell pointed out. "We would have detected their FTL signatures."

"Not if they took an indirect route for most of the journey and cold-coasted the last part," Admiral Marchon protested. "Or had some sort of technology to hide their FTL signatures from our sensors."

"Or they now have jump drives," Admiral Galiardi added.

"We have no evidence of either," Admiral Paretti argued.

"Actually, we do," Admiral Marchon replied. "Do the math, Barb. There's no way they could have cold-coasted all the way to Sol in only seven years."

"If they took an indirect route and..."

"Look at their position at the time of intercept!" Admiral Marchon argued. "*Any* reverse plot you calculate from that point *proves* those ships managed to slip past our sensor nets undetected, and in a short amount of time. That indicates some sort of stealthy FTL. Or jump drives."

Admiral Paretti took a deep breath, letting it out slowly while she forced herself to calm down. As much as she hated to admit it, Admiral Marchon was right. "The Jung outnumber us by at least three to one," she began calmly. "Of that we are certain. And that does not include the ships we don't know about. True, the Jung appear to have violated the cease-fire. But we have suffered no losses, while they have suffered many."

"Compared to the losses the core worlds have suffered under Jung dominance..." Admiral Marchon began.

"The past is not the issue right now," Admiral Paretti replied, cutting Admiral Marchon off mid-sentence. "If, indeed, the Jung violated the terms of the cease-fire, then our response was more than adequate, and it sent a clear message that such violations will not be tolerated." She looked at Admiral Galiardi. "I believe that should be enough. To press further serves no other purpose than to incite another war. Is that truly what we want?"

Admiral Galiardi stared at her for a moment, taking care to respond just as calmly. "What we *want* is to protect the Earth and the worlds of the Sol Alliance. Our enemy has demonstrated both the ability and willingness to penetrate our defenses." Admiral Galiardi put his hand up, cutting Admiral Paretti off. "If, in fact, it was the Jung who committed these acts, then we are obligated to ensure that it does not happen again. If we strike now, and take out their only true means of defeating us, we will have done our duty. If we are wrong, then history will judge us harshly. Personally, I can live with that.

If we are *right*, and we do nothing, our history will be written by our enemy, and they will undoubtedly judge us as fools."

"Assuming we win," Admiral Paretti commented. "Because if you're right, and the Jung *do* have jump drives, you'll be giving them the excuse they need to unleash hell upon us all."

"Jesus, Barb," Admiral Marchon exclaimed, shocked by her remark.

"I'm not going to sugarcoat it for you, Marchon," she defended. "Not for you, not for anyone. That's why we're here."

"She's right," Admiral Galiardi agreed. "I want opinions, as well as facts, even if they do not agree with my own." He looked at Admiral Paretti. "I am aware of the risks," he explained. "But whether the Jung have jump drives or just some sort of stealth FTL capability, they *still* present an intolerable threat to Earth."

"Don't you mean the Alliance?" Admiral Paretti wondered.

Admiral Galiardi's next look was not as supportive. Neither were those of the other admirals in the room, who knew she had overstepped her bounds with her last remark. "I don't need to remind you how you came about your appointment, Admiral Paretti."

"Because Tau Ceti, Sol's biggest ally, wanted to ensure that their interests were given equal consideration by your command...*sir*," she replied respectfully.

Admiral Galiardi stared at Admiral Paretti for a moment before speaking. "I want full intelligence reports from every sector, as well as combat readiness reports from all ships and gunship squadrons," he instructed his staff. "If we are to go to war, I want to be damned sure that we are as ready as possible." He looked around the table for any signs of confusion amongst his staff, but found none. "Dismissed," he added, rising from his seat and leaving the room without another word.

"If you truly have your people's best interests at heart, you'd learn to choose your words more carefully, Barbara," Admiral Marchon commented as he gathered his things to depart.

"We Cetians tend to say what's on our minds," Admiral Paretti stated as she rose from her seat. "It's that whole *honesty* problem that you Terrans seem to have avoided," she added as she left the room.

Admiral Marchon shook his head as she left. "She'll never learn," he mumbled.

"I don't know," Admiral Lewell said. "I think she's figured things out pretty well, all things considered."

Admiral Paretti headed down the corridor, nodding respectfully at Admiral Galiardi and his aide, standing in front of the admiral's office door.

"Her comms are tapped?" Admiral Galiardi asked his aide once Admiral Paretti was out of earshot.

"Since she was first assigned to command," the admiral's aide assured him.

* * *

"And how long do we have to do this?" Vladimir asked Nathan, bracing himself mentally for an answer he did not expect to like.

"Three days," Nathan replied, filling his water bottle from the galley sink.

"It took us nearly three *weeks* to turn her into the Seiiki," Marcus said, also unhappy with Nathan's unrealistic time frame.

"But this time, you don't have to worry about fooling various port authorities or PITA."

"Pain in the ass?" Vladimir asked, confused.

"Pentaurus Interstellar Transportation Authority," Nathan explained. "Same thing, really."

"If it doesn't have to fool PITA, then who?" Neli asked.

"Where are we going?" Josh wondered.

Nathan looked at his crew for a moment. "Earth."

"You're kidding," Josh exclaimed.

"Yes!" Dalen added with excitement. "I've always wanted to go to Earth."

"Uh, I'm a deserter, or a traitor...or something, remember?" Vladimir said. "At the very least, I'm AWOL. I don't think they'll greet me with open arms."

"That's why you're not going," Nathan explained.

"What do you mean I'm not going?" Vladimir said.

"You're going with us, just not all the way to Earth."

Vladimir looked confused.

"You'll be traveling with the strike team," Nathan explained. "We'll hook up with you on the way back."

"Strike team?" Vladimir wondered.

"Everyone in the Sol sector thinks you're dead," Loki reminded Nathan. "Especially the Jung. Do you really think it's a good idea for you to go back there?"

"It's not like I'm going to walk around waving at people," Nathan replied. "I'll keep a low profile... maybe in disguise or something."

"What strike team?" Vladimir pressed.

"Maybe you shouldn't have shaved and cut off that shaggy mop you called hair," Marcus commented.

"Captain, I've got no problem going to Earth," Josh said, "but can I ask *why*?"

"We're going to steal Abby and her family from Galiardi."

"You're in contact with Abby?" Vladimir asked,

astonished. "I thought she was sequestered at Special Projects."

"We're not actually in contact with Doctor Sorenson," Nathan admitted.

"But she knows you're coming for them, right?" Loki asked.

"Not yet, no."

"Is that why we need a strike team?" Vladimir wondered.

"Uh, I don't know anything about Earth law," Marcus said, "but here they call that kidnapping."

"Only if she doesn't want to go," Nathan replied with a smile.

"That's why *you're* going, to talk her into it," Vladimir surmised. "I don't like this plan, Nathan."

"That, and to steal some Cobra gunships," Nathan said. "And, if possible, to see my father."

"I really don't like this plan," Vladimir added, shaking his head.

"You want to steal some Cobra gunships," Loki echoed dryly.

Marcus let out a laugh. "That had to be Nash's idea."

"Actually, it was Cameron's," Nathan explained, taking a drink from his water bottle.

"Gunship crews are fresh out of flight school," Vladimir said. "They're about as loyal to Galiardi and the Alliance as you can get. There's no way you're going to convince them to follow you, Nathan."

"That's why we're planning on stealing brand-new ships, straight from the factory."

"Of course," Vladimir said as if it were obvious.

"What, they ain't guarded or nothin'?" Marcus asked, a skeptical look on his face.

"I'm sure they're guarded," Nathan admitted.

"Heavily," Vladimir added. "With security codes on each ship."

"Which is why you're coming." Nathan looked at Vladimir. "You *can* crack those codes, right?"

"Probably," Vladimir replied. "But if they are still in the inspection yard, they'll all have the same codes, the one used by the inspectors. Once they are put into service, they get codes specific to their crews."

"How do you know?" Nathan wondered.

"I helped design the anti-theft systems during the Aurora's first big refit after your death," Vladimir explained. "The same system is used on all the gunships."

"How many are you planning on stealing?" Josh asked.

"That depends on how many pilots we can bring with us."

"The Aurora's got plenty of pilots," Vladimir said.

"None that she can spare," Nathan disagreed. "She needs to stay at full strength to protect the fleet."

"What about the Avendahl pilots?" Loki wondered.

"They're tasked with fleet threat detection patrols," Nathan explained.

"Then who is left?" Loki asked.

"Well, we were hoping to grab at least four, and there are three pilots right here. So, we need to find at least one more."

Josh and Loki looked at each other.

"Who is going to fly the Seiiki?" Neli wondered.

Nathan hesitated a moment. "I was thinking Marcus."

Neli's eyes widened. "What?"

"Don't worry," Josh said, "a monkey could fly the Seiiki."

"Thanks," Marcus grumbled.

"Doesn't it take two people to fly a gunship?" Loki asked.

"It can be flown by a single pilot," Nathan assured him. "But you need at least one other person to operate the weapons and shields. I'm hoping we won't have to use them, but it *would* be a good idea to have two people in each gunship."

"Neither of us has ever flown a Cobra gunship, Captain," Loki reminded him. "I don't suppose you have a flight manual or anything."

"We don't need a flight manual," Josh insisted. "It's a spaceship...with a jump drive. It flies like any other spaceship. Hell, it's about the same size as *this* ship."

"It's fully automated," Vladimir told them. "The Aurora's flight decks were redesigned to support the gunships. We can hold four of them in the forward deck and four more on the aft apron. We've got complete performance specs, maintenance guides, the works. We've even got the plans to fabricate replacement parts. We may even be able to rig up a flight simulator in the Aurora's sim bay."

"No time," Nathan insisted. "We need to leave as soon as possible."

"Why?" Marcus chimed in. "What's the hurry?"

"The Sol sector is on the verge of an all-out war with the Jung," Nathan reminded them. "If that happens, I suspect that not only will security get a lot tighter, but there won't be any gunships sitting around waiting for crews. They'll be in action. We can't afford to take that chance."

"Then, we're leaving in three days," Vladimir stated. "I guess we'd better get started."

"Actually, we're leaving within the hour," Nathan corrected.

"Then we *really* need to get started."

"We have to take Deliza to Rakuen first. More business stuff."

"I thought you said we were in a hurry," Josh said.

"I thought you said you were giving us three days to turn this ship back into the Mirai," Marcus added.

"I am," Nathan replied. "That's how long it will take us to get to Earth." Nathan took another drink, then turned to head out of the galley. "Spin her up, fellas. I want to liftoff as soon as our passengers arrive."

"Yes, sir," Josh replied.

"How many passengers?" Neli asked.

"Just Jessica and Deliza," Nathan replied. "We jump to Rakuen, take care of business, then return to the Aurora to load up and head for Earth." Nathan moved toward the exit, pausing and turning back at the hatch. "Vlad, make sure you download everything the Aurora has on the Cobra gunships before we depart. We're going to need as much time as possible with those flight manuals."

"*Bozhe*," Vladimir mumbled, as he rose. "This has got to be one of his craziest ideas yet."

"You weren't with us on the Escalon run," Marcus replied.

* * *

Tensen Dalott stepped through the exit of the Mahtize province spaceport, onto the streets of Siniterri. He paused for a moment, looking up at the pale blue sky, breathing in the air of his birth planet. It had been nearly eight years since he had felt the warmth of the Takaran sun on his face. It felt like no other he had known. This planet was home and always had been. And he was here to get it back, once and for all.

But there was much to be done.

Tensen followed the masses toward the nearby transit platforms. Spaceports were rarely located near the center of provincial capitals, and the Mahtize spaceport was no exception. But the transit cars were swift and ran frequently, day and night. Getting to town was nothing more than dragging one's luggage onto a tramcar and enjoying the high-speed ride through the countryside. And it would be the first time, since his arrival at the orbital transfer station hours earlier, that he could relax. Now that he had been chipped by the Dusahn and was on the surface, the risk of being discovered had lessened. He was now just another Takaran going about his life under Dusahn rule.

He had been on Takara for less than an hour, but had already seen signs of Dusahn occupation. Although there had been no soldiers in the spaceport, there were signs everywhere praising the Dusahn. Their propaganda machine had wasted no time spinning up lies to get the population on their side. Tensen would have to work equally as fast, or else it would become difficult to find volunteers still willing to fight. On Takara, just like everywhere else, money and security was the price of loyalty. Give the people both, and they would tolerate considerable oppression. More so on Takara than anywhere else, because oppression was the mainstay of the noble houses. Their wealth was built on the backs of the citizens of their provinces. In exchange for their support, the noble houses rewarded them with the very security they sought, as well as the finances they needed to survive. They even gave them the hope of one day attaining noble status themselves, although such advancements were rare. But they were possible, and that was enough for the masses. At least, most of them.

The same was true under Dusahn occupation: the promise of peace and stability for all, as well as growth and opportunity. The Dusahn had played their hand masterfully, appealing first to the bank accounts of nobility. The thought of greatly increased profits due to military buildup and territorial expansion was enough to buy the loyalty of every noble house in the Takaran system. The one house that had not been willing to bow to the Dusahn had been swiftly and brutally dealt with. The message had been clear: support the Dusahn and prosper; defy them and perish.

It would be a hard sell, of that Tensen was certain. The late Casimir Ta'Akar had died trying to bring true freedom and equality to the masses. And he had only the noble houses of Takara opposing him. With the Dusahn now leading the nobles, such a dream seemed completely unattainable.

But Tensen was committed. Lesser men than he had given their lives to the cause of freedom. He would not be one to exchange his honor for a warm bed, a few credits in his pocket, and false hopes from the mouths of dishonest men who preyed on the weak.

Tensen stepped onto the next available tramcar, moving immediately to the back of the compartment. The fewer eyes facing him, the better. As soon as the car was full, the doors closed, and the vehicle moved forward. It descended under the walkways outside the spaceport's main terminal, accelerating through a long underground tunnel for several minutes before climbing up out of the ground again. As it accelerated, it continued to climb, arcing right to join the main elevated tramway leading into the center of Siniterri.

Once on the main elevated tramway, the tramcar's automated piloting systems settled the vehicle into its cruise speed, positioning it evenly between cars ahead and behind it. Tensen gazed out the window at the landscape. Reddish-brown dirt covered with patches of blue-green grasses, colorful shrubbery, and tall trees of green and gold that swayed in the afternoon breezes. He could make out the suburbs beyond the trees, as well as the Corolis mountain range in the distance. He remembered family trips to those mountains when he was just a boy. He had never had the chance to take his children to those mountains. Work and responsibilities had rarely allowed for such leisurely pursuits. His wife and children had understood, of course, but it did not ease his guilt.

Tensen continued to gaze out the window at the scenery streaking past him, pretending to be lost in the passing vistas as he eavesdropped on other passengers. While most of them were discussing the usual trials and tribulations of daily life, a few were commenting on the Dusahn occupation of the Pentaurus cluster. Their conversations confirmed what he already suspected; those who had accepted rule under the noble houses, and under Caius Ta'Akar, would tolerate the Dusahn in similar fashion. To them, one ruler was just as good or bad as the next, and for the most part, who was in charge did not dramatically affect their lives. To the commoners, it was the nobles who were most affected, and they were quite sure that *those* houses would find ways to make the occupation work in their favor. It was a timeless attitude, one that the nobles themselves had depended upon to maintain their own power.

Their mindset saddened him. Where was the Takaran pride that had settled this region of space and turned it into one of the most populated and advanced sectors in the galaxy?

Tensen was determined to reawaken the pride within them, or die trying.

* * *

Robert Nash stepped through the narrow hatch from his cabin into the central corridor that spanned the length of the Tanna. Although it was the widest corridor on the Alliance destroyer, it was still somewhat narrow, requiring people to turn slightly sideways as they passed to avoid smacking shoulders.

Because of the relatively confined spaces, the usual passing formalities were eschewed in favor of efficiency aboard such a small ship. With a crew of only sixty-eight, most were on a first-name basis. And there just wasn't enough room for people to always be snapping to attention and saluting every time an officer walked past. Instead, a simple nod and polite word was all one ever expected when traversing the ship's spaces.

"Morning, Captain," the Tanna's medical officer, Lieutenant Commander Raska, greeted as the captain started down the corridor.

"Lieutenant Commander," Robert replied, nodding politely as he headed forward. The captain's cabin was only one level down and one compartment aft of the Tanna's bridge, which made for a relatively short trip. The Tanna herself was not very large. Having been upgraded from a frigate, with the addition of her side sections and extra guns, she measured in at just over eight hundred meters in length. While still the same length as her original design, the additional sections added considerable mass, as well as a lot more firepower than she had carried as a missile frigate. It still irked Robert that his ship was originally a Jung frigate, but the addition of four plasma cannon turrets and four plasma torpedo cannons more than made up for it. And while she was smaller than a standard Jung destroyer, she was more nimble. Besides, she had a three-phase jump drive, with a one-minute jump range of eighty light years, making her able to jump from one side of Alliance space and back in a single minute, while still having enough jump energy left to put up a good fight.

All in all, the Tanna was a good ship. But at times, Robert thought fondly of his days on the original FTL scout ships. He missed the closeness of the crew, and he missed flying...although admittedly, flying of spaceships was mostly button pushing. But there had been a few times, especially during his Cobra days, that he had hand-flown his ships even during combat. He had spent the last eight years in command of the Tanna, and it was likely to be the last ship he would ever command. Just like Roselle, he was one of the few officers who had served with Nathan Scott under Admiral Dumar. And just like Gil, he was unlikely to receive another promotion or a larger ship to command. The Tanna was the end of the line for Robert Nash.

It was a big part of why he had not told Command about the message he had received from the captain of the Aurora, Cameron Taylor. He knew he'd have to tell them at some point, and the longer he waited, the deeper he was letting himself get pulled into whatever his baby sister and the others were doing in the Pentaurus cluster. If he didn't fess up soon, he wouldn't be able to without serious repercussions.

Robert had never been a devotee of regulations. He knew procedure had its place, but he also knew that a good leader sometimes bent the rules to get the job done. This was precisely why he had kept Captain Taylor's message secret for nearly seven days. Cameron Taylor was known for being a stickler for the rules. For her to throw the book out completely and go against everything she stood for, there had to be one hell of a reason. And it wasn't just because Nathan Scott had asked for her help. She suspected the same thing Robert did, that they all did: the Jung ships that had recently penetrated Sol Alliance space was actually a false-flag operation. The question was, who had conducted the operation? The Dusahn had the most to gain by renewing hostilities between the Alliance and the Jung Empire. But so did Admiral Galiardi. A renewed war would give Galiardi the support he needed to build up his military to the levels he had recommended more than a decade ago. If Galiardi managed to rebrand himself as a war hero, he would be in a perfect position to run against Dayton Scott to lead the Earth and the entire Sol Alliance.

It was a frightening thought, to be sure. Galiardi's prolific military expertise did not make up for his lack of compassion and patience.

Robert did not believe that Galiardi had colluded

with the Dusahn, but he did suspect that the admiral was withholding information from the Alliance Council for his own purposes. However, there was little Robert could do about it. Galiardi was too smart and too well supported. A single utterance of suspicion would most likely land Robert in a holding cell deep within Port Terra. The people of the Alliance worlds had let their desire to be safe from Jung aggression override their common sense. Galiardi had command of an incredible amount of firepower. It was not enough to repel a full-scale Jung invasion, especially if the Jung *did* have jump drives, but it was powerful enough to overthrow Earth and any other Alliance worlds that might oppose the admiral.

Robert was beginning to feel like a conspiracy theorist. But still, his theories were not beyond reason, and this new train of thought left him feeling uneasy and distracted.

"Morning, Captain," the officer of the watch greeted as Captain Nash stepped onto the Tanna's bridge.

"How's everything, Lieutenant?" Captain Nash asked.

"The threat board is clear, sir. The only contact the entire shift has been the comm-drone we left at the relay point you specified."

"It came back?" Robert said, surprised.

"Yes, sir. There's a personal message in your comms queue."

"And the comm-drone?"

"It's in the bay, ready for dispatch."

"Very well," Captain Nash stated. "I'll be in my ready room."

"Aye, sir."

Captain Nash headed to the back of the bridge,

passing the comms station, stepping through the hatch, and closing it behind him. He pulled the folding seat down in front of the small desk built into the bulkhead and sat down, activating his view screen. After typing in his access code, the screen came to life. He tapped the message on the screen and entered the same decryption key as before. This time, it was a text message. His mouth dropped open and his eyes widened. "They're crazy!" he stated out loud.

* * *

"Goddamn it, Kyle! I can't fight the Jung with only ten ships! Not if they have jump drives!"

"We still don't know for sure if they even *have* jump drives," Admiral Cheggis argued.

"Do you want to bet it all on that?"

"We're up to three hundred and sixty-eight gunships, Mike. And we've got another twenty waiting for crews at the Koharan gunship plant. We're just waiting for her crews to finish up their sim training."

"Gunships," Galiardi grumbled. "Do you really think gunships are going to be enough if the Jung send everything they've got our way?"

"Six gunships have as much firepower as a single destroyer. So, in essence, we've got about sixty destroyers."

"Against mostly cruisers and battleships," Admiral Galiardi reminded his friend. "If they refuse to let us take out those battle platforms first, a thousand gunships wouldn't make a difference."

"We've still got the Benakh," Admiral Cheggis said. "Give her a few dozen gunships, and they can potentially take down a battle platform."

"Not eight of them, they can't," Admiral Galiardi insisted. "I need more capital ships. More destroyers would be nice, but if the Jung do send their battle platforms our way, capital ships are the only real chance we have."

"But the Jung won't leave their core worlds unprotected."

"Battle platforms can't stop super KKVs," Admiral Galiardi said.

"No, but the people who live on those worlds don't know that. Maybe the Jung are keeping those platforms in place to show their people that they are being protected, even if it is a lie."

"I have to find a way to convince the council that taking out those platforms is our only hope. If we sit on our hands, the Jung are going to move those platforms, regardless of what their people think. They are well aware that their battle platforms will be the first assets we target if this goes to all-out hostilities."

"If it was the Jung who penetrated our space, then they either have jump drives or some sort of stealth," Admiral Cheggis reminded his superior.

"It was the Jung, Kyle. You know damn well it was."

"I'm just saying," Kyle defended. "If it was them, they knew we wouldn't target any frontline assets because that would be an escalation we couldn't step back from. They're just waiting to see what we do next. They're trying to get *us* to start the war."

"By violating our territorial space and engaging our warships?" Admiral Galiardi challenged, not following his subordinate's logic.

"We don't have positive identification on any of the ships that penetrated our space," Admiral Cheggis reminded him. "Therefore, they still have plausible deniability. If we take out their battle platforms, that will be an overt act of war, and it will be on our part."

"I don't care," Admiral Galiardi insisted.

"Well, you should...*sir.* Because if the Jung *do* have a lot more ships out there, those platforms will be the least of our worries. We could be forced to defend against a never-ending stream of warships."

"I'd rather bet on *known* assets than *possible* ones," Galiardi insisted. "We *know* we can't stop those battle platforms; not with ten warships and a few hundred gunships." Galiardi sighed, sitting back down in his chair. "I'm betting the Jung *don't* have jump drives, but they *do* have some new stealth capability."

"How did you come to that conclusion?" Admiral Cheggis wondered.

"Because if the Jung *did* have jump drives, you and I wouldn't be having this conversation."

CHAPTER FIVE

In front of Commander Bastyan's desk, Ensigns Walsh and Lowen stood at attention as the commander studied the data pad in her hands. It was the third time they had been called into her office since they had started flight training three months ago.

"Repeatedly demonstrates a lack of understanding of the regulations and respect for operating procedures regarding flight operations of the Cobra gunship." The commander set her data pad down and sighed. "You two just keep coming up with new ways to piss off your instructors, don't you? Is it a hobby of yours or something?"

"No, sir," Ensign Walsh replied.

"Just seems to happen, sir," Ensign Lowen added.

"Just seems to happen," the commander muttered. "Perhaps, if you followed procedures, it *wouldn't* happen."

"Beg your pardon, sir, but the procedures stink," Ensign Walsh stated.

"Is that right?" Commander Bastyan looked at the ensign. "I didn't realize you had become such an expert in the operation of a Cobra gunship, in such a surprisingly short amount of time. On what vast experience do you base this claim?"

"None, sir," Ensign Walsh admitted. "But if you look at all the flight logs and transcriptions of past combat actions, you'll see that these ships are capable of so much more..."

"The procedures exist to provide an operational baseline against which all flight crews can be measured," the commander stated in matter-of-fact fashion. "While I appreciate your enthusiasm, if you hope to ever fly a Cobra gunship the way that you *believe* it can be flown, you must first prove that you are capable of operating one in accordance with established protocols. *That* is the system. If you are unable to follow it, I suggest that you resign from the program. Do I make myself clear?"

"Yes, sir," both ensigns replied in unison.

"You have one week before graduation," the commander continued. "Assuming you two manage to *pass* your final sim checks, you will be given an eight-hundred-million-credit gunship and a crew, all of which will be your responsibility. Those procedures in which you put so little faith are not there to *limit* you, but to help you keep your ship and your crew safe. Try to keep that in mind, gentlemen."

"Yes, sir," the two of them replied.

"Then, I won't be seeing either of you in this office again, will I," the commander stated.

"No, sir," they answered.

"Excellent. Ensign Lowen, you're dismissed."

"Yes, sir," the ensign replied, saluting, then turning and exiting.

Commander Bastyan leaned back in her chair, waiting for Ensign Lowen to close the door behind him on the way out. Finally, she turned her attention back to Ensign Walsh. "Ensign Lowen is a good man."

"The best," Ensign Walsh agreed without hesitation.

"I trust you and he have become friends?"

"Very much so, sir."

"Then, perhaps you should show him some respect and not put his career in jeopardy with your reckless disregard of Alliance regulations."

"That was not my intent, sir," Ensign Walsh defended.

"Your intent is irrelevant, Ensign," the commander explained. "That's what you don't seem to understand."

"Sir?"

The commander paused. "Why do you want to fly your gunship so far outside the established performance envelope?"

"I just want to be the most effective ship out there, sir," the ensign replied with some enthusiasm.

"Have you heard the expression, 'walk before you run'?" the commander asked.

"Not in those words, exactly, but yes, sir."

"Show the Alliance that you can walk, then, in time, you can start running. Is that understood?"

"Yes, sir."

"That will be all, Ensign."

Ensign Walsh looked confused.

"Something on your mind, Ensign?" the commander asked, noticing the look on the young man's face.

"No, sir," he replied, unconvincingly.

"You're a bad liar. Spit it out."

Ensign Walsh hesitated for a moment. "As you said, this is my third time in your office for pretty much the same thing. Yet, you have never even raised your voice."

"Would it help?" the commander asked.

"I don't know," Ensign Walsh admitted. "Maybe."

"Sorry, not my style," the commander explained. "If you can't understand simple logic or follow orders, then I'd just as soon boot you than graduate you. It makes no difference to me. So, I see no reason to raise my blood pressure to get you to do your job." She looked at him for a moment. "Anything else?"

"No, sir." Ensign Walsh snapped to attention,

raising his hand in salute. “Thank you, sir.” Ensign Walsh turned smartly and exited the commander’s office, closing the door behind him. He continued down the corridor, crossing the lobby and exiting the building into the Koharan sunshine. He stood at the top of the steps, looking across the yard, spotting Ensign Lowen sitting on a bench with three other ensigns from their class.

“I don’t get it,” Ensign Wabash said as Ensign Walsh approached. “Both of you still have asses.”

“If Gerlach was still in charge, you’d be on the train back to town,” Ensign Tegg insisted.

“She just doesn’t want to lose the best pilot in the class,” Ensign Walsh bragged.

“Yeah, that’s it,” Ensign Tegg replied, rising to her feet. “I don’t know about the rest of you, but I’m starved, and the mess hall closes in thirty minutes.” She looked at Ensign Walsh. “Are you coming, Aiden?”

“I’ll catch up to you, Char,” Aiden replied. He glanced at Ensign Lowen.

“Alright, but I can’t promise there will be anything left,” Ensign Tegg teased as she and the others departed.

“Ken, you got a moment?” Aiden asked.

Ensign Lowen rolled his eyes, turning to face his friend.

“Listen, Ken…”

“Don’t even start,” Ken interrupted.

“I’m trying to apologize.”

“You don’t need to,” Ken explained. “I could’ve stopped you, but I didn’t. I thought that maneuver was a better choice, too. *I* should be apologizing to *you*.”

“But, it *was* my idea.”

"It usually is," Ken replied, smiling. "But it's my job to reel you in when you lose sight of the big picture. We check each other. That's what we do."

Aiden nodded his head. "It's not going to happen again."

Ken turned further, squaring himself to his friend. "Let's just follow the rules, kiss their asses, and get our ship and crew. Then we can tear up the sky."

"You got a deal," Aiden said, smiling.

* * *

Marcus sat in the pilot's seat of the Seiiki, monitoring the flight displays as the ship came out of its final jump in the series.

"Jump complete," Neli reported.

"Why did you teach her that?" Josh complained from behind Marcus.

Loki stood behind the copilot's seat, ignoring Josh as he watched over Neli's shoulder. "Now, select the arrival point nearest Rakuen," he instructed.

"Shouldn't I wait for Rakuen control to clear me to an arrival point first?" Neli asked.

"Procedurally, yes. But Rakuen only has two," Loki explained, "above and below its poles. They always use the one above the southern pole for arrivals coming from our direction."

"Nothing along the ecliptic?" Marcus asked.

"Most systems save the system ecliptic for interplanetary jump traffic," Loki said. "Rakuen is no different."

"How do you know so much about Rakuen?" Neli asked.

"I did my flight training here," Loki replied.

The sensor screen beeped, displaying a number of fast-moving targets deep within the system.

"What the hell are those?" Marcus wondered, pointing at the sensor display.

"I'm not sure," Josh admitted, "but whatever they are, they're moving pretty fast."

"Gunyoki racers," Loki explained. "They fly a circuit that snakes between Rakuen and Neramese."

"Uh, they're firing weapons, Lok," Josh pointed out.

"Gunyoki races include defending against attack and taking out targets at various points along the course. It's supposed to simulate the old Water Wars."

"Why would anyone want to simulate a war?" Neli commented.

"It's mostly a Rakuen thing," Loki explained. "During the war, members of the upper class financed the construction of their own fighters to help defend Rakuen. Once the war was over, the Gunyoki fighters who survived began racing for fun. Over the centuries, it turned into a really big deal. Vid-drones chase the racers around the course and everything. It's fun to watch, actually. There are about twenty races per year, I think. People even bet on them, especially the championship round."

"Now, *that* sounds like the kind of flying *I'd* be good at," Josh exclaimed.

"I don't know, Josh," Loki said. "The Gunyoki races are dangerous. Five or six crews die every year."

"And fighting the Dusahn is totally safe," Josh commented.

The navigation computer beeped, alerting them of an incoming navigation instruction. Neli leaned forward slightly, reading the message. "You were right. They cleared us to the arrival point over the south pole."

"Go ahead and start the jump plot," Loki instructed.

"You remember how to transfer from a polar orbit to a standard orbit?" Josh asked Marcus.

"Yeah. You select standard orbit and press execute," Marcus replied. "Real tough pilot stuff that is."

"How do we watch those races?" Josh asked Loki. "Can we pick them up from here?"

"Probably."

"Maybe we should concentrate on getting the ship on the ground, first?" Neli suggested.

"Relax," Josh said. "As soon as we jump to the arrival point, Rakuen will take control of our auto-flight systems."

"Humor me, will you?" Neli insisted.

Josh rolled his eyes.

"Don't worry, the races are pretty long," Loki assured him. "And based on the number of ships still in the race, I'd say it just started."

"Jump to the arrival point is plotted and loaded," Neli announced.

Loki looked over her shoulder, double-checking the jump plot for himself. "Looks good. Go ahead and activate the jump sequencer."

"I don't have to change course or speed, or anything?" Marcus asked.

"The jump sequencer and auto-flight systems will take care of it," Loki assured him. "And it can do it far more precisely than we can."

"Just as I thought," Marcus mumbled.

"What?" Josh wondered.

"All this time you've been making out like flying

this thing requires some kinda special talent or something. Turns out all you gotta do is push a few buttons, and the ship does the rest."

"Try jumping it into a cave, old man," Josh said.

"How's it going up here?" Nathan asked as he climbed up onto the Seiiki's flight deck. "Our new pilots getting the hang of things?"

"I'm pushing buttons like a pro," Marcus remarked.

"We're about to jump to the southern arrival point, Captain," Loki reported. "We should be on the ground in about thirty minutes."

"I'll let the others know," Nathan said, turning to head back down the ladder.

"Hey, Cap'n, how long are we going to be on Rakuen, anyway?" Josh asked.

"A few hours, I believe. Just long enough to deposit the funds we collected from the Pentaurus sector into a few of Rakuen's banks and for Deliza to talk to the manager of the Ranni shuttle plant."

"Any chance we could check out the Gunyoki races while we're here?"

"The what?" Nathan wondered.

"Some kind of simulated combat races with old fighters."

"They're not *old*," Loki corrected. "Gunyoki racers are cutting-edge technology around here."

"Really?" Nathan looked at Loki. "Where would we have to go to see them?"

"We?" Josh wondered.

"It sounds interesting."

"You can watch them just about anywhere," Loki explained. "We could probably even pick up the broadcast on the ship's comm-systems."

"What's the best way to see them?" Nathan asked.

"Well, the *best* way is to go to the racing platform. You get to see the ships close-up when they come in for service in between heats," Loki told him. "But you usually need special passes for that, and they are *not* cheap."

"Well, we're carrying a ton of credits," Nathan said.

"Actually, Deliza may have some contacts on Rakuen," Loki realized. "You might want to ask her if she can pull any strings. She's got quite a bit of influence on Rakuen."

"Jumping in twenty seconds," Neli announced.

Loki turned his attention back to the forward consoles, peering over Neli's shoulder again to make sure the jump drive's auto-sequencer was working properly, and that the Seiiki's auto-flight system had the ship on the correct heading and at the correct speed. "Everything looks good," he decided.

"Looks like we're going to the races," Josh exclaimed, clapping his hands together with excitement.

* * *

"We received requests from two more ships," Cameron told General Telles as he entered the bridge. "A mining ship called the Jagaron and a tanker ship called the Villanueva."

"Well, we can certainly use the mining ship," General Telles said, taking a seat across the desk from Cameron.

"We'll need some sort of refining capabilities, as well."

"Most mining ships have basic ore separation capabilities," General Telles said. "It increases their profitability. And we can fabricate whatever systems we need to further refine those raw ores into something the fabricators can utilize."

Cameron nodded. "The Villanueva is carrying several types of propellant."

"Any idea why they are asking to join?" the general wondered.

"The Glendanon checked their registry database. Both ships are owner-operated. The Jagaron is out of Haydon, and the Villanueva operates out of Norwitt. Statements from both ships' captains indicate that they would rather fly with us than hand their ships over to the Dusahn."

"Where are they?" General Telles asked.

"They're holding position about halfway between Yaratru and Korak, a few light years off the shipping lanes, running cold," Cameron explained. "They are waiting for our response."

"How did the message reach us?" General Telles inquired.

"Through Captain Gullen's contacts on Yaratru."

General Telles tilted his head slightly, thinking. "We're getting volunteers faster than I had anticipated."

"Is that a problem?" Cameron wondered.

"No, I suppose not. But it does present additional logistical concerns. More ships and crew to support. More security issues."

"Nothing my people can't handle," Cameron assured him.

"We will need to send a team to intercept and guide them to us," General Telles said.

"I'll dispatch them immediately."

General Telles nodded. "Any reply from Captain Nash?"

"No, but our comm-drone only arrived at the comm-point a couple of hours ago," Cameron replied.

"Have your people come up with any recommendations?"

Cameron leaned back in her chair. "The Cobra plant on Earth is underground, with only three entry and exit points. One for vehicles, one for cargo trains, and the launch ramps for the gunships. It would be nearly impossible to get in there, let alone get out with gunships. Besides, the gunships there rarely spend more than a few days in the inspection yard before launch. Even if we could get our hands on them, we'd probably only get two or three at the most."

"We will only get one chance at this, so we must get as many ships as possible," the general reminded her.

"Agreed. The plants on Kappa Ceti and 82 Eridani have a much lower production rate and also rarely have more than a few ships in the yard, so those are out, as well. That leaves Tau Ceti."

"How many ships do they keep in the yard?"

"Normally, according to my people, the Cetians keep the finished gunships on the ground and have the crews who are going to fly them do the pre-launch inspections, as well as the subsequent shakedown trials. Since their flight crew training program takes three months to complete, and the plant produces one ship per week, there can be as many as twelve ships on the ground, *if* we time it right."

"I assume the Koharan facility is also well guarded," General Telles said.

"Yes, but it is out in the open. Perhaps we should wait for word from Captain Nash? He could have more specific information for us."

"I'd prefer that we move our teams into position closer to the target, even if that means waiting for the right time to execute our plan," General Telles said. "Any ideas on where our teams could safely lie in wait?"

Cameron thought for a moment. "Yes," she finally replied, "but I don't think they're going to like it."

* * *

"What's that?" Marcus asked, pointing at the flashing yellow light in the middle of the Seiiki's console.

"Rakuen Control is querying our auto-flight system, looking for a connection," Loki explained.

"What do I do?" Marcus wondered.

"You accept the control request," Josh chuckled, "unless you want to land the ship on your own."

Marcus cast a menacing glance at Josh.

"Press 'accept remote control' on the auto-flight console," Josh instructed.

Marcus searched the auto-flight section of the center console for a moment, then pushed the appropriate button as instructed. "That's it?"

"That's it."

"That's all you do up here?" Marcus laughed.

"Well, we don't always use auto-flight, you know," Josh defended.

"It can't possibly be that easy," Neli said.

"If everything is working properly, it is," Loki said. "But if something goes wrong, it helps if you know how to hand-fly."

"How often does something go wrong?" Neli wondered.

"On this ship, too often," Josh mumbled.

Neli looked concerned.

"Don't worry," Loki assured her. "All you guys

have to do is one automated takeoff and then an automated landing on the Aurora."

"We gotta land this thing on the Aurora?" Marcus asked, seeming more worried than he was willing to admit.

"Please tell me the Aurora has remote auto-flight capabilities," Neli said.

"Thanks for the vote of confidence," Marcus grumbled.

"Don't worry," Josh said, "it does."

The Seiiki's nose dipped without warning.

"I didn't do that," Marcus said. "Did I?"

"Rakuen Control has taken over," Josh said. "Now, we just sit back and enjoy the ride."

"And keep an eye on all the systems, in case something goes wrong," Loki added.

"That, too," Josh agreed.

Tiny flashes of red, orange, and yellow began to appear around the ship as the Seiiki's thermal shields made contact with the thin upper atmosphere of Rakuen.

"Thermal shields, right?" Neli asked.

"Yup," Josh replied.

"Something that you should probably keep an eye on during atmospheric entry," Loki suggested.

"What happens if it fails?" Neli asked, unsure if she wanted to hear the answer.

"We won't fry, if that's what you're worried about," Josh replied.

"But we will have a lotta shit to fix on the exterior," Marcus added.

"It *could* be a potential problem, depending on the thickness of the atmosphere," Loki told her. "Rakuen's atmosphere is pretty thin, about half that of Earth's. If we lost the shields during descent into Earth's atmosphere, we might have a problem."

"But we're not going to have to land this thing on Earth, right?" Neli asked.

"To be honest, I don't really know," Loki admitted. "The captain hasn't told us what the plan is, yet."

"That's because no one's told *me*, yet," Nathan said as he topped the ladder and stepped in behind Josh, moving to his left to make room for Vladimir coming up the ladder behind him.

"Seriously?" Josh exclaimed.

"We're still waiting for intel from the Sol sector," Nathan added.

The flashes of atmospheric plasma striking the Seiiki's thermal shields began to fade away as the ship penetrated the upper cloud deck, which typically covered the majority of Rakuen's skies. As Vladimir peered forward between Josh and Loki, the clouds parted, revealing a vast ocean peppered with thousands of tiny islands.

"*Bozhe moi*," Vladimir gasped in wonder. "So much water."

"Ninety percent of Rakuen's surface is covered with water," Loki told them.

"Incredible," Vladimir added.

"It's not that deep, though," Josh commented.

Everyone looked at him.

"What?" Josh wondered. "It's not."

"He's right, actually," Loki admitted. "If I remember correctly, the deepest parts are only a few thousand meters."

"It is still a lot of water," Vladimir insisted. "So, the people here live on the islands?"

"Some," Loki replied. "But most of the islands are fairly mountainous. The ones that aren't are used for agriculture. Most of the population live in floating cities."

"Floating?" Vladimir looked skeptical. "How do they keep from floating away?"

"They're anchored in place and usually surrounded by a seawall," Loki explained. "They're commonly positioned in shallower waters around or between islands."

"There," Josh announced, pointing out the port front window.

Everyone looked out at the ocean rising up toward them. Ahead of them was a complex assembly of overlapping circles surrounded by a single, much larger perimeter that encompassed the inner groupings. As the Seiiki descended, details began to appear, each circle revealing spokes that made them look like wheels floating on a calm ocean.

"Amazing," Vladimir gasped.

"Yeah, it's really something," Nathan agreed.

"You've been here before?"

"A few times," Nathan replied, "as Connor Tuplo."

"How many of these floating cities are there?" Vladimir wondered.

"A few hundred, at least," Nathan guessed.

"Actually, there are eleven hundred thirty-eight floating cities on Rakuen," Loki corrected. "Although most of them are not that large, and they're not all circular, either."

"Where are we going to land?" Vladimir asked.

"They don't have big spaceports like most worlds," Nathan told him. "Instead, they have landing pads all over the place. Every city has at least one, while the larger cities have several. That's the city of Yokino."

Loki glanced at the auto-flight data display. "Looks

like we're going to pad eighteen on the northwest side of the city."

"That should put us close to the financial district," Nathan said. "And I'm sure the Ranni plant will send a shuttle for Deliza."

"We should be setting down in a few minutes," Josh announced.

"Do I have to do anything?" Marcus asked, hoping the answer was no.

"When the auto-flight status annunciators flash 'accept landing', press the flashing button to allow them to land us," Josh instructed as if Marcus should have been able to figure that much out for himself.

"After checking that our gear is down and locked," Loki added.

"Well, yeah," Josh replied, rolling his eyes.

"Gentlemen, I'll leave you to get us safely on the ground," Nathan announced, turning to head back down the ladder.

Vladimir moved into the middle of the cockpit after Nathan left, to get a better look at the city below. "This is incredible."

"Yeah, and they've got great seafood, as well," Josh said.

* * *

Robert Nash stopped packing his small travel duffel just long enough to answer the knock at his cabin door.

"You wanted to see me, sir?" Commander Boynton said from the open doorway.

"Come in, Jas," Robert instructed, returning to his packing. "And close the door."

Commander Boynton stepped inside and closed the door. "Going for another excursion?" he asked.

"Yes, only this time, I may be gone for several days."

"Where are you going?"

Robert paused for a second. "Sorry, that's classified."

"I suppose it has something to do with the message you received today?"

"How did you know about that?"

"I'm you're XO," the commander replied. "It's my job to know."

"I'm taking a SAR shuttle this time," Robert said as he closed up his duffel.

"The one that Hardy disabled the transponder on."

Robert looked at the commander, surprised.

"XO," the commander reminded him.

"Right."

"Captain..."

"Don't ask, Jas," Robert interrupted. "You know I can't tell you."

"Why the hell would they send *you*, of all people?"

"Let's just say that I have particular experiences and contacts that are required for this assignment."

"What do I tell the crew?" the commander wondered.

"Nothing. They'll get the hint."

Commander Boynton shook his head. "I'm not liking this, Captain."

"Yeah, well, neither am I, to be honest," Robert said. "But that's life in the service."

"What are your orders while you're gone?" Commander Boynton asked.

"Just maintain our patrol corridor." Robert looked at the young man who had been his right hand for the last fifteen months. He was a good man, one of several who had served under him on their way to getting their own ship. He wanted to tell the commander that he was about to become the Tanna's new commanding officer, but that would raise suspicions; ones the commander would be compelled to report to Command, and that could ruin everything. "One more thing. Go comms silent until I get back."

"If we miss a check-in..."

"Command will think we're on a hot track. They won't bat an eye for at least three or four days. If I'm not back in five..." He looked at the commander.

"Then?"

"Then you take command and report me overdue."

"Now you're really making me nervous, Captain."

"Don't be. You've got this, Commander."

"Yes, sir," Commander Boynton replied, coming to attention. He offered his captain a salute, which Robert happily returned, then offered his hand. "Good luck, sir."

"To us all, Commander." Robert picked up his duffel, grabbed his jacket and cap off the hook, and then opened the door. He turned back to the commander. "See you soon."

* * *

Nathan and Jessica descended the Seiiki's ramp to join the rest of the crew on the landing pad. Nathan took in a deep breath as he stepped off the cargo ramp. A cool, hazy mist seemed to rise off the sea before dissipating into the breezy day, providing a stark contrast to the Seiiki's dryer environment. Since he had left Earth nearly a decade ago, most of his life had been spent in the confines of the Aurora and the Seiiki. He cherished every opportunity to breathe the natural atmosphere of a living world.

He looked around at the nearby buildings, gleaming cleanly in the muted Rakuen sunlight. Rakuen architecture had a unique blend of traditional, Asian styling and high-tech, modern sleekness.

"What's the plan?" Josh asked on behalf of everyone gathered.

"Marcus, Neli, and Dalen, stay with the ship. Make sure she's ready to go on a moment's notice," Nathan instructed.

"You expecting trouble?" Marcus wondered.

"No, but we weren't expecting trouble on Palee, either."

"Fair enough. Can we get some chow first?"

"There's a place just down the street, to the left of the gate," Loki suggested.

Everyone looked at him.

"I've been here before, remember?"

"He's right," Deliza agreed, "about four buildings down, on the right. Try the fried scorridai with topa sauce. You won't be sorry."

"Get it to go," Nathan insisted. "I don't like the idea of leaving the Seiiki unattended."

"I'll stay," Dalen offered. "Just get me some of that scorridai stuff."

"Rossi and Anson will escort Deliza," Jessica announced.

"I don't need an escort," Deliza insisted. "This is Rakuen. It's about as safe a place as you'll find."

"But we got all dressed up," Corporal Rossi said, pulling at his business suit lapels.

"Humor me," Jessica insisted. "Besides, you're carrying a credit chip worth eighty million, remember?"

"It's bio-linked," Deliza reminded her.

"Better to play it safe," Nathan agreed, casting a determined expression toward Deliza.

"Very well," Deliza agreed. "Gentlemen, let's go."

"What about us?" Josh asked, barely able to contain himself.

Nathan smiled. "The rest of us are off to the races."

"Yes!" Josh exclaimed.

* * *

Captain Nash walked across the small shuttle bay and stepped up onto the boarding ladder to the search-and-rescue shuttle.

"Were you just going to leave without saying goodbye?"

Robert turned around to see his chief engineer, Lieutenant Commander Hardison, standing in the hatchway behind him.

"I didn't think anyone was around," Robert answered. "Besides, I'll be back."

"The hell you will," the lieutenant commander disagreed. "A SAR bird, no transponder... You're either doing something covert or something illegal."

"Or both," Robert corrected, stepping back down.

"Are you sure about whatever it is you're about to do, Robert?" the lieutenant commander asked.

"How long have we known each other, Hardy?" Robert asked.

"Five years."

"Have you ever known me to be sure about anything?"

"Nope. Not like that's ever stopped you, though."

"Well, this time's no different, believe me."

The lieutenant commander sighed. "Well, I put extra rations, a heavy assault rifle, and a sidearm in the storage locker behind the cockpit. I hope to God you don't need them."

"Me, too," Robert replied, reaching out to shake his friend's hand. "Don't let the XO do anything stupid, Mike."

"I'll keep an eye on him, Robert." The lieutenant commander stepped back through the hatch. "Clear skies and tailwinds, Captain," he said before he closed the hatch.

Robert turned and climbed up the access ladder into the SAR shuttle, activating the close cycle on the hatch as he stepped inside. He moved forward, squeezing between the forward engine bulkheads and slipped into the pilot's seat on the left side of the cramped cockpit. He flipped several switches, activating the shuttle's start-up sequencer, then punched in his authorization code. The shuttle's control systems flickered to life, and her four engines began to spin up. Within a few seconds, his status lights were all green.

Robert turned to his left, looking out the window to the shuttle bay hatch. He gave the lieutenant commander a thumbs-up. Yellow lights began to flash inside the tiny shuttle bay, warning that the bay was about to depressurize. A few seconds later, the flashing lights changed from yellow to red, and finally, to a softer, steady red.

Robert waited patiently as the deck beneath the shuttle split down the middle and slid out from under him to either side. He leaned as close to the window as he could, looking down to see the star-filled abysm of space.

After one last scan of his systems, Robert reached up with his right hand and pressed the launch button on the overhead console, grabbing onto the handrail next to the overhead console to steady himself. A moment later, the shuttle dropped like a rock out of the bay, propelled downward along short launch rails. He looked up through the overhead window above his left shoulder, watching the Tanna drift quickly up and away from him.

Thirty seconds later, his ship, his home of over seven years, vanished from sight.

* * *

It had taken Nathan and the others less than an hour to catch one of the regular shuttles on the surface of Rakuen and make the trip to the race platform further out in the Rogen system. Immediately, their senses were assaulted by the Gunyoki races' volley of color and noise. Even the tunnel from the shuttle to the race platform was lined with screens displaying the vid-feeds of a dozen vantage points along the racecourse, along with cockpit cameras and cameras mounted on the hulls of Gunyoki racers. There were even a fleet of nimble chase drones following the racers as they snaked and fought their way through the race.

As they made their way through the transfer tunnel nearer to the main concourse, the din of yelling, cheering, and even singing got louder and louder.

The main concourse itself was impressive, at least a hundred meters wide and a full kilometer in diameter. It was a giant, oval tube, completely clear and cylindrical with a flattened walkway, and it completed itself, forming a massive circle. The inside wall, facing the great ring's center, was lined with windows that revealed various race teams' hangar bays. For every four bays, there were smaller, clear conduits that led toward the center of the race platform.

Large view screens were everywhere, strategically placed on the countless structural beams that encircled the concourse tube, ensuring that spectators stayed abreast of every moment of race action as they wandered about the platform.

Outside, ships flew past at speeds so great they appeared as fleeting streaks of multi-colored light on a black backdrop. Slower racers constantly came and went from their hangars back out onto the racecourse, giving the spectators magnificent views of the ships, their thrusters firing as they maneuvered overhead.

Over the clamor, announcers called the heats in progress, providing dramatic, rapid-fire descriptions of the action. Cheers of excitement and cries of disappointment filled the concourse, occasionally drowning out the public-address systems.

The cacophony of the crowds starkly contrasted the silence of the Gunyoki race ships outside. Nathan marveled at the ships as they passed overhead. “This is not what I expected,” he admitted as they walked.

“This is fucking awesome!” Josh exclaimed. “Cap’n, I know what I want to do once we get rid of the Dusahn.”

“Are you kidding?” Loki laughed. “Gunyoki pilots are dedicated, highly disciplined, and highly educated professionals. Not crazy young men who just happen to have a knack for flying. You wouldn’t last a single race.”

“Dude, I’m deeply hurt,” Josh replied, his voice dripping with sarcasm. “A couple weeks of training and I’d give any of them a run for their money.”

"No one ever accused you of lacking confidence, that's for sure," Jessica commented.

"You think Deliza's company would sponsor me?" Josh wondered.

Loki rolled his eyes. "It would be best if you did not belittle the Gunyoki," he urged. "The Rakuens take this sport very seriously. It stems from a long tradition dating back to the Water Wars between Rakuen and Neramese."

"They fought over water?" Josh laughed. "Rakuen's *all* water."

"And Neramese isn't," Loki replied. "It's a long story. The point is, disrespect of the honor and tradition of the Gunyoki will not be appreciated by the Rakuens."

"Hey, I can be as respectful as the next guy," Josh insisted.

"Right," Loki replied.

Vladimir wandered toward the nearest set of windows into one of the Gunyoki hangar bays, drawn to the sight of the ship's uncovered engines. "Look at this thing," he exclaimed. "I've never seen anything like it."

"It looks like the entire engine nacelles articulate in order to direct their thrust," Nathan observed.

"They extend and rotate, as well as angle inward and outward," Loki explained, "also to aim their plasma cannons on the front of the nacelles."

"Wouldn't that screw up their thrust vectoring?" Josh wondered.

"That's one of the things that makes Gunyoki racing so challenging," Loki continued. "You're always having to sacrifice one capability in order to utilize another. The Rakuens have elevated it to an art form."

"Seems like it would be easier to make everything usable at once," Josh insisted.

"It's a Zen-balance sort of thing," Loki said. "You only have so much power available to you, so you have to strike a balance to meet your needs, and you have to constantly adjust that balance as your needs change."

"Sounds like it would make a great vid-game," Josh decided.

"Actually, there are lots of them on Rakuen. There are probably dozens of simulators here on the race platform for the public to use, as well."

"Are those what you're talking about?" Jessica asked, pointing at a row of booths along one side of the concourse ahead of them.

"No, those are full-immersion rooms. You sit inside them and you get a three-dimensional view from any camera of your choosing," Loki explained. "It's pretty impressive, and not cheap."

"What, these passes don't include that kind of stuff?" Nathan wondered.

"Actually, they may have them on the VIP level," Loki admitted. "I've never been there myself, so I wouldn't know."

"Where's the VIP level?" Vladimir asked.

"I think you have to go to the inner hub to get there," Loki said.

"Is it better than here?" Josh wondered.

"Probably. I think you even get to bump elbows with the pilots, crews, owners, and such."

"Maybe we should check it out?" Nathan suggested.

"I think they even have free food," Loki added.

"Then, we definitely should go," Vladimir insisted.

* * *

"Thank you again for the passes," Deliza told Minora as they entered her office. "The crew of the Seiiki has been through a lot recently. I'm sure the excursion will do them good."

"It was not a problem," the plant manager assured her. "We have twelve VIP-level passes. We use them to entertain clients and vendors, and to reward exceptional employees."

"Those cannot be cheap."

"Worth every penny."

"I'm sure," Deliza assured her. "I did not mean to criticize the expenditure. That is certainly not the purpose of my visit."

"Deliza, please. How long have we known each other?" Minora asked.

"Since we started the plant, I suppose," Deliza replied. "Five years?"

"At least. And not once have you ever questioned my financial decisions in regards to the operation of this facility. So, why would I think you were doing so now?"

"You're right, of course," Deliza agreed.

Minora could sense Deliza's stress; it was uncharacteristic for her. "I suspect it is not just the Seiiki's crew that has been through a lot, lately. I heard you had to abandon your headquarters on Corinair."

"Then, news of the Dusahn invasion has reached the Rogen sector."

"I cannot speak for the entire sector, but it has reached Rakuen," Minora said. "I take it you have transferred all Ranni funds out of the Pentaurus cluster?"

"Most, yes." Deliza looked at Minora, cocking her

head to one side, her eyes narrowing. "How did you know?"

"Our bank notified us that you had made a sizable deposit into the parent accounts, just before you arrived."

"I see."

"You *are* planning to move all Ranni funds *out* of the Pentaurus sector, are you not?"

"Time will tell," Deliza replied. "We are hoping that the Dusahn will not spread beyond the cluster itself; at least not for a while."

"Is there reason to believe they will not?"

"Their forces are barely enough to hold the cluster at this point."

"But there is almost no resistance to their expansion, at least not within the Pentaurus sector."

"I wouldn't say there is *no* resistance," Deliza replied.

Minora looked puzzled. Deliza was very good at controlling her facial expressions during negotiations but, today, she was certain that Deliza was smiling ever so slightly. "What *is* the purpose of your visit, Deliza?"

"I can't speak much about it. But I must ask you for a favor." Deliza reached into her bag and pulled out a data pad. "My personal shuttle sustained heavy damage during our escape from Corinair. My assistant, Biarra, was killed. I was hoping that you could provide the parts needed to effect repairs."

"Of course," Minora agreed. She took the data pad and looked over the list. "Wow. I'm surprised anyone survived this much damage."

"I have a very good pilot."

"I would say so," Minora agreed. "But surely this is not the only reason you came? Some spare parts?"

"No, there is more. You will be receiving orders from a new client, The Haxel Group."

"I've never heard of them."

"Their orders may have some unusual modifications."

"What kind of modifications?"

"Nothing too drastic. Most will either be cargo versions, or will have unfinished internal midsections."

"I think we can handle that."

"I would also like you to put the Haxel orders ahead of others, as much as you can."

"The unfinished ones will be easier to move up in the production schedule without ruffling the feathers of our other clients. However, the fully outfitted passenger versions might be a different matter."

"I understand."

"Is there anything else?"

"Yes, upon completion of each unit, send notification, via jump comm-drone, to the coordinates at the bottom of the list."

Minora scrolled down the list to find the coordinates. "That's out in the middle of nowhere."

"And finally, I urge you not to ask too many questions. I know how meticulous you can be, Minora. It's one of the reasons why I hired you to run this plant. But in this case, it would be better for everyone if you put that due diligence of yours aside."

Minora studied Deliza a moment, unsure what to make of her request.

"I assure you that I am not asking you to break any Rakuen laws, nor any of the recently established trade agreements between the Pentaurus and Rogen sectors."

"Of course," Minora nodded.

"Then, we have an understanding?" Deliza wondered.

"I'm assuming that *The Haxel Group* will be picking up their finished units as they become available?"

"Yes. The signed contract from The Haxel Group is also on that data pad."

Minora scrolled further, flipping to the end of the contract to ensure it had been signed. "Huh," she said with a slight smile. "Funny how your signature and that of Mister Jadet Haxel are remarkably similar."

"Similar handwriting styles, I suppose," Deliza replied, but without the smile.

"Well, as a gesture to our newest customer, Ranni Enterprises, Jump Shuttle Division, will get started filling The Haxel Group's orders as soon as possible."

"Thank you," Deliza said, nodding her appreciation. "I'm sure Mister Haxel will be quite pleased."

Minora studied Deliza another moment, her smile growing wider. "You're really not going to tell me, are you?"

"There is nothing to tell," Deliza insisted, her expression still unchanged.

Minora let out a small laugh. "Someday, perhaps?"

"Perhaps."

* * *

Nathan was the first to enter the VIP area, a lavish, circular room covered by a clear dome and supported by beams rising from the top of each of the race platform's spokes. This dome, which itself had multiple stair-like levels, sat as a cupola atop the central hub of the race platform, above the hangar and public concourse levels. More lavishly appointed than the public areas, the room was encircled by a lower level that offered views out into the transition area where Gunyoki racers moved in and out of their service hangars.

The second ring in was two steps up and held countless tables and chairs where VIPs dined while enjoying the events. Waitstaff moved skillfully between tables and guests, delivering the finest foods and beverages that Rakuen had to offer.

Nathan worked his way to the third inner level, higher still. It was on this upper tier that Gunyoki pilots, ship owners, sponsors, and guests mingled while keeping an eye on the holographic projections of heats in progress.

"Now we're talkin'" Josh exclaimed with excitement.

"Oh, please don't embarrass me," Loki begged.

Josh paid him no heed, immediately heading toward the catering tables with Loki hot on his heels.

"Where's he going?" Jessica wondered.

"Probably to the food," Nathan replied.

"That sounds like a very good idea," Vladimir said, turning to follow them.

Nathan quickly acclimatized to the old scene: men in business suits mingling with women in casual, but elegant, attire or pilots still in their flight suits. It appeared to Nathan that most VIPs were there to be seen by others, the races being another excuse to schmooze.

While Jessica, at his side, scanned the crowd for potential threats, Nathan was transfixed by the holographic dance of images overhead. "What do you think this all means?" he wondered.

"First time here?" a woman's voice asked.

Nathan turned toward the woman. "How could you tell?"

The woman moved toward him. She was older

than Nathan by at least a decade, but hid her age well. She was well dressed, with expensive jewelry and perfectly styled hair. A sponsor pass hung around her neck.

She, too, glanced at his clothing and pass. "You're not from Rakuen. Ranni Enterprises. You work at the factory?"

"No, ma'am. I'm, uh... I'm just an independent contractor providing transportation for one of their corporate officers."

"I see."

Jessica moved over next to Nathan. "Hi," she interrupted. "I'm Jessica."

"A pleasure. Jana. Are you also in transportation?" she asked, also noticing Jessica's Ranni pass.

"Not exactly. I'm his bodyguard."

Jana appeared surprised. "I guess that explains that athletic outfit." She turned her attention back to Nathan. "What exactly do you do..."

"Nathan."

"Nathan. What do you do that requires a bodyguard?"

"She's not exactly *my* bodyguard," Nathan corrected. "She's more *in charge* of security for the entire mission."

"*Mission.* That sounds so official."

"Not really," Nathan insisted. "Pilots call every flight a *mission.*"

"Then, you're a pilot."

"Yes."

"Actually, he's the captain of the Seiiki," Jessica told Jana, after reading the information on the woman's pass.

"I'm not familiar with that ship."

"It's an armed utility transport," Jessica

explained. "We've been contracted by the CEO of Ranni Enterprises to provide safe transport. Times being what they are, and all."

"Deliza? You know Deliza Ta'Akar?" The woman seemed quite impressed. "Please, you must come with me. I have some people you *must* meet."

Jana turned to leave, checking behind her to make sure that Nathan and Jessica were following.

"What are you doing?" Nathan said under his breath, so that Jana wouldn't hear him.

"Did you notice her pass?" Jessica whispered back. "She's with the Yokimah race team. That's one of the oldest and most successful racing teams in all Gunyoki history."

"How do you know so much?"

"There's information blaring all over this place," Jessica said. "Aren't you paying attention?"

"Not as much as you are, I guess."

"These are some of the most powerful people in the Rogen sector, Nathan."

"You're thinking they might be willing to provide us with support?"

"I don't know, maybe," she said as they followed Jana between groups and across the top tier. "Just let me do the talking."

Jana walked up to a group of men in business suits, whispering in the ear of one of the elder men. The man looked at Nathan and Jessica, then back at Jana, before heading toward them.

"Hello," the man greeted as he approached. "I'm Ito Yokimah. Jana tells me you are friends of Deliza Ta'Akar."

"That's right," Jessica replied, shaking his hand. "I'm Jessica Nash, and this is Nathan Scott, captain of the jump ship, Seiiki."

The man looked at Nathan, squinting. "A coincidence?"

"I beg your pardon?" Nathan asked.

"You must get this all the time, but you actually *look* like him. So, it's an incredible coincidence that you share the same name, as well."

Jessica smiled. "It's no coincidence."

"What, you changed your name to Nathan Scott?"

Nathan looked at Jessica, trying to hide his confusion.

"He *is* Nathan Scott, formerly the captain of the Aurora," Jessica explained.

"That's impossible. Nathan Scott died in a Jung prison cell. Everyone knows that. Even in the Rogen sector."

"I assure you, Mister Yokimah, I am Nathan Scott. *The* Nathan Scott."

"We rescued him just before his execution," Jessica explained. "Not something that the Jung wanted to admit."

"I chose to keep a low profile, well away from the Sol sector, to avoid embarrassing the Jung and potentially igniting a renewal of hostilities."

"A very noble sacrifice," Jana commented, obviously impressed.

"Not exactly a difficult one," Nathan admitted. "Life is pretty good in this part of the galaxy."

"Thanks to you," Ito insisted. "Because of you, we have the jump drive. Our profits have skyrocketed since Deliza brought the jump drive to Rakuen."

"What business are you in, if you don't mind my asking?" Nathan said.

"We make water purification systems. If there is anything in your water that you don't want, our systems can get rid of it."

"Most of Rakuen uses Yokimah water purifiers," Jana bragged.

"And thanks to the jump drive, most of the worlds within four hundred light years use them, as well," Ito added. "And we're still expanding."

"Well, congratulations on your success," Nathan said in all earnestness. "I imagine your purifiers are improving water quality for millions."

"We like to think so," Ito agreed. "So, is this your first time at the races?"

"Yes, I'm afraid it is," Nathan admitted, sheepishly. "You know, I've been to Rakuen before, briefly, and I've *heard* of the races, but I had no idea they were *this* spectacular."

"Are you enjoying them?" Jana asked.

Nathan laughed. "I don't even understand what's going on," he said, pointing at the holographic display overhead. "How does this all work?"

"Well, the event lasts a full Rakuen day. Qualifying heats start at zero hour, where randomly selected ships are pitted against one another. There are anywhere from thirty to forty ships to start, and over the course of the day, the field gets narrowed down to a handful of leaders. With each round, the runs become progressively longer and more challenging. The final heat is nearly thirty minutes long."

Nathan nodded. "Interesting. Where are we in the process now?"

"We're about to start the first heat of round six, so we're still about ten hours from the final heat. But this is about when they become truly exciting."

"Why is that?" Jessica wondered.

"This is when the targets start shooting back," Jana explained.

"Shooting back?" Nathan was genuinely surprised. "The targets shoot back?"

"Yes," Ito replied. "At the beginning of the sixth round, they activate the target's defenses."

"Isn't that dangerous?" Nathan asked.

"Of course, it is," Jana exclaimed. "That's what makes it so exciting."

"Do the pilots actually get killed?" Jessica wondered.

"It's not as dangerous as it sounds," Ito admitted. "The ships *do* have shields, and the defensive weapons are not as high-powered as they look. But accidents do happen from time to time."

"How often?" Nathan asked.

"Someone is injured at least once per event," Ito admitted. "And at least every third or fourth race, someone dies."

"That's crazy!" Jessica exclaimed.

"That's war," Jana said, brushing it off with ease.

"No, it's not war," Jessica disagreed. "It's a *race*. A *competition*."

"The Gunyoki code states that all of life has risks," Ito explained. "One simply chooses which risks they wish to take. How we face those risks is what defines us."

"Then why aren't you out there risking your life?" Jessica challenged.

"I am not a Gunyoki," Ito replied. "The Rakuen people have incredible respect for the Gunyoki. They once put their lives and their fortunes on the line to defend our world. The competitors of today honor the original Gunyoki warriors by facing similar risks."

"No disrespect intended, Mister Yokimah," Nathan said, "but having experienced the horrors of war firsthand myself, I'm not sure the original Gunyoki warriors would be honored by the glorification of war as a means of turning a profit."

"Our ways may seem unusual to you, Captain, but the Gunyoki are integral to our society. They not only speak to longstanding traditions, but they also serve as a training ground for our military defenses. You see, the Gunyoki racers *are* our frontline defenses. Not only has the presence of the Gunyoki prevented a renewal of hostilities between Rakuen and Neramese, but they have discouraged the very threats that have plagued neighboring systems for more than a century."

"They are your *only* defenses?" Nathan inquired.

"We need no other," Ito assured him.

"No warships. Frigates, destroyers, battleships..."

"Big ships, with lots of guns," Jessica added.

"The Gunyoki fighters are quite formidable," Ito assured them. "A handful of them could easily destroy a much larger warship, if need be."

Nathan looked out the windows as several of the Gunyoki fighters rose from their hangar bays and began to climb out to prepare for the next heat. They were rugged, aggressive-looking ships, to be sure. With twin plasma torpedo cannons on the front of their two engine nacelles and large missile pods fixed under their wings on either side of their fuselage, they were well armed. But they were no match for Dusahn warships, unless...

Nathan turned back to Mister Yokimah. "Are the Gunyoki fighters equipped with jump drives?"

"It is not the Gunyoki way," Mister Yokimah replied. "Besides, doing so would give them offensive capabilities, which would complicate relations with neighboring systems."

"I see." Nathan sighed. "Mister Yokimah, are you

not concerned about the Dusahn presence in the Pentaurus cluster?"

"We do very little business in the Pentaurus sector," Ito replied. "The Takarans have dominated that market for as long as I can remember."

"I was referring to the *military* threat the Dusahn pose."

"We are not ignorant of what is going on outside the Rogen sector," Mister Yokimah insisted. "It is my understanding that the Dusahn have not yet expanded beyond the cluster and are unlikely to do so for some time, if at all."

"May I ask how you came to that conclusion?" Jessica wondered.

"Simple logic, really," Ito replied. "The Pentaurus cluster is the technological, industrial, and economic hub of the entire sector. But once you travel beyond the cluster, levels of those elements decline rapidly. If the Dusahn are seeking to strengthen their empire and expand their forces, logic dictates that they maintain their focus on that which offers the most reward, which is, of course, the Pentaurus *cluster*."

"My experience with the Jung is that they are driven by pride and a sense of entitlement that gives them the right to do whatever is necessary to fulfill what they *believe* to be their destiny. It is the rare occasion that the Jung let logic dictate their actions."

"But the Dusahn are not the Jung," Ito pointed out.

"We believe them to be a rogue caste of the Jung, exiled centuries ago," Nathan explained. "We have seen little difference between the two."

"Yet, thus far, we have seen them take logical steps to achieve their goals," Ito argued.

"Logical steps?" Jessica challenged. "Including the glassing of two worlds?"

"Worlds the Dusahn felt posed significant threats to their empire," Ito replied.

"What?" Jessica was outraged.

"Do not misunderstand my position," Ito insisted. "I do not *approve* of the Dusahn's actions. I am merely asserting that they are *logical,* from their perspective."

"I hope you're correct," Nathan said, "for the sake of Rakuen. Because if they come, they will kill *millions* of your people, if for no other reason than to send a clear message that they are not to be disobeyed by those they conquer."

"I assure you, Captain, that *if* the Dusahn show the slightest *hint* of expansion, the Rakuen will take whatever steps are necessary to defend ourselves."

"Assuming there is a hint," Jessica commented, not quite under her breath.

Jessica's remark did not go unnoticed by their host. He scoffed. "What would you have us do, Miss Nash? Devote our entire economy to a rapid military buildup on the off chance that the Dusahn will take interest in our system? Would not such a buildup run the risk of *attracting* the Dusahn's attention?"

"I thought the Rakuen people were all *about* risk," Jessica remarked sarcastically.

Nathan cast a disapproving glance Jessica's way.

"Please, Ito," Jana urged. "All this talk of war is depressing. We're here to enjoy the races."

"Of course, my dear," Ito replied. "Of course." He turned back to Nathan. "Forgive me, Captain. I did not mean to become adversarial. I guess I have a bit more Gunyoki blood in me than I realized."

"It's quite alright," Nathan assured him. "We did

not mean to intrude on your day. So, if you'll excuse us..."

"Are you sure, Captain?" Ito said. "You are most welcome to stay. I can even introduce you to some of our pilots later."

"A generous offer," Nathan replied, "but I'm afraid our time is limited, and we must rejoin the others in our group."

"Well, it was a genuine honor meeting you, Captain Scott. I cannot wait to tell my children that Na-Tan was in our midst this day."

"The honor was all mine, Mister Yokimah."

"If you ever return to Rakuen and have a bit more time, please do call us," Jana insisted. "You really *must* see the entire event at least once in your lifetime. There is nothing quite like it."

"Of that I am sure," Nathan agreed. "I will make certain to take you up on your generosity on our next visit." Nathan nodded politely, stepping away from the group.

Once out of earshot, Jessica spoke up. "Why did we leave? We never even got to talk about the rebellion."

"You heard him. They don't yet perceive the Dusahn as a threat. And nothing we say is going to change his mind."

"We didn't even try," Jessica argued.

"I've seen his type before. Fifty credits says that guy holds a public office on Rakuen, or is planning on running for one soon."

"How do you figure?"

"I grew up around people like that, remember? I can smell them a kilometer away... *upwind.*"

CHAPTER SIX

"Really?" Robert queried loudly as he approached the end of the dock. "Last time, we at least got to eat and have a few beers."

"I've been looking forward to a day of sailing for weeks now," Gil told him. "I'm not going to give it up just because you decided to bug me again."

Robert stepped onto the twelve-meter sloop, grabbing the side rail to steady himself. It had been decades since he had set foot on a water-going vessel of any kind, let alone a sailboat, but he had grown up in a beach town, and most of his free time had been spent in, on, or around water, so he regained his balance almost immediately.

"Are you sure this thing floats?" he jeered as he stepped down into the stern cockpit.

"Damn thing spent the last three months in dry dock getting overhauled," Gil replied. "She's about as seaworthy as she's ever going to get."

"Not exactly a ringing endorsement," Robert said.

"Shut up and cast off the bowline," Gil instructed. "I want to get a few hours in before the wind peters out."

"Aye, Skipper," Robert replied as he stepped up onto the port side and back onto the dock. He quickly untied the bowline, tossing it across onto the foredeck, and then stepped back over onto the small boat as it began to drift away from the dock.

Gil increased the throttle slightly, and the boat's electric motor pushed it slowly and silently forward through the still marina waters.

Robert neatly coiled the bowline up, just as he

had been taught as a boy, and stored it in the forward locker before returning to the stern cockpit.

"As soon as we clear the breakwater, we'll set sail to the east on a starboard tack," Gil instructed.

"You think I don't know what that means, don't you?" Robert said as he sat on the edge of the cockpit.

"I know damn well you know what that means," Gil replied.

Both men sat in relative silence as Gil guided the boat through the marina, exchanging only common pleasantries about the weather, Gil's girlfriend, and the usual complaints that men in the military shared when in one another's company.

Once clear of the breakwater, Robert raised and trimmed the sails, hearing only a few complaints from Gil. Twenty minutes later, they were a good distance from the marina in wide open waters.

"So, when can we talk?" Robert asked.

"I thought we already were," Gil replied. "Wanna sandwich?"

"Sure," Robert replied, taking the paper-wrapped sandwich offered to him. "And you know what I meant."

Gil looked up, scanning the sky around them. He looked out across the water, his gaze moving slowly around their perimeter. He listened, for a moment, to the sound of the water lapping against the hull, then stood up and moved to the front of the cockpit.

"What are you doing?" Robert asked as Gil started loosening one of the lines. "That sail was trimmed perfectly."

Gil continued to add slack to the line.

"Now you're just luffing," Robert objected as the sail began to beat rapidly in the window.

"I'm making noise," Gil said. "You never know who is listening in."

"We're at least ten clicks from shore, Gil."

"Yup, and we're just two old COs doing a piss-poor job of sailing. Nothing suspicious here." Gil moved aft and sat back down by the wheel. "So, what's the latest?" he asked. "Scott liberate the Pentaurus cluster, yet?" He reached into the cooler and pulled out two beers, offering one to his guest.

Robert moved closer, taking the bottle from Gil and opening it. "They've collected a few more ships, mostly freighters. Oh, and a luxury cruise ship."

"What, is he planning on taking a vacation or something?"

"I think they're using it for personnel housing and support."

"But that's not why you're here, is it?" Gil surmised.

"Hardly." Robert took a drink of his beer and gazed out across the water for a moment. "They want us to help them steal some gunships, Gil."

Gil Roselle nearly spit out his beer. "Are you fucking kidding me?"

"I wish."

Gil thought for a moment. "Makes sense, I guess. It seems unlikely that they could get something bigger, and unlimited strike range *is* more important than firepower at this point."

"That's what Telles said."

"Assuming it can be done, how many do they want to grab?"

"They didn't specify a number," Robert replied. "Just 'as many as possible.'"

"Jesus," Gil sighed. He took another drink of his beer.

"So, is it even possible?"

Gil looked at him. "You're talking about stealing Alliance gunships, Robert. *Gunships*. Not handguns or meal kits or something. Fucking *gunships*. I'm pretty sure they'd throw you in a really deep hole and let you rot for that one."

"Actually, I checked. It would be treason, and we'd probably be executed."

Gil took another long drink, finishing his beer. "We're going to need a lot more of these," he said as he opened up the cooler and pulled out another bottle.

"So, is it possible?"

"I don't know," Gil said. "You'd have to do it a day or two before a batch launch, to make sure there were enough of them there to be worth the risk. And you'd need flight crews."

"Cobras can be flown by one pilot," Robert corrected.

"One *good* pilot," Gil countered. "One who knows the ship well. How many pilots do you think Scott has who fit that bill?"

"Two, as far as I know." Robert looked at Gil.

Gil's eyes widened. "You just keep pulling me in deeper and deeper, don't you?"

"Come on, Gil. You want to stick it to Galiardi as much as I do. What better way than to desert and steal a bunch of gunships on the way out?"

"I'd rather punch the old bastard in the snout and resign," Gil said. "More satisfying, and it wouldn't involve my execution."

"Isn't this more honorable?"

"Following Scott on another quest to save humanity..." Gil took yet another long drink. "You know you've pretty much screwed me already, right?"

"You can always say no."

"But you'll do it anyway. Then Galiardi's henchmen will investigate, find out that I knew about the whole thing and didn't warn them, and I'll fry, anyway. But you already figured all that out, didn't you?"

Robert tried not to smile as he also took a long drink.

"Well, luckily for you, I just happen to be the CO of the very ship tasked with providing security for all Alliance assets in the Tau Ceti system, *including* the Cobra gunship production facility on Kohara."

"You don't say."

Gil sneered. "You and your kid sister are a lot alike, you know that?"

"Then, you're in?"

Gil looked at him again. "You're going to make me say it, aren't you?"

"No insult intended, my friend, but I kind of have to."

Gil sighed. "Yeah, I'm in." He finished off his third bottle and reached for another. "How long do we have?"

"A week, maybe more. They're departing for Sol as soon as I respond to them. They have something to do on Earth first."

"Better make it a week," Gil said. "Cuz there are twenty birds in the yard that will be launched on the twentieth. If they don't do it by then, they'll have to wait a few months before there will be another batch ready to go."

"That doesn't give us much time."

"No, it doesn't." Gil cracked open his fourth beer. "What do they need to do on Earth?" he wondered.

"They plan to smuggle Doctor Sorenson and her

family out of Special Projects and take them back to the Pentaurus sector with them," Robert explained.

Gil shook his head. "And it just keeps getting better."

* * *

Nathan, Jessica, and the others walked onto pad eighteen toward the Seiiki. As they headed up the cargo ramp, Nathan spotted the numerous crates that had been loaded into the bay.

"I take it Deliza was successful," Nathan surmised.

"I sure was," Deliza said, stepping out from behind one of the larger crates. "I got everything we need to fix my shuttle and a few extra parts, for luck."

"Did you reach an agreement with the plant manager?" Jessica asked.

"Yes. The first ship should be ready in about a week."

"And you set up the shell company?" Nathan checked.

"As we discussed," Deliza assured him. "I even rented office space and an answering service to take messages. For all intents and purposes, The Haxel Group is a new, interstellar import/export business dealing in gourmet consumables, complete with their own shipping services."

"Sounds like an expensive operation," Jessica commented.

"Not at all," Deliza explained. "The most expensive items are the shuttle purchases, and that cost is just moving credits from one Ranni account to another, so they're free."

"Why gourmet consumables?" Vladimir wondered.

"We have to eat, don't we?" Deliza replied.

"Yeah, but *gourmet*?" Nathan said, skeptically.

"One man's molo is another man's gourmet meal," Deliza pointed out.

"Oh, God, please," Jessica exclaimed, heading toward the forward ladder.

"We good to go?" Nathan asked Marcus.

"Cargo is secure, and everyone's aboard, Cap'n," Marcus replied.

"Good. Close her up," Nathan instructed.

"Aye, sir."

Nathan turned back toward Josh and Loki, walking backwards as he spoke. "Get us in the air as soon as possible. I want to get back to the Aurora."

"You got it," Josh replied.

"Level three evasion protocols?" Loki asked.

"That should do it," Nathan replied, heading up the forward ladder behind Jessica. He reached the top of the ladder as Jessica stepped through the hatch ahead of him. "Jess, hold up," he called, stepping through the hatch behind her.

Jessica just kept going, turning left to head toward Nathan's cabin, which they had agreed to share during the trip.

"Jess, come on." He followed her into the port corridor and then aft, all the way into his cabin. "What's the deal?"

"You should've asked them," she insisted.

"I'm telling you, it wouldn't have done any good! In fact, it probably would have hurt our cause!"

"The guy has fighters!" Jessica reminded him. "Probably several of them! Did you see them? They were fucking beasts, Nathan. What if he could have gotten other Gunyoki team owners to join us, as well? Do you have any idea what we could do with those ships?"

"Actually, I do," Nathan said. "In fact, I expect I

know better than you what we could do with them. I did graduate from combat school, flight school, and command school, remember?"

"Then how could you not see the advantage the Gunyoki fighters would give us?"

"It might not be as big of an advantage as you think," Nathan explained. "We have no idea just how powerful their weapons are. For all we know, they couldn't take out a cargo hauler."

"But we could have found out," Jessica insisted.

"And we will," Nathan agreed. "But Ito was a businessman *pretending* to be a patriot. He was wrapping himself in the flag of the Gunyoki for the purposes of advancing his own agendas. For all we know, he could already be collaborating with the Dusahn."

"They're more than four hundred light years from the cluster," Jessica argued. "That's too far away for them to be in communication with the Dusahn."

"You're probably right, Jess, but we don't know for sure. That's my point." Nathan paused, waiting for Jessica's next rebuttal, but it didn't come. "Telles will agree, I guarantee it." He put his hands on Jessica's shoulders. "Look, I know how you feel."

"Oh, you do?"

"Yeah, I do. The Dusahn took away your new homeworld. They almost took your family from you, as well, and now you want some payback. I don't blame you. But now is not the time for revenge. It's time to lie low, figure out the landscape and the players, and gather our resources."

"It's been three weeks, Nathan," Jessica pleaded. "*Three weeks*. And all we've done is run around trying to scrounge up credits to feed ourselves. I feel like we've just rolled over and accepted our fate."

"We don't yet have the resources to engage the Dusahn and stand a fighting chance," Nathan reminded her.

"We've got the Aurora! Isn't that enough?"

"If they didn't have jump drives, I'd say yes, the Aurora *is* enough. But they do. We have to be smart about this, Jess. Especially in the beginning, when we are at our weakest. You have to trust me. Telles, Cam, and I all agreed that, as much as we want to start pounding the hell out of the Dusahn, we must wait until the time is right. It just isn't right."

Jessica pushed past Nathan and stepped back through the doorway into the corridor. Before she left, she turned back. "Put me in a room with Lord Dusahn, and I'll end this, just like I ended the reign of Caius Ta'Akar!"

"Jess..." Nathan sighed, watching as Jessica stormed off to be alone with her thoughts.

"Is she going to be alright?" Deliza asked, coming up the corridor behind him.

"She'll be okay," Nathan replied. "She was like this after Tanna was glassed, as well. She needs to punish whoever she thinks is responsible."

"I thought the Ghatazhak had trained that out of her," Deliza said.

"Apparently, she's still a *work in progress*," Nathan replied. They were silent for a moment.

"If it is any consolation, Nathan, I agree with your decision not to discuss the rebellion with Ito Yokimah."

Nathan looked at Deliza, puzzled. "How did you know about that?"

"Are you kidding? We could hear you two arguing all the way back in the cargo bay. I put two and two together... I apologize if I was eavesdropping."

"It doesn't matter."

"Ito Yokimah is not a *bad* man, but he is a shrewd businessman. You are wise not to trust him too easily."

"Thank you," Nathan replied.

"Would you like me to speak with Jessica?" Deliza offered. "Woman to woman, so to speak?"

Nathan let out a small laugh. "Probably better to just let her cool down a bit, but thanks."

"Of course," Deliza replied, heading forward.

Nathan returned to his cabin, stretching out on his bunk as the Seiiki's engines began to spin up. In a few hours, they would be back aboard the Aurora where Telles would talk Jessica down as only he could. Jessica had always been beyond Nathan's influence, and he knew it.

There were some things that even *time* didn't change.

* * *

A direct trip from the Tau Ceti system to the communications rendezvous point that Cameron had designated in her original message would have taken only an hour by jump shuttle. But Robert had selected a different route, one that would be difficult to follow should the Alliance be suspicious of him... He was probably being paranoid. Unless his XO had violated his orders and immediately sent word of Robert's departure to command, no one knew about his illicit movements.

Robert had landed on Kohara dressed as an ensign, not bothering to check in at the Alliance office in Cetia. At the most, an inquiry might be sent to command about an SAR shuttle from the Tanna having come and gone without following procedure, which was not an uncommon occurrence while the fleet was on alert.

So, it had been a long trip; nearly six hours. But it had given him time to think. Gil had told him everything he knew about the layout of the Cobra gunship plant on Kohara and about the specifics of its security measures. For the most part, the plant's security had been designed to keep civilians away and prevent theft of tools and materials by workers. Besides the security codes on the ships themselves and on the launch rail system, no other measures were taken to prevent the theft of gunships. After all, the Tau Ceti system was protected by the second most powerful ship in the Alliance fleet, the mighty Benakh. Only a fool would attempt such a theft.

Robert and Gil had been sailing for hours, further discussing how to do the impossible. In the end, they had agreed that the biggest problem was the contingent of Alliance Marines who guarded the gunship facility. While Robert and Gil both felt that the Ghatazhak would likely defeat them, doing so would involve *killing* most of the marines. Neither man wanted to see Alliance personnel killed, especially by an enemy that could have so easily been an ally. However, Admiral Galiardi had recommended that the Alliance ignore the requests of its member-worlds in the Pentaurus cluster. He had been in favor of protecting the Sol sector worlds, and the Alliance Council had agreed without hesitation. However, turning their backs on member worlds, no matter how distant, had been a direct violation of the Sol-Pentaurus Alliance charter. While the violation was not cause for a *war* between the two sectors, it was *that* decision which might condemn the marines guarding the Cobra plant to their deaths, not the decision whether or not to use deadly force the Ghatazhak would have to make.

Eventually, Robert and Gil had been left with no choice but to let the Ghatazhak wrestle with that decision on their own. No matter what the two of them had decided on that sailboat, the Ghatazhak would do what they *had* to do. While the thought of being complicit in the deaths of Alliance Marines bothered them, being unwilling assistants in whatever Galiardi's end goals were bothered them equally. In the end, the sacrifice that Nathan Scott had made to save them all seven years earlier was what tipped the scales in their minds. If both Nathan *and* General Telles were committing themselves to the fight against the Dusahn, Robert and Gil would back their play.

Robert had been working on the return message to the Aurora during his journey back to the communications rendezvous point, trying to include every trivial detail. He had even included the various ways that he and Gill had come up with to accomplish the mission. Unfortunately, the few plans they had devised all involved considerable risk. However, neither of them truly understood the capabilities of the Ghatazhak. They only hoped they were grossly underestimating those capabilities.

When Robert finally completed the long series of jumps that brought him to the rendezvous point, his message was complete. The jump comm-drone dispatched by the Aurora was still there, waiting for him in deep space, and he wasted no time transferring the message to its queue. Finally, he transmitted the return message, and the drone moved quickly out of sight, its final departure marked only by a distant, almost imperceptible flash of blue-white light.

It would take the drone a few hours to make its way across the thousand-plus light years of space between them, and several more hours for the Ghatazhak to analyze the message and dispatch a response.

Robert powered down his ship, being careful to ensure that his shuttle was not producing any detectable emissions. With only his passive sensors to alert him of company, he settled in for a long wait. Luckily, he had brought plenty of food and water and quite a few vid-plays to waste away the hours.

Thanks to Gil, he even had a few cold beers on hand.

* * *

"I can't believe that all you do is sit here and watch while computers jump this ship over and over across the galaxy," Marcus commented as the Seiiki's windows went opaque again for the next jump.

"It's a bit more complicated than that," Josh defended.

"No, it's not," Loki said.

"Lok..."

"Josh, we both know that once the jump sequencer takes over, we're just passengers like everyone else," Loki insisted. "What makes us pilots is that *if* something went wrong, and the ship could no longer fly itself, *we* would know how to perform the jumps manually."

"You're taking all the glory out of it, Loki," Josh complained. "You're turning us into a couple of button pushers."

"It's all about understanding who you are, and what your role is," Loki insisted.

"Fine," Josh replied. "I'm a pilot, and you're a button pusher. How's that?"

"You're hopeless."

"Uh, guys?" Neli interrupted. "I think we're there."

Loki looked at the sensor screen. "Yup, that's the fleet."

"Just stay on this heading until we're cleared in and given intercept-and-approach instructions," Josh instructed. "You see?" he added, turning to Loki. "*Pilots* know that."

"So do button pushers."

"You two are like an old married couple," Neli commented.

"Yeah, even Neli and I don't argue as much as you two," Marcus added. He glanced at Neli. "Well, not usually, anyway." A disapproving glance from Neli, and Marcus quickly changed the subject. "Maybe we'd better hail the Aurora."

"Good idea," Loki agreed.

Neli quickly changed comm-channels and made the first hail. "Aurora, Aurora, this is the Seiiki. We are at......one five seven by two one five, eight hundred thousand kilometers out, requesting permission to approach for landing."

Neli paused for a response, and looked worried when there was none.

"Gotta give it a minute," Loki reminded her. "We're still a ways out."

"How long?"

"Well, since we've already blown through a hundred thousand clicks since you called, not long," Josh commented.

"At this range, another minute or so," Loki specified. "Go ahead and start decelerating."

"And, how do I do that again?" Marcus asked.

"Select speed, then reduce, then choose fifty percent," Loki reminded Marcus.

"Right. Speed; reduce; fifty percent," Marcus repeated as he performed the steps. "Execute."

The Seiiki's engines reacted immediately, spinning up and firing the deceleration thrusters on the forward portions of the engine nacelles.

"See," Marcus said, smiling, "button pushing."

"Keep it up, smart guy," Josh warned. "We haven't even started your emergency procedures training yet."

* * *

"You wanted to see me?" Michael asked as he entered the makeshift lab, deep inside the old, abandoned terrak mine.

"Yes," Cuddy responded. He finished entering a few more lines of code, then turned from his view screen. "I think I figured out a way to secure your communications over the public networks."

"Already?" Michael replied, surprised. "It's only been a few hours."

"More like fifteen," Birk corrected from his seat in the corner of the lab. "Fifteen...long...boring... hours." Birk stretched, yawning. "Don't you guys have any kind of entertainment around here?"

"We spend most of our time working," Michael replied curtly. He turned back to Cuddy. "What did you discover?"

"Well, you did most of the work for me, to be honest," Cuddy admitted. "All of the message-routing data that you collected over the last ten days is what clued me in. If you compare it with normal message-routing data from *before* the Dusahn, you'll notice..."

Michael studied the two data sets, which were displayed side-by-side on Cuddy's view screen. "There are no messages being pushed through the backup networks," he finally realized.

"Exactly. We switched to the new network infrastructure a few years ago. But we still use the old networks as a backup, and during abnormally high usage periods. Priority traffic sometimes sends the same message on both nets, to ensure that the message arrives intact."

"Why aren't the Dusahn using them?" Michael wondered.

"Probably because they recognize that those nets are based on outdated technology. They probably don't plan on maintaining it. Easier to monitor one high-performance communications system than two, especially when the second one is not as reliable."

"If it isn't reliable, why does it still exist?" Birk asked.

"You never remove the old system in favor of the new one until the new one has proven itself trustworthy," Michael stated. "Not if you don't have to."

"They were going to start dismantling the old networks in a couple years," Cuddy said. "If the Dusahn are not monitoring the old networks, then you'll have your own private messaging system."

"And if they are?" Birk challenged, playing devil's advocate.

"Encryption," Cuddy replied, sarcastically.

"Actually, he has a point," Michael said.

Birk smiled triumphantly.

"It happens on occasion," Cuddy quipped.

"If they *are* monitoring the old networks, we'd be taking a big risk."

"Why not just start flooding the old networks with random copies of messages already being sent on the new networks?" Cuddy suggested. "Give them millions of messages to sort through."

"They would likely shut the secondary network down to avoid complications," Michael insisted.

"But if they are *not* monitoring it..."

"Then they wouldn't even know the messages were there," Michael said. "But how would the recipients know where to look?"

"I'm sure we could create a simple app that would pull the correct messages from the backup networks. Include an algorithm that pulls bits from the other messages and then assembles them on the recipients' comm-unit into a coherent message."

"The algorithm will need to constantly change, never using the same one twice," Michael insisted.

"Of course."

"How long will it take you to create this application?"

"A couple days, maybe," Cuddy answered. "You'll need to send someone out into the wild to receive the message and reply, so that we can test the system."

"That will not be a problem." Michael studied the code on the young man's view screen for a moment. "Nicely done, Cuddy."

"Thank you."

"You know, if you *really* want to make it safe, you could change the chips in all your comm-units," Birk suggested. "Put the master algorithm from which all the iterations are built right on the chip, and encrypt it with an impossibly long key that would take them a decade to break."

"We don't have the ability to create new chips," Michael replied.

"You don't need to create new ones. Just reprogram existing ones, like the ones that were for the old networks. They're redundant now, anyway, right?"

"That *would* make it more secure," Cuddy agreed.

"There's always a chance the Dusahn might capture one of them," Michael pointed out.

"Program a key combo to fry the chip," Birk suggested.

Michael looked at the two young men as he considered the idea. "Very well," he finally said. "Get started...both of you."

"Finally! Something to do!" Birk exclaimed, jumping up from his seat as Michael left the room.

* * *

Without warning, General Telles walked into the flight briefing room on the Aurora's flight operations. All twenty-four Ghatazhak in the room, including Jessica, rose to their feet and came to attention without being prompted. Following suit were Nathan and the crew of the Seiiki, Cameron, Lieutenant Commander Shinoda, and Deliza and Yanni.

"As you were," General Telles instructed, stepping up to the lectern. With the press of a button, the large screen on the wall to his right lit up, displaying an annotated aerial view of a production facility, with what appeared to be a long set of rails traveling down the side of a hill away from the building.

"This is the Cobra gunship production plant on the planet Kohara, in the Tau Ceti system," the general began. "The entire facility is surrounded by a three-layered stun fence and is protected by numerous automated weapons towers. It is monitored by vid-cams and eight different types of sensors, including weapons detectors, infrared, life-sign detectors... You name it, they've got it. In addition, it is also protected by a contingent of fifty Alliance Marines stationed on-site, as well as a wing of Super Eagles and Reapers at the Geraleise spaceport, six hundred kilometers to the southeast. On top of *that*, the Alliance battleship, Benakh, is tasked with the protection of not only the Tau Ceti system, but the Cobra plant itself. Despite the fact that there is seemingly no way for anyone to get into the base without permission, the Cobra gunships themselves are fitted with lockout systems. If launched without authorization, their jump drives will not work, and they will end up in the recovery lake a few hundred meters downrange of the launch track. If any attempt is made to remove a jump drive from the plant, or from any of the completed gunships, the drive's independently powered self-destruct system will detonate, killing anyone within one hundred meters. Quite frankly, the facility is impossible to breach."

Nathan was sure he noticed the faintest of smiles on the general's face.

"*We* are going to breach that facility and steal at least six fully operational gunships."

Nathan looked around at the faces of the other Ghatazhak in attendance, including Jessica. They too had discreet, confident smiles on their faces. Despite their general's description of the target's impenetrable security measures, not a single man—or woman—in the room doubted their leader's assertion.

"As I said, there is only one way to set foot on that compound," General Telles continued, "and *that* is to have *permission.* A team of four will accompany Captain Gil Roselle, commanding officer of the Benakh, on a surprise inspection tour of the facility. Those four will be dressed as Alliance Marines, wearing uniforms and armor provided by Captain Roselle. Once inside, Captain Roselle will use his command codes to disable the compound's security systems, allowing us to safely insert another twenty Ghatazhak into the compound. The disabled security system will automatically trigger a response by the on-site marines, as well as the launch of the air assets at Geraleise. Unencumbered, the marines will be on us in less than a minute, and the air assets in five. Our ground forces will need to deploy and reach proper intercept points *before* the Alliance Marines exit their barracks."

"What about those air assets?" Josh asked rudely.

Nathan cast a disapproving glance at Josh.

"What?" Josh said sheepishly. "It's a fair question."

The general continued, ignoring Josh's comments. "Seconds before Captain Roselle deactivates the facility's security systems, Commander Jarso and his flight of six Rakers will attack the Geraleise spaceport, buying us the time we need to access and launch the gunships."

"That facility isn't designed to rapidly launch the gunships," Lieutenant Commander Shinoda warned. "It normally takes fifteen minutes to get a gunship from the holding area to the launch track."

"Commander Kamenetskiy has assured me that he can alter the control program to accelerate the positioning and launch cycles."

"How much time can you shave off?" Lieutenant Commander Shinoda asked Vladimir.

"The dollies that move the gunships were originally designed for much heavier loads. They are capable of moving a gunship ten times faster than they are currently programmed to do."

"Maybe so, but we're talking about launching six of them," the lieutenant commander reminded him. "How long is *that* going to take?"

"Approximately twenty-one minutes, from the

time we gain access to the gunships to the time the sixth gunship launches," Vladimir replied.

"Twenty-one minutes?" Lieutenant Commander Shinoda looked at General Telles. "You expect to hold off fifty Alliance Marines for twenty-one minutes?"

"Thirty, if you include the time it will take for the flight crews to get to the gunships and bypass their individual security systems," General Telles replied.

"*Thirty* minutes."

"It will not be a problem," the general assured the lieutenant commander.

"Have we considered the ramifications of killing Alliance Marines?" Cameron asked. "Stealing gunships is one thing, but those marines are technically friendlies. If we cross that line, there will be no turning back. Galiardi will declare us to be terrorists, or an enemy state. He may even send ships after us."

"We intend to use non-lethal force to subdue the Alliance Marines on Kohara," General Telles assured her.

"Whoa," Josh whispered. "A kinder, gentler Ghatazhak. Never thought I'd see that."

"However, if lethal force is required to assure the safety of our people," the general continued, "it will be used, regardless of the potential complications."

"Oops, I spoke too soon," Josh muttered.

"And those Super Eagles?" Cameron wondered.

"They will be attacked prior to the alert, and the hour will be late. The loss of life should be minimal."

"Minimal," Cameron said, obviously unsatisfied.

"Commander Jarso and his pilots will be instructed to avoid taking Alliance lives, if possible," General Telles assured her, "but again, we must protect ourselves. Our numbers are few."

Cameron spoke quietly to Nathan. "You're okay with this?"

"I don't see that we have much choice, Cam," Nathan replied. "Galiardi and the Alliance leadership ignored their obligation to defend the Pentaurus sector, knowing damn well that it would cost lives... *innocent* lives."

"Yes, but..."

"Do you honestly think Galiardi would not do the same?" Nathan asked. "Wouldn't *you*, to protect Earth?"

"I didn't say I was opposed, Nathan," Cameron defended. "I just wanted to make sure that we're considering all the facts."

"I assure you, we have," General Telles promised her, and a hush came over them.

"When are we going?" Nathan asked.

"The Seiiki will depart immediately," General Telles replied.

"But we've been running nonstop for twenty hours now," Neli protested.

"It will take you three days to reach Earth," General Telles stated. "You will have plenty of time to rest during your journey. Besides, we need the Seiiki to complete her mission and get Doctor Sorenson and her family off Earth *prior* to our attack on Kohara." General Telles looked at Deliza. "I trust the jump sub is ready?"

"Ready, yes. *Tested...*?"

"Well, if it doesn't work, we'll just bring them back to the Seiiki with us," Jessica said.

"Just like that," Cameron commented dryly.

"Yup," Jessica replied confidently.

"If we're leaving immediately, when are we

supposed to learn how to fly the gunships?" Loki asked.

"We have outfitted several VR units to allow training en route," Cameron told him.

"You'll have additional time at the rendezvous point, as well," General Telles assured Loki.

"I'm not worried," Josh bragged.

"*That's* what worries *me*," Loki said under his breath.

"You spoke of the Rakers," Vladimir commented. "Their jump drives don't have the range to get them to the Sol sector."

"The Morsiko-Tavi departed five hours ago, carrying all six Rakers and their pilots. She will arrive at the rally point two days *after* the rest of our forces, and ahead of the Seiiki."

"Are *we* flying the Seiiki to Earth, or is Marcus?" Josh asked.

"You and Mister Sheehan will pilot the Seiiki all the way through the mission on Earth, and all the way back to the rally point," General Telles explained. "At which point Mister Taggart and Miss Ravel will pilot the Seiiki back to the Aurora, so that you and Mister Hayes can join us on the Kohara mission to pilot gunships."

"So, we're breaking into an impenetrable facility and stealing a bunch of ships that no one knows how to fly," Marcus grumbled. "What could possibly go wrong?"

CHAPTER SEVEN

President Scott sat at the head of the oval conference table in the council chambers, at the Alliance headquarters deep within Port Terra. It was the sixth time the council had assembled since Jung ships began showing up deep within Alliance territory twenty-three days ago. Prior to that, the council met once every three Earth months.

Dayton had always looked forward to these meetings in the past. Most of the representatives from the core worlds were interesting, intelligent people from widely varied cultures; the result of centuries of isolation and independent development after the bio-digital plague had broken their ties to one another. The meetings were literally events, with all the diplomatic pomp and circumstance that one might expect, including the post-meeting dinner. Those dinners would last long into the late hours as they regaled one another with stories from their individual worlds, their tales fueled by the finest wines and spirits available throughout the Sol sector.

But those days were gone. Now, the representatives arrived in their various jump shuttles and hurried straight to the council chambers, their moods foul and their faces worn. They were hardly the same people they had been a month ago, and neither was Dayton. The events of the past three weeks had changed them all, Dayton had felt it. It was the same feeling of dread that he had felt during the original Jung war. He had put on a hopeful and positive face for the people of Earth, and he had tried to instill that same feeling in each of the representatives as their worlds had been liberated by his forces, giving them a taste of freedom for the first time in centuries.

It had taken President Scott months to convince those newly liberated worlds that the Alliance would be able to keep the Jung threat at bay. All of their worlds had recovered. Even Earth, which had been nearly destroyed by repeated attempts by their enemy to erase them from existence, had nearly recovered. His world still had the scars of battle, to be sure, but they were healing. The famine and disease that had plagued Earth for years after their liberation had finally been brought under control, and Earth's people had once again become hopeful.

Until twenty-three days ago.

"Mister President," Admiral Galiardi began, "if I may?"

President Scott nodded, giving the room to the admiral.

"Ladies and gentlemen, I fear that events are forcing us onto a road we'd rather not take but have always known we would eventually have to travel. Our intelligence operatives on Nor-Patri have informed us that the Jung people are calling for an all-out war against the Alliance. There are riots in their streets and on the very steps of the leadership. Even the once-docile isolationist castes are calling for the Alliance to be brought under control."

"I don't understand," President Scott said angrily. "*They* trespassed in *our* territory and, when confronted, *they* fired upon *us*."

"We all know this to be true," Admiral Galiardi agreed, "but the Jung military castes have likely informed their leaders otherwise. And, I suspect, they have leaked as much to the people, as well."

"What about the other Jung worlds?" Minister

Denara asked. "Surely, not all of them are calling for a war."

"We do not have operatives on every Jung world as of yet, I'm afraid," Admiral Galiardi admitted. "But the few we have been able to monitor are of similar minds. They want retribution."

"For responding to their attacks on our ships!" Minister Pinnear exclaimed.

"The Jung do not see things as we do," Admiral Galiardi reminded them all. "They see the entire universe as theirs for the taking and are convinced that it is their destiny to bring order to all of humanity, regardless of the cost."

"Not all the Jung feel that way," President Scott corrected.

"That is true, but unfortunately, they are not the ones who speak the loudest at the moment."

"Perhaps we should send a message to Nor-Patri," Minister Zemar suggested. "A message inviting them to talk."

"They would never respond," Admiral Galiardi insisted.

"It would be worth a try," Minister Zemar argued.

"No, the admiral is correct," President Scott agreed. "To seek a peaceful solution now would appear as a weakness to the Jung and would only embolden them to attack."

"Precisely," Admiral Galiardi agreed.

"We must continue to show our resolve," President Scott added.

"We must do more than that, I'm afraid," Admiral Galiardi said.

President Scott looked at the admiral. He had set the stage nicely and was preparing to make his recommendation, one that President Scott feared most.

"We must strike decisively."

"At which targets?" President Scott asked solemnly.

"We must take out their battle platforms," the admiral replied.

"Which ones?"

"All of them, Mister President."

"There are upwards of five thousand people on each of those platforms," Minister Pinnear gasped.

"We killed far greater numbers in our initial strike," Admiral Galiardi reminded them.

"Why the battle platforms?" President Scott asked.

"Because they are the one thing that we cannot defend against with an acceptable level of certainty," the admiral explained. "If they send them one or two at a time, perhaps, but any more than that, and I'm afraid they will run right over us."

"But as of yet, those platforms have shown no indications that they are preparing to move," President Scott said.

"None that we have been able to detect," Admiral Galiardi agreed. "But if we wait, we may lose track of them."

"I thought we could detect ships in FTL?" Minister Finn said.

"We can, but it is not easy," the admiral explained. "And those platforms are currently in Jung space."

"Then, we have time to prepare," President Scott decided.

"Yes, but again, the longer we wait, the more likely those platforms will slip into FTL," Admiral Galiardi repeated. "Taking them all out now, in a single strike, will send a clear message to the Jung that we are not to be trifled with...that we are willing to do whatever is necessary to protect ourselves and will not tolerate *any* overt aggression...period."

"You are essentially drawing a line in the sand, Admiral," President Scott said.

"The Jung drew that line, Mister President," Admiral Galiardi insisted. "I just want to keep them well on their side. The best way to do that is to break their will to fight."

"And you're convinced that destroying their battle platforms will accomplish that goal?" President Scott wondered.

"At the very least, it will delay their attack for several more years," Admiral Galiardi insisted. "Perhaps even decades. The Jung prefer to use overwhelming force, especially when facing a foe that has already successfully pushed them back."

"The Jung surround us on three sides, Admiral," Minister Finn reminded him as the other men in the room seemed to chew over the proposal. "They could send a hundred ships in at once. If given enough time to move their ships into position, they could strike every Alliance world in the Sol sector with dozens of ships at once."

"But that would take a decade or more," Admiral Galiardi insisted. "By then, we will have several capital ships and nearly a thousand gunships. Not to mention ground-based jump missile defense systems on the surface of every Alliance world. At that point, attacking us would be suicide. The key is those battle platforms. Without them, they may *want* to attack but they will *not.* They will not be willing to sacrifice their ships on a fool's mission."

"Perhaps this is something we should discuss at

length, and then vote on it in a few days," President Scott suggested.

"A few days may be too late," Admiral Galiardi warned.

"You're asking us to authorize a strike against eight of the Jung Empire's most powerful assets. To make that decision in haste, and in fear, would be foolhardy," President Scott insisted. "I appreciate your position, Admiral, but I have made my decision. The council will adjourn for four days, while we study the facts. When we meet again we shall vote, but not before then."

"Yes, Mister President," Admiral Galiardi replied, nearly choking on his response.

"Ladies and gentlemen, I urge you all to give this decision due consideration. I will require a vote when we meet again in four days."

* * *

"A lot seems to hinge on Roselle," Jessica commented as she walked with Nathan and the others back to the Aurora's main hangar deck. "Are we sure he's going to come through?"

"The plan was his idea," Cameron replied. "Ninety percent of the intel about the facility came from him, and my people have verified more than half of it."

"Are we positive we're not being set up?" Jessica asked.

"Good to see you haven't changed," Cameron remarked with a chuckle.

"Hey, I've got to ask, you know that."

"Honestly, I have considered it," Cameron admitted.

"I trust Roselle," Nathan insisted as they headed down the ramp from the command deck.

"I thought you hated him?" Jessica said. "Didn't he chew your ass a few times?"

"I still trust him."

"It does concern me that Roselle is pretty much stuck on the Benakh. Both he and his XO, Martin Ellison, have been passed over for promotion. Gil has pretty much accepted that. Scuttlebutt has it that he has a fiancé on Kohara and is headed for retirement soon. *Ellison,* on the other hand, could use an event to help push him past the old-school hurdle faced by all of us who served with you."

Nathan and the others reached the bottom of the ramp and turned aft toward the main hangar deck. "What are you talking about?" he asked Cameron.

"Galiardi doesn't trust us," Cameron explained. "Me, Vlad, Gil, Robert; pretty much anyone who served under you and Admiral Dumar. That's why he's been promoting anyone with any promise who demonstrates loyalty to his command. You'd be amazed at how quickly your average 'fresh out of the academy ensign' can find themselves in command of a gunship as a newly minted lieutenant."

"So, you think Ellison might give us up to win favor?" Jessica asked.

"Anything is possible," Cameron replied. "That's why I told Robert not to tell anyone but Roselle."

"Gil and Marty *are* pretty close," Jessica commented. "They've served together since before any of us were born."

"Roselle isn't stupid," Nathan insisted. "He wouldn't tell his own mother, if he wasn't sure he could trust her."

"I hope you're right," Jessica said.

"I'm sure I am," Nathan insisted as they entered the Aurora's main hangar deck.

Just ahead, Nathan and Jessica spotted General Telles and a contingent of Ghatazhak. Telles was dressed in full combat armor and was carrying his chest piece and helmet at his side.

"Where are you going?" Jessica asked as they approached.

"This mission is vital to the future of this rebellion," General Telles replied. "Therefore, I am going to ensure its success."

"Great," Cameron said. "What am I supposed to do if all three of you get killed?"

"Protect the fleet and keep harassing the Dusahn however you can," Nathan replied.

"Thanks, I never would have thought of that," she said sarcastically.

"Ghatazhak!" General Telles barked. "Mount up!" He turned back to Nathan and Jessica. "I shall see you at the rally point in a few days."

"Safe flight," Nathan replied. He turned to Cameron. "If we *don't* make it back, the rebellion is in your hands." He looked at her for a moment. "Are you okay with that?"

"I wouldn't be here if I wasn't," Cameron stated confidently.

"I only know two people who I would trust with such a responsibility, and I'm looking at one of them right now," Nathan told her.

"Shouldn't that number be four?" Cameron wondered.

"What, Vlad and Jess?" Nathan laughed. "Hell, no. Vlad's too emotional, and Jess is too damn reckless. Leaders have to see the big picture. They have to think in longer terms than the here and now. That's always been something you have excelled at, Cam. *That's* the *real* reason I asked you to come. Not for the Aurora." After a short pause, he added, "Well, for the Aurora too, I suppose."

Cameron smiled. "Stay safe, and don't let Jess get you into trouble."

"I'll do my best," Nathan replied before turning and heading for the Seiiki in the starboard airlock bay.

Cameron watched as General Telles and the Ghatazhak boarded their cargo shuttle, and Nathan and his crew headed up the Seiiki's cargo ramp. Things were starting to feel like old times. The problem was, those times were always fraught with danger.

* * *

Miri entered her father's office to deliver the documents that he would need to review upon his return. The office was dark, as he had left for another council meeting at Port Terra hours ago.

It was late in the day, and the sun was already setting. Once the papers were on the president's desk, Miri looked forward to being able to spend an evening with her children. She missed listening to them argue, as all teenagers do.

She placed the papers on her father's desk, then picked up the remote to close the curtains over the massive windows that filled the wall behind it.

"Leave them open," her father said.

"Oh, my God," Miri replied with a start.

The high-backed executive desk chair rotated to the left just enough to reveal her father's presence. "I didn't mean to startle you."

"Well, you did," she said, reversing the motion of the curtains. "When did you return?"

"Nearly an hour ago."

Miri set the remote down. "Well, that was a short trip."

"He wants to take out their battle platforms," her father stated.

Miri moved around to sit on the bench seat in front of the big bay window, facing her father. "And that's a *bad* thing, I take it?"

"I never should have reappointed him," Dayton said.

"You didn't have a choice, father."

"I could have opposed him."

"That would have been the end of your presidency, and you know it. Galiardi was going to regain power, no matter what you did. You said so yourself when you decided to put him in command again. At least with you as president, there is someone to hold him back."

"He has been preparing us for a war with the Jung since you were a child. And, now, he is going to get exactly that. And millions will die again."

"Then, you don't believe we can win?"

"Ours or theirs, it matters not. Death is death. War is the most wretched thing humanity has ever conceived, and it is the one thing we can never seem to escape. It is part and parcel to the human animal." He looked at his daughter. "I don't know that I have it in me to lead us through another war, Miri."

"You must," she reminded him. After a moment, she asked, "How did the council vote?"

"I insisted that we take a few days to consider the recommendation."

"Good idea."

"I was stalling for time," Dayton told her, sighing. "I know Galiardi is right. If those platforms *are* jump capable, and if even half of them jump in over Earth at once, we are doomed."

"Then vote to strike," Miri said.

"Which will save the Earth but ensure a long, protracted war with the Jung. How do I live with that?"

Miri sat in silence, unable to find the words to console her father. "If you vote against Galiardi's recommendation, what will happen?"

"The other worlds will likely back me."

"And if Galiardi is right, and we do not strike?"

"Then the Jung *could* walk in and destroy us at any moment...all of us...every Alliance world, one by one."

"And if they do not have jump drives?"

"Then they could still destroy us, but it would probably take a decade for them to get here."

"And if you strike now?"

"War."

"And how soon will that war begin?"

"I do not know. It could be minutes, it could be years. But they *will* come. And Galiardi will recommend that we strike their worlds next, and millions more will die. Not soldiers, but women and children. He will not stop until the threat is completely eliminated. I can see it in his eyes."

"You said that war is something that humanity cannot escape, that it is our nature. Maybe it's up to *you* to break that cycle."

"With such overt aggressions by the Jung, failing to support Galiardi now will only feed his power base."

Miri leaned forward, putting her hand on her father's knee to comfort him. "Not everyone wants to destroy the Jung. Those are the people you represent. If you vote only to retain power, you are lying to yourself and to those who support you. If you vote your conscience, you may be able to protect us from a war we may not *need* to fight."

"Or condemn us to certain destruction. Don't you see, Miri; my duty to *protect* the people supersedes my duty to serve them. Either way, I will carry the responsibility for countless lives that might otherwise be spared. How do I...how do *we* live with that guilt?" Dayton's gaze moved past his youngest daughter, back to the lights of the capital outside his window. "Nathan knew how to live with the guilt of sacrificing the lives of a few, to save the lives of many. If only he were alive..."

He is. The thought tore at her heart. She wanted so much to tell him, but she could not. It was not her decision. Her baby brother, whom she too had believed dead, had asked for her help, for *her* secrecy. She had to honor that request, no matter how much it pained her.

She was beginning to understand the burdens her father and brother both shared.

* * *

Aiden and Ken stood in formation with the rest of their class, outside the Cobra production facility on Kohara. Today was the moment they had all been working toward.

"*Class! Ah-ten-shun!*" the master chief called from the side of the formation as the commander walked out in front of the assembled cadets.

Commander Bastyan came to a stop directly centered in front of the group of men and women, turning sharply to face them. "At ease." After looking them over, she began. "The Cobra-D gunship is the most advanced, most maneuverable, and most deadly ship in the Alliance Fleet. She is a pack hunter, designed to attack a target in concert with as many as twenty elements. She demands your attention to detail and your respect for procedure. Give her the respect she is due, and she will get you home safely. More importantly, she will see that your enemy does not. Today, you will begin your orientation training. You will meet your crews, and you will get to know every nook and cranny of your ships. Do not hesitate to ask the engineers questions about your ships, should you have them. For in five days, you will be riding those ships down that launch rail and jumping them into space."

"Man, I cannot believe this is finally happening," Aiden whispered to Ken.

"I can't believe we actually graduated," Ken replied in similar tone.

"For the next four days, you will be running group simulations in these very ships. Everything will be as it will be in space. It will be your opportunity to become accustomed to the Cobra-D's new flight console, and to practice the pack-hunting tactics using the swarm-attack auto-flight system."

"Yeah, push-button piloting," Aiden mocked under his breath.

"Shut up."

Commander Bastyan paused a moment, turning to look in the direction of Aiden and Ken; both of them turned their eyes straight ahead as if concentrating on the commander's every word. "Do not think for a moment that, because you have passed your initial flight training, that you cannot fail this final stage check. I assure you," she said, looking directly at Aiden, "you can. And some of you will." The commander continued scanning the formation as she spoke. "Once assigned, you will have access to your ships around the clock. You will spend every waking moment of the next four days in your ships, running drill after drill after drill. In between formation simulations, you will be expected to run crew drills. Your crews must be ready to fight. They must be ready to survive in space. You have but four days to prepare. I suggest you use every minute of them wisely."

"I am so damned excited, I'm going to explode," Aiden mumbled.

"Master Chief!" the commander barked.

"Yes, Commander!"

"Give these pilots their ships!"

"Aye, Commander!"

Commander Bastyan turned and strode off toward the training command bunker as the master chief began barking out names.

"Delton, Ferris; Three Eight Zero! Kin, Sangar; Three Eight One!"

As their names were called, the flight teams left the formation and headed toward the holding area to locate their ships and meet their crews.

"Tegg, Wabash; Three Eight Two!" the master chief continued.

Aiden exchanged glances with Charnelle Tegg, her face beaming with anticipation as she and her copilot, Sari Wabash, headed for their ship.

"Walsh, Lowen; Three Eight Three!"

A smile drew itself across Aiden's face as he and Ken marched forward toward the holding area. "Cobra Three Eight Three!" he exclaimed, trying to keep his voice down as they followed Charnelle and Sari toward the rows of waiting gunships. "That's our new call sign, Ken!"

"Yeah, I heard," Ken replied, entertained by his friend's exuberance. "How old are you, Aiden? Four?"

"Tell me you're not excited!"

"Of course, I'm excited," Ken admitted. "I'm just not an idiot about it."

"Cobra Three Eight Three. Has a nice ring to it, doesn't it?"

Ken just looked at him as they continued toward the gunships.

Aiden and Ken followed the others to the holding area. Until now, none of them had actually seen a Cobra gunship up close. They had studied countless technical drawings and models, and had spent at least a hundred hours in the simulators, but had not seen an actual ship up close. The sims were just the front half of the cockpit, with instructors sitting behind them watching their every move. The ships before them were the real thing. Armed combat ships that they would be flying all over the Sol sector.

Aiden felt as if he would explode with excitement. "Three Eight Three," he called out to Charnelle and Sari as they passed.

"I heard," Charnelle replied.

Aiden slowed a moment as he and Ken approached their ship for the first time. She was larger than he expected. The interior mockups they had trained in were cramped, with just enough space to get by, so he had always imagined the ships themselves as equally compact. But now, it seemed enormous. "Holy crap."

"You took the words right out of my mouth," Ken agreed, equally awed by the ship before them.

"It's big."

"Yeah."

Aiden turned to Ken, the smile returning. "And it's ours, Kenji. It's all *ours*."

"It's not ours, Aiden. It belongs to the Alliance. They're just letting us use it. Best you remember that." Ken looked to his left. "Try to look commanding, Aiden. Our crew is coming," he warned, tipping his head in the direction of the approaching group of cadets.

The first to approach was a short, stout woman with high and tight black hair, sporting the rank of chief on her lapels and the symbol of an engineer on her shoulder patch. "You must be our captain," the woman grumbled. She looked Aiden up and down. "You don't look like much. You sure you're old enough to enlist, kid?"

"Are all engineers as old as you?" Aiden quipped. "Or did it just take you longer than most to earn those wrenches on your shoulder?"

Ken looked upward in disbelief.

The woman squinted, staring Aiden in the eyes for what seemed an eternity. Finally, she laughed and extended her hand. "Ashwini Benetti," she greeted. "But you can call me Ash."

"Aiden Walsh," Aiden replied, shaking the woman's rough hand. "You can call me Captain."

She laughed again. "This is Sergeant Dagata, Specialist Brim, and Specialist Leger," she said, introducing the other three members of the group.

"A pleasure," Aiden replied. He approached each of them, shaking their hands one at a time.

"Cowyn Dagata, sir," the first man announced. "Sensors and computers."

"Nice to meet you, Sergeant," Aiden greeted. "This is my first officer, Ensign Lowen."

"Alisanne Brim," the next person said, smiling as

she shook her new captain's hand. "I'm your medic and gunner."

"Nice to meet you, Alisanne."

"Please, call me Ali."

"Very well, Ali, this is Ken Lowen, my first officer."

The last man stepped forward as Ali moved to shake Ken's hand, as well.

"Specialist Cosgrove Leger," the boyish-looking, young man announced, saluting Aiden. "Systems technician and gunner, sir."

"Relax Cosgrove," Aiden insisted as he returned the salute. "A handshake is fine. We're all going to be working together very closely. Can I call you Cos? Cosgrove is a mouthful."

"My friends call me Ledge, sir," the young man replied eagerly. "But you can call me anything you'd like, sir."

"No, Ledge will be fine."

"Yes, sir."

"How old are you, Ledge?" Aiden wondered.

"Seventeen and a half, sir."

"Do your parents know you're here?"

"They signed the age waiver, sir. I can show it to you if you'd like," Ledge offered, reaching into his pocket. "I carry it with me."

"Why?"

"You'd be surprised how many times I get asked how old I am, sir."

"I don't think I would be, Ledge," Aiden replied, holding his hand up. "Keep it in your pocket. I believe you."

"Thank you, sir. Don't worry about my age, Captain. I know my stuff. I won't let you down."

"I'm sure you won't, Ledge."

"Cadets," an older man called as he approached.

"I'm Dahr Mencer. I'll be your orientation engineer for Cobra Three Eight Three. Shall we get started?"

"You bet," Aiden exclaimed. "Aiden Walsh... *Captain* Aiden Walsh."

"Oh, brother," Ken mumbled.

"A pleasure to meet you, Captain," Dahr replied. "Why don't you all climb aboard, and we'll get started with your orientation."

Aiden looked at Ken, that same goofy grin returning.

"Aiden, please get rid of the grin. It's embarrassing."

Aiden laughed. "I can't help it, Kenji."

* * *

Derek walked down the dimly lit corridor from the lab to the secure exit. As usual, he was the last to leave, or so he thought. As he passed the last intersection, he noticed light coming from an open door down a side corridor. He paused a moment, then decided to investigate.

As he approached the open door, he realized it was to the metallurgy lab. He entered the room and found Abby sitting at one of the testing counters, rubbing her eyes. "What are you doing in here?" he wondered.

"Just waiting for the fatigue tests on the last batch of failed emitters."

"Shouldn't you be home by now? Won't your family be worried?" Derek wondered.

"They're at a game at school," she said. "They won't be home for another hour."

"Surely the results can wait until morning."

"I just wanted to get the numbers, so I could start fresh in the morning."

"Yeah, I know what you mean," Derek said,

sitting in a nearby chair. "I really thought the extra terrenium was going to do the trick."

"So did I. That's the reason I wanted to get the test results. I think the terrenium might have held onto the charge longer than expected."

"You think that caused the emitters to fail?"

"Maybe. The discharge curves should tell us," Abby said. "But first, I need to know the true failure points in the emitter structures, and if they were identical across the board."

"Well, *I* can live without that knowledge until morning," Derek yawned. "I can barely keep my eyes open. Honestly, Abby, I don't know how you put in the hours you do." Derek rose from his chair and headed for the door. "I'll see you tomorrow," he said as he departed.

Abby sighed. One of her greatest faults was her inability to let unanswered questions wait. Her calculations had indicated that the extra terrenium *should* have given the emitters the ability to withstand the energy loads without failure of their discharge surfaces. And each of their tests had backed those calculations up...until the last one. That's when reality and the numbers went awry. According to Abby's calculations, the terrenium-enhanced emitters should have been able to handle at least a seventy-percent power load, yet they had all failed at fifty percent; far below their predicted failure points.

She would stay until she had an answer. Her husband would understand. He always did.

Finally, the computer began to display the results. She studied the data on the view screen closely, comparing every value with those predicted by her pretest calculations. They had all failed in precisely the way she had predicted, but at twenty percent less power than expected.

She checked the test data; the power settings showed fifty percent, just as they had the last ten times she checked them.

She leaned back in her chair, dejected. Fifty percent was not enough power for a stealth jump drive to be effective. Specifications called for a stealth jump range of at least ten light years. While fifty percent would get them ten light years, it would require the ship to accelerate considerably. The ten-light-year requirement was without acceleration, and rightfully so. With the advent of the jump drive, warships no longer needed to carry massive propellant stores, as their speeds remained relatively constant.

Abby began gathering up her data pads to place them in their chargers. She was not going to find her answers tonight, that much she would have to accept. But then, something caught her eye as she picked up one of the data pads. The pad contained the output logs for the reactor used for the emitter test chamber. She scrolled through the peak output graph for the day's testing cycles. As expected, each spike was slightly higher than that of the previous test. All the way until the last one, when the spike was drastically higher.

Abby expanded the graph on the data pad. The spike at the moment of the last test, the one that had caused the emitters to fail, did not indicate a fifty-percent power output; it showed a ninety-three-percent power output from the reactor. *Twenty-three percent higher than the predicted failure point.*

"This can't be right," Abby said to herself. The failure patterns on the emitters matched what was expected at seventy percent. At ninety-three percent, the damage should have been much worse.

Of course, while that answered one question, it raised another. Regardless, it meant one thing; she now had a metallurgy formula for creating stealth jump emitters that not only met the ten-light-year criteria but *exceeded* it, likely by at least five light years at average speeds.

"Oh, my God," she exclaimed softly. "We've done it." She looked around, as if to call out to someone to share the moment, and then remembered she was alone. That's when reality hit her.

Admiral Galiardi now has what he needs to attack the Jung with impunity.

The thought terrified her. The Alliance had enjoyed an advantage over the Jung for nine years and, because of it, the two empires had managed to forge a tenuous peace. A stealth jump drive would tip the scales so far in the Alliance's favor that the Jung would not stand a chance. Perhaps worse yet, if the Jung discovered that the Alliance had a working prototype stealth jump emitter large and powerful enough to jump a warship ten to fifteen light years, they would be forced to attack with everything they had *before* the Alliance could outfit their ships with the new technology.

But it would take the Jung years to get their ships to Earth, or to any other Alliance world in the Sol sector.

Assuming they did not yet have their own jump drives.

Abby knew what she had to do. With a few taps, she deleted the reactor output logs.

* * *

Josh sat in the middle of the Seiiki's cargo bay as

Vladimir carefully placed the oddly shaped virtual reality helmet on his head. "I can't see a damned thing," Josh said as Vladimir fastened a strap under Josh's chin and cinched it tight.

"Hold on a minute," Vladimir told him as he moved behind Josh and touched the control pad on the back of the helmet. "First, the system has to make a connection to your brain."

Josh felt the helmet squeezing gently all around his head. "Wait, what kind of connection? This thing isn't going to jack something into my skull, is it?"

"Nothing like that," Vladimir assured him. "It uses a sensor network all around the outside of your head. You should feel them by now."

Josh felt a tingling feeling on his scalp. "Yeah, I do. It's creepy. It feels like bugs crawling all over my head."

"How come we've never heard of this?" Loki wondered.

"It is very new technology," Vladimir explained. "This device has the ability to mimic *any* environment or situation, without requiring all the space that a normal flight simulator needs *or* using a real cockpit in simulation mode."

"*Any* environment or, uh, *situation*?"

"Get your mind out of the gutter, Josh," Nathan scolded.

"This thing is safe, right?" Loki wondered.

"I have used it myself," Vladimir assured him.

"Can this be used for ground combat simulation?" Jessica asked.

"This model, no. It requires the user to be in a sitting position. For use on a moving user, it requires more sophisticated proprioception data processing. But I believe they are working on a model for that purpose." Vladimir checked the control display on the back of the device. "There. It has made the connection. Do you still feel like bugs are crawling on your head?"

"Nope."

"Very well, I am activating the simulation environment."

Josh felt something strange. His hearing faded away, and he felt as if his entire body was going numb. Even his sense of smell had left him. "What the hell?" He held his hands up, touching his fingers to his thumbs one by one. He could feel them, but just barely. Then, his vision came alive. Slowly, at first, as if someone was gradually turning up the lights. But he wasn't in the Seiiki's cargo bay any longer. He was sitting in the pilot's seat of a Cobra gunship.

"Oh...my...God," he said in awe, looking around. Everything around him looked incredibly real. If it wasn't for the fact that everything was too perfect, he wondered if he would be able to tell that this was a virtual reality simulation.

"*Are you okay?*" Vladimir asked.

"What the..." Vladimir's voice sounded different. "You sound like you're on comms."

"*That's because I am,*" Vladimir replied. "*As long as the simulation environment is active, anyone standing near you will sound as if they are on comm-sets.*"

"This is crazy," Josh exclaimed with boyish glee.

"*Okay, the first thing we need to do is get your senses accustomed to the virtual reality environment. It will feel a little different.*"

"Feel?"

"*Yes,*" Vladimir said. "*The system is sending*

sensor input to all three of your primary senses. Sight, sound, and touch."

"I can touch stuff?"

"*Yes. Carefully reach out and touch the console in front of you,*" Vladimir instructed.

Josh reached forward and placed his right forefinger on the edge of the console in front of him. "Whoa," he giggled. "This is *so* cool!" He immediately started touching things—buttons, switches, flight controls—it all felt like the real thing. "Fuck the rebellion!" he exclaimed. "Let's go into the VR sim business! You know how many *credits* you could make with this technology?"

"Try to stay focused on the task at hand, Josh," Nathan urged as he watched Josh reaching out and touching things that were not there.

"This is kind of fun to watch," Loki jeered. "Josh, you look like an idiot."

"Wait till you try this, Lok!" Josh exclaimed, still moving his hands around and touching things. He stopped a moment and touched his fingers to his thumbs again. "Hey, I can feel myself touching myself."

"You sure you don't want to rephrase that?" Loki teased.

"You know what I mean."

"The system still allows sensory input from the real world around you," Vladimir explained. "Primarily your sense of touch and balance, although the balance part is limited. That is why you must be seated, so that you don't fall over. But sight and sound are completely overridden."

"Where did this tech come from?" Jessica asked.

"The Data Ark," Loki guessed.

"Correct," Vladimir confirmed. "It was in widespread use just before the bio-digital plague hit. Of course, it was far more sophisticated; they had complete worlds in which they could exist, regardless of their position within the real world. You could be sitting still and feel like you were walking, running, jumping..."

"Among other things," Josh giggled.

"Do you remember how to start up the ship's systems?" Vladimir asked.

"Please," Josh replied. His head titled upward and to his right as he reached for an imaginary overhead panel.

Josh began activating systems in the sequence he had memorized from the Cobra gunship operating manual he and Loki had been studying since they left the Aurora for Earth thirty hours ago. Every switch he touched felt real. He could even feel the resistance of the switches, the *click* sensation in his finger, and the sound of the switch in his ears. The sound even had direction to it, being louder in his right ear than in his left. "This shit is amazing," he commented as he continued activating systems. "APUs are hot. Reactors are spinning up. Start-up sequencer is active. Initiating engine start-up sequence."

"*You don't need the engines to be active to jump from the launch rails into space,*" Loki reminded him.

"Maybe not, but there's no reason *not* to start them now," Josh replied. "Besides, I feel better knowing they're at least in the start-up sequence before we head down that rail. I don't want to become a submarine if the jump drive fails."

"*There may not be enough propellant on board*

to power you to orbit if the jump drive fails," Loki pointed out.

"Maybe, but it certainly won't be an option if the engines aren't spooled up," Josh argued.

"*Good point.*"

"*How's it going?*" Vladimir wondered. "*Is your body getting used to the simulation?*"

"Are you kidding? This shit feels real."

"*Just don't get up from your chair,*" Vladimir warned.

"Why?" Josh asked.

"*Just don't.*"

Josh couldn't help himself. He had to try. As soon as he stood, his head began to spin, and everything began to change shape, distorting in odd ways. "Whoa." He immediately sat back down and closed his eyes, keeping them closed while he waited for his head to stop spinning.

"*I warned you,*" Vladimir said.

"You knew damn well I was gonna stand as soon as you told me not to, didn't you?"

"*Who, me?*" Vladimir replied sheepishly.

Josh opened his eyes again. Everything appeared normal, but his fingers were tingling once again.

"*It will take a moment for the system to realign with your body's proprioception centers. You disturbed them when you stood up,*" Vladimir explained.

"*I can see why this thing can't be used for combat training,*" Jessica commented.

Josh felt the tingling subside and continued with his start-up procedures. "Okay, the reactors are at fifty percent and rising. Main propulsion is online, and maneuvering is online. Jump drive will be ready in one minute." Josh felt the cockpit shake slightly. "What was that?" He looked out the window and noticed that the scenery outside the ship was sliding to one side. "We're moving...I think."

"*That is correct,*" Vladimir assured him. "*I am moving your ship to the launch rails, as planned in the mission.*"

"But I'm not ready yet."

"*Then I suggest you get ready,*" Nathan urged. "*There will be little time.*"

"No problem," Josh replied. "Hey, I can actually feel us rolling on the dolly-thingy. I can feel it in my ass."

Loki shook his head.

"Is there any way we can see what he sees?" Nathan asked.

"Yes, but it requires additional equipment, which we did not bring," Vladimir replied.

"Why not?" Jessica wondered.

"The point is to give everyone an opportunity to practice operating a gunship," Vladimir explained. "As none of us are instructors, visually monitoring the user's actions would be of little benefit."

"How much were you able to shorten the transit time from parking to launch position?" Nathan wondered.

"Five minutes per ship, with one minute between each ship," Vladimir said.

"One minute?" Loki wondered. "That's pretty tight spacing, isn't it?"

"You would rather stay on the ground and remain a target a little longer?" Vladimir asked.

"One minute it is."

"Okay, now I'm bored," Josh declared, his hands on his legs, his helmeted head slowly turning from side to side as he scanned the VR environment that only he could see. “This thing have in-flight vid-plays?”

“I notice you didn’t include the process of overriding the lockout codes in the simulation,” Jessica commented.

“I didn’t program this simulation,” Vladimir told her. “All I did to it was speed up the transit time to the launch position. That will be accomplished at the launch controller shack, not in the cockpit.”

“But shouldn’t they be practicing the override sequence?” Nathan wondered.

“It’s just entering the sequences I give them, once I figure it out on the first ship,” Vladimir explained. “I don’t see the need to simulate that.”

“I’m coming up to the launch position now,” Josh reported from under his VR helmet.

“Are you ready to launch?” Loki asked.

Josh scanned his console, checking that everything was ready. “Flight dynamics display is good; main propulsion and maneuvering are up; reactors are at eighty percent.”

“*How’s your jump drive?*” Loki asked over the simulated comms.

Josh tapped the jump control screen on the center console, calling up the launch jump. “Looks like there’s an initial launch program already in the jump drive’s database, just like the manual said.” Josh called up the program and started entering the parameters. “Looks like you can either choose the default distance or enter one of your own.”

“*Better to enter one of your own,*” Nathan suggested. “*Something further out. If they send Super Eagles to intercept, they’ll probably start with the default jump distance programmed into the launch jump sequence.*"

"Good thinking," Josh agreed, dialing up a different distance. "I'm doubling the default distance for now."

"*We should probably come up with prearranged distances and post-jump turn-outs for the actual mission,*" Loki said. "*That way, we won't jump into one another.*"

"*Telles already thought of that,*" Jessica told them.

"Figures." Josh glanced up at the flashing warning light on the annunciator panel. "I'm in launch position. I'm showing a ten-degree-down angle." He looked around. "Isn't there a manual dolly brake release around here somewhere?"

"*Flip open the side panel on the center pedestal,*" Loki reminded him. "*Then twist and pull.*"

"Oh, yeah." Josh looked down to his right and opened the panel. Inside was the red lever, right where Loki said it was. "Here we go," Josh declared as he twisted the lever and pulled.

There was a distant, mechanical *clunk* sound, and the ship again began to move, gravity pulling it down the steadily increasing decline. The scenery outside began moving past the windows more quickly as the ship picked up speed. He could feel the ship shaking as the dolly, on which it rode, barreled down the launch rails. He glanced at the jump sequencer, noting that it was counting down as expected. "This is wild," he commented with amusement. "But I thought it would be moving a lot faster than this."

"*You don't need much forward momentum to jump to orbit,*" Nathan commented. "*Just enough to ride up the incline at the end and off the rails, so that the dolly will fall away from you before you jump.*"

"What happens to the dolly?" Josh asked as he watched the bottom of the hill race toward him at an ever-increasing rate.

"It falls into the recovery lake below," Nathan replied.

"Just like you will, if your ship fails to jump," Loki added.

"Twenty seconds to the jump," Josh reported, one eye on the jump sequencer. "Coming to the bottom of the run!" Josh could feel his adrenaline rising, despite the knowledge that it was only a simulation. It just felt so real, he felt himself leaning back in his chair, preparing for the jump. "Bottom of the run! Starting up the ramp!" He watched the forward window as the ship started up the final hill, the sky coming into view. "Oh, shit!" he exclaimed as the tracks disappeared under him, and the ship became airborne. A second later, the simulated windows turned opaque, and the jump sequencer reached zero. The jump light on the console lit up, indicating that the jump drive had fired. One second later, the windows cleared again, and the blue sky was gone, replaced by the starry black void of outer space. "Jump complete!" he exclaimed with excitement. He reached forward and fired his main engines, pushing his throttles to full power. "Good burn on the mains! Launch is complete! Initiating a turn to port and preparing an escape jump! What a fucking ride!"

Nathan looked at Jessica and Vladimir. "So, I guess Josh won't be a problem." He turned to Loki. "Do you want to go next, or should I?"

* * *

Robert sat on the white, sandy beach, listening to the waves crashing against the shore. He had been sitting in this spot for as long as he could remember, which was strange because he couldn't recall how he had gotten there.

He looked around, suddenly realizing that he had no idea where exactly he was. The spot looked familiar, much like the beaches he had grown up around. But those beaches had never been empty. Even during storms, there were always the die-hards who would be out there, bonfire blazing, music blasting, and alcohol flowing. But this beach was absolutely empty. Nothing. No signs that anyone had ever set foot there. No footprints, no garbage, no burnt-out wood.

Robert turned to look behind him, to see if he could retrace his steps. To his surprise, there were no footprints leading to the spot in which he sat. There was a breeze, but it certainly wasn't enough to erase his tracks, at least not in...

Just how long have I been sitting here?

A flash of light far out on the water caught his eye. *A sail?* He couldn't tell. It came again. *A blue-white light? A flash, or a reflection?* It came several more times over the next few minutes, yet it did not appear to change position.

A buoy?

At least it was a sign of something. Robert looked up at the sky; brilliant blue, with only a few fluffy, white clouds drifting by. Birds floated about, riding endless currents of air as they scoured the beach for sustenance.

He noticed that he was not wearing a uniform. Instead, he was dressed in swim trunks, tank top, and flip-flops, with sunglasses and a cap to complete his ensemble. The color of the water, the temperate climate, the pristine sands... Wherever he was, it was a tropical environment, that much he was sure of. *Then why am I so cold?*

Robert could feel the sun beating down on his skin. If anything, he should be hot. But he *felt* cold, quite cold in fact.

And what is that beeping sound?

Robert looked around for the source of the sound, but it seemed to be coming from all directions. He stood up, wrapping his arms around his body to ward off the frigid temperatures.

This can't be happening, he thought. *This doesn't make sense.*

Robert's eyes popped open, the repeated beeping finally waking him. He looked around. *The SAR shuttle. Running cold.* It all came back to him.

A message.

Robert sat up, leaned forward, and pulled his flight seat back into position. The comms panel showed a new message, one that had been transmitted from a nearby jump comm-drone only moments ago. He accessed the message and entered the encryption key. The message played out across his screen as it decoded, one word at a time.

Time to go, he thought, reaching for the reactor console to begin the start-up process.

* * *

Nathan climbed up the access ladder into the Seiiki's cockpit, squeezing in beside Loki who was sitting at the auxiliary station just behind Neli. "How's it going?" he asked no one in particular.

"They're doing pretty well," Loki replied.

"We're not *doing* anything," Marcus insisted. "Just watching the displays and watching the windows fog up and clear, and fog up and clear, and fog up and clear, and..."

"I get the idea," Nathan said.

"How was your VR training?" Loki asked.

"Did three cycles. Flubbed one, but only because Vlad threw a low-power issue in the jump drive at me at the last moment."

"Did you end up in the lake?" Loki wondered.

"No. I tried firing the mains, like Josh, and ended up slamming into the far shore."

"Survivable?"

"Hell, no."

"You realize what you did wrong?" Loki wondered, already knowing the answer himself.

"Yup, after I was already dead. Electrically accelerated propulsion systems don't work very well when your main power is low."

"Who's up now?" Loki asked.

"Josh is doing another run, then it's your turn," Nathan explained. "Jess is running the sim, so they shouldn't be as hard. I don't think she knows how to throw curve balls at us."

"Where's Vlad?" Loki wondered.

"He and Dalen needed to get back to work on converting the Seiiki back into the Mirai." Nathan turned to Marcus. "He could use your help, if you don't mind taking a break from piloting."

"Sure," Marcus replied. "Watching this ship jump again and again is boring. And it makes my teeth hurt even worse from up here."

"You can take a break, as well," Nathan told Loki. "I can keep an eye on Neli for a while."

"Sounds good," Loki agreed, rising from his seat.

Nathan moved out of Loki's way, staying far to the port side of the cramped cockpit while first Loki, then Marcus, passed by and headed down the access ladder to the main deck below. He moved into the pilot's seat on the left and sat down. He looked around at the display, letting out a sigh. "It seems like forever since I've sat up here."

"I guess so," Neli replied. "Jump forty-seven, in thirty seconds."

"So, how are you holding up, Nel?"

"I'm okay, Connor... I mean, Nathan."

"It's okay. I don't mind being called Connor, if it makes you feel better. I still *am* Connor Tuplo, after all. I think in some way, part of me always will be."

"It was just a slip of the tongue, really," Neli insisted. "I don't mind calling you Nathan. It *is* your *real* name, after all." She looked at him. "Now that you've shaved and all, you *do* seem more like Nathan than Connor. Are you letting it grow back?"

"Not on purpose," Nathan admitted. "I just haven't had a chance to shave lately."

"You might want to keep a little stubble going. It makes you look older."

"I'll remember that." Nathan looked over the flight data displays. "Are you getting the hang of this?"

"Not really," she replied. The windows turned opaque and the jump sequencer triggered the next jump. "Jump forty-seven, complete."

"You don't need to announce all the jumps, you know."

"Marcus said the same thing. It must run in the family. But Loki taught me to, so..."

"Loki likes procedure."

"So do I," she admitted. "At least when I'm doing this. To be honest, this scares the hell out of me. Jumping light years at a time, over and over again. I'm always afraid we're going to come out in the middle of a star, or in front of a black hole or something."

"Yeah, not fun," Nathan commented, remembering

the last time he made the journey from the Pentaurus sector back to Earth. “Don’t worry, Neli. We’re flying a completely charted jump course. There won’t be any surprises.”

“Still, announcing each jump makes me feel better. I hope you don’t mind.”

“No problem,” Nathan replied.

“Position has been confirmed. Jump forty-eight has been calculated. Jumping in one minute.”

Nathan sat quietly, his eyes darting around the displays, checking that his ship was functioning properly and that the multi-jump system was doing its job. The Seiiki rarely did more than ten or twenty jumps in a series. She’d never had the need. At least not until recently. But her auto-jump system was working perfectly, thanks to Vladimir’s efforts since joining his crew. In fact, his ship had never been in better shape.

For a brief moment, he wondered what it would be like if the situation was different. His crew, with the addition of Vlad, Jessica, and Cameron, jumping all over the lost colonies of Earth in the Seiiki, bringing jump drive technology to everyone. He wondered what the galaxy would be like, if every human civilization had jump drives. He imagined vast networks of jump ships, moving people and goods between every inhabited world in the Milky Way.

Or beyond? After all, if the jump drive could be made to jump repeatedly, over hundreds, thousands, or even tens of thousands of jumps, could they travel to yet *another* galaxy?

Nathan laughed to himself. It was a ridiculous idea. The Andromeda galaxy was something like two point five million light years away. With the Seiiki’s limited jump range, it would take more than a billion jumps, at a jump every few minutes, to get there. They couldn't even get there within their own lifetime.

An automated ship, maybe? With SA pods?

"Jump forty-eight, in thirty seconds," Neli announced.

Nathan shook off his silly daydreams of intergalactic exploration, turning his attention to the task at hand. A quick scan of his displays told him everything was as it should be for the next jump. Once again, the windows of the Seiiki turned opaque, and the jump drive activated.

"Jump forty-eight, complete," Neli announced. "I'm showing an overheat warning on the starboard jump field generator's energy transfer bus." She looked at Nathan. "Should I pause the jump sequencer?"

"As soon as it verifies our position, yes. It'll cool down in about ten minutes," Nathan assured her.

"Is it supposed to do that?" she wondered.

"It isn't really designed to do so many jumps in a row."

"We were trying for fifty jumps before taking a break," she admitted.

"It might help if we dialed down the jump range a bit and took a few minutes to accelerate."

"Marcus was the one doing the piloting," Neli admitted.

"No problem. I'll do it." Nathan made some quick calculations in his head and then checked them on the flight computer. To his surprise, his mental calculations were correct. A few touches to the flight displays and the auto-flight systems, and the Seiiki's main engines were burning at fifty percent. "We don't want to accelerate too much, or we're going to have to burn more propellant to slow down when we get to the rally point."

"Where exactly *is* the rally point?" Neli wondered.

"Need to know basis," Nathan replied. "Besides, I doubt you'd recognize the name even if I could tell you."

"You people love your secrets, don't you?"

"Actually, I pretty much don't," Nathan admitted.

"Position is verified," Neli reported. "Pausing the jump sequencer." She looked at him again. "That comes as a surprise."

"I hate secrets. Growing up, my family was full of them. Always putting on a proper front for the media. Hiding all our ugly truths from public eye. I just hated it."

"You had ugly truths?"

"Everybody does," Nathan insisted. "Even if they don't want to admit it."

"What's yours?" Neli asked.

Nathan looked at her.

"Sorry, I didn't mean to..."

"No, that's alright." Nathan thought for a moment as he looked at the stars outside his window. "I guess my ugly truth is that I don't want to be a leader. I'll do it. I can't help myself. It's who I am, even if it's not who I *want* to be."

Neli was surprised. "Who do you *want* to be?"

Nathan thought for another moment. "You know, I've always been jealous of the guy who can just go about his business, happy in his little bubble of a world. You know the type. The guy who doesn't really have any great aspirations. He just wants a happy life. The kind of guy whose only excitement is watching sporting events or something."

"Your average, working-class guy, then," Neli said.

"Yeah. They always seem so happy, like all the

terrible things going on in the galaxy don't really exist."

Now it was Neli who thought for a moment. "Did you ever imagine *that* guy might be looking at *you,* wishing that *he* had *your* life?"

"If they knew the truth, they wouldn't."

"Don't be so sure, Nathan. Everyone wants to be a hero."

"I'm not a hero, Neli. I'm a figurehead. I'm a poster boy for the rebellion. A recruiting gimmick."

"You regularly put your life at risk for others," Neli reminded him. "Isn't that what heroes do?"

"So do you," Nathan replied, trying to deflect the spotlight from himself. "You, and everyone else aboard."

"We're just following your lead, Nathan."

Nathan looked at her. "Why?"

"Well... To be honest, I don't know. Marcus and Josh believe in you. Dalen, well, he's young. He just wants excitement."

"And you?"

Neli shrugged. "I go where Marcus goes."

Nathan smiled. "You really do love him, don't you?"

"It's not always an easy thing to do," she admitted. "But yeah, I guess I do."

"Yeah, he takes some getting used to," Nathan agreed.

"Can I ask you something?"

"Sure," Nathan assured her.

"Do you know anything about Marcus, from *before* you met him? As Nathan, I mean."

"Not much. I know he raised Josh when Josh's mother died. And I know he has gone by more than one name in the past. And I know that he has been involved with some nefarious types in the past, but that's it. But none of that really matters, because what I *do* know is that I can trust him with my life, just as you can."

"I'm not so sure."

"I am. As gruff as he likes to come across, there's a good guy deep inside of him."

"Really deep," Neli commented. "The temps are back to normal on that energy transfer bus."

Nathan shut down the main engines. "Go ahead and start the jump sequencer again," he instructed.

"What about our speed?" Neli asked. "Do I need to adjust anything?"

"The auto-sequencer will reassess our flight data and adjust the jump drive to maintain the same distance per jump based on our new speed."

Neli shook her head.

"What?" Nathan asked.

"I always imagined this as being a lot more complicated."

"It's not," Nathan admitted, "until something goes wrong," he added with a grin.

CHAPTER EIGHT

The windows on Robert's shuttle cleared as the ship came out of its final jump in the series. Before him lay the once-inhabited planet Tanna, shrouded in the same swirling haze of dust and ash that had clouded its atmosphere since the Jung had wiped almost all life from its surface nearly eight years ago.

The sight of the world he had once fought, and failed, to defend stirred up more emotions in him than he had expected. He had spent months on Tanna, training crews to fly the original Cobra gunships being built there. He had grown close to those men, and to the Tannan culture itself. Those three months on Tanna had been the most he had spent on the surface of any world since he had first left Earth in an FTL scout ship more than twenty years earlier.

The Tannans had been a proud people with a unique culture. They had been some of the warmest, most genuine people he had ever known. And now, the survivors of their world were scattered among the core worlds. All that was left of their culture were the various "Little Tanna" neighborhoods that popped up in every city in which the survivors had settled.

Robert had meant to visit at least one of those neighborhoods over the years, but had never gotten around to it. Now, he wished he had. The last emergency workers left the surface six years ago, so he didn't know what he was going to see when he broke through those clouds.

He activated his sensors and scanned the atmosphere. The radiation level was still too high for prolonged exposure, but he didn't intend on taking long hikes in the desolated landscape. He was only there because it was a good rally point, it was within an hour's multi-jump range of the Tau Ceti system, and it was someplace that no one ever went. In fact, the current Alliance borders didn't even include the 72 Herculis system, as it was beyond their current fleet's one-minute jump range. Besides that, there was nothing left there to defend. Although the Jung had not completely glassed the surface, they had plastered it with enough nukes to make it unlivable for centuries.

If so many other worlds had not been trying to rebuild, more effort might have been made to clean up Tanna and make it livable sooner. But the Jung had done so much damage across the core that the resources to save a distant, obviously doomed world were just not available. Hence, a massive evacuation had taken place. Less than ten percent of the Tannans had survived. But many swore that, someday, their children's children would return and repopulate their homeworld. Robert honestly hoped they would be able to keep that promise.

Robert used the SAR shuttle's navigation computer to calculate a course to the old, abandoned evacuation center near Tanna's capital city. If it was still standing, there would be a flight apron, a nav beacon, and a large hangar that could be sealed up against the radiation outside. It wouldn't be pretty, but it would be a safe place for the rebel forces from the Pentaurus sector to hold up for a few days.

Robert accepted the course, loaded it into the auto-flight system, and activated it, letting the system take him down into the clouds of Tanna.

* * *

"You've got twenty seconds to get that damned hatch open and get him out of there, or we're all fucked!" Aiden yelled over his comm-set.

"*Just do the burn, Captain!*" Specialist Leger insisted.

"Shut up, Ledge! Nobody's asking you!" Aiden barked.

"He's right, Aiden," Ken said.

"Eyes on that track, Kenji," Aiden barked. "Ten seconds!"

"*It's stuck!*" Ali exclaimed.

"Blow the primary!" Aiden reminded her, barely able to contain his frustration.

"*Shit!*"

"Five seconds!" Aiden warned.

"Roll us, Aiden!" Ken insisted.

"Damn it!" Aiden cursed, pushing his flight control stick hard to the left.

"The missile passed over us!" Ken announced with relief.

Klaxons began to sound, and red lights began to flash along the walls of the gunship's interior.

"Hull breach!" Ash announced.

"Visors down!" Aiden ordered, pulling his helmet visor down and locking it in place.

"*Explosive decompression in the starboard gun tunnel!*" Ashwini reported. "Sealing it off!"

"*Ali!*" Aiden called out.

"*I'm not getting any vitals from Ali or Ledge!*" Sergeant Dagata reported.

"*Are you sure?*" Aiden demanded.

"*They got sucked out, Aiden,*" Ashwini told him.

"*Dags! Scan outside! See if you can find them!*"

"*It's too late, Aiden,*" Kenji told him.

"*They're gunners! Their visors were closed!*"

"*More incoming!*" Sergeant Dagata warned. "*Starboard side, two hundred clicks! Fifteen seconds!*"

"*We've got to jump!*" Ken insisted.

"*Spinners and flashers!*" Aiden ordered. "*Ten each! Pop'em now!*"

"*Popping countermeasures!*" Ken replied.

Aiden pushed his flight control stick forward, twisting it to the right at the same time. "*Bring all guns on those missiles!*" he added. "*Just watch out for Ali and Ledge!*"

"*We've got to jump, Aiden!*" Ken insisted.

"*No!*" Aiden argued. "*Not if there's still a chance they're alive!*"

"*It's a fucking simulation, Aiden!*" Ken reminded him. "*They're sitting in the airlock, with their comm-sets shut down!*"

"*Missiles are locked!*" Sergeant Dagata cried out.

Aiden pulled his flight control stick back, pushing the main propulsion throttles to full power. Suddenly, everything went dead; their flight consoles, their helmet comms, the interior lighting...even the simulated view outside their cockpit windows.

A moment later, the lights came back on.

"*You're all dead,*" the controller's voice announced over their helmet comms.

Aiden leaned back in his flight seat and sighed. "*Fuck.*"

"*You should have jumped the ship before those missiles closed on you,*" the controller explained.

"*I was afraid the jump fields would kill Specialist Leger,*" Aiden defended, lifting his helmet visor. "I thought I could shake the missiles and buy Specialist Brim enough time to get the hatch open and get him back inside before we jumped away."

"*You don't know for sure that Specialist Ledge*

would not have survived the jump. What you did know for sure was that your ship and your crew would be destroyed if you took another missile hit while your shields were down...which you just did."

Aiden removed his helmet and set it aside. "I know."

"*Being captain means making the hard calls,*" the controller reminded Aiden. "*That means being able to let one die to save many.*"

"I know."

"*Then show me that you know.*"

"Yes, sir," Aiden replied.

"If it helps, Captain, I appreciate that you were trying to save me," Ledge said as he and Ali stepped into Cobra Three Eight Three's flight deck.

"Well, I don't," Ashwini said. "And I'm pretty sure Dags doesn't either." She turned to look at Ken. "How about you, Ensign? You appreciate being dead?"

"Knock it off, Chief," Ken ordered.

Aiden turned his seat around to face aft, looking at his crew. "I don't give a damn what the book says. I'm not going to leave anyone behind, not if I don't have to."

"Then maybe you shouldn't be in command, sir," Ashwini stated bluntly.

"You're out of line, Chief," Ken warned, backing up his friend.

"And maybe you shouldn't be on this crew," Aiden replied, looking straight at his engineer. "We're a team," he continued, looking at each of his crew one by one as he spoke. "We take *care* of each other. We *back* each other up. We risk our *lives* for each other. That's the way it is. We're a fucking warship, people. We're going to be attacking ships ten times our size and a hundred times our firepower. I expect you all to do whatever I ask of you, *without* hesitation. The only way I know of to deserve *that* kind of loyalty is to promise you that I will *not* leave you behind. If *one* of us goes down, we *all* go down, even if it's you, Benetti." He looked back at Chief Benetti. "If that doesn't work for you, then you'd better transfer off this ship now, *before* we launch. You got that?"

"Yes, sir," Chief Benetti replied, begrudgingly.

"Very well," Aiden said. "Everyone, get back to your stations and set everything back up. We're going to run this again."

"How much longer are we going to do this, Captain?" Sergeant Dagata asked. "It's getting late."

"We run it until we get it right, or until we can no longer keep our eyes open," Aiden insisted. "So, let's get this one right." Aiden turned back around to face forward, picking up his helmet and putting it back on. "Control, Cobra Three Eight Three. I'd like to reset and run this again in five."

"*You want me to order you some sandwiches, or are you guys going to eat the e-rations you have on board?*"

"Sandwiches will be fine," Aiden replied, using the same sarcastic tone as the controller. He looked at Ken. "You good?"

"I'm with you, Aiden. You know that."

"Alright, then, let's reset."

* * *

Robert opened the hatch of his shuttle and was immediately met with the foul stench that had become Tanna. Dust swirled about the tarmac, spilling in through the open hatch. He quickly stepped out, closing the hatch behind him. He dropped the half meter to the surface and paused to look around.

The tarmac was dry and dusty, with dead weeds

poking up through the many cracks in its surface. The green and brown mountainsides that were once present on Tanna were now brown and gray. If you squinted, you could make out the dried trunks of trees in the distance, like barren needles dotting the landscape, their foliage long dried and fallen.

The sky above was as gray as the tarmac on which Robert stood. Clouds of dirt and ash swirled past, swept up by the winds that constantly scrubbed the surface of this now-dead world. Robert wondered if it ever rained on Tanna anymore. It felt as if a single spark could ignite a global fire.

Robert headed for the largest hangar, only fifty meters in front of him. It was an enormous metal structure, the kind that was built rapidly using a kit. It had one massive split door at the front, which was large enough for all of their shuttles to pass through. Jutting out of one side was a secondary building; it was less than half the larger building's height with a single door and window in front, with more windows along the side. That was where he would start.

Robert quickly moved to the front door of the building, wanting to get out of the radioactive environment as quickly as possible. As expected, the door was unlocked. There was no one left on Tanna to lock it against, and had there been, it was better to leave them access, so that they might benefit from its shelter.

The door opened into a large foyer of sorts. The purpose of the room was immediately evident. To one side there were empty lockers and benches, and to the other, decontamination showers.

Robert didn't bother with decon procedures. The radiation levels outside, although not conducive to long-term survival, were not high enough to warrant the extra effort. He would be here but a few days, most of which would be spent inside.

He moved through the next door. On the other side was yet another foyer, with even more lockers but without showers. This room was where the crews would have changed into their interior clothing.

He passed through that room, as well, and into the next, which was much larger with desks, a long counter, a small kitchenette in the corner, and several chairs along one wall. He looked around but saw nothing of interest, so he proceeded through the next door. He followed the corridor past several empty rooms—possibly examination rooms—until he reached what he was looking for; a door into the main hangar.

The process of evacuation had been to bring evacuees in, decontaminate them, examine them, then load them into a shuttle parked inside the hangar bay. Once loaded, the hangar doors would open, and the shuttle would roll out and lift off. It was a standard procedure that all EDF officers had been taught back at the academy. It wasn't perfect, but it was efficient and quick. Complete decontamination and quarantine procedures would have been observed once the evacuees reached their transport ship in orbit, and then again upon arrival at their destination.

Robert entered the cavernous hangar. It seemed even larger from the inside and included a decon chamber that was big enough for a single cargo shuttle. He walked out into the middle of the hangar, which was remarkably clean for having been unoccupied for seven years.

Yes, this will do nicely, he thought. Now, he just

needed to get his shuttle inside so that he could use its reactor to power the facility. His guests would be arriving soon enough.

* * *

Michael Willard stood in the makeshift, underground electronics lab, studying the circuit board of the comm-unit that Birk and Cuddy had been working on for the last two days. "You changed the chipset on this yourself?"

"I could've done a better job if I had the automated solder rig," Birk defended.

"No, it looks quite good," Michael assured him. "I doubt anyone would notice that it wasn't off-the-shelf gear without special diagnostic equipment. It's very clean work."

"Thanks," Birk replied.

"You haven't powered it up, yet, have you?"

"Yes, but without the internal antenna attached," Birk explained. He became defensive when Michael cast a disapproving glance his way. "I had to put power to the board to test it," he defended. "Besides, without the internal antenna, there is no way the signal would get through all this rock."

"True enough," Michael agreed. "But in the future, do not take it upon yourself to make decisions that could affect us all. That is *my* responsibility."

"Understood," Birk agreed apologetically.

"How soon can you test it?" Cuddy wondered.

"That will be difficult," Michael explained. "We must send two men into the city, far from this facility, in case it is not as secure as you claim."

"It's secure," Cuddy insisted. "I'd bet my life on it." Both Michael and Birk looked at him. "Sorry. Poor choice of words."

"How long will it take you to create, say, four more of these?" Michael asked.

"A few days," Birk replied. "Now that we know how. Faster if we had the rig."

"If these devices work, then I will get you that soldering rig," Michael promised. "Good work, gentlemen."

"Now what?" Birk called to Michael as he turned to leave.

"Now, we wait."

"For how long?" Birk asked impatiently.

"For as long as it takes," Michael replied, appearing somewhat annoyed.

Birk sighed, rolling his eyes.

"By its very nature, a rebellion is *more* waiting than it is *action*," Michael told them. "Trust me when I say that, *eventually*, you will prefer the waiting."

* * *

"How's the flight training going?" Jessica asked Nathan as she entered the Seiiki's galley.

"I finally managed a successful launch," Nathan replied in between sips of tea.

"Just one?" Jessica teased. She opened the cold box and pulled out a piece of omla fruit, taking a bite as she closed the door.

"Yeah, well, Vlad *loves* to throw curve balls at us."

"Are you going to be able to get us off Kohara alive?" Jessica jeered as she sat down across the table from him.

"I think I can handle it," Nathan replied. "Actually, as surprising as it seems, stealing those gunships will probably be the *easiest* part of this trip."

"You're not looking forward to seeing Earth again?" she asked, taking another bite.

"A little. I don't know," Nathan continued, "maybe I'm a little worried. There are so many things that could go wrong."

"Such as?"

"Well, this face, for one," Nathan said, pointing at himself. "I'm not exactly an unknown on Earth."

"You've been dead for seven years, Nathan," Jessica said with a small laugh. "No offense, but I'm pretty sure most people have forgotten your face by now."

"Yeah, you're probably right," Nathan admitted. "Then, there's the plane."

"I thought you said it was still there."

"It probably is. I mean, it was before I died. But it's been seven years, Jess."

"You think your father sold it?"

"Not likely. But he could've moved it. Even if he hasn't, it has been sitting for seven years. Planes need to be flown to stay in good condition."

"You don't know that it hasn't," Jessica argued. "Didn't you say that your grandfather used to pay a local pilot to take his plane up every once in a while, when he didn't have the time?"

"Yeah, but that was when he was alive. With all his responsibilities, I doubt my father bothered to make similar arrangements. Even if it's still there, it might not even start."

"Then we find another means of transportation," Jessica said. "At the most, we lose a few hours."

"And increase the risk of being recognized."

"Jesus, get over yourself, Nathan," Jessica jeered.

"Sorry. I guess it comes from growing up in a very public family."

"You know what *I* think?" Jessica asked.

"I wouldn't even hazard a guess."

"I think that *you* don't know what you're going say to your father, and *that's* what's bothering you."

"So, you're not bothered by all the things that could go wrong," Nathan said.

"In spec-ops training, we learn to identify the risks and decide how to mitigate them should they occur. Once you've done that, you can analyze the probability of a successful outcome. If the probability is unacceptably low, and the *need* for a successful outcome is high, then you come up with a new plan."

"Simple as that."

"Simple as that," Jessica repeated. "There are three goals to this mission," she continued in surprisingly analytical fashion. "Speak to your father; try to convince Abby to join us, and if she agrees, get her off of Earth; and steal a bunch of gunships. Item one hinges on two things: transportation to Winnipeg and help from your sister. If the plane is a no-go, then we have just enough money with us to book passage on high-speed rail. Either way, we get to Winnipeg by the next day."

"Why not just jump in closer?"

"Because the closer you get to Winnipeg, the tighter the security. Hell, we're pushing our luck with Vancouver. Japan would have been better, but transportation would have been a nightmare."

"And item two?" Nathan asked.

"It all hinges on your ability to convince Abby to join us, nothing else. At least not anything that we can control."

"And what if the jump sub isn't there when we need it?"

Jessica sighed. "Okay, I admit, *that* would complicate things a bit."

* * *

It had taken Robert more than an hour just to get his shuttle into the main hangar. Without working power in the facility, the process had involved running a power cable from his shuttle to the motor for the outer doors, pulling inside and closing them, and then repeating the process for the inner doors. The process itself was not difficult, just tedious.

Once inside, he was able to move his shuttle to the back corner of the hangar, close to the main power distribution panel. Once there, he was able to connect the power cable to the distribution panel and use the fusion reactor in his SAR shuttle to power the entire facility, including the motorized hangar doors and the navigation beacon outside.

Despite its size, he only had to run his reactor at five percent to power everything. It took a few hours, but the interior of the evacuation facility was finally at a comfortable temperature, and the air inside had been through the cleaning filters enough times to rid the building of its annoying aroma. Of course, it was also possible that he was just getting used to the smell of desolation, but he preferred to believe the former.

Once everything was up and running, Robert had managed to choke down another round of e-rations and get a half-decent nap in, as well. His sleep had been fitful at best, and when he woke, he had felt as if the ghosts of those he had failed to protect on Tanna had somehow been responsible for his restlessness.

He sat in the front office, staring out the window at the barren landscape. There had once been a thriving city just outside, full of Tannans *and* Terrans going about their daily lives. Hundreds of thousands of people, none of whom had ever done anything to deserve the punishment the Jung had inflicted upon them.

Robert tried to convince himself that he had done everything he could at the time; and that had been true. There had just been too little time to truly prepare a proper defense. A few more months and things might have been completely different. He might even have retired on this world...

Had it survived.

Luckily, his morose contemplations were interrupted before they became overwhelming. A screeching crack of distant thunder, followed by the sonic boom of a jump ship entering the atmosphere at greater than the local speed of sound.

"*Tanna Base, Bulldog One. How do you copy?*" the voice called over Robert's comm-set.

"Bulldog One, Tanna Base," Robert replied. "Copy you five by five. What's your status?"

"*Bulldog One is inbound, with flight of three. Wheels down in three.*"

"Copy you, Bulldog One. The doors will be open. Pull all the way in."

"*Roger that, Tanna Base. See you in a few.*"

Robert jumped from his seat to head to the hangar and open the doors. The ghosts of Tanna would have to wait.

* * *

"*Three Eight Zero to all Cobras, prepare for swarm attack.*"

"Again?" Aiden complained. "I hate swarm attack."

"It works, Aiden."

"I didn't say it didn't work, Kenji. But this is the third swarm attack simulation today. Why do we need to practice pressing a button to engage auto-flight? Why the hell do they even need six bodies on board if they're just going to have a computer flying the attacks?"

"Uh, for those times when the auto-flight AI *doesn't* work," Ken commented.

"Have you ever heard of it failing?"

"Nope."

"Exactly," Aiden said. "I'm telling you, we're going to get out there, and we're going to become passengers; spectators with targets on our backs."

"You can always fly manually, Aiden," Kenji pointed out.

"Sure, if I want to get written up."

"I thought getting in trouble was your primary form of entertainment," Ken joked.

"Funny."

"*Cobra Three Eight Three, is your auto-flight active?*"

"Three Eight Three, affirmative," Aiden replied with a sigh, as he switched his auto-flight system into swarm mode and activated it. "Remember to keep your hands and feet inside the ride at all times, boys and girls."

"Come on, Aiden, it isn't that bad."

"Ninety percent of the time, we push buttons to fly this thing," Aiden said. "The only time we're allowed to hand-fly is *during* combat, and *now* they are taking that away from us with this automated swarm AI crap. This is not what I signed up for, Kenji. I signed up to be a pilot, not a button pusher."

"You *are* a pilot," Kenji insisted. "Pushing buttons is what pilots do these days. You'd better get used to that; otherwise, you're going to be one unhappy, young man."

"I already am an unhappy, young man," Aiden insisted.

"Ten seconds to swarm attack," Ken announced.

"Yippee," Aiden exclaimed, poorly feigning excitement.

* * *

The Seiiki rolled quietly backwards into the main hangar at the Tanna rally point, coming to a stop just inside the hangar doors. As the doors closed, the Seiiki's cargo ramp began to descend, coming to the ground as Robert and General Telles, who had just disembarked from Combat One moments earlier, approached.

As Robert came to the bottom of the ramp, his baby sister, whom he had not seen in seven years, came down the ramp, a smile spreading across her face. A similar expression immediately came upon him as she opened her arms in greeting.

"Bobert," she greeted as she wrapped her arms around him.

"God, it's good to see you," Robert said, almost gushing. He broke their embrace and stepped back, his hands on her shoulders. "Jesus, Jess, you're solid as a rock!"

"And you're not!" she said, pinching the fat around his midsection. "What the hell is this?"

"Too much time in space, I suppose."

Jessica stepped aside. "Look who I brought," she beamed as Nathan came down the ramp behind her.

Again, Robert couldn't help but smile. "The infamous Captain Kid," he greeted, reaching out to shake Nathan's hand. "I've got to admit, I wasn't sure I believed it when I first heard you were alive." Robert decided a handshake wasn't enough, hugging him, as well. "And they say *Nash's* are hard to kill."

"Good to see you again, Robert."

"I hope you're taking good care of my baby sister, here," Robert added.

"More like she's taking care of me," Nathan admitted.

"Commander Kamenetskiy," Robert said, noticing Vladimir coming down the ramp to join them. "Why am I not surprised that you became a rebel, as well?"

"I blame him," Vladimir said, pointing at Nathan. "How are you doing, Robert?" he greeted, also shaking Robert's hand.

"How is everyone?" Robert asked Jessica. "Mom, Dad, Ania, the guys?"

"Everyone is fine, Robert," Jessica assured him. "They're all living on the Mystic. The guys are helping to convert her. But we can talk about all that later."

"She's right," General Telles said. "They must complete their mission on Earth before we can conduct our mission on Kohara."

"Of course," Robert agreed. "You know that we only have four days before those gunships launch, right?"

"We are aware," General Telles assured him.

"It would be best if we took them on the eve of their launch, when they will be fueled and ready."

"That is the plan."

"Where's Roselle?" Nathan asked, looking around.

"Gil is sticking to his usual schedule aboard the Benakh. He will be here when the time comes."

"What if we have to move up the mission?" Jessica wondered.

"I have a jump comm-drone, reprogrammed to transmit a Fleet Command identifier, so that I can send him an urgent message without arousing suspicion."

"I trust that Deliza has completed the jump sub modifications?" General Telles inquired.

"She and my crew have been working nonstop since we departed the Aurora," Nathan assured him. "She says it's ready. I just wish we had time to test the remote recall device."

"If that thing doesn't work, it'll be a bitch of a dive to get to the sub and bring it ashore," Jessica added.

"And the Seiiki has been reconfigured as the Mirai?" the general asked.

"Yes, she has," Vladimir assured him.

"Very well," General Telles said. "Let's get your crew changed and get your ship ready for departure. The sooner you're on your way to Earth, the better."

* * *

Gil Roselle sat in the officers' mess, picking at his dinner. He rarely ate in his private mess, since he hated to eat alone in an empty room. Here he sat within earshot of others, allowing him to keep abreast of what was going on with his junior officers.

Of course, he was quite sure that his officers were careful about their topics of conversation when their commanding officer was around. Nevertheless, he was able to tell which officers got along well, and which ones did not.

None of this was his concern, of course, as matters of personnel were the purview of his longtime executive officer, Commander Ellison, who, as usual, was sitting across the table from him.

"You and Shari have a fight?"

"No," Gil replied. "Why do you ask?"

"Well, you haven't been your usual, loud, obnoxious self the last few days...since the last time you were on Kohara."

"Nothing like that," Gill assured his XO.

"Then, what's got you in a mood?"

"A mood?" Gil huffed. "What am I, a teenager or something?"

"Well, something's bugging you."

Gil thought for a moment. He had known Martin for twenty years. They had served together on an FTL scout ship and on the Benakh. Martin had been his right-hand man the entire time. If there was ever anyone he could trust, it was Martin Ellison. But Marty was also his friend, and there was still a chance he might finally get a command of his own, especially if Gil resigned, or...

On the other hand, if the Alliance discovered that Gil had helped the Karuzari steal gunships from the Kohara plant, it would give Galiardi the excuse he needed to get rid of Martin once and for all. After all, Gil, Martin, and Robert Nash were the last of those who had served under Nathan Scott and Travon Dumar. They were the final three who were still in uniform and serving under Galiardi's command. Even if Galiardi's investigators were unable to come up with any hard evidence against Martin, they'd probably pass him over for command of the Benakh simply because of their close association. It wasn't fair, but it was what it was.

"Maybe I'm just contemplating my retirement," Gil finally said.

"What's to contemplate?" Martin wondered. "Sailing, fishing, drinking, screwing..."

"Not necessarily in that order..."

"Of course. Sounds like the good life to me," Martin commented.

"Yeah, it does. But you know, all that stuff is great as a break from all this. But as a full-time occupation?" Gil shook his head in uncertainty. "I've been commanding this bucket for too long, Marty. And the scout ship before her. Being in space is what I know. It's what I'm good at. People like you, I get along with. Civilians? Jesus, they're just a bunch of whiny, self-indulgent idiots."

"I'm sure Shari appreciates that assessment."

"You know what I mean, Marty."

"You don't have to retire, you know. As long as you pass your annual medical reviews, they can't force you out. Besides, wouldn't you love to outlast Galiardi? Stay a thorn in his side till the day *he* retires?"

"The thought *did* occur to me," Gil admitted, a mischievous smile on his face. "But there's a good chance we're going to war again, Marty. I'm not sure how I feel about that."

"What do you mean, *how you feel* about that?"

"I mean, I'm not sure how I feel about following Galloping Galiardi into the fire," Gil explained.

"How do you feel about defending Tau Ceti? Or Sol, or any of the other Alliance worlds?"

"Oh, hell, Marty. I'm not talking about that. Of course, I'd defend them. I'm talking about going on the offensive."

Martin looked around the officer's mess, ensuring that no one was eavesdropping on their conversation which, if taken out of context, might be misinterpreted, especially by an overzealous young officer looking for a way to move up the ranks. "Look, Gil, I hear what you're saying," Martin continued, keeping his voice low, "but what choice do we have? Like you said; this is what we do."

Gil contemplated his reply carefully. Finally, he spoke, in an even lower volume. "But maybe we don't have to do it for *him*?"

"What?"

"Maybe there is someone, or *something*, that is more worthy of our loyalties."

"What are you talking about, Gil? Becoming mercenaries or something? Who the fuck would hire a couple old farts like us?"

"You'd be surprised," Gil said, finally taking a bite of his meal. "*Really* surprised." Gil chewed his food for a moment, thinking. "You know you're not going to get your own command, right?"

"Yeah, I figured that one out. Thanks for rubbing salt in my wounds, though."

"And you're okay with that?"

"Well, I was still hoping they might give me this bucket when you retire, but..."

"Yeah."

"What's this all about, Gil?" Martin asked.

Gil took another bite, casually looking around the room as he chewed. "What if I told you I could get you your own ship? Not a big one, mind you, but your own ship."

"I'd say, 'What's the catch?'"

"The catch is, you'd have to give up all this," Gil replied. "Your billet, your commission... Hell, the entire Sol sector for that matter."

"Out of the Sol sector?" Martin was suddenly intrigued. "What, like a cargo ship or something?"

Gil looked around again. The last few officers had finished their meals and were rising to depart. He waited for them to leave and then continued. "A warship. Again, not a big one."

"You *are* talking about turning merc, aren't you?" Martin was shocked. "Jesus, Gil. What does Shari have to say about all this?"

"I haven't talked to her about it, yet."

"You are planning to, right?"

"I haven't decided," Gil admitted.

"And you wonder why your relationships never last," Marty commented. "Mercs get paid pretty well, right?"

"Doubtful," Gil said. "At least not with this outfit. But at least it would be for a good cause."

"A good *cause*?" Martin suddenly put it together. "Shit. You're talking about going to the Pentaurus sector, aren't you? Are you nuts? Gil, if the Jung have jump drives, they need us *here*."

"Bullshit," Gil argued. "Galiardi's got hundreds of jump missiles sitting on launchers on the surface of Earth, and he's cranking more of them out every day. Not to mention all the jump KKVs he's got trained on Nor-Patri. Any war we fight will likely be for show, to pump up his damned resume so he can run for the position of God someday. Eventually, he'll pull the trigger on those JKKVs and flatten Nor-Patri, Nor-Doray, Nor-Essona, and every other Nor in the Jung sector. Then, he'll look like he tried to keep it conventional for as long as possible, but the Jung didn't give him a choice. Hell, if he wanted, he could send a handful of JKKVs over to the Pentaurus sector and take care of the Jung there, as well. Of course, collateral damage would probably tally in the millions, but he doesn't give a rat's ass. We all know that."

"Slow down, Gil," Martin begged. "You're starting to scare me. Is this some kind of a midlife crisis or something?"

"Please."

"Then what is it? You're talking crazy."

"I'm talking about fighting for someone *worth*

fighting for, instead of helping Michael Galiardi climb to power."

"For who?"

Gil shook his head. "I can't tell you that. Not yet. All I can tell you is that I may be resigning earlier than I thought."

"How soon?"

"A week...maybe two." Gil sighed, wondering if he had said too much. "Listen, Marty, the only reason I'm even telling you all this is because you're my friend, and I don't want you to get screwed by Galiardi when I retire."

Martin thought for a moment. "So, you really don't think they'll give me the Benakh, do you?"

"No, I don't," Gil admitted. "I think they'll put another politically connected dumbass like Stettner in command, knowing full well that you'll resign because of it. And that will give Galiardi what he wants... To be free of all of us."

"Except for Robert, of course."

Gil said nothing. He didn't have to.

"Shit, Nash is leaving, too?"

"I didn't say that."

"Christ, I need a drink," Martin exclaimed.

Gil smiled. He was pretty sure he'd just found another pilot.

* * *

Nathan and Jessica stood in the Seiiki's cockpit behind Josh and Loki, watching the cargo bay's vid-cam on the view screen in the center of the console. As planned, the launch-and-recovery arm was slowly extending, sending the jump sub out the back of the open cargo bay in preparation for launch.

"Course is good...and speed, *if* you can call it that, is holding steady," Josh reported.

"We're on a perfect intercept trajectory for Earth," Deliza added from the auxiliary station behind Loki. "Entry point of twenty-eight point five degrees north, by seventy-seven point three degrees west. That puts it between one hundred and two hundred nautical miles off the coast of Florida."

"Same latitude as the Academy?"

"That's where Special Projects is located now," Jessica said. "That's where Abby should be."

"That's not too far out, is it?" Nathan asked.

"The jump sub should be able to navigate to within a few miles of the coast within a day or two, so it should be there when you need it," Deliza assured them.

"Assuming it works the way it's supposed to," Jessica commented.

"It will," Deliza insisted. "Jump sub is in release position. All systems show ready. We're go to release. You guys ready?"

"What do you think?" Josh chided.

"Very well, initiating release." Deliza pressed a button, and the clamps securing the jump sub to the launch-and-recovery arm disengaged from the jump sub's hardpoints. "Clamps are disengaged."

"Thrusting up and forward," Josh announced. Tiny spurts of thrust fired in response to his manipulation of the Seiiki's flight controls.

The jump sub drifted slowly away from the cargo bay's vid-cam. As it disappeared into the shadows, Deliza activated the aft floodlights, lighting the little sub up again.

"Good sep rate, good trajectory," Loki reported, keeping a close eye on the sensor display directly below the view screen containing the cargo bay vid-cam view. "Clear to translate to port."

"Sliding to port," Josh announced, pushing the base of his flight control stick to the left. Again, the Seiiki's thrusters fired, only longer this time, causing the ship to move to the left of the jump sub's course.

"One minute to the jump point," Deliza reported.

"We'll be clear in thirty seconds," Loki assured her.

Nathan watched as the cargo ramp came back up, closing up the bay and blocking their view of the jump sub.

"*Cargo bay is secure,*" Marcus reported over comms. "*Repressurizing.*"

"Jump point in thirty seconds," Deliza announced.

"We are clear," Loki reported.

Deliza looked back over her shoulder, feeling the tension from Nathan and Jessica. "Relax, guys. It'll work."

"It better," Jessica said. "That's our ride back."

"Jumping in three......two......one...... Jump sub is away," Deliza announced triumphantly. She turned to look at Nathan and Jessica. "Told you it would work."

"When I push this button, and that sub squawks back at me, *then* I'll celebrate," Jessica said, holding up the jump sub's tiny remote-control unit.

"It'll take us about ten minutes to get back up to normal transit speed," Loki warned.

"We'd better get suited up," Jessica said. "We don't want them to pick up two more life signs than they find on board when the Seiiki lands," Jessica reminded Nathan.

"You mean, when the *Mirai* lands," Nathan corrected, turning to head down the ladder.

CHAPTER NINE

"Tell me again why we didn't take the jump sub down?" Nathan wondered as Marcus checked the exterior of Nathan's space jumpsuit.

"*Logistics and potentials,*" Jessica replied over his helmet comms. "*Vancouver is a hell of a lot closer to Winnipeg than Cocoa Beach and has the potential for low profile transportation.*"

"I don't know," Nathan argued.

"*Don't be a wuss. You've space-jumped before, right?*"

"Yeah, in flight training. But never through a fiery plasma wake."

"*I promise you, these suits can handle it,*" Jessica assured him. "*It'll get toasty, but you'll survive.*"

"How *toasty*?"

"*Let's just say you're going to lose a few pounds on the way down,*" Jessica mused.

"*Jumping to Sol system in thirty seconds,*" Loki announced.

"You sure they won't pick us up in these things?"

"*These rigs are as stealthy as it gets,*" Jessica insisted. "*The material does not give any sensor returns, and they radiate no emissions of their own, other than comms, which we'll shut down before we jump. The only way we can be detected is visually; hence, the plasma wake.*"

"Remind me not to listen to any more of Vlad's harebrained ideas."

"*Five seconds,*" Loki warned.

Marcus lowered his helmet visor, as did Dalen.

"*Three......two......one......jumping...*"

"...Jump complete," Loki finished as the Seiiki's cockpit windows cleared.

Josh looked up, spotting a tiny blue dot ahead of them. "There she is."

"Activating transponder," Loki announced. "We want to look as non-threatening as possible." Loki called up the correct comms channel next. "Sol Control, this is the Mirai. We have just jumped into your system at eight hundred thousand and fifty kilometers from Earth, stellar bearing of three two seven, eighteen degrees up relative. We are an armed, personal transport vessel, and we mean you no harm. How do you copy?"

Josh and Loki looked at one another.

"How many seconds will it take?" Josh wondered.

"A few."

After nearly a minute, a response came.

"*Mirai, Sol Control. State your intentions.*"

"Sol Control, Mirai. We are carrying Deliza Ta'Akar, heir to House Ta'Akar, president of Ranni Enterprises, and diplomatic representative for the Karuzari rebellion. She is requesting an audience with President Scott."

Again, they waited. Thirty seconds later, four flashes of blue-white light appeared no more than a hundred meters away on all four sides of them.

"Oh, shit!" Josh exclaimed, startled. "I hope that's not their answer."

"*What's going on?*" Jessica asked over comms.

"Four Super Eagles just jumped in. Two on either side and two moving in behind us. They're painting us," Loki reported.

"*That's okay,*" Jessica assured them. "*We were expecting this.*"

"*Mirai, Eagle Four One Seven. Hold course and*

speed. Do not attempt to maneuver, or you will be fired upon. Do not power up shields or weapons, or you will be fired upon. Do not attempt any further communications with Sol Control, or you will be fired upon. Is that understood?"

"Eagle Four One Seven, Mirai," Loki replied calmly, "instructions received. We will comply."

"*Mirai, Four One Seven, switch to local, ship-to-ship laser comms, narrow beam.*"

Loki immediately reconfigured the ship's communications as instructed. "Four One Seven, Mirai, on local, ship-to-ship laser, narrow beam. How do you copy?"

"*Copy you five by five, Mirai. Stand by for further instructions.*"

"Mirai, standing by." Loki looked at Josh.

"Is it my imagination, or do those Super Eagles look meaner than they used to?"

* * *

"To be honest, Mister President, I'm not so sure he *wouldn't* use his forces against this administration," Mister Dalton said.

President Scott sat in his armchair by the fireplace in his office at the North American Union's capital in Winnipeg. Sam Dalton was one of his top advisors. He was a brilliant man and was well respected throughout the core worlds of Earth. But he despised Michael Galiardi and, because of this, tended to see conspiracies involving the admiral around every corner. "Although I have no doubt the admiral *would* do whatever he felt was necessary to ensure the safety of the Earth and her allies in the Sol sector, I do not believe he would do as you suggest, Mister Dalton. To do so would be a direct violation of his oath..."

"Or the ultimate adherence to it," Mister Dalton said, interrupting. "It depends on your point of view."

President Scott nodded his understanding of Mister Dalton's point, continuing his reply. "...*And*, it would potentially weaken his support from his base, thus costing him the election."

"Assuming he ever *held* an election," Miri pointed out.

"The people of Earth would never stand for a dictatorship," President Scott insisted.

"A dictatorship doesn't *care* what its citizens think," Mister Dalton pointed out. "And how would they stop him? He controls all the military."

"Admiral Galiardi will not stage a coup against this administration," President Scott insisted. "Not unless we give him a justifiable *reason* to. One that convinces the *public* that a coup was necessary for *their* own safety."

One of the doors opened, and a man in a suit entered the room rather urgently. "Excuse me, Mister President, but we've just received word that a ship, the *Mirai*, carrying Deliza Ta'Akar, has just jumped into the system. Miss Ta'Akar is requesting an audience with you, sir."

Miri felt her pulse quicken.

"She will no doubt be making a public plea for support in the Pentaurus sector," Mister Dalton surmised. "The Alliance Council has agreed that we cannot afford to send any ships at this time, not with the threat of a renewed war with the Jung here in *our* sector."

"We might be able to give her *something*," the president said. "Small arms, consumables, propellant. A rebellion needs more than just ships, after all."

"It would at least be a gesture," Miri said. "It might even help us maintain relations with the Pentaurus sector, after all of this is over. I think you should give her a chance to make her plea...in public. Perhaps a state lunch?"

"Security would require time to quarantine and process both ship and crew," Mister Dalton reminded them. "There are procedures to follow in such cases."

"Of course," the president agreed. "Allow them to land," he instructed the gentleman who had delivered the message.

"But *here,* in Winnipeg," Mister Dalton insisted. "Not at Port Terra. We should *not* give Galiardi any control over this meeting."

"Agreed."

* * *

"*Mirai, Eagle Four One Seven, you are cleared to approach Earth. Are you familiar with Earth's approved standard approach orbits?*"

"Eagle Four One Seven, Mirai, affirmative," Loki replied. "However, we were hoping for a straight-in approach to Winnipeg, west to east. We're low on propellant, and we'd prefer not to land on fumes."

"Not bad," Josh said, congratulating Loki for a believable lie.

After a moment, their escort responded. "*Mirai, Four One Seven, maintain current heading. Decrease speed to minimum reentry speed.*"

"Ask them if we can jump down into the atmosphere," Josh suggested.

Loki looked at him, confused. "We need the reentry to cover..."

"...I know, I know. But you gotta sell a lie to make it work. Trust me."

"Eagle Four One Seven, Mirai, any chance we can jump past the reentry? It's been a long trip, and..."

"*Negative,*" their escort replied, cutting him off. "*Do not attempt to power up your jump drive, or you will be fired upon.*"

"Understood," Loki replied. He turned to Josh. "I'm not sure that helped."

"For a lie to work, you've got to surround it with what they expect," Josh insisted.

"Well, you would know."

"*We're cleared straight down to Winnipeg, west to east, just like we planned,*" Loki reported over Nathan's helmet comms. "*Are you guys ready back there?*"

"No," Nathan admitted, "but let's do it anyway." Nathan rose to his feet, feeling the full weight of the Ghatazhak space-jump rig for the first time. "Whoa. How are we supposed to manage all this on Earth?"

"*Half of it will be gone by the time we land,*" Jessica reminded him.

"*And the gravity in here is only at half a G right now,*" Marcus added.

Nathan and Jessica moved to the back of the Seiiki's cargo bay, stepping up to the sharply angled cargo ramp. As he approached the nearly vertical ramp, he felt the pull of its separate gravity field on him. He put one foot against the ramp, then leaned forward and put both hands on it, as well. "Ready," he reported.

"*Ready,*" Jessica echoed.

Marcus touched the control panel on the wall next to the ramp, dialing down the cargo bay's gravity to one quarter normal, while he increased that of the ramp to one half normal. "*Go ahead,*" he instructed, activating his mag-boots to hold him down as he dialed back the cargo bay's artificial gravity to zero.

Nathan and Jessica both placed their other feet on the ramp and then stood up, their bodies nearly perpendicular to Marcus's.

"*Now this ain't something you see every day,*" Marcus commented.

"*Thirty seconds to atmospheric interface,*" Loki warned.

Nathan and Jessica walked up the steeply-angled ramp, moving as close to the ceiling as possible, in preparation for their deployment.

"*Loading the pop-open sequence into the ramp motor controller,*" Marcus announced. "*Craziest thing I ever heard of, and I've seen a lot of crazy, believe me.*"

"Don't forget to hook up, Marcus," Nathan reminded him.

"*Don't you worry,*" Marcus assured him as he reached down and clipped the safety hook on his belt to the bulkhead in front of him.

"*Fifteen seconds,*" Loki reported.

"*If either of you are so inclined, now would be a good time to start praying,*" Marcus advised.

The Seiiki shook slightly.

"Atmospheric interface," Loki announced.

"It's your thing, isn't it," Josh said. "Reporting the obvious?"

"Thirty seconds to simulated failure point," Loki said. "Be ready, it's going to get bumpy."

Josh looked out the window to his left. The Super Eagles were still flying close on either side of them. A quick glance at the sensor display confirmed that the two Super Eagles in the kill slot behind them were still there, as well.

"Alright Dalen, do your thing," Loki instructed.

"First time I ever tried to make something fail on purpose," Dalen replied.

"I'm showing a fluctuation in our ventral thermal shields," Loki reported.

Josh looked at him. "Seriously?"

"Just playing the part," Loki insisted. "It's getting worse." He keyed the Seiiki's comms. "Eagle Four One Seven, Mirai, we're showing a fluctuation in our ventral thermal shields. It's probably nothing, but you might want to have your trailers move off a bit, just to be..." Loki stopped mid-sentence as the Seiiki began to shake violently. "Four One Seven! Our ventral thermal shield is down! Repeat, our shield is down! We're losing exterior hull integrity, ventral side, aft!"

"Eagle Leader to trailers! Move off! Move off! But maintain weapons lock!"

"Eagle Four One Five, moving below and away, maintaining lock."

"Four One Six, breaking off! Unable to maintain lock! The Mirai's hull is burning off! She's leaving a big plasma wake behind her!"

"Say when," Marcus urged.

"Not yet," Loki warned, his eyes on the sensor display. He waited for the two trailing Super Eagles to move away, then gave the command. "Now!"

"Good luck," Marcus bid them. He grabbed the rail with his left hand and then pressed the activation button with his right, immediately grabbing the right rail afterward.

Nathan and Jessica both bent over on their hands

and knees. A split second later, the cargo ramp dropped open a full two meters in a single second, causing a sudden decompression of the cargo bay that sucked them both out the back of the ship into the fiery plasma wake behind the Seiiki.

"Jumpers away!" Marcus reported. He carefully wrestled his right hand free and pressed the button to reverse the ramp's action. A few seconds later, the ramp was closed, and the bay began to repressurize. "Like I said, not something you see every day."

"*Mirai, Four One Seven, do you wish to declare an emergency?*"

"Give us a minute," Loki begged. "We're working the problem."

"*Mirai, Four One Six, you're losing a lot of hull coating aft of your heat exchangers. Can you pitch down slightly to let your nose take some of the heat, instead?*"

"We'll give it a try, Four One Six," Loki replied. He nodded at Josh to comply.

"He probably thinks he's *soooo* clever," Josh said as he pushed the Seiiki's nose down slightly.

"*Say the word,*" Dalen reminded Loki.

"Give it a few more seconds, just to make sure they're well clear of us," Loki instructed.

"*We're taking some real damage to the hull, you know,*" Marcus pointed out.

"Right now, you're the only one at risk, Marcus," Loki replied.

"*Yeah, that's why I'm worried.*"

"*Mirai, state your intentions. Can you make it to Winnipeg?*"

"Okay, Dalen. Bring it back online, but only at

twenty percent power, then bring it up a little at a time."

"*You got it,*" Dalen replied.

Loki watched the shield status display as the ventral thermal shielding powered back up, and the shaking became less violent. "Eagle Four One Seven, Mirai, we've got partial power to our ventral thermal shield restored. I think we can make it down. Yes... It's working. It's coming back up. I think we're alright."

"*Good to hear, Mirai,*" the escort replied. "*Continue inbound to Winnipeg as planned.*"

"Understood," Loki replied.

"*Trailers, close back up.*"

Loki looked at Josh and smiled. "I guess I'm picking up some of your skills, huh?"

"I'm so proud." Josh replied, grinning.

* * *

The first few seconds had been hair-raising. Passing through a long tail of burning plasma and bits of the extra coating, which Vladimir and Marcus had applied to the underside of the Seiiki's hull back on Tanna, had seemed like the fires of hell itself. Luckily, it had been short-lived.

Five seconds after being sucked out the back of the Seiiki, they had passed aft of her plasma wake. At that moment, the Seiiki and her fighter escorts had been tiny dots, all of which faded from view in seconds. After that, it had simply been a long free-fall.

The Ghatazhak space-jump rigs were completely automated. Although they appeared as if they were nothing more than heavy-duty body armor, they were, in fact, fully actuated flight systems, complete with automated piloting. Servos moved Nathan's arms, legs, and torso, using them like control surfaces on a guided missile. Onboard navigation computers guided him and Jessica down through the atmosphere, controlling their trajectory, and, as much as they could, their rate of descent, ensuring that they would reach their selected touchdown point.

The journey through the evening skies over the Pacific Ocean had been incredible. At higher altitudes, Nathan could see the sun to the east ahead of them, but as they descended, they eventually fell into darkness as the sun quickly fell below the horizon.

There was no communication between them on the way down. As planned, their comms had been shut down prior to departure. The electronics running their jump rigs were sealed, generating no detectable emissions, and their flat-black finish made them invisible once they fell into the predawn darkness.

As they descended, Nathan was able to make out the lights of Vancouver as they approached. He had not seen the city in which he had been raised since he'd left Earth nine years earlier, just after graduating from the Earth Defense Force Academy. He had *never* seen it from this vantage point. He suspected few people ever had.

Eventually, they passed over Vancouver, traveling east of the city. One by one, braking chutes deployed, slowing him from just below the speed of sound down to a speed that would not tear his main chute to pieces. Finally, his main chute opened a mere one thousand meters above the northeast tip of Boundary Bay. A minute later, he found himself touching down, more gently than he anticipated, thirty meters to one side of the runway at White Rock Airfield.

A press of a button on his chest control pack reeled his chute back in, preventing the morning breeze off the bay from dragging him across the field. Nathan quickly removed his helmet, taking in the first breath of his native atmosphere in more than seven years. Dripping with sweat, he fell to his knees and dropped his helmet on the ground beside him. He looked to his left and spotted Jessica, who was already removing her chute-pack. He followed suit, flipping both release lever below each shoulder as he leaned back slightly to allow the pack to fall away.

"You okay?" Jessica asked as she approached, her helmet in one hand and her chute-pack in the other. Despite the remaining bulk of her space-jump rig, she moved with relative ease. He envied her physical condition and made a mental note to start working on his own physique upon their return to the Aurora.

"Yeah, I think so. Hell of a ride, though."

"You can say that again. Drink up," she instructed, tipping her head to one side and using the hydration tube sticking up from her collar-ring and taking a long drink.

Nathan tipped his chin down and right, taking a drink from his own hydration tube, not stopping until he had emptied the bladder.

"We need to get to cover," Jessica urged. "Can you walk?"

"Of course," Nathan replied, struggling to get to his feet.

"Where's your grandpa's plane?"

"Hangar B eight," Nathan said, pointing toward the hangars along the taxiway on the opposite side of the runway from them. "Second row back from the taxiway."

Jessica looked around. The sky was already beginning to lighten slightly. "What time does this place open?"

"Probably just after sunrise, for the public," Nathan answered. "But people who have hangars here can come and go night and day."

"Then we'd better get moving," Jessica reiterated.

* * *

The Seiiki settled gently on landing pad one four at the Winnipeg spaceport's NAU flight operations center. The four Super Eagles that had escorted them down pitched up and disappeared behind blue-white jump flashes just after the Seiiki's wheels had touched the tarmac.

"*Mirai, Winnipeg Ground, shut down all systems and prepare to be boarded for inspection.*"

Josh and Loki watched as several security vehicles pulled up on either side of the ship, and what appeared to be some sort of tracked plasma turret rolled into position fifty meters away, bringing their barrels around to take aim on them.

"Holy shit," Josh exclaimed. "These guys don't fuck around."

"Winnipeg Ground, Mirai. We copy and will comply." Loki quickly shut down the Seiiki's engines and reactor, switching her basic systems to run on batteries for the time being.

"Is everyone in uniform?" Josh asked over his comm-set. "Marcus?"

"*Yeah, I'm ready. You want me to drop the ramp?*"

"Yeah. And please tell me you're not armed."

"*How dumb do you think I am?*"

"Deliza? Is Nathan's cabin ready?"

"*You'd never know it wasn't my cabin,*" she replied. "*It even smells like me now.*"

"Oh, Nathan's going to love that," Josh chuckled. "Okay," Josh said, climbing out of the pilot's seat. "Everyone report to the cargo bay and prepare to be inspected."

Josh and Loki were the last ones to make it to the cargo bay, sliding down the forward ladder as an NAU security officer and a squad of armed guards came marching up the ramp. Josh went to the right, standing in line next to Marcus and Neli, while Loki went left to stand alongside Dalen and Yanni.

"Welcome aboard the Mirai," Deliza greeted from the center of the cargo bay. "I am Deliza Ta'Akar, heir to House Ta'Akar of Takara, president of Ranni Enterprises, and diplomatic representative of the Karuzari rebellion. I am formally requesting an audience with President Dayton Scott of Earth."

The NAU officer did not seem impressed. He signaled his men to begin their search, sending them in pairs up the port and starboard ladders, as well as up the forward ladder behind Deliza. "Is there anyone else aboard this ship?"

"No, sir. Everyone is here with me. You are free to search this vessel."

"Are all your systems powered down, as instructed?" the officer asked.

"Yes," Loki replied. "We are running on battery power only. We would appreciate it if you could provide us with a ground line. Our batteries will only last an hour or two, at best."

"We will provide one once we are satisfied that your vessel is secure and is not a threat."

"I assure you, sir, we are no threat," Deliza promised.

"Yet, two plasma cannons sit atop your ship," the officer stated.

"Recently added for our protection," Deliza explained. "The Pentaurus sector has become a dangerous place, as of late."

"I assume you have forms of identification for everyone aboard?" the officer asked.

"Yes, although I do not know if they will suffice for your purposes," Deliza told him. "However, I assure you President Scott knows us quite well. Perhaps you should send him images of us so that *he* can verify our identities."

"I will decide how to verify your identities," the officer snapped, unaccustomed to being told how to perform his duties by someone from another world.

"If I may," Yanni interrupted. "I am still a citizen of Earth. You should be able to verify *my* identity." He looked at Deliza. "It's a start."

The officer turned his attention to his comm-set. A moment later, he spoke. "My men have confirmed that there is no one else on this vessel, and my superiors have already sent your images from my body-cam to the president's aide. *She* has confirmed your identity." The officer's demeanor suddenly changed. "I apologize for the inconvenience, Miss Ta'Akar. As the hour is late, the president's aide, Miri Scott-Thornton, has arranged accommodations for you and your crew for the night. When you are ready, transportation will be waiting just outside."

"We will require time to gather our things and secure the ship," Deliza told him.

"Please, take all the time you need," the officer

replied. "Meanwhile, I will see to your ship's power needs. Is one of you the ship's engineer?"

"Uh, that would be me," Dalen stated, meekly raising his hand.

"If you will follow Sergeant Turner here, he will provide whatever you need to keep your ship properly powered throughout your stay. He can also provide whatever assistance you need to repair your vessel. I understand you experienced some difficulties on the way down?"

"Nothing I can't handle, but...cool," Dalen exclaimed.

"Are we going to stay here, on the landing pad?" Loki asked.

"For security reasons, we cannot allow an armed vessel to park within the common operations area. However, a detail will be assigned to shuttle you to and from your ship and the COA as needed, day and night."

"We could use some propellant, as well," Josh suggested.

"We will be happy to replenish your propellant stores just prior to your departure," the officer explained. "My name is Lieutenant Dupra. I will be on duty until twenty-three hundred hours, local time. If you need anything, please use this comm-unit to contact myself or my assistant, Sergeant Turner." The lieutenant bowed his head politely. "Welcome to Winnipeg."

* * *

Nathan and Jessica made their way along the row of hangars, moving in and out of the shadows of the dimly lit airport. Finally, Nathan came to a stop in front of one of the control pads next to a set of hangar doors. "This is it, or at least it should be."

"What do you mean, it should be?" Jessica asked. "I thought you said your father would never get rid of it?"

"Yes, but I never said he wouldn't *move* it," Nathan defended. "Either way, we'll find out in a moment." He flipped open the keypad cover and typed in his six-digit code.

Nothing happened.

"Huh," he commented.

"Maybe they changed the code?"

"The code has been the same since I was a kid." He tried the code again, but still nothing happened. "Maybe they did move it after all," he said. He looked at Jessica, thinking.

"What?"

"If I punch it in a third time and it doesn't work, I *think* it's designed to automatically notify the owner of the hangar, or set off the alarm, or lock out the control pad... I don't really know for sure."

"Are you sure you put in the correct code?" Jessica asked.

"I'm sure," Nathan insisted. "But the system is old, and sometimes you really have to push hard, but..."

"But what?" Jessica asked, looking back over her shoulder to make sure they were still alone.

"If someone else owns this hangar..."

"There's only one way to find out," she said.

"Alright." Nathan carefully entered his code a third and final time, pressing each key firmly, and in an even cadence. After pushing the sixth button, he held his breath, waiting. But again...

"Shit," Jessica cursed.

The red light on the control pad flashed three

times, then turned green, and the doors began to retract. Nathan turned to Jessica and smiled.

The hangar doors rolled open to either side, turning into the walls on either side of the hangar as they parted. Overhead lights flickered to life revealing a sleek, white aircraft with swept-back upper and lower wings, each with winglets on the ends that pointed up from the top wing and down from the bottom one. There were two red and gold stripes that came from the propeller hub at the front, running along the sides and under the edge of the cockpit canopy, eventually turning up across the tail of the aircraft at a forty-five-degree angle.

The aircraft was small and sat atop three small wheels—one under each wing, and one under the nose—all of which appeared insufficient for the task.

"*This* is the plane you were talking about?" Jessica asked in disbelief. "Are you joking? It's a toy. It isn't even big enough to hold two people. What were you going to do with me? Strap me to the wing or something?"

"Relax, Jess, it seats two."

"Where does the second person sit, in the tail?"

"You sit right behind me," Nathan explained. "It's tight, but you'll fit."

Jessica shook her head. "Where do we wind it up?"

"It's a high-performance solar-electric," Nathan explained as he moved around the right wing. "It's got a battery bank in the bottom wing and solar cells built into the top wing. With a full charge, the engine will produce full thrust for an hour; cruise for an hour and a half. On a sunny day, you can cruise forever."

"How fast is it?" Jessica asked, hoping to be impressed.

"With two of us, maybe three hundred and sixty to three hundred and seventy KPH."

"Great, it's a fucking turtle."

"It's an aerobatic plane, Jess, not a jump shuttle."

"And you learned to fly in *this*?"

"Yup."

"Will it fly now?"

"If it's got a charge, it should, but unless it's been plugged in all these years..." Nathan looked back at the tail, bending over to look under the stabilator. "Damn."

"What's wrong?" Jessica asked.

"It's not plugged in."

"Why not?"

"Well, if you're not going to fly it for a long time, it's better to let the batteries completely discharge. It keeps them healthy."

"So, what do we do now?"

"We plug it in and wait," Nathan explained. "Doesn't matter, really. We couldn't fly until sunrise anyway."

"Oh, yeah, because it's solar-powered," Jessica realized.

"No, because it doesn't have any running lights. It's an aerobatic plane," Nathan said. "Just as well, really. It will give us time to give her a *really* thorough preflight. Close the doors, so we don't attract attention."

Jessica turned around and headed for the door controls on the side wall. "I was *really* picturing something else when you said your grandfather had a plane, Nathan."

* * *

Nathan and Jessica pushed the small aerobatic plane out of the hangar and into the breaking dawn. After closing the hangar doors, they climbed up into the cramped cockpit of the aircraft.

"You weren't kidding when you said this was cramped," Jessica said as she squeezed down into her seat behind Nathan. "You have to be a contortionist to get into this thing."

"Needless to say, I didn't give many rides to friends," Nathan admitted as he pulled Jessica's harness over her shoulders. "This goes into the buckle between your legs."

"I got it."

Nathan moved forward, stepped over the edge of the cockpit, and slid down into the pilot's seat with ease. It felt more familiar than he had anticipated, which helped to ease his nerves.

"How long has it been since you flew this thing?" Jessica wondered.

"Do you really want to know?" Nathan replied as he went through his checklist.

"What, ten years maybe?"

"Honestly, the last time I flew this thing was the summer before I started college. You do the math."

"You're right, I didn't want to know," Jessica admitted.

"But I flew the hell out of it that summer. I even entered an aerobatic contest."

"Did you win?" she asked, hoping for anything encouraging.

"Not even close," Nathan replied. "Actually, I almost crashed."

"Not helping."

"I'm kidding, Jess. But just in case, you should know that your seat has a parachute built into it. If we have to bail, I'll jettison the canopy, and then you pull the yellow handle to your right to release your pack from the airframe, so you can jump out."

"You're kidding again, right?"

"Nope. You'll jump first, then I'll jump."

"I am not liking this, Nathan."

"Jesus, Jess, you just jumped from orbit...and that was how many times? Four or five?"

"More like twenty."

Nathan shook his head as he turned on the plane's main power. He checked his energy levels, which indicated he had about an hour of flight time. If he kept their speed down, he could squeeze an hour and a half out of his current charge, thereby giving the sun time to rise enough so that their solar cells would start producing sufficient power to keep them aloft.

He leaned his head out and hollered, "Clear prop!"

"Uh, there's no one out there," Jessica reminded him.

"Old habit." Nathan pressed the engine start button and the propeller immediately began to spin, sending a rush of air across them. Nathan scanned his flight display, checking that all the systems were functioning properly. "Pull the canopy forward over your head," he told Jessica.

Jessica reached back, grabbing hold of the leading edge of the canopy and slid it forward as far as she could reach. Nathan reached back and took the canopy from her, pulling it the rest of the way forward and latching it closed.

"Wow, it's really quiet in here," Jessica commented. "I expected it to be a lot noisier."

"It was when I first learned to fly it," Nathan assured her. "My grandfather replaced the combustion engine with an electric one when I was about sixteen or seventeen."

"You're telling me the engine in this bucket is twenty years old?"

"Closer to thirty, actually," Nathan corrected as he pushed the throttle forward to test the engine. "But these engines are practically bulletproof."

"Why aren't we moving?"

"I'm doing my run-up."

"Okay."

A minute later, Nathan backed the throttle down and released the parking brake, and the plane started rolling forward. The tail shifted left and right without warning. "Oops," he apologized. "I forgot how squirrelly the steering is on this thing."

Jessica said nothing.

Nathan guided the small aircraft down the row of hangars, paused for a moment to check the windsock, and then increased power and turned right onto the taxiway.

Jessica bounced along in the back seat as the plane seemed to jump upward with every little rock or bump in the taxiway. "What are we doing? Why aren't we airborne?"

"This is an airplane, Jessica," Nathan explained. "Wings, lift, thrust... We need a runway to take off and land. No vertical thrust on these things."

"Why do they even make these things anymore?" she wondered.

"They don't, at least not commercially. Not in more than two hundred years."

"Are you telling me this fucking thing is two hundred years old?" she demanded, suddenly feeling like she wanted out.

Nathan laughed. "No, my grandfather built this one himself, about thirty years ago."

"Oh, great."

"From a kit, actually."

"Even better."

Nathan turned from the taxiway toward the runway, barely able to see in the predawn light. "White Rock Airfield, Allen Aerobat niner two, niner four, Quebec, on the roll, runway two five, for a right downwind departure."

"Are you making radio calls?" Jessica asked, shocked. "We are supposed to be covert, remember?"

"We'll attract more attention if we collide with someone or cause a near-miss incident, trust me," Nathan explained. "Besides, on the ground, these comms have a *very* short range."

Nathan guided the small plane onto the runway and pushed his throttle all the way forward. The plane surged down the runway, and Nathan had to fight to keep it on the centerline in the face of a considerable left-quartering crosswind. His eyes danced up and down, dividing his attention equally between the view forward and his flight data display.

"This runway looks short," Jessica exclaimed, peering over Nathan's left shoulder to see forward.

"We won't even need half of it," Nathan assured her, glancing down at his airspeed tape. In a single smooth motion, Nathan pulled his control stick back slightly and to the left while adding right rudder with the pedals. The plane rose slightly off the ground, and his left wing dipped. The plane yawed left, weather-vaning into the crosswind as it began to climb slowly off the ground. Everything was suddenly coming back to him as he pulled back on the stick a little more and guided the tiny aircraft silently into the steadily lightening sky.

After a minute, Nathan rolled the aircraft to the left, bringing it around until they were traveling due east toward the rising sun. He leveled off and then retrimmed the plane, settling the throttle back to a power level that would give them the greatest flying time.

"What's wrong?" Jessica asked. "Why aren't we climbing?"

"Climbing takes more power," Nathan explained. "Besides, it's better if we stay low. Air traffic tracking sensors generally don't look below two hundred meters. Too much ground clutter."

"Are you planning on flying this low all the way to Winnipeg?"

"You wanted to be covert, right?"

"Yeah, but..."

"Just keep your eyes peeled for high towers and low-flying drones, and we should be fine."

"How long will it take to get there?" Jessica asked as she gazed outside at the dimly-lit countryside passing below them.

"At this speed, six or seven hours," Nathan replied. "But we should be able to increase our speed a bit once the sun comes up and we start producing more power."

"Six hours? This thing have auto-flight?"

"Nope. It's an aerobatic plane, remember?"

"You're going to hand-fly this thing for six hours?"

"We'll stop along the way for a break or two," Nathan assured her.

Jessica shook her head. "We should've just stolen a shuttle or something."

"And miss out on all this?" Nathan laughed. "This

is *real* flying, Jess. Nothing like it. Balancing the four forces; lift against gravity; thrust against drag. None of that pushing buttons and overpowering your way from place to place. In *this*, you *feel* every little ripple and current of the air as you pass through it."

"Yeah, I noticed," Jessica grumbled as the plane bounced in the gentle, morning turbulence.

* * *

Dressed in conservative Corinairan business attire, Deliza sat next to President Scott, smiling and pretending to talk about important matters as dozens of cameras took hundreds of images that would appear all over the core worlds of Earth within the hour. News of her plea, if not the actual content, would reach every citizen and every politician throughout the Alliance. Citizens would question whether or not their world should risk weakening their own defenses in order to support their fellow member worlds in the Pentaurus sector. They would have to wrestle with the moral implications of turning their backs on those worlds.

"How long do we have to keep this up?" Deliza asked the president while trying to move her mouth as little as possible to prevent others from lip reading her words.

"A few more minutes, at least," the president replied. "It's all part of the process, I'm afraid."

"When will we be free to discuss the Pentaurus sector's problems?"

"At lunch, I expect. That will be a private affair, in sealed chambers, so that we may speak freely."

"I look forward to it," Deliza replied, continuing to smile for the cameras. "To be honest, I was not expecting this."

"What were you expecting?" the president wondered.

"I don't know. A podium; an audience; a well-prepared speech, perhaps?"

"I'll be happy to listen to it, *after* the media has departed, I assure you," the president replied.

* * *

Nathan and Jessica walked into the office building at the tiny airport just north of Winnipeg. The building had seen better days, but it had all the usual comforts that pilots of small aircraft hoped for when flying cross-country.

"Can I help you?" the old man behind the counter asked.

"Yes," Nathan replied. "We were wondering if there was a way to get into Winnipeg from here? Some kind of public transportation?"

"You here for the playoffs?"

"Uh..."

"You a Wolves fan?"

"Actually, I'm originally from Vancouver."

"Vancouver, huh? Shame about the Beavers. If they just could've pulled out at least one good season, they wouldn't have had to fold up the club."

"Yeah, a real shame," Nathan agreed, not knowing what the man was talking about.

"At least we got Buchard and Tisdale out of it," the old man laughed. "Without them, I don't think there would be a game seven tonight."

"You're probably right," Nathan agreed, going along with him for appearances sake. "About that transportation..."

"There's a bus stop about a kilometer down the road. Just head west out the front gate. Right hand side...can't miss it. Buses to Winnipeg run every hour. There's a cafe next to the bus stop, if you have much of a wait." The old man looked out the window at Nathan's plane. "That your Allen out there?"

"Yup."

"She's a nice one. Haven't seen one in ages. You build her?"

"My grandfather did, when I was a kid. Taught me how to fly her. Left her to me when he died."

"You're a lucky fella, aren't you? That's real flying right there."

"That's what I've been trying to tell her," Nathan agreed, tilting his head toward Jessica behind him. "How much to leave her tied down for a couple days?"

"No way I'd charge for a vintage kit like that," the old man laughed. "Makes my little strip look pretty. Besides, I'll make plenty off the shuttles that come in for the game later."

"Thanks," Nathan said. He turned to Jessica, pointing toward the door. "Shall we?" He followed her outside where they both headed down the drive for the airport's main gate.

"What was that all about?" Jessica wondered.

"Just small talk," Nathan replied. "But it gave me an idea."

* * *

Lunch with President Scott, Miri Scott-Thornton, and the president's advisors had been a very delicate affair. Deliza had been given strict instructions *not* to reveal that Nathan was alive and leading the rebellion. Nor was she to disclose that it was the Dusahn who had invaded the Pentaurus cluster and not the Jung, as they had originally reported. Both General Telles and Nathan had felt that this information was best shared with Dayton Scott in private, by the son he had long believed dead.

They also did not know who among the president's staff could be trusted. It was entirely possible that Galiardi had a mole inside the NAU administration, perhaps even one close to the president. As far as they were concerned, only the president and his aide, Nathan's sister, Miri, could be trusted. It was an attitude that Deliza was unaccustomed to. As the leader of Ranni Enterprises, she had dealt with her fair share of unscrupulous businessmen, but those stakes had involved profit, not lives.

Lunch itself seemed a pretense. No one was really eating, just poking at their food and nibbling here and there in between words. In fact, the first hour of their meal had been spent discussing the current state of the Pentaurus cluster and what the new Karuzari hoped to accomplish.

"If you hope to run a guerilla campaign, you will need considerable resources," the president's advisor, Mister Dalton, said. "Not just weapons, but basic consumables like food, water, medicine, communications equipment, building materials, portable sensor devices...the list is endless. You will need specialists, as well. And I don't mean combat specialists. I'm talking about technicals, like construction, electrical, comms..."

"Many of these skills can be learned," Deliza insisted. "But I agree with your assessment of our needs for the basics. As word spreads about how the Jung punish worlds who aid and abet the Karuzari, it will become harder to acquire resources. If we have to travel to find them, it will limit our ability to sustain an effective, armed conflict."

"We can likely help you with the basics," President Scott promised, "as doing so will not jeopardize our security in the Sol sector. Food and water, especially, is once again in abundance across the core worlds, thanks in large part to the jump drive."

"What about medicine?" Deliza wondered. "We are in dire need of medical supplies."

"We can spare enough to keep you going for a few months, I expect," the president replied.

"And propellant?"

"*That* might be more difficult," Mister Dalton admitted.

"Mister President, I hope you realize that the Karuzari are not asking for handouts. We are willing to pay a fair price for all that you are willing to sell us."

"Where are you getting your funds, if you don't mind my asking?" Mister Dalton wondered.

"I used the remainder of my father's holdings to develop several technologies that were lacking in the Pentaurus sector, for which Ranni Enterprises holds the patents," Deliza explained. "Those patents provided substantial income, which we invested in other commodities. Some of those investments are within the Pentaurus cluster itself and are still paying considerable dividends. In fact, the invasion of the cluster may even increase our profits in those divisions."

"Kind of ironic, wouldn't you say?" Miri commented.

"Indeed," Deliza agreed. "However, we fear that it is only a matter of time until our enemies discover this, at which time those dividends will cease to exist."

"We have spent the last week moving the bulk of our assets to financial institutions well outside the Pentaurus cluster," Yanni explained. "Which is why it is so important for us to *keep* our enemy's influence contained *within* the cluster itself. If it spreads beyond, or perhaps even beyond the Pentaurus sector itself..."

"Your ability to fund your rebellion will disappear," Mister Dalton realized.

"Precisely," Deliza agreed.

"The fact that it would be a *business* arrangement, and not just a gift, will give us a lot more leverage," Mister Dalton surmised. "Many providers would welcome a chance to open up new markets."

"Transportation of goods to the Pentaurus region will be a challenge," President Scott warned. "We barely have enough ships to move goods between the core worlds."

"We can provide transportation," Deliza assured him. "Many of the jump ships whose home ports are now under enemy control are afraid to return for fear of seizure. We are slowly accumulating these ships into our fleet. At the time of our departure for Earth, there were at least six cargo ships that had yet to be tasked. The problem is, we cannot send them on a six-week, round-trip journey unless we are quite sure they will have sufficient propellant to return."

"Then we will have to ensure that is the case," President Scott promised.

An aide entered the president's private dining room and approached the president, whispering in his ear.

"My apologies, Miss Ta'Akar," the president said, dabbing at his mouth with his napkin. "I'm afraid the duties of my office call."

"Of course," Deliza replied.

"Anything I can help with?" Miri wondered.

"A minor matter," the president assured her. "Please, finish your lunch." The president turned to Deliza. "I hope I get a chance to speak with you further before your departure, Miss Ta'Akar, Mister Hiller." The president bowed his head respectfully before turning to exit, followed by Mister Dalton.

Deliza's comm-unit vibrated. She looked at the device's screen, reading the message.

"Don't tell me you have to leave, as well?" Miri said.

"Not at all," Deliza assured her. "It was just my pilot. The repairs on the ventral section of my ship have been completed."

"I heard about that. It must have been a frightening experience."

"It was a bit bumpy for a while," Deliza replied. "But the Mirai is a sturdy vessel that has served me well all these years, and will likely continue to serve me for many more."

"Personally, *all* space travel makes me nervous," Miri admitted. "So much energy being manipulated with such precision, and in such a harsh environment. It seems like a recipe for disaster."

"You get accustomed to it after a while," Yanni assured her.

"It has been some time since you were on Earth, Mister Hiller," Miri observed. "Do you miss your homeworld?"

"To some extent, yes."

"What do you miss most?" Miri wondered.

"Oh, I don't know. The food, maybe. I miss snow skiing. They don't have that on Corinair."

"He misses hockey terribly," Deliza added.

"I do?"

"He's always talking about it. He even tried to get an ice rink built on Corinair, but was unable to generate any interest. He even has several jerseys from your World Hockey League."

"Uh, yeah, I do," Yanni agreed, playing along.

"You're in luck," Miri told them. "Game seven of the finals is tonight, right here in Winnipeg. The Wolves are playing the Swords. The entire city is buzzing over it."

"Really?" She looked at Yanni, feigning excitement. "What do you think, Yanni?"

"Is it even possible to get tickets?"

"I can do better," Miri replied. "The president is a fan. We have a skybox at the arena."

"Didn't Nathan play hockey as a child?" Deliza asked.

"He did," Miri confirmed. "He wasn't very good, though."

"If only he were still alive," Deliza said wistfully. "He would love to see the game, I'm sure."

"Yes, he would," Miri agreed, understanding Deliza's meaning.

"Maybe the president would like to go, as well?" Deliza suggested. "It might give us a chance to continue our discussions. I think it is important for us both to fully understand *all* sides of the problems we face, both together *and* separately."

"I'll be sure to suggest it to him," Miri agreed. "To be honest, I think it would do him some good to take at least *one* evening off. And it wouldn't hurt his public image to be there when the Wolves win the cup."

"I'm looking forward to it," Deliza said, smiling. She turned to look at Yanni. "Aren't you?"

"Oh, yes," Yanni agreed. "Very much so."

CHAPTER TEN

Nathan stepped through the doors into the main arena, pausing for a moment to take in the view. It seemed a lifetime since he had seen the inside of a professional ice hockey arena. He had missed the game, but until this moment, he never realized how much.

The building was packed with spectators, upwards of twenty thousand by his estimation. Giant view screens hung over the center of the ice, playing exciting images from past games. Graphic effects using team colors of blue and gold streaked around the perimeters of each seating deck, all choreographed in time with music that played at such volume you could scarcely hear someone talking next to you.

The excitement of the crowd was palpable, despite the fact that the final game had yet to begin. Vendors roamed the aisles, hawking all manner of snacks, beverages, and souvenirs, while ushers helped fans wearing mostly Wolves jerseys find their seats.

The Winnipeg Wolves had been struggling more than most to rebuild their franchise. This was the first time since the Jung invasion that the Wolves had made it to the finals. With the series tied at three games each, the stage had been set for a glorious victory on home ice.

"Wow," Jessica commented as she stepped up next to Nathan. "I knew these things were big events, but I never expected *this*."

"Honestly, this is even more over the top than I remembered," Nathan commented.

An usher asked for Nathan's ticket, which he

promptly displayed. He and Jessica followed the usher to their seats, only a few rows down.

Unfortunately, they were about as far away from the ice as possible, but considering that it was the final game of the championship series, they were lucky to get them at all. They had been forced to purchase their tickets from a scalper, which had not been cheap. If they were unsuccessful in their attempt to meet with Nathan's father and sister, they wouldn't have enough money to get back to their plane, let alone the funds needed to complete their business in Cocoa Beach.

It was a calculated risk. Nathan was reasonably certain that his father would have a skybox at the arena. The entire Scott clan, having lived in the Vancouver area for generations, were avid ice hockey fans. Considering how much they all loved the game, Nathan had always found it odd that he had been the only member of the family who had actually played it as a child.

Even if they were unable to meet with his father, Jessica was certain they could find a way to acquire additional funds. Nathan had chosen not to inquire how she might do so.

"I thought it would be colder in here," Jessica said as they took their seats.

"It's only cold down closer to the ice," Nathan explained.

"Why do people pay such prices to sit this far away?" she wondered. "You'd see more in the broadcast, wouldn't you?"

"It's about being here, being part of it when it happens," Nathan explained.

"When what happens?"

"When they win the cup."

"What if they lose? Then you spent two thousand credits to watch them lose."

"Didn't you ever go to games?"

"Not hockey games," Jessica replied.

"Well, any game."

"No. We always watched them at home," she explained. "The whole family and, usually, several of my brother's friends. Probably about twenty people, all in all. It was sort of an event at our house."

"Well, that's the same thing, just on a much smaller scale, right?" Nathan said.

"Yeah, I guess so." Jessica looked around. "So, how does this work. Are there four quarters or something?"

"You know nothing about hockey, do you?"

"I'm from Florida, Nathan. We wore shorts and swimsuits most of the time, not parkas like all you Canucks."

"Well, you're in for a treat, then."

"Try not to forget why we're here," Jessica reminded him.

"Don't ruin it for me," Nathan objected.

* * *

After passing through several layers of security, Deliza and Yanni entered the presidential skybox at the Wolves' arena. The room, located right along the arena's center line, was a lot bigger than either of them had imagined.

The skybox was deeper than it was in width and was divided into four sections. At the back were catering counters, complete with servers and a bartender. Between them and the bar were four standing-height tables with barstools.

"So glad you could make it, Miss Ta'Akar," a man in suit and bowtie greeted. "I am Mister Solvang, your host. If there is anything you need, simply squeeze the clip on your security badge lanyard, and one of my staff will respond promptly. May I show you to your seats?"

"Yes, thank you," Deliza replied, smiling. The man was very pleasant and likable, and his demeanor put her immediately at ease in an unfamiliar environment.

Deliza and Yanni followed Mister Solvang toward the front of the room, down two steps to the next level. This level contained two rows of seats that appeared roomy and comfortable, with sidearms that had beverage holders and a small table that folded away. And there was plenty of room to walk past those already seated without bothering them, unlike the seats she remembered at the polon games back on Corinair.

Each row of seats was nearly a meter lower than the other, giving the spectators unobstructed views of the arena below. There was a clear partition between them and the next two rows of seats, which were on a balcony in front of the skybox itself.

"You may sit anywhere you like, with the exception of this row here," Mister Solvang explained, touching the back of the row behind him, "which is reserved for the president. You may also go out and sit in the balcony. Some prefer it, as they feel it makes them more a *part* of the event. However, I must warn you that the crowd can be quite loud."

"I think here will be fine," Deliza said. "Yanni?"

"Yes, this is wonderful."

"Thank you, Mister Solvang."

"It is my pleasure, ma'am. Enjoy the game."

Deliza and Yanni moved to take their seats but

were immediately interrupted by a voice from behind them.

"Miss Ta'Akar," Miri called.

Deliza turned to look. "Please, call me Deliza," she insisted.

"Of course," Miri agreed. "Miranda, but I go by Miri."

"Yes, Nathan spoke of you often."

"Were you close to Nathan?" Miri asked, as if fishing for cues.

"I *am*," Deliza replied, purposefully using the present tense. "I mean, I was. In all honesty, I feel like he is still with us, even now."

That was all Miri needed to hear. "Please sit with me in the president's row," she instructed, gesturing for her to move to the next row forward.

Deliza and Yanni moved down to the next row and made their way along several seats before sitting. Miri sat down next to Deliza, then pressed a button on the side of her chair. A second later, the din of the crowd outside, and of the people talking in the skybox, faded away completely, leaving them in silence.

"We are within an acoustical shield," Miri explained, speaking quickly. "No one can hear us. Please face me while you speak, so that no one observing from across the arena can read our lips."

Deliza turned in her seat toward Miri, trying to do so in a natural fashion as if engaging in a normal, personal conversation.

"Is he here?" Miri asked.

"Section three one two, row twenty-three, seats fifteen and sixteen."

"Who is with him?"

"Jessica Nash," Deliza replied. "He wishes to

speak to you and the president, in private. Is that possible?"

"Here? Now?"

"Yes," Deliza replied. "He is on a tight schedule and must depart Winnipeg tonight. He still has much to do on Earth before his departure."

"Then you are not *really* here to request aid, are you?"

"No. We are here to provide you with critical information about the Jung incursions into the Sol sector. Nathan insists on explaining it to your father in person. Can you arrange this?"

Miri thought furiously. "Yes, I think so. Give me a few minutes."

"We have the entire game," Deliza replied. "However long *that* is."

* * *

"*And now, let's welcome, your Winnipeg Wolves!*" the announcer called in dramatic fashion meant to excite the crowd.

It worked, as nearly every person in attendance rose to their feet to cheer as their team took the ice—Nathan included.

Jessica also rose, but more to blend in. "I thought you weren't a Wolves fan?" she said, leaning in close to be heard.

"What?"

Jessica shook her head. She felt a tug on her sleeve and turned to the man next to her, who pointed toward the aisle. Jessica looked, spotting an usher gesturing for her to get the attention of Nathan. She touched Nathan's shoulder and tipped her head toward the usher at the end of the row. "I think she wants to speak to us!"

"Do you think she wants to speak to us?" Nathan

hollered, not hearing what Jessica had said above the roar of the crowd.

Jessica pulled at his jacket, urging him to follow as she began squeezing past the spectators between her and the usher at the end. Once they reached the aisle, the usher leaned closer to Nathan.

"Are you Connor Tuplo?" she asked, also yelling to be heard over all the noise.

Nathan was taken aback by the question, but immediately realized the significance. "Yes," he replied, nodding.

"Someone needs to speak with you, sir. If you would both please follow me."

"Of course," Nathan agreed. He exchanged glances with Jessica and then followed the usher up the aisle and into the perimeter corridor, where they were met by two gentlemen dressed in the same blue blazers as the usher. These two, however, were both wearing comm-sets.

"What's this about?" Nathan asked the usher, once they were sheltered in the corridor from the roar of the crowd.

"Someone wishes to speak with you, Mister Tuplo," one of the men repeated.

"Who?" Jessica asked.

"We do not know," the man replied. "Arena management has instructed us to escort the two of you to a more private location. That is all we know."

"Are we in some kind of trouble?" Nathan wondered.

"No, sir. It's probably some sort of prize. Like an invitation to view the game from the team skybox. The Wolves do that kind of thing a lot."

"Great!" Nathan exclaimed. He didn't believe him

for a moment; there was only one person who could have asked for Connor Tuplo. "Lead the way, fellas!"

Nathan, Jessica, and the men wove their way through the crowds still making their way into the inner arena. After a few minutes, the men led them to a set of secure doors. One of the men punched in a short code and opened the doors, stepping aside to allow Nathan and Jessica to enter. Once their charges had entered, the men closed the doors, remaining outside.

Another man promptly greeted them. "Mister Tuplo, I presume?"

"Yes," Nathan replied.

"If you'll please follow me," the man said, turning and continuing deeper into the complex. He led them into an elevator that took them up two more levels, opening into yet another service corridor, one bustling with activity. In addition to arena staff, there were a lot more security personnel, including men in black suits wearing discrete comms earpieces. Nathan immediately recognized them as NAU presidential security. He looked at Jessica, who also recognized the role of the black-suited men.

The man led them into a large, industrial kitchen also bustling with activity. They made their way across the back of the kitchen and into a locker room, where they were met by a very serious-looking young man in similar black attire.

The man who had brought them to this locker room left without another word, leaving Nathan and Jessica alone in the locker room with the young man. Once the door was closed, the young man spoke.

"I am Mister Graves. Miss Scott-Thornton has instructed me to bring you to a private location, so that she may speak with you directly. However, in order to do so, I must ask you both to strip down to your underwear and put on these catering uniforms."

"Our underwear?" Nathan asked.

"My apologies to you both for the inconvenience," the young man replied, "but it is necessary for purposes of security."

"Of course," Nathan said, unzipping his jacket. He looked at Jessica, who was already removing her top, apparently untroubled by the request.

* * *

Vladimir walked up to Robert's SAR shuttle parked in the back of the hangar at the evacuation complex on Tanna. "Hello?" he called as he approached.

Robert stuck his head out of the side hatch a moment later. "Commander."

"I am just Vladimir, at the moment," Vladimir corrected. "There are no ranks aboard the Seiiki. And since, technically, I am a deserter..."

Robert chuckled. "As am I."

Vladimir smiled. "Then I am in good company, I suppose. I was told you were having problems with the output regulator on your shoreline?"

"Yes, I am."

"Probably because the regulator was designed to control the power levels coming *into* your ship, not those going out."

"I wasn't aware."

"It is a common mistake," Vladimir assured him. "May I?"

"Of course." Robert hopped down out of his shuttle, following Vladimir aft to the reactor bay access panel on his port side.

"It was actually a very clever idea," Vladimir congratulated him. "Powering this facility with your reactor. You just needed to take a few additional steps, was all."

"Well, it's been a while since I had to do any engineering work on my own," Robert admitted.

Vladimir tapped his comm-set. "General, this is Vladimir. There will be a momentary interruption in power throughout the building. It will be brief."

"*Understood,*" the general replied.

"What do you have to do?" Robert asked as the general's voice warned everyone on comms of the impending power outage.

Vladimir raised the hatch to the SAR shuttle's reactor bay, propping it open and turning on the work light inside the bay. "I just need to reverse the polarity of the inline regulator and then make a few adjustments," he explained as he worked.

"That easy, huh?"

"That easy." Vladimir reached inside the reactor bay and killed the power switch, plunging the entire facility into relative darkness.

"Can I ask you something?" Robert wondered.

"Of course."

"How hard was it for you? You know, to leave it all behind? To go AWOL, desert, whatever you want to call it."

"It was easy," Vladimir said as he made adjustments to the inline regulator. "My best friend was asking for my help, just like your sister was asking for yours, yes?"

"In a manner of speaking, I suppose."

"Perhaps it is even easier for you," Vladimir suggested. "All your family is there, are they not? I mean, you have no ties on Earth?"

"How did you know?"

"I know your type," Vladimir explained.

"My type?"

"Career man, Captain. You chose to go on long, deep-space missions, far from home. You decided long ago that family could wait until retirement. Am I right?"

"Pretty much," Robert admitted. "I didn't realize engineers were such good judges of human nature."

"I cheated," Vladimir admitted. "Your sister has spoken of you often." He smiled, then turned the power back on. "All good."

"Thanks."

"I trust everything is working properly now?" General Telles asked as he approached.

"There should be no more interruptions," Vladimir promised.

"Excellent," General Telles said. "We still have much to do."

"I thought we just had to wait until Nathan and Jessica returned," Vladimir said.

"We are teaching as many of my men as possible how to operate the Cobra gunship," the general explained.

"In two days?" Robert wondered. "Are any of them at least pilots?"

"No. However, they are all intelligent, highly educated men, and it is my understanding that most of the basic flight operations are automated."

"Yes, but the launch cycle is one of the riskiest operations in a gunship's service life," Robert warned.

"Which is precisely why that operation is fully automated. It is my understanding that those gunships *could* be launched under auto-flight, *without* a crew."

"Yes, but that capability is only available in case of crew incapacitation," Robert insisted. "You *need* a crew, especially a *pilot*, in case something goes wrong after departure."

"I agree," the general replied. "However, since we will only get one chance at this, it makes sense to try to steal as many ships as possible."

Robert nodded. "I see your point. But how do you propose to get those gunships back to the Pentaurus sector? I doubt they have a jump series profile for the PC in their database already."

"Our plan is to jump the ships to a rally point a few light years away from the Tau Ceti system, then have the lead ship, which would be piloted by you, calculate the jump series plot and transmit it to the ships piloted by my men."

"They still have to get those ships onto the proper speed and course for it to work. If they are off by even the slightest..."

"Then the jump drive sequencer will not engage," Vladimir pointed out.

"You're right, it won't," Robert agreed. "And then what?"

"They come about and try again," General Telles suggested.

"Not quite as easy as it sounds, General. It's not like driving a boat," Robert objected.

"Actually, it is very similar," Vladimir argued. "I mean, it is not the same, of course, but the jump drive sequencer is designed to take small errors in course and speed into consideration. True, it will abort the jump if the gunship is *too* far off, but it will first attempt to recalculate the jump and make adjustments. If it can do so and still get the gunship to the destination with reasonable accuracy, the jump will initiate."

"So, essentially, you just want to play 'follow the

leader' all the way back to the Pentaurus sector?" Robert scratched his head. "That's got to be one of the craziest ideas I've ever heard."

"Crazier than stealing the gunships to begin with?" Vladimir wondered.

"No, I guess not," Robert admitted.

"We don't have to get the gunships all the way back to the Karuzari fleet," General Telles explained. "We just need to get them far enough away from the Alliance, so they can safely await either a recovery ship or more qualified flight crews to retrieve them."

"That makes sense, I guess," Robert admitted. "But it still seems risky."

"I admit there is risk involved," the general stated. "But there is also risk involved with the theft to begin with. I am only seeking to extract maximum benefit from the mission."

Robert sighed. "You know, while Gil and I were figuring this thing out, there was one variable we couldn't quantify."

"What was that?" General Telles wondered.

"Just how good the Ghatazhak really are," Robert replied. "There are at least fifty Alliance Marines stationed there, sometimes more. And I'm not talking about the ones you trained seven years ago. These guys are much better. They are probably the closest thing the Alliance has to Ghatazhak."

"How long ago was such a program implemented?" General Telles wondered.

"A couple years after you guys left, I guess. So, maybe five years?"

"Ghatazhak train for more than a decade prior to beginning their first tour of duty. We start just before puberty, both mentally and physically. We not only learn how to fight, we also learn how to *think.*

Physical sciences, philosophy, economics, political sciences, psychology, physics, medical sciences... You name it, the Ghatazhak know it."

"I was not aware," Robert admitted.

"There is far more to being a soldier than pressing a trigger on a weapon," General Telles said. "Knowledge, understanding, and insight...*those* are what separate the Ghatazhak from any other soldier. We act as one, we think as one, and we understand *everything*...more rapidly than others."

"Then you are not afraid of failure?" Robert asked.

"If the information you and Captain Roselle provided is accurate, then I am confident we will be successful. What I do *not* know, is how many men I will lose in the process."

"I thought the Ghatazhak were not afraid of dying," Vladimir said.

"We are not," General Telles confirmed. "To die in battle is the ultimate honor for a Ghatazhak. My concerns are logistical. There are no more Ghatazhak, only those who escaped Lawrence. The more of them we lose, the lower our chances of defeating the Dusahn become. It is as simple as that." General Telles turned and departed without another word.

Vladimir looked at Robert. "I am glad he is not *my* commanding officer."

"I should go help him," Robert said, "I am type-rated for Cobra gunships, after all. And there are only so many of the Ghatazhak left, right?" Robert added, patting Vladimir on the shoulder as he departed to follow the general.

* * *

Miri paced nervously across one of the catering staging rooms just down the corridor from the president's skybox, at the Winnipeg Wolves' arena.

She could hear the muffled sounds of the crowd and the voices of the broadcasters calling the play-by-play action that was piped into all the skyboxes. Her heart was beating a mile a minute, her palms were sweaty, and she felt light-headed, the same way she had felt when she had first seen Nathan on that first vid-message a few weeks ago.

Until yesterday, she was beginning to believe the message had been a hoax; an elaborate plan to get her to relay a message to the Aurora.

But he had looked so real.

His hair had been longer, and he had been wearing that god-awful mess of a beard, but the *eyes* were unmistakable. It *was* Nathan.

Or so she had thought.

When she heard nothing back from Doctor Chen or Captain Taylor, she began to doubt she had ever even *received* that message. *Perhaps it had been a dream*? It wouldn't have been the first time she had dreamt that her baby brother was still alive.

She had to shake the doubts away. Given the events of the past twenty-four hours, it *had* to have been him. It *had* to be...

The door swung open, and two black-suited NAU security officers entered the room, followed by...

"Oh, my God," Miri gasped, her hands coming to her mouth.

The black-suited men stepped back out, closing the door behind them.

It was that smile...that same smile.

"Hi, Miri," Nathan said, raising his arms, inviting her embrace.

"Nathan," she whispered, almost crying as she fell into his outstretched arms. "You *are* alive."

Nathan held her tightly. "God, it's good to see you again," he whispered back.

Miri pulled back from him a bit, just enough to look at his face. "You look terrible," she laughed, rubbing the stubble on his cheek.

"It's been a rough few weeks."

She laughed again. "It's been *seven years*, Nathan. Why haven't you..."

"It's a long story," Nathan interrupted. "One that can wait for another time. Just know that there was no other way and leave it at that, for now."

"But..."

"I need you to trust me, Miri," Nathan urged.

"Of course, I trust you, Nathan."

"Where's Pop?"

"He's nearby," Miri assured him. "I had to... I had to be sure it was *really* you. He's been through so much. Your death has been *really* hard on him. I didn't want to take the chance..."

"You don't have to explain," Nathan said, interrupting her again. "I understand."

Miri pulled back further, turning to look at Jessica. "It's good to see you again, Jessica. I hope you're taking good care of him."

"I'm trying," Jessica replied. "He doesn't make it easy, though."

"I can imagine."

"I hate to rush your reunion, but the faster we get this done, the better," Jessica reminded Nathan.

"She's right," Nathan sighed.

"Of course," Miri replied, reaching into her pocket and pulling out her comm-unit. "Scott-Thornton, one one five seven, alpha four, echo two two five. Bring the president to room four one seven. There is someone he needs to speak to, as soon as possible.

Yes, the room is secure. Two agents are at the door. Thank you." She ended the call and returned the comm-unit to her pocket. "He should be here shortly. Meanwhile, you want to tell me how you managed to get out of a Jung cell on Nor-Patri, on the eve of your execution?"

"He had some help," Jessica told her.

"Yeah, I figured that much."

"Like I said, it's a long story, and we don't have time to go into details at the moment," Nathan repeated.

"Well, what the hell is going on in the Pentaurus cluster?" Miri asked instead. "It must be important, if you decided to come all the way back to Earth after all these years in hiding."

"Look, Miri, I realize you're probably mad at me for not letting you know I was alive sooner..."

"Oh, just a little, yes."

The door opened, and two more NAU security stepped in, quickly checking the room.

"Miss Scott-Thornton, I have the president outside," the first man said.

"Please, bring him in," Miri instructed, stepping around to stand between Nathan, his back turned, and the door.

Nathan did not turn around, instead keeping his back to the door as his father entered the room.

President Scott, accustomed to private discussions taking place at various locations behind one closed door or another, instinctively waited for the door to close behind him before speaking. "What's going on here, Miri?" he asked. He looked at Jessica, suddenly recognizing her. "Jessica Nash?"

"Yes, Mister President," Jessica replied. "It's good to see you again, sir."

"Are you the one I am supposed to speak with?" he asked.

"No, sir," she replied, stepping to one side.

Miri also stepped to the side as Nathan turned around to face his father.

"Hello, Mister President," Nathan greeted.

President Scott was speechless, his mouth agape and his eyes wide in disbelief. "This can't be," he said, mumbling his words as if he were half speaking them and half thinking them. "Nathan?"

"Yes, sir, it's me."

"But...but... I thought..." He looked at Miri, his eyes welling up. "Miri?"

"It's him," she told him, her eyes tearing up, as well. "It's really Nathan."

"My God..." he whispered, his voice trembling as he opened his arms to embrace the son he believed long dead.

CHAPTER ELEVEN

Abby picked at her breakfast, her mind elsewhere as her husband recited his itinerary for the day in his usual fashion. It had been four days since she had sabotaged the results of the terrenium-enhanced emitter tests, and every day that she had gone to work since then, she had expected to be her last.

"Abby?"

She had been positive that someone would discover the missing reactor logs. After all, there were people who checked those things. Ever since her father had discovered a discrepancy in a shield test from before the bio-digital plague, and that accidental discovery had led to the development of the jump drive, independent data audits had become standard on all research and development projects.

"Abby!"

Erik's tone startled her. "What?"

"Did you hear a single word I said?"

"I'm sorry, my mind was elsewhere." Abby took a bite of her breakfast, despite her lack of appetite.

"What's gotten into you lately?" her husband asked.

"I'm fine," Abby insisted.

"You've been distant; you haven't been eating or sleeping. Is something wrong? Something at work?"

"No, everything is fine."

"Is it about the last emitter test?" Erik surmised. "You always say that sometimes the numbers are wrong; that they don't account for unknown variables, right? That's why everything has to be tested and not just computer-modeled."

"You're right."

"Well, now I *know* something is wrong," Erik joked. When she didn't respond, he pressed. "Is it possible that there *isn't* a way to make stealth emitters for large ships?" Again, he waited, but got nothing. "That's it, isn't it?" Erik fell back in his chair in desperation. "My God, we're never going to get out of this place."

"That's not it, Erik," Abby finally said.

"Then what *is* it?"

"I already know how to make the stealth emitters work," she admitted.

Erik looked confused. "But... When did you figure it out?"

"Four days ago. The night you and the kids were at the game."

"Isn't that the day the emitters failed?"

"Yes, at least that's what we thought."

"I'm confused."

"Everyone *thinks* they failed," Abby explained, "but I know they didn't. The test environment was flawed. The energy levels were too high."

"Then why isn't everyone celebrating?" he wondered. "Why have you been so glum the last few days? Is it because of what you were talking about the other day? Because you're afraid of what Galiardi will do with it? Abby, I thought we agreed that it's not your responsibility. If you hadn't figured it out, someone else would have."

Abby just looked at him, a guilty expression on her face.

Erik's eyes widened. "You didn't tell them, did you?"

"No."

"Jesus, Abby, you know they'll figure it out sooner or later."

"Maybe." Abby looked at him again. "But probably not, considering..."

"Considering what?"

"I deleted the evidence."

"You what?"

"I deleted the file."

"You can't delete test data, can you?" Erik challenged. "I thought all that stuff was protected; backed up and all that."

"The test data is protected *and* has a multi-level backup. But the reactor logs are not as well protected. And I didn't actually *delete* them. I just corrupted them so that they're useless."

Erik took a slow, deep breath. "Abby, why would you do that? You know they'll eventually figure it out, and the Alliance *will have* their stealth jump ships."

"I know, but now that they think the terrenium is a dead end, they'll have to start over with a new coating. That will take another month just to get to the full-power testing phase. And that will fail, as well, which means they'll try something else, and so on... It could take them *years* to figure it out."

"And what if the Jung attack us before then?" Erik asked. "It should be easy for them, now that they have jump drives."

"Then I can give them what they want."

"And go to prison."

"They don't put people in prison for corrupting reactor logs, Erik."

"Don't be so sure."

"I don't have to tell them that I steered them away from it. I just have to make them believe that I want to try the terrenium again."

Erik did not look pleased. "Did it ever occur to

you that maybe you don't have the *right* to decide what gets invented, and what doesn't? Or who gets it and who doesn't?"

"Now you sound like my father," Abby said.

"Your father was a wise man, Abby. He believed that a scientist's job was to discover truths, and that it was society's decision what to do with them."

"He had the luxury of not having seen the evil that humans can do with those discoveries, Erik. I do not. I've seen it, and so have you, and so have our children! I, for one, do not want to be a party to that! Not again!"

"Abby, I understand that. I really do. I lived through the invasion of Earth and the bombardment during the liberation. I kept our children safe while you were jumping around the stars."

"That's not fair."

"I never said it was. But it still isn't your fault, nor your father's. If it's anyone's fault, it's the Jung's." Erik sat back again, taking a moment to lessen the tension. "I know you don't trust Galiardi. I don't blame you. I don't trust him, either. But is there anyone that you *do* trust with this technology?"

Abby thought for a moment. "No, I suppose not." She turned toward him. "You think I should give Galiardi his stealth jump drive."

"That's *your* decision, Abby." He reached across the table and took her hand in his. "Just think about it."

"That's all I've *been* thinking about," she insisted.

Erik smiled, rising from his chair. "I have to get the kids to school." He paused in passing, kissing her on the head. "Don't forget, you're cooking dinner tomorrow night, so you need to go to the store sometime soon."

Abby stared at her half-eaten breakfast, thinking. Her husband reminded her so much of her father. Both had never-ending faith in humanity. Both believed that things always worked out in the end. She wanted to feel the same way, but she couldn't figure out how. Trust was not something that came easily for her, and trusting Admiral Galiardi with a stealth jump drive felt wrong.

* * *

The flight from Winnipeg to Cocoa Beach had been grueling. Nathan and Jessica had left at the break of dawn, flying for as long as their fully charged battery would take them, before landing and recharging while they napped. Once the sun was high enough, they continued their journey with a new charge, and the knowledge that their aircraft would have the energy to complete their three-thousand-kilometer, cross-country trek.

They had chosen to divide the journey into a series of two-hour hops; neither of them wanted to endure the uncomfortable cockpit of the Allen Aerobat longer than they had to. Miri had provided them with all the funds they would need for the remainder of their stay on Earth, despite the fact that Nathan had refused to tell them what they were planning.

Although the conversation with his father had lasted for hours, Nathan wished he could have spent more time with him. Nathan and Jessica had shared nearly everything with the president and Miri: the Dusahn, the false-flag operation in the Sol sector, and the fact that Galiardi *knew* that it was not the Jung who had trespassed in Alliance space, nor had they invaded the Pentaurus cluster. They even told him about the Aurora's defection to the Karuzari.

What they did *not* tell him were their plans to convince Abby to join them and to steal a half dozen Cobra gunships. Not that the president would have tried to stop them, but to provide him with plausible deniability should the need arise.

They also didn't tell them what *Nathan* considered the most important thing of all: that Nathan was a clone. He and Jessica had discussed that topic for the entire flight from Vancouver to Winnipeg. In the end, they had somberly agreed that the truth might complicate matters, which was a risk they could not take. Under any other circumstances, Nathan would certainly have told them. He knew that it would not change how his family felt about him. But there was far more at stake than his relationship with them, and he did not have the right to risk it all to satisfy his own conscience. When it was all over, assuming they survived, there would be plenty of time for truths.

Due to headwinds and numerous stops en route, the trip had taken them nearly sixteen hours to complete. Surprisingly, the journey had been more enjoyable than expected...at least to *Nathan*. He had forgotten the joy of true, aerodynamic flight. The balancing of a small aircraft against the forces of nature was a difficult skill that had long since become obsolete in the face of the brute force of modern propulsion systems. Lift was no longer a function of airspeed and airfoils. These days, it was lift fans and thrusters, and even they would soon be replaced by the new anti-gravity lift engines being developed, based on designs from the Data Ark. Nathan doubted he would ever have a chance to fly the old aerobat again.

Jessica had not enjoyed the journey at all and

had spent most of her waking hours complaining. Luckily, she had chosen to sleep most of way, which had given Nathan plenty of time with his own thoughts; something he'd not had the pleasure of since regaining his memories a mere ten days ago. He had not realized how much he *needed* the time to figure it all out within his own mind. He carried the memories and experiences of two men within him. Two separate identities that had to be reconciled.

Connor Tuplo lacked the dramatic life experiences and diplomatic environment in which Nathan Scott had been raised. He had been a clean slate; an identity that he did not know was false, and had been sent off to live a life that was a lie. Part of him still resented that, although he both understood and agreed with the reasons his friends had made that decision for him.

More than anything else, the time in the air had given him a chance to truly experience his own senses in a way that the demands upon him had not allowed. He saw things *differently* than before. He *felt* and *heard* things differently. He even felt as if he *processed information* differently. The question was: *was it a change for the better?*

Now, nearly twenty exhausting hours after he had bid his father and sister farewell, Nathan found himself standing on a moonlit, secluded stretch of beach, watching the waves roll in. But it wasn't the waves that interested him; it was what was supposed to be under them.

"Are you sure this is the spot?" Nathan asked.

"Yup," Jessica replied confidently. "We used to call this 'make-out beach' when I was young."

"Good spot for it."

"Here goes nothing," Jessica announced. She

held up the remote-control device in her right hand, pointed it toward the ocean, and pressed the query button firmly, holding it down for a full second. She brought it back close to her, both of them looking down at the device, waiting for a response. Fifteen seconds later, a light on the remote blinked three times, paused, and then blinked three more times.

"Yes!" Jessica exclaimed triumphantly.

"Chalk up another win for Ranni Enterprises," Nathan joked.

"Tug would be so proud," Jessica added.

"Let's go find a hotel and get some sleep," Nathan said. "We'll start looking for Abby first thing in the morning."

* * *

"Jump plot to first rally point received," General Telles reported. "Loading plot into jump-navigation computer."

"*We call it the 'jump-nav com',*" Robert corrected over the general's comm-set.

"The word 'com' usually refers to communications," the general argued.

"*True, but in this case, 'com' is short for 'computer'.*"

"As long as it is used in conjunction with 'jump' and 'nav' preceding it, it shouldn't cause confusion."

"*Of course.*"

A red failure light began to flash on the jump-nav com screen. "The jump-nav com did not accept the plot," Telles reported as he attempted to load the plot a second time.

"*Try reloading the plot,*" Robert suggested.

"I have already done so," Telles replied. "It failed a second time; I am now running a file repair utility. There may have been some signal degradation during transmission."

"*Ask the sending ship to retransmit the plot,*" Robert instructed.

"That ship has already jumped away," Telles reported. "As have the others."

"*They are supposed to wait until you have confirmed a good plot load,*" Robert said.

"I am aware of that requirement," Telles replied. "Perhaps they had a... I have a new sensor contact. A Jung frigate; ten kilometers. They are locking missiles on me." General Telles quickly dialed up an escape jump and pressed execute. "Initiating emergency escape jump."

"*If you jump, you won't be able to use the plot they sent you.*"

"I am aware of that, as well." General Telles dialed up another escape jump, with a different jump distance than before, then throttled up his engines and initiated a turn to starboard.

"*What are you doing, General?*" Robert asked.

"I am taking evasive measures, in case the frigate attempts to track my escape."

"*The further you get off your original jump track, the greater the chance that you will not be able to rejoin the group,*" Robert warned.

"Must you continue to state the obvious, Captain?"

"*Sorry, sir. May I ask if you have a plan?*"

"I am Ghatazhak. I *always* have a plan," the general assured him as he punched commands into the ship's auxiliary computer to his left.

"*Care to share it with me?*" Robert wondered.

"As I execute a series of turns and escape jumps to shake any pursuers, I am parsing the damaged file in an attempt to recover the destination coordinates. If I am unable to do so, I will simply begin executing jumps along a direct line to the Pentaurus sector.

Once there, I will execute Mister Sheehan's evasion algorithm, and work my way back to the Aurora on my own."

"*Just like that? Navigate your way across the galaxy?*"

"The jump-navigation computer in this gunship is quite capable of making the calculations."

"*And if the jump-nav com fails?*"

"There are backups," the general replied. "Two of them, if memory serves."

"*And if they fail?*"

"Then I will perform a series of manual escape jumps, keeping the proper constellations in my forward window, adjusting along the way for distance and stellar drift. With any luck, I will eventually find my way home."

"*If you live long enough.*"

"The gunships should be loaded with enough food and water to support a crew of six for at least a month, which means a crew of two should be able to last at least three times that length. A crew of two Ghatazhak, six times that length."

"*Unless you get swallowed up by an uncharted black hole or something,*" Robert mused.

"In which case, I will never know it."

"*General, I'm pretty sure you've got this under control,*" Robert admitted. "*Maybe you don't need the sim time?*"

"Nonsense. Practice can only improve one's performance."

"*True, but we only have two units, and others may need the practice more than you do.*"

General Telles stopped what he was doing. "*That* is a very good point, Captain. Please end the simulation."

"As you wish."

General Telles placed his hands in his lap as the images around him faded away to black, and the muffled sounds of the activity around him returned. A moment later, the VR helmet was removed from his head, allowing him to see the room around him again. "A very useful device. I appreciate your attempts to make the simulation more challenging, Captain."

"My pleasure," Robert replied, setting the VR helmet on the table next to him. "Apparently, I didn't try hard enough."

"I look forward to the version that can simulate more complex motions in order to simulate physical combat."

Robert and Vladimir exchanged glances.

"That will be interesting to watch," Vladimir commented.

"*Telles, Anwar,*" the master sergeant called over the general's comm-set.

"Go for Telles."

"*We just received a transmission from the Morsiko-Tavi. She has entered the 72 Herculis system and is requesting instructions.*"

"Tell them there has been no change and to continue to the staging point outside of the Tau Ceti system," the general instructed.

"*Yes, sir,*" Master Sergeant Anwar replied.

"What if the Seiiki doesn't make it back in time?" Robert wondered.

"Precisely why we must train as many potential pilots as possible," the general replied calmly. "With or without the crew of the Seiiki, the mission will be executed as planned."

* * *

"God, I miss this stuff," Jessica exclaimed as she sat in the driver's seat, sipping her coffee.

"This isn't even *good* coffee," Nathan said.

"When you haven't had *any* coffee in seven years, *all* coffee is good coffee." Jessica reached into the bag and pulled out a donut, taking a big bite. "And donuts...don't even get me started."

"You keep eating those donuts, and you're going to ruin that rock-hard body the Ghatazhak helped you build," Nathan teased.

"No way," Jessica insisted. "I'm an ectomorph, with just a touch of meso. I can eat like a pig and not gain a pound."

"Really?"

"Yeah. My friends all hated me. My mom used to say that I could eat more than all my brothers combined."

"High metabolism, huh?"

"Yup," she said, reaching for another donut. "The Ghatazhak training just made it worse. The more I exercise, the more I eat."

Nathan looked to his right as a sedan with military plates drove by. "Military plates," he pointed out, keeping his eyes on the vehicle as it pulled into the driveway of Abby's house. "They've got to be picking her up."

Jessica watched as she sipped her coffee. In the distance, she noticed Abby come out of the house and head for the car that had just pulled up in her driveway.

"That's her," Nathan said. "I guess we have the right place."

"Score one for Miri." Jessica quickly finished her donut and placed her coffee in the cup holder.

"Are we going to follow her, or what?" Nathan asked. "You want me to drive, so you can eat?"

"I'm on it," Jessica insisted, starting up the car. She waited for the car to back out of the driveway and depart, and then pulled out to follow them.

"What's the plan here?" Nathan wondered.

"We follow her and hope she makes a stop on the way to work."

"And if she doesn't?"

"Then we wait until she gets off work, and follow her again."

"And if she still doesn't stop somewhere?"

"Then we wait until dark and find a way to make contact with her *without* showing up on any of the Alliance surveillance systems."

"You're sure they've got them?"

"Positive," she said as she turned the corner to follow the vehicle carrying Abby.

"Don't get too close," Nathan warned. "You don't want them to know they're being followed."

Jessica looked at him. "Who here has spec-ops training?" When he didn't answer, she queried him again. "Who?"

"You do."

"That's right."

"Well, I got the car."

"Your *sister* got us the car, Nathan."

* * *

Gil Roselle walked down the corridors of his battleship, the Benakh. The ship had been his command, his home, for over seven years. Together, he and Marty had taken the captured Jung battleship and turned her into the most powerful ship in the Alliance Fleet, at least until the launch of the Alliance's newest Protector-class ship, the Cape Town, a month earlier.

The Jar-Benakh. In Jung, it meant 'the battleship Benakh'; hence, the prefix had been dropped. He had tried for years to get her name changed, but Galiardi wouldn't allow it. To Admiral Galiardi, the Benakh was a five-kilometer-long reminder of just how dangerous the Jung were. His plan was to eventually use the captured warship as a training vessel. She would be stripped of all weapons, and her jump drives would be replaced with her original, linear faster-than-light systems. She would also be fitted with override systems that would prevent her Jung crew from stealing the ship back and using her to return home.

As much as Gil hated to admit it, the admiral's plan was a good one. Assuming that the Jung who crewed the Benakh did their jobs as agreed, it would provide invaluable combat experience for Alliance warship crews. There were still more than thirty Jung battleships in the Jung fleet, possibly more. Galiardi's plan would ensure that Alliance crews would be ready for them.

That was one of the main reasons Gil was retiring. He could wait another five years, when the conversion was scheduled to take place, but that meant his executive officer, and best friend, would never get a command of his own. Galiardi wanted to be rid of Martin just as much as he wanted rid of Gil and Robert Nash, the last of the old guard. At least, if Gil retired now, Marty would get command of the Benakh and a promotion, which meant a more comfortable retirement when the Benakh was taken out of frontline service. Unfortunately, it was not going to work out that way.

"You going somewhere, Gil?" Martin called from behind as he jogged a few steps to catch up with his friend.

"Just heading down to spend a few days with Shari," Gil replied without breaking stride.

"Technically, we're still on alert, you know."

"The rest of the fleet is on alert. The only way the Benakh moves is if all the other ships are destroyed or we're attacked. Besides, it didn't stop me the last three times I went down."

"Sooner or later, Galiardi's going to have your ass for it, Gil."

"Galiardi can kiss my ass," Gil snickered.

"I thought Shari was on assignment on Sorenson."

Gil glanced at him out of the corner of his eye. "I'm going to meet her there and fly her home when she's done."

"Right," Martin replied. "With four sets of class-alpha Marine armor and four pulse rifles? You and Shari planning on robbing a bank?"

"I don't know what you're talking about, Martin," Gil insisted, a deadpan look on his face.

"And the timed charges you set on our sensor arrays?"

Gil glanced at him as they walked.

"I'm the XO. Nothing happens on this ship without me knowing about it."

"Bullshit. You've been watching me, Marty."

"You tipped your hand on purpose, Gil. Who's bullshitting who, here?"

Gil said nothing, just kept on walking.

"You're setting me up, Gil. Whatever you're about to do, you need the Benakh's sensors down to pull it off. And guess who's going to take the blame when that happens?"

"Then, I guess you don't have any choice, do you?" Gil said, a small smile creeping onto his face, knowing he'd just outsmarted his friend.

"I could still arrest you, you know."

Gil finally stopped walking. "But you won't. And you know why? Because you hate what's happening to this Alliance as much as I do...as much as Nash does."

Martin glared at Gil, unsure how to feel.

"Come with me, Marty," Gil urged, grabbing his friend by the shoulders. "Fight for someone *worth* fighting for."

"Who?"

"I can't tell you that," Gil replied. "All I can tell you is that when you find out, you'll understand why I'm going."

Martin shook his head, confused. Gil had warned him that he was thinking of leaving, but not like this. "What about Shari?"

"That was never going to last," Gil confessed. "Christ, she's thirty years younger than I am. She's going to want kids, someday. What's she going to do, change diapers on her kids *and* her husband at the same time?" Gil looked at him. "Last chance, Marty."

Martin stared at his friend for nearly a minute. "What do I need to bring?"

Gil smiled. "Just a fearless attitude, my friend."

* * *

Nathan and Jessica had spent the entire day sitting in their vehicle, parked in a shopping mall where they had a good view of the only road in and out of the base. All day long, they had taken turns watching vehicles depart, checking each of them using a small, telescopic viewing device, to determine if Abby was a passenger. It was a long shot, as they were not always able to see well enough to be sure, but it was better than trying to slip into her home at night without being detected by Alliance surveillance systems.

Luck had been with them. Finally, as the sun was setting, they had spotted her leaving the base and had followed her. Much to their surprise, and their good fortune, Abby did not appear to be going straight home.

Jessica drove their car down the street, past the parking lot that Abby's driver had pulled into. "Keep your eyes on them," she instructed Nathan, "they may be trying to shake us."

"I think he's parking," Nathan said, his head turned to his right to keep his eye on the car. "Yup, he's parking."

Jessica pulled into the next parking lot, pausing just inside the entrance. "Is he getting out?"

"Driver's door is open."

Jessica eased their car forward as if looking for a parking spot.

"He's getting out. The other guy is getting out, as well."

"What about Abby?"

"Wait......front passenger guy is opening Abby's door...... Yup, she's getting out, too."

"Are you sure it's Abby?" Jessica asked.

"I'm sure."

Jessica pulled into an empty spot.

"She's headed for the grocery store," Nathan said.

"Are they going in with her?"

"No, it doesn't look like it." Nathan continued watching. "No, they're both staying with the car."

"Definitely not spec-ops trained," Jessica observed. "Hat and coat."

"What?"

"Put them on."

Nathan reached over and grabbed his hat and coat from the back seat. "It's not even cold."

"It's Florida. It's never cold."

"Won't we look odd?"

"I doubt they'll even notice," Jessica insisted. "Besides, there's a breeze out this evening." Jessica pulled a light jacket on and then placed a ball cap on her head, tucking her hair up underneath.

"What are you doing?" Nathan asked as he donned his hat and coat.

"Trying to look like a guy."

Nathan giggled. "You're kidding, right?"

"Don't make me smack you around," Jessica said as she got out of the car. She closed the door, zipped up her jacket, and pulled her cap down snugly. She hunched up her shoulders a bit, pushing them forward and putting her hands in her jacket pockets, spreading the jacket slightly outward to either side.

Nathan got out of the car, as well. He closed the door and put on his cap, walking around to Jessica who was already walking toward the buildings nearby. "You don't look like a guy, you know. Just a girl with mental problems and no fashion sense."

"From up close, maybe," Jessica replied. "Follow me, and don't look at them."

Nathan followed her toward the buildings and then along the front. At the end of the building, they turned to the left and headed for the back edge of the store. "Where are we going?" he asked.

"Trust me."

They continued to the back of the store, then along the side street to the next intersection, well out of sight of Abby's escorts. They crossed the street to the same side as the store Abby had gone into and headed back in the direction they had come, but on the opposite side of the street. Jessica removed her hat and jacket, tossing them into the bushes.

"Lose them," Jessica said.

"The hat and coat?"

"Duh."

Nathan removed his hat and coat, as well, tossing them into the next bush they passed.

Jessica pulled her shirt down tight, accentuating her bosom, and tucked it into her pants. With her shoulders pulled back and hanging normally, and an entirely female gait, she had changed her appearance completely in less than a minute.

"Impressive," Nathan commented.

"Poorly trained escorts only notice surface details," she explained. "Two men, hats and jackets. Man and hot girl. Two completely different profiles."

"And you're certain they're not spec-ops?"

"Mid-thirties, bad back, potbelly; mid-twenties, lanky, perfect uniform: not even close."

Nathan and Jessica continued down the street to the corner of the grocery store.

"Take my hand," Jessica instructed.

Nathan did as instructed, immediately recognizing the role she was having him play.

They turned the corner, headed to the front door, in full view of the two men standing at Abby's car, and entered the grocery store.

"Grab a basket, honey," Jessica instructed in an affectionate tone.

Nathan picked up a basket and followed her inside. They turned down the first aisle, where Jessica immediately grabbed a few items and placed them in the basket. They continued to the end of the aisle and turned right, toward the center of the store, strolling along as if they were trying to determine which aisle they needed. As they passed the third aisle in, they spotted Abby reading the back of a package.

"Do you need to go to the bathroom?" Jessica asked.

"Uh, sure?"

Jessica stopped at the meat department, smiling at the man behind the counter. "Excuse me, is there a public restroom?"

"Yes, ma'am," the young man replied. "Straight ahead and to the left, down the corridor. You can't miss it."

"Thank you." Jessica returned to Nathan's side, took his hand, and the two of them continued down to the far side of the store and down the corridor. "Perfect," she said. "A single, unisex bathroom. Lock the door and wait in here. I'll send Abby to you."

"If the door's locked, how is she going to get in?"

"She'll knock, you open," Jessica explained, rolling her eyes.

"Of course," Nathan replied, feeling stupid.

Abby turned the corner and made her way around the end of the aisle, not noticing Jessica coming out of the corridor at the far side of the store. She continued deeper into the aisle, stopping at the dried pasta section. The store was not very busy, which was not surprising for a Friday evening. Cocoa Beach had a young demographic, most of whom would be going out that evening. As she browsed the different pastas, a familiar voice spoke to her from the periphery.

"I prefer the penne, myself," Jessica said. Then,

in a hushed tone, she added. "Keep your voice low, and don't overreact, Abby."

Abby suddenly became concerned and turned to look at the person talking to her. Her eyes widened when she realized who it was. "Jessica?"

"Surprise."

"I thought you moved to..."

"I did."

"What are you doing back on..."

"No time to chat, Abby. I need you to go to the bathroom, back right corner of the store. There's someone who needs to speak with you...covertly. Knock on the door, and he'll let you in."

"What's going on?"

"Trust me, Abby...just go," Jessica urged, moving on as if she was continuing to shop after exchanging pleasantries with a stranger.

Abby looked around trying, but failing, to look inconspicuous. She had no idea what was going on, or who Jessica was asking her to meet with. She wasn't even sure if she should go, or immediately run to her escorts and report the incident.

But it's Jessica. If there was anyone she could trust, it was she.

There was barely enough room to pace back and forth in the small bathroom, but that didn't stop Nathan. It had been hard enough to figure out what to say to his father. But there was a family bond there, one that had been strengthened by all they had endured together. Although he and Abby had been through a lot together, as well, it was different.

Or was it?

Three barely audible knocks came at the bathroom door. Nathan took a deep breath, unlocked the door, and pulled it open, taking care to stay behind the door, out of Abby's sight, until she was all the way inside.

Abby entered the bathroom, immediately looking around the door and spotting Nathan. Her eyes became even wider than when she had seen Jessica a few minutes ago. "Oh, my God," she exclaimed in a near whisper, her breath escaping her.

Nathan pushed the door closed behind her, quickly locking it.

"Is it really you?" she whispered.

Nathan turned on the water in the sink, letting it run to hide their voices from anyone who should pass by in the corridor. "It's me."

"Nathan?"

"The one and only." Nathan held his arms open just enough to invite an embrace, which he immediately received.

"How is this possible?" Abby asked as she hugged him. "We all thought you were dead."

"Actually, I was...technically."

"What?"

"It's a long story."

"Does your father know you're alive?"

"Yes, I met with my father and sister two days ago," Nathan told her.

"Then, everyone knows?"

"No, only a handful of people in the Sol sector know I'm alive," Nathan explained. "But it may not be that way for long, I'm afraid."

"Why are you here?" Abby asked. "Don't get me wrong, I'm terribly happy to see you, especially since I thought you were dead, but..."

"I need your help, Abby," Nathan began. "*We* need your help."

"We?"

"Me, Jessica, Telles, Vlad, Cameron, Deliza, the Aurora...all of us."

"The *Aurora* is in the Pentaurus sector?" Abby asked. "I thought the Alliance decided they couldn't afford to send..."

"We've reformed the Karuzari to fight the Dusahn in the Pentaurus cluster."

"Who are the Dusahn?"

"A rogue caste of the Jung, exiled centuries ago. Somehow, they got their hands on a jump drive, upgraded their fleet, and captured the entire cluster. We're trying to keep them from spreading, becoming more powerful, but we need your help. We *need* a stealth jump drive for the Aurora."

"Then, the Jung are *not* about to attack us?"

"No, it's a false-flag operation by the Dusahn to make the Alliance *think* they are about to be attacked, so that they won't send ships to the Pentaurus sector."

"I don't understand," Abby said. "If that's the case, then just tell Galiardi..."

"Galiardi already *knows*," Nathan interrupted. "Jessica and the Ghatazhak sent him that intel a few days after the invasion, but he kept that information to himself. He *wants* a war with the Jung, because he knows if he defeats the Jung once and for all, he'll be a shoo-in at the next election cycle. Galiardi *wants* power. Why? I don't know and, frankly, I don't care. What I *do* know is that he's willing to sacrifice millions of lives, both here and in the Pentaurus sector, in order to *get* that power. For all we know, he could even be working *with* the Dusahn."

"You don't really think..."

"I admit, it's only speculation at this point,"

Nathan admitted, "but anything is possible. One thing is for sure, he is purposefully hiding the truth from the Alliance Council. That alone is reason enough to distrust him."

"Oh, I've never trusted Galiardi," Abby agreed.

"Then, help us," Nathan begged. "Help us develop and implement a stealth jump drive on the Aurora. Give us the edge we need to defeat the Dusahn, or at least buy us time until my father can get Galiardi under control and send ships to help us."

"How am I supposed to help you?" Abby asked. "I'm here, and you're..." She suddenly realized what he was asking her to do. "Nathan, no. You can't possibly ask me to..."

"I know I'm asking a lot, Abby, but...we *need* you."

"But my family..."

"Bring them. They'll live on a luxury cruise ship right next door. You'll see them every day, I promise."

"I don't see them every day now," Abby commented, her mind racing.

"Now, you'll be able to," Nathan pointed out, reaching for anything that might help sell her on the idea.

"I don't know, Nathan. Erik has been trying to get me to give Galiardi the stealth jump drive and walk away, so we can get on with our lives. What you're asking will just suck us back in more deeply...and on the other side of the galaxy. How am I supposed to convince him... How do I ask my children to give up their lives...*again*?"

"You'll think of something, Abby," Nathan assured her. He could see the despair in her eyes. "Just bring your family to Harris Cove tomorrow, at noon."

"What? Why?"

"Tell them it's a picnic at the beach or something.

Jess and I will be there. We'll help you convince your family to go."

"Just like that?"

"Hopefully."

"I don't know, Nathan." She touched his cheek. "I want to help you, I really do. I hate Galiardi, and I'm afraid of what he'll do with a stealth jump drive, but Erik. My children..."

"Just be there, Abby, that's all I ask."

"And if they don't want to go?"

"Then Jess and I will leave you alone, I promise."

Abby looked at him, sighing. "We'll be there," she finally said. "But that's all I can promise."

"I'll take it." Nathan reached around behind her and flushed the toilet, then turned off the water in the sink. "You'd better go finish your shopping, so your escorts don't get suspicious."

"Right." Abby stepped over to the door, pausing to look back at Nathan. "I am so glad you're alive, Nathan."

Nathan smiled at her as she turned and headed out the door.

* * *

Loki walked down the corridor of the Capital Hotel in Winnipeg, where President Scott's administration had put them up during their stay. It was a grand hotel, by far the finest that Loki had ever stayed in. He only wished that he could have brought his wife along. She would love to have seen Earth, even if all they were seeing was this hotel and the Winnipeg spaceport.

Josh, of course, had made himself right at home in their suite, ordering room service almost hourly and watching every vid-play on the menu. He had even ordered an in-room massage, although he had been considerably disappointed when the masseuse turned out to be a man.

Loki knocked on the door to room eight zero nine. A moment later, the door opened, revealing Yanni.

"Loki," Yanni greeted, stepping aside to let his friend in. "What's going on?"

Loki entered Yanni and Deliza's suite, waiting for the door to close before speaking. "I just wanted to let you know that the ship is fully repaired, and we will be departing tomorrow, no later than eleven hundred hours."

"I see," Yanni replied. "Did you hear that, Deliza?"

"Yes, I did," Deliza replied, walking toward them with a piece of paper and pencil in hand. She handed it to Loki, who immediately wrote a message on the paper and gave it back.

> *They made contact. Will depart tomorrow on schedule. Unknown if additional passengers.*

Deliza nodded, taking the paper to the desk. "Thank you for keeping me updated, Mister Sheehan." She stuck the scrap of paper into the small shredder next to the desk, which silently devoured it, leaving only a pile of dust in the basket below. "We will see you in the morning, then."

"Yes, ma'am," Loki replied, turning to exit.

CHAPTER TWELVE

A convoy of six black NAU vehicles drove across the tarmac at the Winnipeg spaceport, toward landing pad one four.

"We're popular today," Marcus said to Josh as they watched the local ground crew finish loading the Seiiki's cargo bay.

The convoy pulled up to the landing pad and stopped. The two middle cars pulled inside the outer four, positioning themselves between the Seiiki and the other four vehicles in the convoy. Four black-suited men got out of each of the four outside vehicles, moving in well-rehearsed fashion into their assigned positions.

Once in place, two more men got out of each of the two inner vehicles, opening the rear doors to allow their passengers to exit.

Deliza and Yanni stepped out of the first vehicle, pausing to wait for the president and his aide, Miri, to get out of the second vehicle.

Once out of his vehicle, Dayton Scott paused to take in the full view of the Seiiki. "So, this is his ship," he said, low enough that only those next to him could hear.

"Yes, Mister President," Deliza confirmed. "She is only using her former name for the purposes of this trip. She has been the Seiiki for the last five years."

The president smiled, imagining his son walking down the cargo ramp to greet him, his customary debonair smile on his face. "Jumping around from port to port, never knowing if you'll make enough to get by, let alone get ahead." He walked up to the starboard engine nacelle, putting his hand against it. "Fits him, doesn't it."

"It does," Miri agreed, smiling.

"Mister President," one of the men in black suits said as he approached. "Shall we load the items?"

"Yes, please," the president replied.

"Even more?" Deliza asked. "You're too kind, Mister President."

"A few...*sentimental*...items, that your captain will find particularly useful," the president explained. He looked at Deliza, taking her hands in his. "I cannot thank you enough for all you have done for him. You have renewed the hope of an old man who was barely holding on."

"He would do the same for any of us," she insisted.

"Take care of him, Miss Ta'Akar," the president said.

"I shall, Mister President."

"Safe travels to you all," the president said, shaking her hand. "I hope we will meet again."

"As do I, Mister President."

The president turned and headed back to his vehicle as Miri bid Deliza farewell, as well.

"We will monitor the comms exchange point for word from you," she assured them. "Safe travels."

"Thank you," Deliza replied. She waited for Miri to get into the vehicle before turning and heading for the Seiiki.

The last of the ground crew came down the cargo ramp, climbed into their now-empty trucks, and drove away.

"We may have a problem," Josh told Deliza as she came up the ramp. He looked up the ramp at the cargo bay, which was packed full of supplies provided by the NAU as a gesture of support.

"We'll just have to jump back to Tanna and offload it," Deliza said.

"It's going to be cutting it close," Josh warned. "I really wish you would've given us a heads up on this."

"I didn't know until we were already on our way here," Deliza replied. She reached the top of the ramp, taking in the full view of the cargo. "Maybe we can move some of it inside?"

"The inside is stuffed, as well," Marcus said. "There's hardly enough room to get around."

"We're barely going to be able to get off the ground," Josh added. "If they don't give us permission to jump clear of Earth's gravity well, instead of burning propellant to get there, we'll be lucky to have enough to land on Tanna, let alone get back up and recover the jump sub."

"I'm sure we can transfer propellant from one of the ships on Tanna," Deliza assured him.

"Better we get the jump clearance," Josh insisted.

"I'll make a call and see what I can do," Deliza promised. "Meanwhile, let's get buttoned-up and ready for departure."

* * *

Aiden could barely keep his eyes open. He had been staring at the Cobra-D operations manual for hours, after spending a *full day* running drills in their actual ship. The Cobra-D was the most automated version to date. It literally could fly itself, if given permission. It even had the ability to jump back to base on its own, should the crew become incapacitated.

It was a gunship with training wheels.

Aiden put his data pad down and rubbed his eyes, rising when a knock came at his door. He opened the door and found Kenji standing in the hallway. "What's going on?"

"Just checking on you," Kenji replied, entering Aiden's room. "You studying the manual, like you promised?"

"Yes, mother, I'm doing my homework," Aiden mocked as he plopped down on his bunk.

"What's the problem?" Kenji asked, noticing his friend's frustration.

"It's *too* damned automated," Aiden insisted. "I could literally fly an entire mission without ever touching the flight controls!"

"Auto-flight can respond faster than we can, Aiden. Using it gives us all a better chance of staying alive."

"If it's so damned good, why do they even need crews? Why not just use drones?"

"Because drones can't fix themselves," Kenji replied. "And they can't take over if the auto-flight fails, or if the ship encounters a situation the auto-flight isn't programmed to handle. It doesn't have an AI, you know."

Aiden suddenly sat up. "*That*'s what I'm talking about! How am I supposed to *manually* fly a ship with *any* level of competency, if they never *let* me do it to *maintain* competency?"

"You've already demonstrated competency at manual flight, Aiden. That's why the training sims didn't emphasize using the auto-flight systems. Hell, you flew the sims better than anyone. *Now*, it's about proving you can operate the ship the way Command *wants* you to operate the ship, and *that* is by using auto-flight. Prove to them you can keep your hands off the flight controls and operate your ship according to procedures, and they'll let us launch."

"They'll let us launch no matter what," Aiden insisted. "They need to get the ships into orbit, and they're short on crews. That's how *I* managed to get in, remember? Besides, they'll just yank me as soon as we dock at the ready base."

"I don't get you, Aiden," Kenji exclaimed. "You say you want to fly. You say you want to go into space. All you have to do is use the auto-flight, and you're there."

"Riding in a computer-controlled warship, right into battle."

"You can take manual control whenever you'd like," Kenji reminded him.

"And the Alliance will question every instance where I do," Aiden argued.

"You're exaggerating things again."

"I don't know, Kenji."

Kenji sighed. "Look, just run through the drills a few more times so that they're automatic...just to be sure we pass the pre-launch sim testing in the morning."

"I can pass them," Aiden insisted.

"By a few seconds' margin, yes," Kenji agreed. "But *you* need to pass them with a *much* better margin than everyone else. You can't risk giving Commander Bastyan an excuse to can you."

Aiden sighed, looking at the clock on the wall. "It's zero one hundred, Kenji."

"That gives us seven hours before pre-launches."

"What about sleep?"

"We can sleep *after* we reach the ready base."

Aiden smiled. He knew Kenji would keep his position, even if Aiden got canned. He might even take command of Cobra Three Eight Three. Yet he was willing to stay up all night to help Aiden pass their final pre-launch simulation tests. They had only known each other a few months, but Kenji Lowen had become the best friend Aiden ever had. "Alright, let's do it," Aiden agreed, rising to his feet. "But can we get some coffee first?"

* * *

Jessica stared out across the ocean from their vantage point on the hillside, just north of Harris Cove. It was a typical day on the Florida coast, and it felt good to wear a bikini again. Jessica had grown up on these very shores, and she felt at home here, more than anywhere else she had lived.

Nathan, on the other hand, looked completely out of place in swim trunks and tank top. Between the two of them, any Floridian would peg them as tourists, if not for her faded tan, then definitely for his complete lack thereof. Nathan was as pale as could be.

"I really miss this place," Jessica commented as she stared at the pounding surf.

"I can see why," Nathan said, also admiring the beauty of the ocean. "It's strange...such complete opposites, and yet so similar."

"What are you talking about?" Jessica asked.

"Oceans are huge bodies of water, with mass and currents, carrying entire ecosystems within them. Those at the poles are completely different than those at the equator. The oceans contain enormous amounts of life and energy, just like space. We sail ships on, and within, the ocean, just like we do in space. Space has gravity currents. Space has entire ecosystems, each one unique. Each one vastly different than the others, yet many sharing multiple similarities. Different, yet the same, really."

"You always get this way when you're sleep-deprived?" Jessica wondered.

"I slept fine," Nathan insisted. "I just haven't seen an ocean—not a real one, anyway—for a long time. It makes you think."

"Over there," Jessica said, nodding to their right. "That looks like Abby and her family."

"I wasn't sure she'd show up," Nathan admitted.

"She's got a tail," Jessica added. "Two goons in uniform on the ridge."

"You think they follow her everywhere?" Nathan wondered.

"No, but they probably do if she takes her entire family somewhere," Jessica explained. "I'm sure Galiardi is worried about her skipping out or, even worse, about Jung operatives."

"You think they know what we're up to?" Nathan asked.

"Doubtful," Jessica said. "Even if Galiardi has spies in your father's administration that reported us as having spoken to the president, guessing that we're going to try to recruit Abby would be a hell of a leap. The most I would expect would be increased security everywhere, which I haven't seen any indications of."

"What's the plan?"

Jessica looked around, failing to spot any other escorts. "All we're doing is talking to some people on the beach," she finally said. "No crime in that, right?"

"I just figured you'd want to take them out or something."

"Don't be so dramatic, Nathan. Besides, we don't even know if she's willing to go with us yet. And for the record, I don't plan on killing anyone. Not if I don't have to."

"Well, that's good to know," Nathan replied.

Jessica suddenly changed her expression. "Let's go for a walk on the beach, honey."

"Sure, sweetie," he replied without hesitation. He was really starting to get the hang of this game.

* * *

General Telles walked up to the Seiiki as she landed just outside the hangar at the abandoned evacuation center on Tanna, bracing himself against her thruster wash. Before her engines had even begun to spool down, her cargo ramp was lowering.

The general moved around to the back of the ship as her engines wound down, just in time to see Marcus and Dalen coming down the ramp dragging large cargo crates. "It might have been better to pull the ship inside," he said. "You cannot survive more than fifteen minutes outside with these radiation levels."

"We don't plan on being here that long," Marcus insisted.

Deliza and Yanni came down the ramp next, carrying the smaller boxes that President Scott had brought for Nathan.

"President Scott gave us a going-away present," Deliza said. "Unfortunately, that didn't leave enough room for the jump sub."

"I see." General Telles tapped his comm-set. "Telles to all Ghatazhak. Report to the front of the hangar immediately."

"Where should we stack this crap?" Marcus asked.

"Bottom of the ramp, Mister Taggart," General Telles replied. "We'll take it from there."

"Orders, General?" Master Sergeant Anwar asked as he approached from the hangar door.

"We need to get this ship unloaded as quickly as possible, Master Sergeant...starting with the cargo bay."

"We'll get right on it, sir."

General Telles turned to Deliza. "We'll have her unloaded in no time," he assured her. "Did you receive word from Captain Scott and Lieutenant Nash?"

"Only that they are due at the recovery point on schedule," Deliza replied.

"No word on Doctor Sorenson?"

"They didn't say."

* * *

Abby knelt on the blanket on the beach, unpacking the picnic lunch they had brought, while her husband and their two teenage children explored the nearby tide pools. She stopped suddenly when her daughter squealed, looking in the child's direction only to see her older brother waving a sea creature of some sort in front of his sister's face.

That's when she noticed the young couple in swimsuits coming toward her. At first, she thought nothing of them. Beaches here were rarely unoccupied. But she was expecting Nathan and Jessica to make contact with her. That's when it clicked.

Abby looked at the couple again, realizing it was Nathan and Jessica. She looked at her husband and children, still undecided on what to do.

"Why so surprised?" Jessica asked as they approached.

Abby didn't respond.

"What is it, Abby?" Nathan asked.

"I didn't talk to them yet," she admitted.

"Not even your husband?" Nathan wondered.

"How did you get them to come?" Jessica asked.

"They love the tide pools," she answered, looking past Nathan and Jessica at her family having fun together. "And I'm going to ask them to never see them again."

"There are many other wondrous things to see in the universe," Nathan pointed out. "The planet Paradar has three moons, all in orbits half the distance of Earth's moon. It has an ocean that wraps around the entire planet. It's like a giant river that encircles it along the equator. Those moons cause crazy tide patterns. The tide pools there are like ones you've never dreamed."

"So, I'm supposed to sell them on the idea of leaving their homeworld just because of some tide pools a thousand light years away?"

"No, you're supposed to sell them on the idea that going with us will save millions of lives, possibly billions, both in the Pentaurus sector *and* the Sol sector," Nathan explained.

"And what about my husband?" Abby asked. "He's *finally* got a career he loves, and now I'm going to ask him to give *that* up?" Abby looked frustrated. "It's not fair," she said, looking up at Nathan.

"I used to ask myself the same thing," Nathan said as he sat down on the sand next to Abby. "Especially when I was sitting in that Jung prison cell, awaiting execution."

"You're going to play *that* card?" Abby asked. "Already?"

Nathan smiled. "I'm not trying to *play* that card, Abby. I'm just trying to show you it's *okay* to feel that way. I could give you the old 'no one said life was fair' or 'you have a responsibility to the human race'..."

"Or 'fate has chosen you,'" Jessica added. "I hate that one."

"You're right," Nathan said. "There's nothing fair about it. Not for you, not for me, not for Jessica, not for your family...the list goes on and on. It isn't fair... it just is what it is. Simple as that. Trying to make anything more of it than that is a waste of time. The big bang or God. The chicken or the egg. There is no answer, and there never will be. All there is, is here and now. That's it. And here and now, you have a decision to make."

"How do I know what the right decision is?" Abby asked. "How do I know what's best for them?"

"You don't," Nathan answered. He looked out at the waves crashing into the rocks on the opposite side of the cove from the tide pools. "Have you ever wondered where I get my answers?"

"Yes, actually, I have," Abby admitted.

"So have I," Jessica added.

Nathan put his hand on his chest. "Here. At first, command was overwhelming. Every decision was surrounded by variables and possible consequences. And every decision meant someone would die. Sometimes only a few people, sometimes many. I simply followed my instincts. I simply did what I felt was right, and dealt with the consequences as they came."

"But that almost got you killed, Nathan," Abby reminded him.

"Actually, it *did* get me killed. At least, that's what I'm told. I don't really remember it."

"You're going to have to explain that to me sometime," Abby said.

"Come with us, and I promise I'll explain everything."

"I want to," she finally admitted. "But..."

"But is right," Jessica said. "Your husband's coming."

Nathan stood up, brushed the sand from himself, and offered Abby his hand.

"Everything alright?" Erik asked as he approached.

Nathan kept facing Abby, purposefully angling himself to keep his back toward the two men watching Abby and her family on the nearby hill.

"Jessica?" Erik said, recognizing her as he approached. "Oh, my God, what are you doing here?" he said, embracing her. "I thought you joined the Ghatazhak and moved to the Pentaurus sector."

"I did," Jessica replied. "I'm back on business."

"Business. What kind of business?" he asked.

"I brought a friend," Jessica said, turning toward Nathan.

Erik's eye widened and his mouth fell open when he saw Nathan. "I don't believe it," he finally gasped. "Nathan?"

"Hello, Erik," Nathan said, stepping up to shake his hand. "It's good to see you again."

"I thought you were dead. We *all* thought you were dead. The whole *world* thought you were..."

"I know," Nathan said cutting him off.

Erik looked at his wife, expecting her to appear happy that Nathan was alive, but instead, she looked scared, and a bit guilty. "Abby? What's wrong?"

"Our business is with your wife, I'm afraid," Nathan explained.

Erik suddenly became suspicious. "Abby, no..."

"Erik," Nathan began, "we wouldn't be here if it wasn't important, you *know* that."

"Important to whom, Nathan, you? Jessica? The people of some distant world?"

"Erik," Abby said, trying to intervene.

"What about what is important here?" Erik asked. "What about *our* lives?"

"This isn't about *our* lives, Erik. It's about millions of lives."

"Those lives are not your responsibility, Abby. I thought we agreed on that."

"No, *you* agreed on that, Erik," Abby insisted. "You and my father."

"But you're a scientist. Your job is to..."

"...discover truths, I know," Abby finished for him. "It's not about being a scientist, Erik. It's about being a good *person.* If I hand Galiardi a stealth jump drive, I don't know what he'll do with it."

"You don't know what *he'll* do with it, either," Erik insisted, pointing to Nathan. "No offense, Nathan, but there are some who blame *you* for the Jung having the jump drive."

"Why don't they blame me?" Abby asked. "My father and I invented it."

"Abby..."

"Erik, the other day you asked me if there was anyone I trusted with the stealth jump drive technology."

"And you said there was no one," Erik replied.

"Because I didn't know Nathan was *alive,*" she said. "Now, I may not know for sure what Nathan will *do* with this technology, but I *do* know that I trust him *far* more than Michael Galiardi. And I cannot, in good conscience, do something that I *strongly* feel will be detrimental to the human race."

"Oh, don't put yourself on such a pedestal, Abby," Erik insisted. "You know damn well that if you *don't* create a stealth jump drive for Galiardi, someone *else* will."

"You're right," Abby agreed. "But there *is* something I can do about *that.* I can create one for Nathan and the Karuzari. I can help them maintain the balance of power in the Pentaurus sector...until they figure out how to drive the Dusahn out of the sector."

"Who the hell are the Dusahn?" Erik said, throwing his hands up, becoming even more aggravated.

Jessica glanced up at the hill. "They're coming this way, Nathan," she warned. "We need to wrap this up."

"We need a decision, Abby," Nathan insisted.

Abby looked at him with pleading eyes, then looked at her husband. "Erik, please..."

* * *

"You see? That didn't hurt at all, did it?" Kenji said from the copilot's seat.

"Don't be a smart-ass," Aiden replied. "We should probably run that sequence again."

"Damn right, we'll run it again," Kenji agreed. "Wait," he said, noticing a warning light on his side panel. "I've got an open hatch light, ventral side." He quickly switched on the exterior cameras.

"Is that Char?" Aiden asked, leaning over to better see the view screen to the right of Kenji.

"And Sari."

"What are they doing up?" Aiden wondered. He looked at the local time display. "It's zero two twenty." He unbuckled his restraints and climbed up out of his seat to go meet them.

Aiden made his way aft, past the sensor and engineering stations, into the airlock that separated the cockpit from the aft section of the gunship, arriving as Charnelle climbed up the access ladder. "What are you guys doing here?" Aiden asked, reaching down to take her hand, helping her up into the ship.

"I saw the lights in your cockpit windows from the head," Char explained. "So, I thought I'd see what you two were doing."

"You can see gunship row from your bathroom window?" Kenji asked as he joined them in the airlock.

"My room faces south, so, yes," Charnelle said.

"Yours too, Sari?" Aiden asked.

"*No. She woke me up,*" Sari called from the tunnel below. "*Take this,*" he added, handing a bag up to them.

"What's this?" Aiden asked, bending over and taking the bag from Sari.

"Polkies," Charnelle said. "I bought them in town yesterday. I thought you two might be hungry."

"Yes," Aiden exclaimed, reaching into the bag and pulling out one of the pastries.

"Pass that bag over here," Kenji insisted.

"There's more," Sari announced, his hand holding a large beverage cylinder.

"Oh, please tell me that's coffee," Aiden begged, taking the cylinder from Sari as he climbed up into the airlock. "Where'd you get it? The mess hall doesn't open until six."

"I have a coffee maker in my room," Charnelle said.

"I thought we weren't allowed to have food or drinks in our rooms?" Kenji said.

"Polkies either," Charnelle replied, smiling. "But as soon as you finish, you get right back to it," she demanded. "Sari and I will act as your evaluators."

"Deal," Aiden replied, his mouth full of polkie.

* * *

"Excuse me, Doctor Sorenson," one of the escorts said as they approached. "Are these people bothering you?"

"It's okay, we're old friends," Jessica said, stepping toward the two officers.

"I'm afraid I'm going to have to ask you both to leave the area..."

"It's alright, officer," Abby assured the two men in uniform. "These people are my friends."

"It didn't appear that way," the officer said.

"Oh, that?" Jessica said as she continued toward them, playing the innocent female...in a bikini. "We were just arguing about where to go for dinner tonight..." Jessica pretended to suddenly trip in the sand, stumbling forward toward the surprised officer. She grabbed his uniform as he caught her. "God, I'm so clumsy," she apologized, right before she pulled on his shirt, butted her head into his nose, and rammed her knee into his groin.

The guard doubled over in pain, his nose bleeding. The pain was short-lived, as Jessica's fist drove upward into his jaw, knocking him backward.

As the first officer fell, the second one came charging to his rescue, intending to subdue Jessica. She immediately went into a squatting position, spinning around in the sand and sweeping with her outstretched leg, catching the second guard's leg, sending him tumbling forward.

Nathan was immediately on the second guard, punching him hard in the back of the head as he tried to get up, knocking him unconscious. Nathan turned and looked at Jessica, who was falling backward, driving her elbow into the stunned first guard, knocking him out, as well.

"Are you two crazy?" Erik exclaimed. He turned to look at his children who had been approaching, but stopped ten meters away when the attack began, unsure of what to do.

"If there aren't others nearby, there will be soon," Jessica warned as she rose to her feet. "Hit the recall button, Nathan. We've got to go now."

"You need to decide, Abby," Nathan insisted as he pulled out the remote control, pointed it at the ocean, and pushed the button.

Abby looked at the two downed officers, her mind racing a mile a minute.

"Abby, if you thought you were on a tight leash before, you're definitely going to be on one now," Jessica warned as she searched the officer.

"Thanks to you two!" Erik exclaimed. "This is what I'm talking about, Abby. These people are nothing but trouble!"

"Because they are willing to do what needs to be done?" Abby replied.

"Abby," Nathan began.

"You were supposed to help me talk them into going, Nathan, not scare the hell out of them!" Abby exclaimed.

"You *knew* he was going to be here? Is that why you suggested we go to the beach today?" Erik was furious. "Why didn't you tell me?"

"Because I knew you'd object, Erik. And once your mind is made up about something, there's no convincing you otherwise!"

"They've got body monitors built into their comms, Nathan," Jessica announced, searching the officers. "That means backup is on the way."

"Abby, we don't have time for this," Nathan urged. "I'm sorry we're putting you on the spot here, but with or without you, we have to go...now."

Abby turned back to her husband. "I need to do this, Erik. I know it isn't fair to you or the kids. But it isn't fair to me, either. You can't ask me to stay here, knowing how I feel about it. You just can't."

"Abby..." Erik started to plead.

"I've had enough of this shit," Jessica decided, moving back toward the group. "Abby, do you want to go or not?"

"Yes, but..."

"That's all I need to know," Jessica said as she walked past her. "Erik, you've got two choices," she said, staring at him intently, face-to-face. "You can be a good husband and stand by your wife while she does the right thing, or I can knock you out and drag your ass back to the PC. Either way makes no difference to me."

Erik stood there, staring at a determined-looking Jessica, unsure of how to respond.

The jump sub broke the surface and drove itself up onto the beach.

"What's that?" Abby asked.

"Our ride," Nathan replied. "She's not bluffing, Erik," Nathan warned.

Erik looked at the two unconscious guards, then at his wife.

"Erik," Abby begged.

"Kids!" Erik called out. "We're taking a little ride!"

"Good choice, Erik," Jessica said. She winked at him, then headed for the jump sub.

"We're leaving, just like that?" Abby asked, her head spinning from all the excitement.

"Just like that," Nathan replied. Nathan noticed

distant sirens. "We've got to get going, Abby," he urged, taking her arm.

"Follow your father," Abby ordered her children as she and Nathan headed for the water.

Erik herded his confused children toward Jessica, who was already splashing through the surf to get to the jump sub. Once she reached it, she began pushing it back into the surf to turn it around. "Give me a hand!" she ordered Erik.

Erik joined her, helping her push the nose of the small watercraft around so that it was facing outward.

"What's going on?" Abby's son, Nikolas, asked as they ran toward their father and Jessica.

"We have to go," Abby explained. "It's not safe here, anymore."

"Are the Jung coming again?" her daughter asked.

It nearly broke Abby's heart to hear the fear in her daughter's voice. "Take my hand, sweetie," she insisted, taking her daughter's hand.

Abby's daughter looked at Nathan as they walked quickly into the knee-deep surf. "I know you," Kirsten said. "Aren't you supposed to be dead?"

"I got better," Nathan told her as they ran into the surf.

Jessica already had the jump sub's hatch open and was climbing inside. "Abby goes behind me, kids in the middle row, then you and Nathan in the back," she instructed Erik.

"Got it."

Jessica slipped down into the jump sub, immediately noticing that the controls had been completely upgraded. A light flashed on the annunciator panel at the upper middle of the console.

"Sweet," she commented, noticing the added sensor display. "We've got incoming drones!" she yelled.

"Hurry up!" Erik urged. By now, he realized that he had no choice. For the safety of his family, he had to cooperate, and deep down inside, he knew his wife was right. Galiardi could not be trusted. "Drones are coming!" he warned Nathan and Abby.

Jessica grabbed an energy rifle tucked in between the single pilot's seat and the side wall of the narrow bow of the jump sub. "Hand this to Nathan," she ordered Erik, passing it back toward the open hatch.

Erik reached down inside and took the rifle. "Oh, my God," he exclaimed, realizing what was in his hands. "Nathan!" he called out.

Nathan held up his hands, and Erik tossed him the rifle.

"Come on!" Erik urged his family. "Abby, you have to get in first!"

Abby splashed up to the sub, now thigh-deep in the surging surf, clutching her daughter tightly. Her son, Nikolas, grabbed his sister's other hand, holding on to the side of the sub to steady himself in the surf as his mother climbed up onto the bouncing jump sub.

Nathan turned the energy rifle on, spinning around to face the shore as the targeting screen on the weapon came to life. A second later, three small icons appeared, all of them about forty meters above the ground and heading toward them. The words 'select mode' flashed on the screen in Takaran. Nathan quickly scrolled through the selections, settling on an acronym which he knew indicated 'self-guided, self-propelled rounds'.

Abby climbed down into the jump sub, slipping

into the single seat directly behind Jessica. "Is this thing..."

"Jump equipped?" Jessica said, finishing Abby's question for her. "You bet."

"Incredible," she said as Kirsten dropped down into the seat behind her and to her right. A moment later, Nikolas came down and slid into the seat next to his sister. "Help strap her in, Niko," Abby instructed.

"What's going on, Mom?" Nikolas asked as he helped his sister with her shoulder harness.

"I can do it myself," Kirsten insisted.

"I'll explain it to you later, once we're safe," Abby promised as her husband came down the hatch and took his seat at the back right of the compartment.

The drones were less than a half mile away now, and the targeting system indicated that two of them were armed. Nathan selected all three targets, raised his rifle skyward, and pulled the trigger once. A small projectile, only a few centimeters in length, leapt from the secondary barrel at the bottom of the weapon and streaked skyward on a tiny trail of thrust. Nathan pulled the trigger two more times, sending additional projectiles skyward. He didn't wait to watch the projectiles wind their way up to their targets, instead turning and splashing his way through the surf to the jump sub, and climbing up onto it.

Nathan stepped into the hatch, pausing to look toward the drones just as three small explosions appeared in the sky just above the abandoned picnic that Abby had been setting up for her family.

Jessica turned her head, checking that Nathan was aboard, and then gunned the throttles forward. "Close it up!" she ordered.

Nathan handed Erik the energy rifle and slid down into the seat next to him, pulling the hatch above them closed and locking it. "Hatch is secure!" he told Jessica, taking the rifle back from Erik to stow it properly.

"Taking her down!" Jessica announced, adjusting the sub's dive planes. Water splashed on her forward windows as the jump sub submerged. The water was clear, and the visibility was good enough that she didn't need the terrain-following sensors at this point. "Engaging the auto-flight systems," she reported.

"This thing has auto-flight?" Abby wondered, surprised.

"You really think they'd let me drive this thing if it didn't?" Jessica replied.

* * *

"For someone who is so good at hand-flying, you'd think you'd be a lot better at piloting a ship using auto-flight," Charnelle teased.

"Very funny," Aiden said. "Just give me the straight critique...and without the wisecracks, if you don't mind."

"Aren't *you* touchy?" she teased.

"Are you kidding me?" Kenji said, looking at his view screen. "We've got more company."

"What?" Aiden leaned over again.

"Who is it?" Sari wondered.

"It's our crew," Aiden realized. "It's only zero four forty-five; they shouldn't be here for at least three more hours."

Again, Aiden unbuckled himself and climbed out of his seat. "I'm never going to get any practice in if this keeps up," he complained as he headed aft. Aiden moved past Charnelle and Sari, into the airlock, as Sergeant Dagata came climbing up the ladder.

The sergeant paused when he looked up and saw his captain standing above him. "What are you doing here, Captain?"

"I was about to ask you the same thing, Dags."

"Uh, we're fueling the ship, remember?"

"I thought all the gunships were fueled last night?"

"Ash didn't tell you?" the sergeant said as he finished climbing up into the airlock. "Ours had a bad seal on the starboard tank, so they had to replace it. By the time they finished, the fuel crews were off duty."

"So, you're fueling at five in the morning?" Aiden wondered.

"Oh, five fifteen, actually," the sergeant corrected. He spotted Kenji in the forward hatchway. "Morning, sir."

"Morning, Sergeant."

"How many of you does it take to oversee a refuel?" Aiden asked, annoyed.

"On the surface? All four of us, sir. The chief oversees the juice jerks, I watch the systems, and Ali and Ledge are on fire watch."

"Standard procedure, Aiden," Kenji reminded him.

"Of course."

Sergeant Dagata noticed Charnelle and Sari behind Kenji. "Sirs." He looked at the captain. "Probably none of my business, Captain, but what are all of *you* doing here this time of night?"

"Just going over some flight procedures," Aiden admitted. "I want to make sure we shine from the moment we launch this thing."

"Yes, sir." The sergeant moved forward. "If I could just squeeze past you all, I have to be at the engineering station during the refuel."

"We can't practice while they're fueling us up, Aiden," Kenji said.

"What are we supposed to do in the meantime?"

"The mess hall opened early for us and the juice jerks," Sergeant Dagata told them, overhearing their conversation.

Aiden looked at his friends. "I could eat."

* * *

The sub slid along smoothly through the depths of the Atlantic, heading swiftly for her launch point. They had been in the cramped little sub for nearly an hour, and during all that time, only a few words had been spoken, and none of them by Erik or Abby. In fact, most of the talking had been by her children, both of whom desperately wanted to know where they were going and why.

Nathan wanted to answer them, to explain everything that was going on and how much he and Jessica needed their mother's help. But it was not his place, it was their parents'.

"Coming up on the launch point," Jessica reported. "Depth is three hundred meters, speed is forty KPH. Jump plot is loaded; jump drive is charged and ready. Pitching up in three......two......one......"

The jump sub's nose began to rise as the tiny submersible headed for the surface at a twenty-degree angle.

"Here we go," Jessica announced, "in three...... two......one......"

The jump sub's only windows up front turned opaque. The slight rocking motion of their underwater motion suddenly ceased, and the occupants of the jump sub suddenly found themselves in a weightless environment.

"Neat," Nikolas exclaimed as the chain he wore around his neck began to rise from his body.

"Good thing I had a light breakfast," Erik said, looking a little uncomfortable.

Nathan reached for an emesis bag, handing it to Erik.

"How long until we're picked up?" Abby asked Jessica.

"Shouldn't be long," Jessica assured her.

"I can't believe we're doing this," Erik said, trying to hold it together.

"Mom, Dad doesn't look so good," Nikolas warned, looking over his shoulder at his father.

"I've got them on sensors," Jessica announced. "A jump flash. It's the Seiiki, or at least I *think* it's them." She turned on the comms, waiting for a friendly voice, and was quickly rewarded.

"*Jump Sub, Seiiki. How do you copy?*" Loki called over comms. "*Hope you didn't have to wait long.*"

"What kept you?" Jessica joked.

"*We had to run back to the rally point to make room for you. President Scott stuffed us to the ceiling with 'aid'.*"

Nathan smiled. "Just a few more minutes, Erik, and we'll be back in near-normal gravity."

"Hurry," Erik whispered.

CHAPTER THIRTEEN

Captain Tobas and Commander Jarso stood on the Morsiko-Tavi's bridge, looking forward over the cargo pods stacked on the ship's long, flat cargo deck. While she could carry up to twelve pods, stacked three pods high in four columns, on this trip, she carried only two layers on her deck. The pods on the lower layer were connected and pressurized, and contained additional crew accommodations, emergency medical bays, and finally the six Rakers that had escaped when the Avendahl fell. The second layer contained additional propellant, since this journey was well beyond the ship's normal range, and Captain Tobas wanted to be sure he could get home again.

The Morsiko-Tavi's windows did not turn opaque, like most ships. By design, hers merely filtered out extreme luminosity. The result was a subdued flash that filled the bridge whenever she jumped, but was not blinding to her crew.

"Jump complete," the pilot reported after the jump flash subsided. "We are at the staging point, two light years outside of the Tau Ceti system."

Captain Tobas looked at his watch. "You have about thirty minutes before you launch," he told Commander Jarso. "You and your men best get to your ships."

"I'm not sure how I feel about flying a mission against the Alliance," Commander Jarso admitted.

"We do what we must for our own," Captain Tobas said. "The Alliance does the same."

"You served with the Alliance," Commander Jarso said, wondering how Captain Tobas felt.

"*I* served in the Sol-Pentaurus Alliance, under Admiral Travon Dumar," Captain Tobas corrected. "This is *not* that alliance."

"I suppose you're right," the commander said, turning to exit.

"Good hunting, Commander."

Commander Jarso nodded. He departed the bridge, wondering if the phrase had been appropriate, given the circumstances.

* * *

"It's small, but it'll get you through till you get back to the fleet," Nathan told Abby and Erik. "The kids can have the next cabin. Marcus, Neli, and Dalen are all bunked on the other side of the ship, so you'll have this side to yourselves for the entire trip. If you need anything, just ask Neli. She'll take good care of you. Oh, and don't eat anything that Marcus or Dalen cooks. Don't ask how I know."

"How long will it take us to get there?" Erik asked.

"Three days," Nathan answered.

Erik scratched his head, sighing. "That far, huh?"

"Over a thousand light years," Nathan said.

"I thought the Pentaurus sector was just *under* a thousand light years," Abby questioned.

"You're not going to the Pentaurus sector," Nathan explained. "The fleet is two sectors away, out of immediate reach of the Dusahn, and it doesn't stay in the same place for long."

"How will we find it?" Erik asked.

"They're holding position until we get back," Nathan assured him. "And if they *should* have to move before then, Marcus knows how to find them."

"Then, you're not going back with us," Abby surmised.

"No. We have another mission in the Sol sector to

complete before we can return. We'll see you in four or five days."

"How soon do you want me to start work on the stealth emitters?" Abby asked. "I'm pretty sure I already have them figured out. I just need to do some more testing."

"Get your family settled on the Mystic Empress, first. That's more important at the moment."

"Thanks," Erik said.

"*Reload is almost complete, Captain,*" Dalen reported over Nathan's comm-set. "*We should be ready to depart in a few minutes.*"

"Understood," Nathan replied. He turned his attention back to Abby and Erik. "Thanks again...to *both* of you."

Nathan turned and exited the cabin, making his way aft down the port corridor, stepping through the aft hatch onto the cargo bay's port catwalk landing, and then headed down the ladder. "Safe journey," he told Dalen, patting him on the shoulder as he passed.

"You too, Captain," Dalen replied.

Nathan headed down the cargo ramp, onto the dusty, wind-blown tarmac in front of the Tannan evacuation facility, moving quickly inside to get out of the higher radiation levels.

"As I live and breathe," Gil bellowed from inside. "If it isn't Captain Kid, back from the dead." There was an uncharacteristic smile on Gil's face, one that Nathan didn't remember ever seeing.

"Captain Roselle," Nathan greeted, extending his hand.

"I'm pretty sure you've earned the right to call me Gil, kid," Gil insisted as he vigorously shook Nathan's hand. "It's good to see you."

"You, as well," Nathan replied. "You too, Commander," Nathan said to Commander Ellison.

"Marty," the commander insisted, shaking Nathan's hand.

"I can't thank either of you enough for the risks you're taking. It's a hell of a sacrifice you're both making."

"Our jobs are a dead end, kid. It's time for a change. A *big* one," Gil added with a chuckle.

"You on your way out?" Nathan asked.

"You bet," Gil replied. "I understand you talked the good doctor and her family into joining the cause, as well. Nice work."

"Thanks."

"Gotta run, kid," Gil said with enthusiasm. "Time to start my life of crime," he joked as he turned to face the four Ghatazhak standing behind him, dressed in Alliance Marine armor. "Marines!" he bellowed. "Let's move out!"

Nathan and Martin watched Gil and his squad of fake marines march out into the open, headed for the shuttle Gil and Marty had taken from the Benakh a few hours ago.

"I haven't seen him this excited about something in a long time," Martin commented.

"I've *never* seen him this excited," Nathan said. "I take it you're going to fly a gunship for us?"

"Yes, indeed."

"Glad to have you with us, Marty," Nathan said as they watched Gil's shuttle lift off.

"*Strike Team!*" Master Sergeant Anwar's voice called from further inside the hangar. "*Time to mount up!*"

"I guess it's time to go to work," Nathan said.

"Do criminals call it work?" Martin wondered as

they turned and headed for the Ghatazhak troop shuttle waiting inside.

* * *

"I trust the ship is properly fueled, Chief?" Aiden asked his engineer as he, Kenji, Charnelle, and Sari returned to Cobra Three Eight Three.

"She's good to go, Captain," Chief Benetti replied as she closed the access cover on the starboard propellant tank's transfer fitting. "Are you going to run some more simulations?"

Aiden looked at Kenji. "We still have two hours before the pre-launch quals begin. We could do at least four or five more runs through the launch and docking sims."

"What's a few more hours without sleep," Kenji agreed.

"We'll evaluate you for two or three of them, but then we have to get to our own ship to get ready," Charnelle said.

"You don't have to stay," Aiden insisted.

"It's no trouble. Besides, I rather like watching you screw up," she said with a grin as she headed up the access ladder toward the ventral access hatch.

Aiden glanced at Charnelle as she climbed the ladder, then back at Kenji. "I'm not *that* bad, am I?"

"Don't listen to her," Kenji told him. "She likes to mess with your head."

Aiden watched as Kenji and Sari both headed up the ladder, as well.

"She does it because she likes you, Captain," Chief Benetti commented. "Trust me, I'm a woman, I can tell."

Aiden glared at her, grabbing hold of the ladder to start up.

"Captain, if you don't mind, I'd like to run the

crew through some drills in the engineering spaces. We're still a little slow doing the emergency manual reactor shutdowns."

"Very well, Chief," Aiden agreed. "Just don't get in our way up front," he added as he started up the ladder.

"Yes, sir."

Aiden stopped just short of the hatch above him, looking back at the chief. "She *likes* me?"

"Bet a week's pay on it, sir."

"Huh," Aiden said, continuing up the ladder.

* * *

The cargo shuttle, loaded with two, two-squad strike teams of Ghatazhak, was the first to roll out of the evacuation base hangar on Tanna. Following it was the much smaller combat jump shuttle, carrying General Telles and three more Ghatazhak. Along with the four Ghatazhak who left previously with Captain Roselle and Commander Ellison, dressed as Alliance Marines, the total number of Ghatazhak taking part in the mission on Kohara was twenty-eight.

Finally, the last ship, the search and rescue shuttle that Commander Nash had taken from the ironically named Tanna, rolled out of the hangar. Robert and Nathan were at the SAR shuttle's controls, while Jessica, Vladimir, Deliza, Yanni, Josh, and Loki rode in the back.

One by one, the three shuttles lifted off the dusty tarmac, slowly climbing skyward. As each ship reached a safe altitude, they disappeared, one after the other, behind flashes of blue-white light.

Three screeching claps of thunder were heard, a split second later, as the sound of their departure arrived. Once again, the evacuation facility was silent, abandoned to the winds and radiation of Tanna.

* * *

Commander Jarso led his men into the massive cargo pod, toward their waiting fighters. They had spent the last week as passengers aboard the Morsiko-Tavi while the ship jumped its way across the galaxy to its current position, two light years outside the Tau Ceti system.

The old, flatbed cargo ship was not as spacious and clean as the Avendahl had been, nor was she as advanced. But her crew had been very accommodating, and the additional living quarters inside two of the class-one cargo pods had been quite spacious for the six of them and the medical team of three that the Aurora had sent along. It would not be as spacious on the way back, however, since the additional housing would be filled with at least twenty Ghatazhak.

Commander Jarso climbed up into his fighter, sliding down into the cockpit. He pulled on his flight helmet, securing it to his flight suit's mating collar around his neck. As he activated the start-up sequence on his fighter's reactors, the lights inside the massive pod began to flash red, warning them of pending depressurization.

The commander pressed a button on his console, causing his canopy to slide forward, sealing him inside. He checked his life support system, noting that both his suit and the cockpit were at the proper temperature, pressure, and oxygen saturation.

"Raker Leader to all Rakers, count off."

"*Raker Two, secured and spinning up,*" Ensign Viorol, the commander's wingman reported.

"*Raker Three, secured and spinning up,*" Lieutenant Commander Giortone announced.

"*Raker Four, secured and spinning up,*" Ensign Baylor, the lieutenant commander's wingman said, following suit.

"*Raker Five, secured and spinning up,*" Ensign Hebron said.

"*Raker Six, buttoned up and running hot,*" Ensign Dakus, Ensign Hebron's wingman reported.

"Morsiko-Tavi, Raker One. Raker Flight is ready for depress."

"*Understood, Raker Flight,*" Mister Kellog, the cargo ship's comms officer replied. "*Depressurizing the Raker bay.*"

Commander Jarso continued preparing for flight as the lights in the cargo pod changed to steady red, indicating depressurization of the bay was under way. He checked all systems, tested his flight instruments, and verified his weapons systems were all operational while waiting for his reactors to come to full power.

A few minutes later, the red lights suddenly reduced their intensity by fifty percent, and the massive pod doors began to fold open, slowly turning into a ramp which extended the cargo pod's deck out another eight meters into space.

"*Raker Flight, bay door is opening. Be ready to launch as soon as we jump into the target system,*" Mister Kellog warned. "*Jumping in seven minutes, forty-seven seconds.*"

"Understood," Commander Jarso replied. "Seven minutes, gentlemen."

* * *

Two officers and four armed guards burst through the door of the control center at the Cobra production plant on Kohara, moving quickly toward the nearby landing pad.

"Since when do they do security inspections at five thirty in the morning?" Lieutenant Commander Kessler complained as he and his men hurried across the yard. "And on launch day, of all days!" He looked back at his second. "Are you sure it was Roselle?"

"Gave his clearance codes and everything, sir."

"Damn that man. I knew I shouldn't have traded shifts with Ekholm."

"It's not like it's the first time Captain Roselle has conducted a surprise inspection," the lieutenant reminded his commander.

"You'd think the old fart would be sleeping this time of the morning. The sun won't even be up for almost two hours."

"These inspections never take more than thirty or forty minutes, sir," the lieutenant assured him. "He's just hoping to catch us with our guard down, so he can rack up a few points with the brass before retiring."

"Roselle's retiring?" the lieutenant commander asked, surprised.

"That's what I heard."

"About time," Lieutenant Commander Kessler grumbled as he came to a stop a few meters from the landing pad.

The shuttle appeared in a blue-white flash that lit up the pre-dawn sky over the compound, followed a split second later by a thunderous clap due to the sudden displacement of air caused by the shuttle's arrival. The shuttle descended quickly as it passed over the outer fence. A minute later, it settled onto the landing pad and spun down its engines.

As the whine of the shuttle's engines faded, its

boarding hatch opened, and two Alliance Marines in standard battle armor stepped out. The marines stepped to either side, taking up protective positions as Captain Roselle stepped out of the shuttle, followed by two more marines.

The captain and the two marines marched confidently toward the control center, with determined looks on their faces. "Are you the duty officer?" Captain Roselle barked at the lieutenant commander, obviously in a foul mood.

"Yes, sir!" the lieutenant commander replied. "Lieutenant Commander Kessler, sir!"

"What the hell are you yelling for, Kessler?"

"Sorry, sir. Allow me to introduce Lieutenant Sauntor..."

"Yeah, yeah. This damned inspection wasn't my idea, gentlemen. Came down from Fleet an hour ago; no idea why. So, let's just get this over with as quickly as possible," Captain Roselle said as Commander Ellison came down out of the shuttle.

Lieutenant Commander Kessler exchanged glances with Lieutenant Sauntor when the commander appeared. "Commander," he greeted.

"Commander Ellison will be taking command of the Benakh in a few weeks, when I retire, which means he'll be doing these inspection tours. So, I figured I'd wake his ass up, as well. Besides, two command officers can get it done twice as fast, and we can all get back to work, right?"

"Of course, sir," the lieutenant commander agreed.

"How about *you* show me the control center and security command, and the lieutenant shows Commander Ellison the launch control tower."

"The control tower, sir?" the lieutenant commander asked.

"You're launching twenty-odd birds in a few hours, aren't you?" Captain Roselle said. "Tower security had *better* be up to snuff. In fact, I suspect *that* is why Fleet woke my wrinkled, old ass up before dawn."

"Of course, Captain," Lieutenant Commander Kessler replied. He turned nervously to the lieutenant. "Lieutenant Sauntor, please show Commander Ellison the launch control tower, and make sure he has access to everything he needs to complete his inspection."

"Yes, sir," the lieutenant replied. "Commander, if you'll follow me."

"Excellent," Captain Roselle said. "Let's get this over with, shall we, Lieutenant Commander?"

"If you'll follow me, sir."

Captain Roselle and two of the marines followed the lieutenant commander and one of his men toward the control center. Once at the door, the lieutenant commander punched in his security code and opened the door, holding it for Captain Roselle and his men.

Gil stepped aside, waiting for the lieutenant commander to take the lead. "Let's start with security command," he instructed.

"As you wish, sir," the lieutenant commander agreed, leading them down the corridor.

"How many men are currently on duty?" Gil inquired.

"We're short-staffed at the moment. Normally, the plant runs around the clock. But the alerts delayed some of the flight training, and the yard got backed up with ready ships, so production has been halted for the last week. Night staff is currently ten guards and four officers."

"And how many marines are stationed on base?"

"Fifty, give or take a few," the lieutenant commander replied. "They work three-day rotations, and some of them live on the other side of the lake, so they come in the night before. The current rotation ends at zero eight hundred today."

Lieutenant Commander Kessler stopped at the entrance to security command, punching his code into the door lock. Again, he opened the door and allowed the captain and his men to enter.

"This is security command," the lieutenant commander stated. "Of course, you know that, sir."

"I see that two of your cameras are down," Captain Roselle said, feigning concern. "How long?"

"Camera four went down yesterday afternoon, and camera twenty-one went down a few hours ago. There are work orders waiting for maintenance when they report in at zero nine hundred, and I have stationed an additional guard at each of the camera locations as a precaution."

"Very good." Gil felt the comm-unit in his pocket vibrate.

"Is there anything in particular you'd like me to show you, Captain?" the lieutenant commander asked.

"Two things," Captain Roselle began. "First, I'd like you to transmit this message to my ship. Narrow band, blind transmission, no response or acknowledgment required." Gil handed him a data card.

"Sir?"

"I'm taking advantage of being up, and initiating

a surprise drill for the Benakh," Gil explained, a sinister smile on his face.

"Of course," the lieutenant commander said, handing the data card to one of the technicians. "Transmit this, per the captain's instructions."

The technician slid the data card into a slot on his console, then initiated the transmission. "Message is being sent," he assured the lieutenant commander.

Lieutenant Commander Kessler turned back to Captain Roselle. "You said there were two things, sir?"

"Indeed," Gil replied. "Do you have a secure closet? One large enough to accommodate, say..." Gil looked around the room, counting heads, "...five men?"

"Sir?"

"A closet, Lieutenant Commander. A secure closet. Do you have one?"

"Uh, yes, sir, over there," the lieutenant commander replied, pointing toward the corner of the room. "Why do you ask?"

"Because I need someplace to lock you all up in," Captain Roselle said plainly, a smile on his face.

The guard next to the lieutenant commander made a move for his gun, but stopped when the two marines flanking Captain Roselle quickly raised their weapons and charged them to full power.

"Hands high!" one of the marines barked. "Nobody touches anything!"

"What's going on, Captain?" the lieutenant commander asked, bewildered. "What kind of an inspection is this?"

"It's not an inspection," Gil said, smiling, "it's a heist."

* * *

"Sir, our sensor array just went down," Ensign Vukovic stated.

Lieutenant Commander Norath moved across the Benakh's bridge toward the sensor station, his fourth cup of coffee of the night in hand. "The entire array?"

"Yes, sir."

"How is that possible?"

"I'm running diagnostics now," the sensor operator replied. "We should know in a minute or two."

Lieutenant Commander Norath thought for a moment. It wasn't the first time the Benakh's antiquated sensor array had gone down unexpectedly, and every time it had done so in the past, it had come back online a few minutes later. Engineering had spent countless hours trying to troubleshoot the cause of the intermittent failures. The best they could come up with was 'unexplained overheating of power relays'. They had supposedly resolved the issue, and there were plans to take the entire system down and replace it after the Aurora's overhaul was completed. But just like the Aurora's overhaul, those plans had been postponed when the Jung began showing up deep inside Alliance space a few weeks ago.

"Link us into Tau Ceti's sensor net," Lieutenant Commander Norath ordered. "I'd rather not be blind."

"The data from the Tau Ceti system-wide sensor net will be a few minutes old," the sensor officer reminded the lieutenant commander. "I may have this resolved by then."

"I'll buy you breakfast if you do, Ensign. But I'd still like to have the connection as a backup, just in case."

"Should I notify the XO?" the communications officer wondered.

"Not yet," Lieutenant Commander Norath said. "Let's see if we can get it fixed in short order. Besides, this may be one of those *surprise* tests he is so fond of."

"Regulations state that the commanding officer is *supposed* to be notified when any systems critical to ship's operations are not functioning properly," the tactical officer stated.

"*Should* be notified, Lieutenant, not *supposed* to be notified," the lieutenant commander corrected. "Two entirely different meanings, the latter of which gives me discretion as officer of the watch."

"Of course, sir," the tactical officer agreed, feeling properly chastised and somewhat embarrassed for having misquoted the regulation.

"Make that diagnostic quick, Ensign," the lieutenant commander urged, his voice a bit tense.

"Aye, sir."

"Comms, warn flight ops that we may have to launch an additional patrol, close in."

"Yes, sir," the communications officer replied.

The more Lieutenant Commander Norath thought about it, the more he was certain that he was being tested. *Early morning, the captain's off-ship, near the end of the watch, when everyone is tired...* If this *was* one of Commander Ellison's little surprise tests, he was determined not to fail it.

* * *

The inside of the cargo pod lit up briefly as the light from the Morsiko-Tavi's jump spilled in through the opening before Commander Jarso and his Rakers.

"*Raker Leader, Morsiko-Tavi. Jump complete. You are clear to launch. See you at the recovery point.*"

"Tavi, Raker Leader. Don't be late," Commander Jarso replied. "Leader to all Rakers, follow me out."

Commander Jarso applied slight upward thrust, then forward, sending his fighter sliding out of the cargo bay into open space. He waited several seconds for his ship to completely clear the cargo pod's exit, then applied enough thrust to bring him up to insertion speed.

The commander glanced over his right shoulder, looking back to see the other five Rakers following him out. "Leader to all Rakers, turn to jump heading."

Commander Jarso initiated the turn, coming to the course they had calculated would bring them to their target in a single half-light-year jump.

A quick glance at his squadron status display told him that all his men's ships were on course and speed, and were ready to jump. "Leader to all Rakers, jump in three......two......one..."

Commander Jarso touched the jump button on his flight control stick. His canopy suddenly turned opaque, and he felt as if his ship had hit a wall, throwing him forward against his restraints. As his ship shook violently, his canopy cleared, revealing the lights of Geraleise Spaceport directly below them.

The commander quickly activated his targeting system, selecting the four leftmost targets, as planned. A few seconds later, his targeting systems verified the targets had been acquired, and his weapons were ready to fire. He reached forward, pressing the auto-attack button on his console, transferring control of his diving fighter to the combat computers. The ship began flying itself as the plasma cannons on either wing sent a barrage of plasma bolts streaking toward the surface. His combat flight computers made tiny adjustments much more quickly and accurately than any human pilot could, allowing him to destroy all four targets on the ground before the men stationed at the spaceport could even realize just what the alert klaxons they were hearing truly meant.

Once his targets were obliterated, he took back control of his ship, pitched his nose up level to end his dive toward the spaceport, and pressed the jump button to clear the immediate area before the surface defenses could lock onto him and seek their revenge.

As Sergeant Ayers and Sergeant Morano herded the stunned lieutenant commander and his men into the closet, Gil Roselle inserted a data chip into the security console and typed in his command codes.

As he waited for the data to download onto the data chip, he pulled out his comm-unit to check his messages. As the officer tasked to protect the entire Tau Ceti system, he would be notified if anything within the system was amiss. As expected, he was receiving flash traffic about an attack at the Geraleise spaceport by an unknown enemy.

"All personnel have been secured," Sergeant Ayers reported.

The console beeped, and Gil removed the data chip, inserting it into his comm-unit. "I've got the codes," he told them. "Get into position, and I'll join you in a moment."

The two Ghatazhak sergeants, both dressed in Alliance Marine combat armor, exited the room, securing their escape route.

Gil typed in several commands, causing the security system to go into an emergency restart cycle. As soon as the cycle started, he turned and went to the server rack and planted several small, remotely-triggered charges. "That should do it," he decided, taking one last look around.

Just then, the security console went dark, and Gil smiled and exited.

Neither Ghatazhak sergeant bothered restraining or imprisoning the officer and guard who had brought them to the launch control tower, choosing simply to stun them instead.

"You sure that will keep them out long enough?" Commander Ellison wondered as he uploaded Vladimir's improved control program into the ground movement and launch control system.

"By the time they wake, we'll be long gone, or long dead," Sergeant Notoni assured the commander. The light next to the data card slot blinked green, and the system beeped, indicating the upload was complete.

Commander Ellison typed in execution instructions, then activated the time-delayed program. He turned to look at the two Ghatazhak sergeants dressed in Alliance Marine combat armor. "So far, this is going too easily."

"Don't say that," Sergeant Notoni said. "Things usually start to go terribly wrong immediately afterwards."

"Superstitious Ghatazhak," the commander scoffed as he headed for the exit. "Now I've heard everything."

The windows on the combat jump shuttle turned opaque, and the entire ship suddenly jolted as if it had struck something in the air.

"*Twenty seconds,*" Lieutenant Latfee warned over General Telles's helmet comms. The general reached over and released the latch on the port side door, allowing it to slide aft. At the same time, Lieutenant Jessup, sitting next to him, did the same with the starboard door.

The cool pre-dawn air of Kohara swirled into the cabin of the combat jump shuttle as it swooped in low over the rolling hills of the Geraleise province. The general checked his weapon, then dropped his visor to check the tactical data it was designed to display.

"*Ten seconds,*" the lieutenant updated.

The fact that the automated weapons towers were not already firing at them told General Telles that Captain Roselle, and likely Commander Ellison, had completed the first and most critical phase of the operation without incident.

"*Five seconds,*" the lieutenant warned.

"*Good luck, boys,*" Sergeant Torwell said from the topside weapons turret.

General Telles tapped the trusted sergeant's boot as a response as he turned toward the open doorway in preparation.

"Go, go, go," Lieutenant Latfee ordered calmly.

Neither General Telles nor any of the three men with him bothered to look out the door before they leapt out. Their trust in the skill of their pilots was complete.

On the way out the door, General Lucius Telles glanced at the time display on his tactical visor. The local time was zero five forty-five thirty, ninety minutes before sunrise.

"What was that?" Charnelle wondered.

"What was what?" Aiden asked as he continued with the simulation.

"I thought I saw a flash of light outside, like a jump flash."

"Probably just a shuttle on approach. Cargo or something," Kenji said. "They come and go at all hours."

"Yeah, but you probably don't know that because *your* rooms face the gunship yard instead of the landing pads, like ours," Aiden complained.

"Let's finish up this sim," Sari urged. "We need to think about getting to our own ship to get ready."

The lights in the marine barracks at the Kohara Cobra plant suddenly came on as an alert klaxon sounded.

"Are you fucking kidding me?" Corporal Travis moaned, pulling his blanket up over his head.

All over the barracks, marines immediately got out of their bunks and began pulling on their pants and boots, preparing to respond to the alert.

"Get your lazy ass up, Travis!" Sergeant Beechum urged his bunk neighbor. "It's an alert."

"It's a fucking drill, Sarge," the corporal complained. "And I'm not even on duty, yet."

"You take a bunk, you respond to an alert, Corporal. Those are the rules," the sergeant insisted, ripping the blanket off the corporal. "Move your ass."

"LET'S MOVE, MARINES!" the duty officer barked as he stormed into the barracks. "ALL SECURITY SYSTEMS ARE OFFLINE! THIS IS NOT A FUCKING DRILL!"

Corporal Travis reluctantly sat up, swinging his legs over the edge of the bed and pulling on his pants. "Next time, I'm staying at a hotel in town."

"Ghatazhak!" Commander Kellen barked from the front of the cargo shuttle's main bay. "Stand ready!"

The nineteen other soldiers immediately stood, dropping their helmet visors and checking their weapons.

"Ten seconds," Lieutenant Quinlan warned.

"Dropping the ramp," the crew chief announced.

The ramp at the back of the cargo shuttle began to open, allowing the outside air to come swirling into the long cargo bay full of Ghatazhak. The ship rocked as it touched down, and the ramp hit the ground a moment later.

"MOVE OUT!" the commander ordered.

Ghatazhak soldiers ran down the ramp in two lines, raising their weapons to ready position and breaking off to the right and left as their feet touched the ground.

Commander Kellen was the last man out, following Delta team to the right as the two squads headed for the gunships.

The commander glanced at his visor, noting the local time was zero five forty-six.

Jessica sat next to the boarding hatch of the SAR shuttle. She scanned the faces of everyone sitting with her. She knew that Deliza, Yanni, and Loki would do as they were told. They were too scared to do otherwise. She also knew that Vladimir had spent six years in the Russian military as a foot soldier prior to joining the Earth Defense Force and attending the academy, so she expected him to be fine, as well. Josh, on the other hand, was always unpredictable. The young man had amazing skills as a pilot, but his overconfidence often blinded him to his inabilities in other areas.

Robert, of course, was a well-trained, highly-experienced officer. Although he had no field operations experience, she knew that she could count on him to keep cool and remain effective if the mission took an unexpected turn.

The wild card, as usual, was Nathan. Although he appeared to be his old self again, there were times that Connor's personality reared its head, causing momentary confusions within him. This only added to his unpredictable and impulsive nature. Unfortunately, once they stepped out the door, they would all be headed to different ships, and she would not be able to protect him and keep him under control, as if she ever could.

The SAR shuttle touched down, bouncing slightly. Robert and Nathan immediately began shutting everything down, since they planned to abandon the SAR shuttle.

Jessica popped the hatch open and jumped out, falling the last meter to the soft grass below rather than using the single step that had deployed out of the shuttle's fuselage. Her weapon raised, she immediately moved to the left in the direction from which the responding marines would come, dropping down to one knee at the aft end of the shuttle to scan for threats.

Vladimir was next out, jumping to the ground and landing in a crouch, the same as Jessica had done. He raised his weapon, and moved to the right, also dropping down to one knee at the nose of the shuttle, scanning for threats.

Nathan, having quickly climbed from the copilot's seat to the open hatch, stood waiting for signals from Jessica and Vladimir indicating it was safe for everyone to deploy. After a few seconds, Jessica's hand went up, signaling it was clear on her side. Nathan looked to Vladimir, who gave a similar hand sign. "Let's go," Nathan said, turning back to the other passengers.

Jessica continued to scan the area, using her tactical visor to help detect targets. There were plenty of them, all clustered in the marine barracks at the other end of the gunship yard. For the moment, they were not a threat, but they soon would be. Jessica quickly returned to the task at hand. The Alliance Marines were the responsibility of Alpha and Delta teams, not hers.

She glanced over her shoulder, noting that the rest of the passengers were out of the SAR shuttle and ready to move. She then glanced at the time display on her tactical visor. The local time was zero five forty-six thirty.

By the time the first few Alliance Marines exited their barracks onto the porch which opened into the north end of the gunship yard, Commander Kellen and Alpha team were already in position. Tucked tightly against the massive, motorized dollies that the gunships rode on during production and eventual launch, they had a protected, clear line of fire on the unsuspecting marines. To the Ghatazhak's surprise, the Alliance Marines were better prepared than expected.

The first two marines came out in a low crouch, moving with the confidence and precision that only repetitive training could provide. They exited in pairs; one man low and aiming left, the second one, a step behind the first, not quite as low and aiming right. The first pair moved immediately to the left, staying low enough that the half-wall in front of the barracks left the Ghatazhak little to target.

Within seconds, a half dozen marines had spread out along the half-wall. One marine, obviously an officer, rose slightly to be heard. "You have trespassed on an Alliance installation!" the officer ordered at the top of his lungs. "Drop your weapons and stand down, or we will use deadly force!"

Master Sergeant Willem looked at Commander Kellen. "Seriously? Who the hell gives verbal warnings to the enemy before opening fire?"

"Alpha Team, Alpha Actual," the commander called over his helmet comms. "Stunners only, fire at will."

"This is your final warn..."

The officer's words were cut short as a dozen blue stunner beams streaked across the gap between the two forces, one of which struck the officer square in the face. Had he not raised his visor in order to yell out a warning to the enemy, he might not have ended up unconscious at the start of the battle.

The marines, however, were relentless and determined, and their body armor had much to do with that. One after another, the Ghatazhak stunner bolts bounced off the marines' helmets, visors, and upper body armor. After thirty seconds of stunner barrage, only two marines had fallen; the officer who had shouted the warning and a marine who had stood a little too high while coming out of the barracks and trying to get to the firing line.

"This isn't working," Commander Kellen observed.

As the number of marines at the wall doubled, the first group, having realized that their armor was offering them an acceptable level of protection against the invaders, rose and advanced toward the enemy firing positions. Again, in pairs, they advanced, the forward marine holding a blast shield that protected both of them from the midsection down, and the second marine following behind him, firing over the first marine's head.

Four pairs of marines advanced, firing relentlessly. The lead man of one pair let his shield come off the ground just enough that a stunner shot slipped underneath, striking him in the foot. He did not fall, but the pair did stop their advance.

As more marines reached the wall, more shielded pairs began to advance. A Ghatazhak fell to their energy weapons fire, taking too many simultaneous hits in his abdomen for his body armor to withstand.

"*Alpha Blue One is down!*" Sergeant Yanna, Alpha Blue squad's leader reported. "*Alpha Blue Two is pulling him back!*"

"Alpha Red Leader, Alpha Bravo," Master Sergeant Willem called as he fired. "Pinch in to the north to cover retreat of Alpha Blue One and Two."

"*Alpha Red Leader, pinching in to the north!*" Sergeant Rattan acknowledged.

"*Alpha Actual, Delta Actual,*" Lieutenant Commander Lazo called. "*Marines moving in from between buildings three and four.*"

"There's no gate there," Commander Kellen replied.

"*There is now, sir. We're taking heavy fire. They're advancing using shields. These damned stunners are barely slowing them down, Commander.*"

"I knew this wasn't going to fucking work," Commander Kellen cursed as he tapped his helmet to call up another tactical channel. "Strike Actual, Alpha Actual..."

"*Yitzo is down hard!*" Corporal Mahado reported.

"He's bleeding out! Alpha Red Three is down! I'm pulling him..."

"Alpha Red Two is down!" Sergeant Rattan reported. *"Alpha Red is ineffective!"*

"Fuck this," Commander Kellen cursed as red plasma bolts slammed into the ground around him and the body of the dolly behind which he was taking cover. "Alpha Actual to Alpha Team. Switch to plasma pulse rifles and shock grenades! Low power! Let's stop those marines in their tracks!"

"Strike Team, Strike Actual," General Telles called over comms. *"Deadly force is authorized. I repeat, deadly force is authorized."*

Commander Kellen glanced at the time display on the inside of his tactical visor. The local time was zero five forty-eight. It had taken only three minutes for him to decrease his force by two men, possibly four. Stunners had been a bad idea.

Captain Roselle ran from the security building toward the back row of gunships, flanked by two Ghatazhak sergeants dressed as Alliance Marines. Surprisingly, no one took a shot at them. Gil wondered if the real marines took them to be friendlies trying to flank the enemy, or if they were just preoccupied with the enemy directly before them, pinning them down with heavy plasma weapons fire. He didn't care which...as long as they made it to their gunship.

Gil ran under the nose of the third gunship from the end, bending over slightly to keep from hitting his head as he got to the ventral access hatch. He looked around, first spotting those who had arrived on Robert's SAR shuttle running for their assigned gunships, and then his XO, Martin, along with Martin's two Ghatazhak in marine armor, running from the launch control tower to their gunship, as well. Behind him, the Ghatazhak strike teams were exchanging weapons fire with the marines pouring out of their barracks. Red-orange bolts of energy streaked from the Ghatazhak positions toward the marines while red energy bolts flew in the opposite direction, slamming into the ground and the gunship dollies the Ghatazhak were taking cover behind.

Gil reached up and entered the access code for his particular gunship. The hatch opened, and he headed up the ladder. "Cobra Six is in," he reported over his comm-set. "Let's go, boys," he called to his two Ghatazhak escorts as he continued up the ladder.

"What the hell is going on out there?" Charnelle wondered, her attention no longer focused on Aiden's performance, instead standing on her toes to try to see what was going on outside. "Is that weapons fire?"

"What?" Kenji asked.

"If you're trying to distract me, it's working," Aiden complained.

"Seriously, Aiden, there's something going..." She stopped suddenly when she saw several soldiers in flat-black body armor, the likes of which she had never seen, go running past the front of their ship, weapons held high. "Who the hell is..."

"Are we being attacked?" Sari wondered, also straining to see the movement on the ground outside.

"*Captain!*" Ali called over comms. "*Sorry to bother you, sir, but there's a gunfight going on outside, and soldiers in black armor are running around all over the place!*"

Aiden looked at Kenji. "Well, who are they?"

"I have no idea, sir, but they're kind of scary looking."

"*Holy shit!*" Ledge exclaimed. "*They're Ghatazhak, Captain!*"

"Are you sure?" Aiden asked in disbelief.

"*No, but they look just like the pictures I've seen of them. And Ali's right...they're scary as hell!*"

"*Captain!*" Ali interrupted. "*There are two people trying to get into Cobra Three Eight Two!*"

"That's my ship!" Charnelle yelled, turning to leave.

"Char! Wait!" Aiden warned. "If those are Ghatazhak out there..."

"But..."

"Chief! Break out the small arms!" Aiden ordered as he unbuckled his restraints and started climbing out of the pilot's seat.

"We don't have any small arms!" Chief Benetti replied. "We don't get them until after launch, with the rest of our provisions at the ops platform!"

"Seems like I should have known that, doesn't it," Aiden admitted.

"What are we going to do?" Charnelle wondered, a bit panicked. She caught a glimpse of the side view screen behind Kenji as he was climbing out of the copilot's seat. "Who is *that*?" she exclaimed, pointing at the view screen.

Kenji turned around just in time to see two men climbing up the ladder to the ventral access hatch.

"Oh, shit," Aiden exclaimed. "Close the hatch, Kenji!"

Kenji moved to activate the hatch motor, but it was too late. He looked at Aiden, "It's too late."

"*Deadly force is authorized. I repeat, deadly force is authorized,*" General Telles instructed over comms.

"I knew it," Jessica muttered as she pulled out her comm-unit.

"*Cobra Five is in,*" Martin reported over comm-sets.

"Read me the codes," Robert said.

"One four seven, two two five, eight one eight," Jessica finished reading the access code, sent to her by Gil on her comm-unit, to Robert as he punched the code into the gunship's ventral access hatch control pad. There was a metallic click, and the red light on the control pad turned green, after which the hatch slid open, disappearing into the hull and revealing a dimly lit vertical tunnel above them.

"Cobra One is in," Jessica reported over comms. She stayed on the ground, her weapon up, scanning left and right as Robert ascended the ladder and opened the inner hatch at the top of the access tunnel.

"*I'm in,*" Robert's voice crackled over her comm-set. One last look around, and she started up the ladder, pausing to activate the hatch controls from the inside to close the outer hatch behind her.

"Did he just tell them to use deadly force?" Nathan wondered.

"Yes," Vladimir confirmed.

"Damn it," Nathan cursed.

"Why is the outer hatch already open?" Vladimir wondered as he ascended the access tunnel. He stopped at the control pad for the inner hatch at the top of the tunnel. "This one is locked," he said, pulling out his comm-unit. "Which ship was this?"

"Three Eight Three," Nathan stated.

"*Da, da, da.*" He typed in the appropriate access

code, and the inner hatch above him slid open, revealing a pitch-black interior. "That is strange," he said. "The lights are supposed to come on automatically when the hatch is opened."

"Hey, as long as the thing flies, that's all I care about," Nathan said as he closed the outer hatch underneath him. When he noticed that his friend wasn't moving, he asked, "What are you, afraid of the dark? Get moving."

Vladimir continued up into the pitch-black airlock compartment, and immediately started feeling his way along the bulkhead, looking for the lighting controls.

Nathan climbed up after him, pulling his sidearm and turning on its targeting light. It was a narrow, white beam that did little to illuminate the entire compartment, but it was better than complete darkness.

"The lights don't work," Vladimir announced. "Something's wrong here."

Nathan panned his targeting light from side to side when suddenly his light flashed across an angry female face charging toward him.

A bloodcurdling battle cry pierced the relative silence inside the gunship as the woman charged forward in the narrow beam of light. Nathan fired his stunner, striking the woman in the chest, causing her to stumble forward into him. He caught the full force of her weight and was nearly knocked over, but managed to sidestep and roll her off to the side.

Two more battle cries were heard. Nathan spun around, his light flashing across two more attackers, a male and a female, both young, and both of them doing their best to attack Vladimir. In the flash of his beam light, he saw Vladimir toss the female aside, then punch the skinny, young male in the face, knocking him over.

Nathan fired upward, sending three blue stunner bolts bouncing off the overhead and deck, headed aft away from the cockpit, which he preferred to keep undamaged. "Stand down! Or I shoot to kill!" he warned.

The compartment fell silent.

"*Who are you?*" a voice called from the darkness.

Nathan turned to face the bow of the ship, the direction in which the voice had come from.

Vladimir pulled his weapon, as well, and was pointing aft with the targeting light on. "I've got aft."

"Decide!" Nathan ordered.

"*Don't shoot,*" the voice begged.

"Step out where I can see you!" Nathan demanded.

Four young men and a young woman stepped out from either side of the hatch, revealing themselves in the dark cockpit on the other side.

"Turn the lights on," Nathan instructed.

"Move into the back," Vladimir instructed the man and woman who had attacked him.

"What about her?" the young woman asked.

"She'll be fine," Vladimir insisted. "She's only stunned."

Nathan watched as the young man wearing the rank insignia of a sergeant leaned over slowly and activated the lighting. The lights flickered to life, giving Nathan a better look at the five people standing in the cockpit, hands held high, scared looks on their faces. "Four strapping young men, and you send in the skinny kid and the little girl, first?" Nathan admonished.

Aiden stood in the cockpit, hands held high, the light from the intruder's weapon shining in his eyes.

"Uh, actually, we sent the chief in first. She's tougher than all of us."

"Are you the captain of this gunship?" Nathan asked.

"Uh, yeah."

"What's your name?"

"Uh, Walsh. Aiden Walsh. *Ensign* Aiden Walsh."

Nathan shined his targeting light in the young man's face. "Since none of you opened fire on us, I'm guessing you don't have any weapons. Am I right?"

"Uh, yes, sir," Aiden replied.

"Jesus, Aiden," Charnelle said. "What did you tell him that for?"

"He's going to figure it out eventually, Char," Aiden insisted.

Nathan turned off the targeting light on his stunner, lowering his weapon a bit. "I'm going to do you all a favor and let you leave."

"You are?" Kenji said in disbelief.

"Yes, but do yourselves a favor, and run *away* from all the shooting," Nathan urged. "You'll live longer."

"What about the chief?" Ali asked from the aft compartment.

"She's not going to wake up for at least an hour, I'm afraid," Nathan explained. "So, you're going to have to carry her out."

"But she's gotta weigh about..." Ali started.

"We'll take her," Aiden promised.

Nathan turned back forward. "Good call, kid."

Aiden stared at Nathan for a moment. "Oh, my God," he finally exclaimed. He looked at Kenji and Charnelle. "That's... He's..." he stuttered. He looked back at Nathan.

"Spit it out, kid," Nathan said.

"You're Nathan Scott."

Yanni stumbled nearly every other step as he and Josh ran to the next gunship in line, energy weapons fire streaking across the yard. The shots were not aimed at them, but those that missed their targets came flying across the compound, some of them ricocheting off the gunships they were attempting to steal.

"This is insane!" Yanni exclaimed as they huddled under the gunship they were to steal.

"Hurry up and get this thing open," Josh urged, squatting with his gun out, ready to defend them both.

"Why me?" Yanni wondered, not wanting to move from the little cubby he had found in the front edge of the dolly the gunship sat upon.

"Fine. You take the gun and protect us, and I'll open the hatch," Josh suggested.

Yanni wanted nothing to do with any weapons. He took the comm-unit out of his pocket, nearly dropping it as an errant energy bolt streaked past him, slamming into the dirt on the other side of the gunship. "Oh, my God!" he exclaimed, moving to enter the access codes for their ship. A moment later, the hatch slid open. "I got it! It's open!"

"Then go!" Josh urged. "Up the ladder! Quick! Before I get my ass shot off out here!"

"*Cobra Four is in,*" Loki announced over their comm-sets.

Josh looked around quickly, then headed up the ladder after Yanni. "Cobra Three is in," he reported over his comm-set as he closed the outer hatch under him.

Delta team switched to plasma pulse rifles and opened fire, sending short staccato bursts of red-orange plasma into the line of advancing marines. The deadly plasma bounced off the enemy's shields at first, but repeated impacts quickly caused the shields to overheat, making them unusable. Once they were too hot to handle, they were cast aside, leaving the pairs of marines defenseless as they scrambled to fall back to the safety of the meter-high barrier wall.

One by one, the Ghatazhak mowed the marines down, aiming for the weak points in the very same Alliance armor they had helped design years ago. Kill shots only took a single combatant out of play and left bodies on the ground that made good cover. Shots that only incapacitated took out at least two, sometimes three men, as the injured man's comrades came to his aid. As they did so, more marines came out with shields attempting to protect both the injured and the men rescuing them. It was a mistake that too many armed forces made, and it only put more of them at greater risk.

Lieutenant Commander Lazo almost felt guilty as his men picked off the marines, one by one, killing some, but incapacitating most. Finally, he had to give the order. "Check your fire! Only target those who are firing. Otherwise, fire around them to keep them falling back!" It was not the Ghatazhak way, but these were unusual times. Those marines were not truly their enemy. They were simply the unfortunate, misguided followers of a leader who had no honor, and while Toray Lazo had no problem killing them if need be, he preferred not to.

"Sir!" Ensign Bussard called from the Benakh's

communications station. “Incoming message from Geraleise Spaceport! They’ve been attacked! Their entire squadron of Super Eagles has been destroyed!”

“Wake the XO!” Lieutenant Commander Norath ordered. “Set general quarters. Launch the alert fighters.”

“General quarters, aye,” the comms officer replied as the red trim lighting around the bridge activated.

“Mister Bussard, any word from the Cobra plant?”

“No, sir,” the comms officer replied. “And I’m no longer receiving their security status signal.”

“Mister Tikodan, prepare a jump back to Koharan orbit,” the lieutenant commander continued. “Lieutenant Moratt, execute the course change and jump us as soon as the alert fighters are away.”

“Captain,” the navigator interrupted. “Without the main sensor array, we can’t be sure our jump line is clear.”

“Damn it,” the lieutenant commander swore, more because he hadn’t realized the risk he was about to take. “Ensign Vukovic, launch a recon drone along the course that Mister Tikodan gives you. Once you verify that our jump course is clear, we jump back to Kohara.”

“Aye, sir.”

“All stations report general quarters, sir,” the tactical officer reported.

“Where the hell’s the XO?” the lieutenant commander demanded. He tapped his comm-set. “Commander Ellison, Officer of the Watch. How do you copy?”

“Sir, the message from Geraleise was at least four minutes old by the time we received it,” the tactical officer reminded the lieutenant commander. “Whatever happened is already over.”

"At the spaceport, yes," Lieutenant Commander Norath agreed. "But what if that's just the start?"

"The Cobra plant?" the tactical officer guessed.

The lieutenant commander tapped his comm-set. "Security, Officer of the Watch. Send a man to the XO's quarters and get him to the bridge," he ordered firmly.

"*Immediately, sir.*"

"First four alert fighters are away," the tactical officer reported. "Next four will be launching in one minute."

"Recon drone is away, sir," the sensor officer reported. "We should get data back in a few minutes."

"Mister Bussard, anything more from the spaceport at Geraleise?" the lieutenant commander asked.

"Only that six fighters of unknown type jumped in and blew the hell out of everything. They jumped out less than a minute afterward."

"*Bridge, Security. The XO is not in his quarters, sir.*"

"Jesus," the lieutenant commander exclaimed. "If this is a drill, it's a damned good one."

"This isn't a drill, sir," the comms officer insisted. "Geraleise sent video."

The lieutenant commander spun around. "Put it up," he insisted. A moment later, video from the attack on Geraleise appeared on the view screen above the communications station, showing Super Eagles, parked on the tarmac, getting blown apart by a barrage of red-orange plasma raining down on them from above. "My God," the lieutenant commander exclaimed. "Prepare a jump comm-drone. Flash traffic for Fleet Command. Message reads: Attack on Kohara. Geraleise squadron is destroyed. Contact with Cobra plant lost. Moving to defensive position over Kohara. End message." His eyes rolled as he turned. "And please, Mister Vukovic, get our damned sensors back on line."

"Sorry, kid," Nathan said, pushing past him on his way to the cockpit. "You're mistaken."

"No, I'm sure of it," Aiden insisted. "You're Captain Nathan Scott."

"Aiden, Nathan Scott died seven years ago, in a Jung prison cell, no less," Charnelle argued.

"Yeah, I know," Aiden exclaimed. "That's what's so amazing."

"Shouldn't we be going?" Sari urged.

"There have been all kinds of conspiracy theories about his death," Aiden continued. "The Jung say he was executed, but there was no public execution as planned. Why?"

"I'm with Sari, Aiden," Kenji said. "Let's go while we still can."

"Some people say he took his own life the night before, and *that's* why there was no *public* execution."

"Captain," Sergeant Dagata pleaded.

Nathan turned around, mistakenly responding to his familiar hail, which didn't go unnoticed by Aiden.

"You see?" Aiden exclaimed, excited. "You *are* Nathan Scott, aren't you? A lot of us believed you had somehow escaped, but everyone thought we were nuts...called us crazy conspiracy theorists, like those wackos who believe the Pentaurus cluster was all an elaborate ruse to cover up why the Aurora wasn't there to protect Earth when the Jung invaded."

"The Pentaurus cluster is real," Vladimir insisted.

"Vlad..." Nathan warned.

"And we did everything we could to get back

in time," Vladimir continued, ignoring Nathan's warning. "If it wasn't for him, the Aurora wouldn't even be here, and the Earth would still belong to the Jung, just like Tau Ceti and all the other core worlds."

"I *knew* it!" Aiden exclaimed.

"Holy crap," Charnelle added, turning like everyone else to look at the famous savior of the Pentaurus cluster and the core worlds of Earth.

"You *are* Nathan Scott," Aiden proclaimed triumphantly. Then it occurred to him. "What are you doing here, on *my* gunship?"

Nathan turned to look at him. "I'm stealing it," he said, a little grin on his face. "Along with nine more, if you'll all just get the hell off *my* gunship."

"You're stealing gunships?" Kenji asked, dumbfounded. "Why?"

"Because the Alliance refuses to help the very worlds that saved their ass eight years ago, that's why," Nathan explained. "So, we have no choice but to *take* what we need in order to save our worlds ourselves."

"But, isn't *Earth* your world?" Charnelle asked.

"It was," Nathan replied. "But I had to give it up seven years ago. Now, either get the hell out of here, or strap in and shut up, because with or without you, this gunship is departing in about five minutes."

Everyone turned to leave... Everyone *except* Aiden.

"Take me with you?" Aiden asked, stepping forward.

"What?" Charnelle exclaimed, turning back around.

"Are you nuts?" Kenji asked.

"Aiden..." Sari started.

"There are twenty gunships here," Aiden told Nathan, ignoring his friends. "If you're only stealing ten of them, it's because you don't have enough pilots. Well, I'm a pilot. Hell, I've got a whole crew here! Take us all!"

"Aiden!" Kenji objected.

"Come on, Kenji," Aiden begged, turning to his friend. "Guys, let's all go. Char, Sari, you guys take Three Eight Two."

"You're being ridiculous, Aiden," Sari insisted.

"I don't know," Charnelle said, becoming intrigued.

Sari looked at Charnelle. "Are you serious?"

"Yeah, she's serious," Aiden insisted, latching onto the momentum that was building.

"I kind of think I am," Charnelle admitted.

"I don't think any of you realize what you're getting into," Nathan warned. "We're going to fight a war. A bunch of scrubs like you don't stand a chance."

"You were a scrub, and look what you've accomplished," Aiden argued. "Besides, if we stay here, we're likely going to war anyway. Either way, we're fighting the Jung in the Sol sector or in the Pentaurus sector. What's the difference?"

"*We're* not fighting the *Jung*," Nathan corrected. "We're fighting the Dusahn."

"Who are the Dusahn?" Aiden asked.

"Think Jung with jump drives."

"See, same difference," Aiden insisted.

"No, it's not," Nathan corrected. "How many gunships does the Alliance have?"

"Including the ones launching today, four hundred, I think. How many do you have?"

"Including the ten we're stealing today...ten," Nathan replied.

Aiden suddenly became very quiet. "But you have other warships, right?"

"One," Nathan replied. "The Aurora."

"What?" Aiden exclaimed. "The Aurora's an Alliance ship."

"Not anymore," Nathan replied.

"No way," Kenji said in disbelief.

"It's true," Vladimir insisted. "I should know. I'm her chief engineer."

All of them looked at Vladimir, including Nathan.

"What?" Vladimir wondered. "Nathan, we need to get going, either in this ship or another."

"If you only have the Aurora and the ten ships you're stealing now, you need every ship you can get," Aiden insisted. "You *need* two more ships. And do you have crews?"

Nathan said nothing.

"Well, I have a full crew. We can help train your other crews, if you don't have them already." Aiden spun around to look at his friends and his crew... except for Chief Benetti, who was still unconscious. "Come on, guys. This is our chance to do something *really* exciting. We'll be fighting alongside *Nathan Scott* and the *Ghatazhak*!"

"I kind of like this kid," Vladimir exclaimed. "He reminds me of you."

"I'm in," Ledge offered.

"Yes!" Aiden exclaimed.

"I'm in, as well," Charnelle said.

Aiden smiled at her. "Sari, are you going to leave your captain hanging?"

Sari sighed. "I'm in."

"I'm in, too," Ali announced.

"Dags?" Aiden asked.

"You're a certified nut job...sir."

"Is that a yes or a no, Dags?" Aiden wondered.

"Fine, I'll go... But I need to send a message to my parents, first."

Aiden looked at his best friend. "What do you say, Kenji? Want to go on a grand adventure?"

Kenji looked at Aiden. "You are the only person who would call defecting, stealing a gunship, and going off to fight a war on the other side of the galaxy, an *adventure*."

"Well, it *kinda* is," Aiden insisted. "You in?"

Kenji looked at Aiden, and then at Charnelle and Sari. "I'm in," he finally sighed.

"Yes!" Aiden exclaimed, spinning around to look at Nathan.

Nathan stood there, arms crossed and one eyebrow raised, a disapproving look on his face.

"That's, *if* you'll take us, of course," Aiden said. After a long pause, he added, "*Please*, take us..."

Nathan thought for a moment. "Vlad, how many ships did Roselle send us the codes for?"

"Holy shit!" Aiden exclaimed. "Captain Roselle's in on this?"

"All of them," Vladimir replied.

Nathan tapped his comm-set. "Strike Actual, Cobra Two Actual."

"*Go for Strike Actual,*" Telles replied.

"I've got a flight crew and an entire gunship crew volunteering to join us."

"*Specify, Two Actual,*" Telles insisted. "*Do you mean join our fight, or just fly out a couple ships for us?*"

"Does it matter?" Nathan wondered.

After a moment, the general replied, "*I suppose not. Can they be trusted?*"

"I believe so, but I can't be sure," Nathan replied. "It *is* a way to get two more gunships, though."

"*It is your call,*" the general said. "*But I will send a Ghatazhak to each ship, just to be safe.*"

"*Cobra Two Actual, Cobra One Bravo, are you sure about this?*" Jessica asked.

"Am I ever?" Nathan looked at Aiden and his friends.

"*How do we get two more gunships to cycle to the launch deck?*" Jessica asked.

"I hadn't thought of that," Nathan admitted.

"I did," Vladimir told him. "I wrote the program to cycle the first ten as planned, and then the last four ships in the last row, just in case we ended up with more pilots than we anticipated."

"Good thinking," Nathan replied.

"I also figured it would make it more difficult for them to get the ships launched to come after us, if their crews have to run all the way to the launch deck to get in. And they won't launch without someone in the pilot's seat to push the button."

"Vlad says the rest of the ships in the back row will cycle, as well," Nathan announced over his comm-set.

"*Again; your call, Two Actual,*" General Telles repeated. "*But I suggest you decide quickly. We start rolling in ninety seconds.*"

Nathan sighed. "Very well, you're in." He looked at Charnelle. "Which ship is yours?"

"Three Eight Two," Charnelle replied. "The one directly in front of us."

"One Bravo, the ship you're in belongs to one of the flight crews who are volunteering to join us," Nathan reported over his comm-set. "Do you want me to escort them to another ship, or do you want to change ships?"

"*You're kidding,*" Jessica replied.

"No, I'm not."

"*If they have to go to a different ship, they'll probably get their asses shot off before they get there,*" Jessica said. "*We'll change ships.*"

"Understood," Nathan replied. He looked at Aiden and his friends and crew. "Ladies and gentlemen, welcome to the Karuzari."

"Yes!" Aiden exclaimed triumphantly. He was the only one who seemed excited.

Nathan headed aft, passing between them. He stopped in the airlock chamber, turning back to look at them, a serious expression on his face. "I warn you, if any of you show the *slightest* sign of aggression, I will blow you out of the sky myself."

Nathan turned and headed down the ladder without another word.

"What did Jess mean by that?" Vladimir asked as he followed Nathan down the ladder. "Are *we* going to get *our* asses shot off?"

Commander Jarso skimmed the hills of Kohara as his fighter streaked toward one of eight jump missile launchers in the greater Geraleise area. Before the gunships could safely launch, those missile launchers needed to be destroyed. If even one of them was in operation, they would target the fleeing gunships before they could override the jump safeties, destroying the gunships and their crews before they escaped.

The commander kept one eye on his terrain-following sensor display, the other on his targeting systems. His auto-flight systems guided his fighter along, weaving it between hills, never flying more than thirty meters above the surface, in order to stay off the targeting sensors of the missile launchers' antiaircraft defenses. At the speed he was flying, no human would ever be able to keep the ship as low as the auto-flight systems could, and although it was not the first time the commander had flown this low, it was still a bit unnerving.

"*Raker Three, strike one,*" Lieutenant Commander Giortone reported, signaling he had taken out one of the eight launchers.

Commander Jarso resisted the urge to increase the range of his targeting sensors, knowing that doing so would allow the antiaircraft batteries to lock onto him. Instead, he rode his automated ship on its wild ride through the hills of Geraleise, weaving and bobbing along, trees and landscapes whizzing past him at blurring speeds.

"*Raker Four, strike one,*" Ensign Baylor reported.

"*Nicely done, Peanut,*" Lieutenant Commander Giortone congratulated.

Finally, just as Commander Jarso was becoming overwhelmed by the intensity of the flight, his targeting systems began to lock on to the first approaching missile launcher. At his current speed, he would be in firing range of the first battery in ten seconds, but he needed to climb.

The commander took a deep breath and pulled sharply back on his flight control stick. His fighter pitched up sharply, pushing him into his seat despite the efforts of his inertial dampeners to maintain a steady level of G-forces in his cockpit. His ship began to buffet violently as the airflow separated from the top of his wings and his fighter threatened to stall. He pushed his throttles all the way forward, powering his ship through the stall. The sudden surge of thrust sent him skyward like a missile, climbing more than a full kilometer in the blink of an eye. A split second later, he pulled his throttles back to zero thrust and deployed his air brakes. Seconds later, his ship had lost half its airspeed and was fifteen hundred meters above the ground. His threat warning systems began blaring as the sky around him filled with explosions from antiaircraft fire. He would be most vulnerable at the top of his climb, when most of his airspeed was gone and he would be leveled off as he transitioned into an attack dive. At that moment, he would be an easy target.

But Commander Jarso had other plans. He pulled his stick back hard, then manually tied in the thrusters normally used during spaceflight. The thrusters forced his tail to slide out from under him, causing him to flip over and bring his nose back down toward the antiaircraft batteries now two kilometers below him and four kilometers downrange.

His ship rocked from nearby explosions as it finished flipping over. His targeting systems lit up and he opened fire, holding the trigger for his plasma cannons down as he angled his ship ever so slightly to walk the plasma bolts onto his first target.

It was a bold and dangerous maneuver, but it was the only way to take out these two particular jump missile launchers. They had been placed at *that* location for precisely *that* reason. But it hadn't been good enough.

The first icon on his targeting screen disappeared. As antiaircraft rounds exploded all around him, the commander eased his nose off to the right, and pulled it up a bit more, bringing his ship to a forty-five-degree angle to the surface, now twenty-five hundred meters below, inverted. He pressed his trigger again, sending a stream of red-orange plasma bolts raining down on the second emplacement. The second icon disappeared.

"Raker One, strike two," Commander Jarso stated proudly. He rolled his ship over and eased his throttles forward again, adding just enough thrust to get sufficient air flowing over his wings and restore lift.

Once stable flight had been reestablished, Commander Jarso turned toward the gunship plant and jumped ahead a few kilometers to escape the antiaircraft fire, confident that his pilots would destroy the other four launchers in similar fashion.

As soon as Nathan and Vladimir had left Cobra Three Eight Three, Kenji said what was *really* on his mind. "Aiden, are you insane? You're talking about treason, here!"

"Let me explain..." Aiden begged.

"You know what they do to traitors?"

"You're not seeing the big picture here, Kenji..."

"...And as usual, *you're* not seeing the risks. And now you're dragging Char and Sari into this, too? And our crew?"

"This is a once-in-a-lifetime opportunity..." Aiden tried to explain, but Kenji wasn't hearing any of it.

"You're not thinking this through. Is *this* the sort of captain you're going to be, Aiden?"

"No, you're the one who's not thinking this through," Charnelle interrupted, coming to Aiden's defense. "Aiden's right. This *is* a once-in-a-lifetime opportunity."

Kenji looked at Charnelle, dumbfounded. "Come again?"

"Yeah, come again?" Sari agreed.

"Don't you see? These people *must* have already taken out all the local defenses, otherwise they'd never get away. And if *Roselle* is in on this, then the Benakh is likely unable to stop them, as well."

"I'm not following you, Char," Sari said.

"We're the *only* ones who *can* stop them." She looked at Aiden. "Isn't that right, Aiden?"

"Uh, exactly," Aiden agreed.

Kenji looked at Charnelle, then Aiden, then back at Charnelle. "Are you proposing we shoot them down?"

"Our ships are the first in line for the launch ramp," Charnelle explained. "Maybe we can shoot them down one by one, as they jump."

"You heard Captain Scott," Sergeant Dagata warned. "He said if we try anything, he'll shoot *us* down himself."

"Maybe we can blow up the tracks behind us as we launch," Ledge chimed in, "that way, they can't even get off the ground."

"What if they have more ships waiting in orbit?" Kenji argued. "They'd mow us down."

"Captain Scott said all they had was the Aurora, and that she was in the Pentaurus sector," Sergeant Dagata said.

"Actually, he didn't say *where* the Aurora was," Kenji corrected. "She could be in orbit right now."

"He's right," Charnelle realized.

"Would *you* be crazy enough to try and steal a bunch of gunships without a ship like the Aurora to back you up?" Kenji asked, looking at Aiden. "Jesus. Look who I'm asking."

"Then we play it by ear," Aiden decided. "We play along and launch. If the Aurora *isn't* here, and the opportunity presents itself, we take them out one by one as they jump out."

"And if we can't?" Kenji wondered.

"Then we follow them back to the Pentaurus sector."

"And do what?" Kenji asked. "Fight for the Karuzari?"

"If we have to," Aiden insisted. "At least until we figure out a way to steal the Aurora back and return her to Earth, or let Fleet Command know where she's at so they can come and get her."

"Any way you slice it, we'll be heroes," Charnelle said, trying to convince Kenji.

"Or we'll end up fighting alongside the Karuzari and be traitors," Kenji countered.

"Would you rather die as passengers in an automated pack fight?" Aiden wondered.

"There is a third option," Sari pointed out. "We could just leave. Run the opposite way from the fight."

"And where will that leave us?" Aiden asked. "What do you think Fleet Command will say? If we can figure out how to turn this into a win, they can, as well. We'll be crucified for *not* trying to stop them."

"I say we go!" Ledge exclaimed.

"Nobody asked you, Specialist," Sergeant Dagata chided.

"I'm with Ledge," Ali added.

Charnelle looked at Sari, who nodded his approval. She then looked at Aiden, who was smiling. Finally, all three of them looked at Kenji.

Kenji felt the full weight of their stares. "Surprisingly, it's not as crazy an idea as I'd first thought," Kenji admitted.

"Then, you're in?" Aiden asked.

Kenji sighed. "It doesn't appear that I have much choice. Yeah, I'm in."

"Dags?" Aiden asked.

"What the hell," the sergeant replied. "But what about Ash? She can't vote."

"Ah, she'll be fine with it," Aiden insisted.

"Or she'll kick all our asses when she wakes up," Kenji said, climbing into the copilot's seat.

"We'd better get to our ship," Charnelle said. She looked at Aiden. "Keep channel four active and scrambled, so we have secure comms between us," she suggested.

"Good idea," Aiden agreed. "And, thanks Char."

Charnelle smiled at Aiden and then turned to depart, Sari following behind her.

Josh and Yanni reached the cockpit of their gunship, quickly climbing into their seats.

Josh looked at the console, confused.

"What's wrong?" Yanni asked.

"Uh..." Josh tapped his comm-set. "Hey guys? Is it just me, or is there something different about these consoles?"

"Reactors are spinning up," Kenji reported.

"Hey, Captain," Sergeant Dagata said. "Maybe we should strap the chief into her seat, so she doesn't roll around the deck after we jump."

"Good idea..." Aiden looked out the front windows. "Three Eight Two's dolly lights just came on."

"What?" Kenji also sat up straighter to see. "Oh, shit, they're already moving. Are they even on board yet?"

Jessica crouched low, weapon held high and

ready, walking alongside the dolly for the first gunship as it rolled slowly forward.

Robert tapped her on the shoulder. "Here come the volunteers," he said.

Jessica spun around and spotted a young man and woman, both in Alliance uniforms, both sporting the rank of ensign.

The two volunteers slowed their pace as Jessica turned to watch them, likely afraid of the plasma rifle she was holding at the ready. There was a sudden jump flash to their left that lit up the area momentarily. An armed shuttle slid sideways to their right, pounding the marine barracks with weapons fire from above.

"Move your ass!" Jessica yelled at the two volunteers.

"*Cobra Seven is in,*" Lieutenant Jessup reported over Jessica's comm-set.

"Are you the volunteers?" Robert asked as Charnelle and Sari approached.

"Yes, sir," Charnelle replied, noticing the captain's insignia on the man's Alliance uniform. She also noticed the ship patch on his shoulder, and the name plate on his chest. "Captain Nash, sir?"

"That would be me, yes. You two are doing the right thing, here."

"Yes, sir," Charnelle replied. "We're trying, sir."

"We've got to go!" Jessica insisted, pushing her older brother along. She looked at Charnelle and Sari. "You try to pull any shit, and I will *end* you both!" she warned in no uncertain terms. "You got that?"

"Yes, sir!" both of them replied. They watched Jessica leave, looked at each other, and then headed up the ladder into their ship.

"What the hell are we getting ourselves into?" Sari wondered as they ascended.

The closet door in the security control room suddenly burst open, pieces of the door frame flying about as the door itself fell forward, the man who had knocked it open falling clumsily on top of the door.

Lieutenant Commander Kessler came charging out of the closet, followed by one of his guards and two technicians. "Get the system back online! NOW!" he ordered.

One of the technicians looked at the console, shaking his head. "No way, sir. The entire console is dead."

"The servers are fried," the other technician reported from the other side of the room. "They must have set off some type of charge in the racks."

"Can you fix it?" the lieutenant commander demanded.

"Sure, but it will take a few weeks."

Lieutenant Commander Kessler looked out the windows at the firefight going on in the gunship yard. He also noticed that gunship Three Eight Three was moving. "They're trying to steal the gunships!" He looked at the two technicians. "We've got to do something!"

"We might be able to send signals to the weapons towers," one of the technicians suggested. "Maybe trigger them to go into independent mode?"

"What will that do?" the lieutenant commander asked.

"If they're running independently, we can transmit targeting commands."

"Can you have them target the gunships?"

"Yeah, but..."

"Do it!" the lieutenant commander ordered.

"I cannot believe this is happening," Sari said as he climbed into the copilot's seat of Cobra Three Eight Two.

"How quickly can you spin up the reactors?" Charnelle asked.

Sari looked at his console. "They're already spinning up," he said, surprised.

"They must have already started prepping for launch," Charnelle realized.

The ship lurched suddenly, its motion apparently stopping. Just as suddenly, it started moving again but to the side instead.

Charnelle looked at Sari. "We're headed for the launch deck." She immediately started working furiously. "We *really* need to get ready."

Nathan crouched next to gunship eleven's dolly, looking left and right as Vladimir entered the access codes into the ventral hatch control pad. Straight ahead and on the other side of the first row of gunships, the ones they were not planning on stealing, the Ghatazhak strike teams were holding the marines at bay, buying them time to get the gunships away. To his left, he could see Robert and Jessica opening the ventral hatch to gunship ten, and to his right he could see General Telles and Master Sergeant Anwar entering gunship twelve.

"*Cobra One is in...again,*" Jessica announced over their comm-sets.

"Twelve gunships," Nathan said. "Twelve. You know what we can do with a dozen gunships?"

"*Cobra Nine is in,*" Master Sergeant Todd reported.

"We don't have them yet, my friend," Vladimir said as the hatch opened.

"But we will shortly," Nathan muttered. He tapped his comm-set as he headed up the ladder after Vladimir. "Cobra Two is in."

Four Ghatazhak charged across the gunship yard as the firefight raged behind them. A flash of blue-white light illuminated the area as another ship jumped in overhead, followed a split second later by a clap of thunder.

"*Bulldog One is on the attack,*" the copilot's voice reported calmly.

Heavy weapons fire erupted from the cargo jump shuttle's starboard door gun and the aft gun on her open cargo ramp. She drifted across the yard slowly, pummeling the marine line and sending them back for cover, allowing the Ghatazhak still on the firing line to maintain their positions until the gunships could get moving.

Lieutenant Commander Lazo was the first of the two pairs of Ghatazhak to reach their assigned gunship, quickly entering the access code, provided to everyone by Captain Roselle, and getting the hatch open.

To his right, between Lazo and Roselle's gunships, General Telles's new executive officer, Commander Kellen, was just getting to his gunship, crouching low while Master Sergeant Willem entered the access codes.

Lazo didn't wait to see if they gained access. Master Sergeant Todd already had their hatch open and was headed up into the gunship, and Lazo followed.

"We're moving," Aiden said as the ship lurched forward slightly.

"Is Three Eight Two even out of the way yet?" Kenji wondered.

"It doesn't look like it, does it," Aiden said. "Dags, can you tell if we're going to clear Three Eight Two?"

"Sensors don't work very well on the ground, sir," the sergeant replied, coming forward to look out the window. "That isn't standard speed."

"What are you talking about?" Aiden wondered.

"These things are supposed to crawl their way to the launch ramp. They're moving a lot faster than a crawl."

"He's right." Kenji agreed.

"*Hey, the ship next to us is moving,*" Ledge reported over comm-sets. "*Aren't they supposed to wait until we're already on the main track before they pull out?*"

"Apparently not," Aiden said. "These guys aren't messing around, are they?"

The interior of the cockpit suddenly flashed repeatedly with blue-white light in a staccato, non-rhythmic fashion as muffled claps of thunder were heard in the distance.

"What the..." Aiden started as he looked outside and saw eight Super Eagles streak overhead, firing at the area of the gunship yard between the first row of gunships and the buildings. Explosions ensued, spreading reddish-yellow flashes of light across the yard and into their cockpit.

"Shit," Aiden exclaimed.

"They're going to shoot at *us*, too, Aiden!" Kenji exclaimed.

"We'll try to hail them and tell them we're friendlies!" Aiden insisted.

"You really think they're going to believe us?"

"At least try!" Aiden insisted. The ship suddenly stopped moving with a jolt, then started moving to the left. Aiden looked out the left window, his eyes widening as he saw Cobra Three Eight Two no more than a few meters away from them. "Jesus!" he exclaimed, nearly climbing out of his seat. "We really shouldn't be this close!"

"*Aiden! Do you copy?*" Charnelle called over comms.

"Yeah! I copy! Jesus, Char! We're really close together!"

"*Go secure!*"

"Oh, yeah." Aiden activated the comm-scrambler. "We're secure!"

"*Aiden, one of those Ghatazhak just boarded us! We tried locking him out, but it didn't do any good. He's coming up the ladder now. I'm not going to be able to help you!*" After a pause, she added. "*I'm sorry. Good luck.*"

Aiden just stared straight ahead, dumbfounded.

"What are we going to do?" Kenji wondered.

"*There are a couple of those Ghatazhak headed for us, Captain,*" Ledge warned.

"I can change the access codes on the outer hatch," Sergeant Dagata said, moving to the systems console where the unconscious Chief Benetti was strapped in.

"No," Aiden ordered.

"Aiden..." Kenji started to object.

"If they think we're trying to double-cross them, they might do something to Char and Sari."

"*They're moving under us,*" Ledge warned.

"We play along," Aiden insisted, "for now."

Sergeant Torwell swung his turret around as he

continued firing at the Super Eagle fighters who had just jumped in behind them. "What the fuck, guys? Are we gonna jump out of here or what?"

"I'm trying to lead them away from the gunships," Commander Kainan replied over comm-sets. *"Just keep firing!"*

"No problem there, Skipper!" the sergeant replied. "No fucking problem at all."

The combat jump shuttle jinked hard right, then back left, changing its altitude just as drastically as bolts of plasma and rail gun fire from the attacking Super Eagles streaked past them on all sides.

The ship shuddered as rail gun fire slammed into it, walking across the top, just in front of Sergeant Torwell's gun turret, piercing the hull and passing out the bottom.

"That was too fucking close, guys!" the sergeant exclaimed.

"Our hull's breached!" Lieutenant Latfee reported. *"We're going to be suits only all the way home."*

"For three days?" Sergeant Torwell complained. "Fuck that! I can patch us up!" Several more rail gun rounds slammed into the hull just behind the sergeant. "But not if you keep letting them punch holes in us! I've only got so many patches!"

"Raker Flight, Leader!" Commander Jarso called over comms. *"Engage and destroy all Super Eagles!"*

"Oh, yeah!" Sergeant Torwell exclaimed.

"NOW we can jump," Commander Kainan announced as the jump energy washed over their hull.

"These are Cobra-D gunships," Roselle explained to Josh over comms. *"Didn't you guys train on the new interfaces?"*

"I thought they weren't going in until they started production on the four hundred group," Vladimir defended.

"How the hell do I start up the reactors?" Josh demanded. "We're already moving, here!"

"Calm down, kid!" Roselle insisted. *"The layout is basically the same. But instead of having a crap load of separate physical consoles, you just tap the button for the section you want, and it appears below the button. You can call up any screen you want, on any console you want. Reactor controls, weapons, sensors, flight systems...whatever."*

"How do you know all this?" Josh wondered as he started pushing the buttons along the top of the console directly in front of him. "I thought you were a battleship captain."

"I spent nearly twenty years in the scout ships these things are based on, remember? I sorta kept up, for old times' sake."

"Thank God," Josh muttered as he began to get the hang of it.

"Did you figure it out?" Yanni asked.

"Yeah, I think so," Josh said as he continued changing screens. "This is actually kinda cool." Finally, he found the reactor control screen. "Got it. Starting up the reactors."

"Will they be ready in time?" Yanni wondered.

"I sure fucking hope so," Josh replied as he reached over to the center console and started cycling through screens there, as well.

Sergeant Dagata sat at his station just behind Cobra Three Eight Three's cockpit, wide-eyed, staring at the armor-clad Ghatazhak soldier as he stepped from the center airlock compartment onto the flight deck. The soldier carried a complex and menacing-looking rifle with three barrels, as well as an assortment of grenades attached to his body armor at easily accessible locations.

The Ghatazhak soldier's visor rose, revealing the face behind it. "I am Corporal Chesen, of the Ghatazhak. I am here to ensure your cooperation."

"Well, I am *Sergeant* Dagata," the sergeant began.

Corporal Chesen looked at the uppity, young sergeant, raising a disapproving eyebrow.

"Uh...no problem, Corporal. We're on your side."

"That is good to hear," the corporal replied. "We can use all the help we can get."

The corporal continued forward to the cockpit. Sergeant Dagata watched as he passed by.

"*Is he in?*" Ledge asked over comm-sets.

"Uh, yeah."

"*What's he like?*"

"Uh...not as big as I expected?" the sergeant replied. "But *definitely* scary."

"*Put your flight systems and dynamics on the console in front of you, weapons and sensors in the center, and power and propulsion on the right,*" Robert suggested over comms. "*That way, you can see everything you need to keep an eye on, and then just call up whatever you need to control on the center console.*"

"Is everyone supposed to be moving at the same time?" Nathan asked as he started their gunship's reactors.

"The first eight had to be layered in, because they were on opposite rows," Vladimir explained. "But the last six all move forward at the same time."

"Isn't that going to put more time between launches for the last of us?"

"Trust me, Nathan. I know what I'm doing."

"Of course," Nathan agreed as he continued working on setting up his console.

"*Be warned,*" Commander Ellison stated over comms, "*stay at least ten kilometers away from the Benakh. Her main sensor array is down, and she'll be blind beyond that. Her big guns and missiles will be useless without the main array, but her point-defenses each have their own targeting sensors. Get closer than ten clicks, and she'll own you.*"

"Good to know," Nathan replied. "Hey, kid," he called over comms. "The guy that volunteered everyone. Did you copy all that?"

"*Three Eight Three, affirmative,*" Aiden replied.

"*Three Eight Two, we copied, as well,*" Charnelle replied.

"*Strike Actual, Raker Leader,*" Commander Jarso called over comms. "*Eight more Super Eagles just jumped in. We now have a total of twelve bandits in the air. If you can put some people in your gun turrets, it would sure help.*"

"Vlad?" Nathan said.

"Are you okay by yourself?"

"I'm good," Nathan assured him. "The launch sequence is all automated anyway. Go."

"*Raker Leader, Strike Actual. Understood,*" General Telles replied. "*Strike Actual to all Cobras. Put whomever you have available in your gun turrets, and target those Super Eagles.*"

"*Those Super Eagles aren't trying to kill us,*" Commander Ellison insisted, "*they're trying to scare us.*"

"How can you be sure of that?" Nathan asked.

"*No way Norath is going to authorize blowing up Alliance assets without orders,*" Martin replied. "*The kid doesn't have the balls. But if we start shooting at them, he may grow a pair.*"

"*We have no choice,*" General Telles stated. "*Shoot them down.*"

"*He's right, Marty,*" Gil agreed. "*The minute the first gunship gets to the launch deck, those Super Eagles will shoot to kill. It's standing orders. No jump-equipped ship is allowed to fall into enemy hands. For all they know, we're Jung operatives.*"

"Uh, guys," Aiden called over his comm-set. "You have to target those Super Eagles."

"*What?*" Ali exclaimed from her turret on the starboard side.

"*You want us to shoot down friendlies?*" Ledge asked from the port turret. "*Captain, we can't do that.*"

Kenji grabbed Aiden's right arm to get his attention. "Aiden, stealing a gunship and going to help fight a war on the other side of the galaxy is one thing, but shooting at our own people?"

"I know, but..."

"We might *know* some of those pilots," Sergeant Dagata pointed out.

"Gentlemen," Corporal Chesen began, "I understand your hesitation, but if you do not defend yourselves, your comrades *will* kill you...*without* hesitation. Of this I am certain."

"He's right," Aiden said. He looked at Kenji. "I don't like it any more than you do, guys. But those Super Eagles are no longer friendlies, and *I'm* going to fight them. If you want to live, you'll all fight them, too."

Ledge sat in his turret, staring at the targeting display on his turret control pedestal. His mind was racing. He hadn't anticipated this. None of them had. And he wasn't sure he could do it. He looked to his left, spotting Sari climbing into the starboard turret of Cobra Three Eight Two, not more than six meters away, as both ships rolled along the tracks toward the launch platform in unison. Sari locked eyes with him, exchanging a painful look. He was feeling the same way as Ledge, only he was still doing what had to be done to survive.

Ledge watched as Sari strapped himself in and swung his turret around to face aft, his barrels rising toward the sky in preparation to defend his ship. "Let's do it," Ledge said, grabbing his control yoke and bringing his weapon around, as well. He looked to Sari, who nodded at him, and Ledge nodded back.

Nathan quickly called up his gunship's point-defenses. A quick look at his available weapons display told him that he had eight double-barreled energy pulse cannons; four on top and four on the bottom. He selected all four top point-defense turrets, locking onto the nearest attacking Super Eagle and authorizing the system to attack it and all similar targets. But every time he tried to do so, the system rejected his commands. "What the hell is wrong with this system?" he complained. He tapped his comm-set. "Roselle! Why can't I assign Super Eagles as targets to engage on the point-defense weapons?"

"*Automated systems won't accept friendlies as targets,*" Gil replied. "*You'd have to hack the code to circumvent it.*"

"Shit."

"Strike Actual to all ground forces," General Telles called over comms as he set up the consoles in his gunship. "Begin falling back to gunships eight through twelve. Bulldog One, begin ground suppression fire to cover their withdrawal."

"*Bulldog One, understood.*"

"The first Ghatazhak to get to their gunships, man the gunship turrets and target the Super Eagles."

"*Bulldog One, starting our attack run.*"

"*Strike Actual, Combat One,*" Lieutenant Latfee called over the general's comm-set. "*We can come in behind Bulldog One and provide additional cover fire.*"

"Combat One, Strike Actual. Approved," the general replied, continuing his preparations.

Sari fired his plasma cannons repeatedly, doing his best to keep his gun sights on the Super Eagle that was diving on him and firing. Red-orange energy bolts slammed into the ground around him and into his gunship's shields, rocking the ship on its dolly as it rolled toward the launch deck.

The diving Super Eagle exploded, passing over him and crashing into the downhill side of the base compound. Sari felt a sudden wave of exhilaration surge over him, replaced a second later by a feeling of guilt for taking the life of someone who might very well be from his own world.

"*We're almost to the launch deck,*" Charnelle warned over Sari's comm-set. "*I have to retract the turrets.*"

"Understood," Sari replied solemnly, swinging his turret around to face forward. As he unbuckled his restraints, he looked to his right at Ledge in the port turret of Cobra Three Eight Three next to him, firing away in his own battle with attacking Super Eagles. He hoped the young man wouldn't have to wrestle with the same guilt he currently felt.

Charnelle glanced out the window to her left as the two-kilometer-long, downhill launch track slid toward her. "Cobra Three Eight Two is approaching launch position," she reported over comms.

"*Three Eight Two, Cobra Two, did you receive the override codes I transmitted?*" Vladimir asked. "*You will need them to override your initial jump restrictions and escape the system.*"

Charnelle looked to Sari, who nodded. "Three Eight Two, we have them."

"*Three Eight Two, Strike Actual. Immediate launch, no delay. Do you understand?*"

"Three Eight Two, affirmative," she replied.

The launch track slid from the left into the center of her forward window, and her gunship stopped moving. Three seconds later, a green light appeared on her launch status display, indicating the movement dolly her gunship rode on had disengaged its motors and was ready to roll freely down the launch track.

Ensign Charnelle Tegg had spent two years in the Cetian Alliance Academy and another four months in the Cobra flight school, preparing for this very moment. Never in a million years had she expected it to go this way.

All she had to do now was press the button.

* * *

"Do we still have a track on the Mirai?" Admiral Galiardi asked his staff in the Alliance Command Center.

"No, sir," Admiral Cheggis replied. "We lost her

about three jumps out. She had to have changed course several times for us to lose her track, though."

"So, they were *trying* to shake us," Galiardi observed.

"Undoubtedly," Admiral Cheggis agreed. "But what does the Mirai have to do with the attack on Kohara? There have been no sightings of the Mirai anywhere near the Tau Ceti system."

"A surprise visit from Deliza Ta'Akar?" Galiardi began. "Doctor Sorenson and her family are abducted on the very day the Mirai departs? And now an attempt to steal gunships? Tell me that's a coincidence, Kyle."

"It could very well be," Admiral Cheggis insisted. "Or, two or more of the incidents could be connected. But for all we know, the Jung took Doctor Sorenson."

"The only Jung left on Earth are sitting in cells in Winnipeg," Galiardi insisted.

"It *could* be the Jung trying to steal our gunships," Admiral Cheggis added. "The Cetians have never been very good at detecting spies."

Admiral Galiardi sighed, his face a study of concentration. "Dispatch two squadrons of gunships to Tau Ceti, with orders to destroy any gunships that manage to launch from the plant on Kohara, and pursue any that get away." He looked at Admiral Cheggis. "And they'd better *not* get away."

"Yes, sir."

"And tell Roselle to dispatch two of his quick-response marine units to the Koharan Cobra plant to take control of the situation."

"Roselle isn't aboard the Benakh, Admiral," Admiral Cheggis said. "He was *at* the plant on Kohara doing a surprise security inspection when the attack started."

"What about his XO?"

"They can't find him," Admiral Cheggis said. "Lieutenant Commander Norath's in command."

Admiral Galiardi looked at Admiral Cheggis. "Coincidence, huh?" The admiral sighed again. "Tell whoever is in command of the Benakh to *stop* whatever the hell is happening on Kohara dead in its tracks. Not a single gunship gets out of the Tau Ceti system!"

"Admiral, there's no way those ships can jump *out* of the system. We have safety protocols, security codes...all to *prevent* such a thing from happening."

"And yet, it's happening as we speak, isn't it, Kyle?" Admiral Galiardi said, losing his patience. "Not a single gunship! I don't care if he has to blow up the whole damned plant to stop them!"

"Yes, sir," Admiral Cheggis agreed.

"And find the damned Mirai while you're at it!"

CHAPTER FOURTEEN

"*Cobra Three Eight Two is rolling,*" Charnelle reported.

Aiden and Kenji both looked out the windows as Charnelle's gunship began to roll slowly down the hill. Once it began to pick up speed, their own ship started to move again, continuing left to the launch deck.

"*Cobra on the launch deck, Raker Five!*" Ensign Hebron called over comms. "*Two bandits on your six high. I'm moving in for the shot. Open fire and shake them up before they get a clear shot at you.*"

"Ledge; Ali!" Aiden called out.

"*I'm on it!*" Ledge answered from the port gun turret.

"*Swinging aft!*" Ali added from starboard.

The launch tracks moved into the center of their forward windows, and their ship came to an abrupt stop.

"Three Eight Three is on deck," Aiden announced.

"*I can't get an angle on them,*" Ledge exclaimed. "*We need to extend!*"

"Not during launch!" Kenji insisted. "It's too dangerous!"

Commander Jarso pulled his fighter into a tight, descending left turn, rolling out and jumping in a fluid motion. In an instant, the view outside changed from clear dawn skies and rolling farmland to the Cobra production plant; complete with explosions, energy weapons fire, and a sky full of Super Eagles looking to tear apart the row of closely spaced, slowly moving gunships crawling along the surface on their way to the launch track.

"Raker Five, engaging two!" Ensign Hebron reported.

The commander glanced at his tactical display, then out the window to his left. "Five, Leader! Two bandits dropping into your six! Take the shot and jump!"

"Five, fi..."

There was a fireball in front of Commander Jarso, about a kilometer away, where Raker Five had just been. The explosion caused the two Super Eagles the ensign had been attacking to roll out in opposite directions, forcing them off the attack run on the Cobra gunship parked on the launch deck. The commander's targeting systems flashed, and he pressed his cannon trigger. Red-orange plasma bolts shot out, striking the lead Super Eagle that had just killed one of his men. The second Super Eagle turned toward the commander, looking to line up a shot of his own.

Commander Jarso waited just long enough to lure the Super Eagle far enough away from the Cobra launch track that he wouldn't be able to change his mind and attack the surface targets. As soon as the Alliance fighter lined up, the commander pitched up and jumped five kilometers ahead, immediately bringing his fighter into another tight turn to head back to the Cobra plant.

"Five is down, hard," Ensign Dakus reported. *"Moving in to protect the launch slot."*

The mission was a mere fifteen minutes old, and he had already lost one pilot.

Cobra Three Eight Two rocked and swayed as it

continued to pick up speed. Charnelle scanned her console displays as they approached the bottom of the downhill portion of their launch roll. Their reactors were at full power, their propulsion and maneuvering systems were ready, and the automated launch sequencer showed ready and was monitoring their progress along their launch roll. All she had to do was sit back and enjoy the ride, at least until they got to orbit.

"*Three Eight Three, start your roll now!*" Nathan ordered over the comms.

"*But the track isn't clear yet!*" Aiden argued.

"*It will be by the time you get to the bottom of the hill! Now get going!*"

"Char!" Sari exclaimed as they entered the short, level portion of the launch track, just before it started to pitch up to put them on a skyward trajectory. "The towers!"

"*Three Eight Three is rolling,*" Aiden announced.

Charnelle looked at the towers streaking past them as they started the uphill portion of their launch run. The automated weapons turrets at the top of the towers were moving, and they were swinging around to take aim at her. "Leader! Three Eight Two! The weapons towers are active!" she reported as her ship rode off the end of the track.

The rocking and swaying suddenly stopped as the gunship became airborne. There was a sudden clunk, and what sounded like several tiny explosions under their hull, as their launch dolly disconnected and was pushed downward toward the approaching recovery lake. A split second later, their windows turned opaque, and the gunship's auto-launch sequencer triggered their jump to orbit.

"She made it!" Aiden exclaimed, reaching over and shaking Kenji by the shoulder.

"*Three Eight Three! Target the towers! Target the towers!*" Nathan instructed.

"*Hey, Captain...*" Ledge started.

"Shoot the weapons towers! Shoot them now!" Aiden instructed as he looked out the forward windows and saw the nearest weapons atop their towers turning to take aim on them as they rolled down the track, picking up speed.

Aiden's eyes widened as the weapons at the top of the approaching towers on either side of the tracks brought their barrels to bear on them. Before they could fire, streaks of red-orange plasma streaked forward from behind them, from both port and starboard, slamming into the menacing weapons, blowing them apart.

Two Alliance shuttles jumped in just above the gunship yard, one on each side of gunship row. They descended quickly, touching down only long enough to deploy two teams of quick-response marines. Men jumped out of the sides of the shuttles, five at a time, two waves each, deploying a total of twenty armor-clad soldiers from each specially-designed shuttle.

The marines deployed in choreographed fashion, the first wave of men holding blast shields, the next tucking in behind them to one side, the third to the other. They spread out in formations, extending further out toward the fence line to improve their firing angles on the enemy tucked in beside the moving gunships.

The fourth wave of soldiers carried much larger weapons, powered by packs on their backs. Each of them dropped to one knee, after which legs telescoped out from their weapons, followed by blast shields that deployed around the weapon itself, thereby shielding the soldier.

These larger weapons were the first to open fire, sending rapid-fire streams of bright-orange plasma bolts toward the moving gunships.

Ghatazhak soldiers scurried under the moving gunships as they rolled toward the launch deck. While some fired on the newly arrived marines, others climbed up the gunships' ventral access hatches, scrambling to quickly reach the gun turrets to defend against the attacking Super Eagles.

Three Ghatazhak soldiers climbed up into the airlock compartment of Nathan's gunship.

"Permission to come aboard, sir," Corporal Estabol joked, leaning forward into the flight deck.

"Permission granted," Nathan replied. "Would you mind getting on those guns, fellas?"

"We'll get right on it, sir," the corporal assured him, turning to head down the access tube to the port gun turret.

Several energy bolts slammed into the top of their hull, just forward of the windows, ricocheting up and over their heads, causing both Nathan and Vladimir to duck.

"Christ!" Nathan exclaimed. "What the hell are they shooting?"

"HFR personal assault weapons," Vladimir explained, flinching as another round glanced off the side of the ship, causing it to shake slightly. "High fire rate, high power, their own automatically deployed tripods and shields. Very deadly."

"Can they hurt us?"

"Yes, if they score several direct hits in a critical area. And they *know* where those areas are, trust me."

"Corporal, can you guys get a firing angle on those HFRs?" Nathan asked over his comm-set.

"*Negative sir,*" the corporal replied. "*Only Cobra Ten's starboard turret can engage them, and I don't think it's manned just yet.*"

"I hope someone gets in there soon."

"*Cobra Line, Raker Two!*" Ensign Viorol called. "*Four bandits coming in low, treetop level, from your six. Suggest all guns engage!*"

"*We're on it!*" the corporal assured Nathan.

"Can we use our plasma torpedo cannons while we're on the ground?" Nathan wondered.

"Yes, but we can't really aim, and there's a city in that direction, about twenty kilometers. We might blow the hell out of it," Vladimir warned.

"*Cobra Three is rolling,*" Josh's voice announced over comms.

Nathan looked out the windows, leaning forward to see to his left. He could barely make out Josh's gunship at the far end of the line as it started rolling slowly off the launch deck and down the tracks.

"*There are three more weapons towers on your side,*" Josh explained over comm-sets as Yanni climbed into the gun turret and sat in the gunner's chair. "*You have to take them out before they take us out!*"

"No pressure, no pressure, no pressure," Yanni kept repeating to himself as he tried to figure out how to power up the plasma cannon that he was practically straddling. He tried not to look outside, but he was surrounded by a clear bubble, and the ground was passing under him at an ever-increasing rate, which wasn't helping. "Ah," he exclaimed, finding the power switch. The weapon began to hum, and the entire apparatus pitched up and swung outward when he grabbed the control yoke with both hands to hold on. He quickly fastened his restraints, then grabbed hold of the yoke again.

"*Start shooting, Yanni!*" Josh insisted. "*The first tower is coming up!*"

"I'm working on it!" Yanni pulled the yoke back, twisting it to the left. The weapon pitched up and left, but too far left. He brought it back down and right.

"*Would you fire already!*" Josh pleaded as they picked up speed.

Yanni glanced up and saw the first weapons tower, the turret at the top swinging around to take aim at them. He pressed the firing trigger and held it. His cannon began spitting out red-orange bolts of plasma that slammed into the ground just ahead of them. He struggled to get the weapon to come up and slightly left again, intending to shoot the weapons turret. Instead, his plasma bolts struck the base of the tower, causing it to fall toward the tracks...and them.

"*Oh, shit!*" Josh exclaimed.

Yanni didn't let go of the trigger as he continued to try controlling his plasma cannon. The tower was falling right toward them, and he was certain it was going to hit their gunship, at the very least derailing them, possibly even destroying them.

As the tower fell, it passed right through Yanni's plasma bolt barrage, blowing it apart just before it hit their ship. Burning debris bounced harmlessly off their hull.

"*Hell, yes!*" Josh exclaimed. "*Do the same thing to the two at the...*"

Yanni flinched at the deafening sound of an explosion to his left as the inside of his turret lit up. He looked to his left as the nose section of a Raker bounced off the ground, its fuselage a burning broken hulk behind it, headed straight for him.

As Yanni instinctively raised his hands in front of his face to shield himself, he caught a glimpse of the pilot, a look of horror on the officer's face as he met his fate.

"Yanni!" Deliza screamed in horror from the cockpit of Cobra Four.

"Cobra Four...rolling," Loki announced, calmly. Josh and Yanni's ship was already half a kilometer away, too far for them to see exactly what happened, but it didn't look good. "Josh?"

"Oh, my God," Deliza exclaimed in shock as she saw debris spreading across the top of Josh and Yanni's gunship down the hill ahead of them.

"Josh!" Loki called again. "Strike, Cobra Three is hit, but they still appear to be rolling."

"*Cobra Three, Cobra Two,*" Nathan called. "*How do you copy?*"

Loki tried to stay calm. He didn't know if Josh and Yanni were alive or dead, nor did he know if their ship would be able to jump or even clear the end of the launch ramp and make it to the recovery lake beyond. The only thing he did know was that he needed to be ready for anything.

"*Combat One, Strike Actual. Do you have a clear visual on Cobra Three? They're approaching the bottom of the hill on the launch roll,*" General Telles said.

Lieutenant Latfee tapped the controls on the side of his helmet, causing his visor to magnify. He looked to his right, spotting the rolling gunship. "Affirmative. Cobra Three is still at speed. She'll clear the ramp."

"*Damage report,*" the general requested.

"Cobra Three's starboard turret is obliterated, and it looks like she's got hull damage just aft of her turret. She's leaking propellant, and it's burning. Her slip stream is the only thing keeping the fire from igniting her starboard propellant tank."

"Sarge!" Commander Kainan called. "Two more weapons towers at the end of the run. I'll drop down and take the one on the left, you take the one on the right!"

"*Got it,*" Sergeant Torwell replied.

"*Cobra Three,*" Nathan continued to call. "*Talk to me, Josh!*"

"*We've got to raise shields!*" Jessica insisted over comms. "*We're getting pounded!*"

"Can we do that on the ground?" Nathan asked Vladimir, as their gunship continued to roll in line toward the launch deck.

"I don't know," Vladimir admitted, throwing up his hands. "They were not designed to be used in contact with the surface. The energy may damage the tracks."

"General, Vlad says the shields may damage the tracks," Nathan warned over comms.

"*These tracks are designed to take direct plasma hits!*" Gil said. "*The most the shields are going to do is fuck up the grass......and maybe set the launch deck on fire!"*

"No choice," the general decided. "Strike Leader to all Ghatazhak. Get under the gunships so they can raise their shields. All gunships, cycle the appropriate shields off and back on as they pass over the launch deck."

"Seems like we should've thought of that beforehand," Vladimir commented as he reached for the shield controls.

Ghatazhak soldiers crept under the gunships, crouched low, staying close to the dollies, to use them as cover as they returned fire against the advancing marines. Energy weapons fire streaked back and forth, slamming into buildings, the ground, and the gunships themselves.

Two Ghatazhak soldiers fell to enemy fire and were helped to the access ladders and up into the gunships.

Suddenly, the enemy weapons fire began bouncing off invisible shields, causing the barriers to shimmer in reds and oranges as the enemy weapons fire slammed into them. The grass sizzled and burnt as the shields of the moving gunships slid across them, creating an acrid smoke that wafted about within the shielded area under the gunships and beyond.

Now protected, the Ghatazhak soldiers clinging to the cover of the moving dollies were able to move out into better firing positions. They immediately found strategic points along the inner perimeter of the shields, being careful to stay in unison with the movement of the gunships, firing away at the enemy, preventing them from advancing any further than they already had.

Aiden braced himself as their gunship started up the launch ramp at the end of the run, their ship vibrating and swaying as it sped up toward their final destination. He was finally going to get there... outer space.

The last two towers at the end of the run disappeared in fiery explosions, his gunners yelling triumphantly.

Aiden glanced at Kenji, "Here we go!"

The gunship rolled off the end of the launch ramp, the vibrations stopping suddenly as they became airborne. The mooring clamps on the dolly beneath them automatically released their hold on the underside of their hull, and their separation thrusters fired their brief charges in unison, causing the dolly to fall quickly away from Cobra Three Eight Three.

Aiden felt his pulse quicken. He held his breath as his ship's momentum carried it skyward. Then, their windows turned opaque, and their auto-launch sequencer triggered their jump.

A moment later, their windows cleared, revealing the black, starry background of outer space.

"Oh, my God!" Aiden exclaimed.

Alarms started sounding, ones he hadn't expected.

"Multiple contacts!" Sergeant Dagata called from the sensor station behind them.

"Where?" Aiden asked.

"Everywhere!" the sergeant replied.

"*Three Eight Three, Three Eight Two!*" Sari called over comms. "*Break left and go to full power! You have three Super Eagles diving on you from your three o'clock high!*"

"*I've got them in sight!*" Ledge announced.

"Four more to port!" Sergeant Dagata reported. "Below us, ten kilometers and closing fast."

"Powering up," Aiden said as he pushed the throttles to full power.

"*Extend us!*" Ali pleaded.

"Extending the turrets!" Kenji announced. He glanced at the threat display. "Char's got six chasing her, Aiden. She's maneuvering wildly."

"She doesn't have any gunners," Aiden realized. He yanked his flight control stick hard to the right. "We're coming to help you, Char!"

"Enter the override codes for the jump drive!" Corporal Chesen insisted as he unbuckled Chief Benetti's restraints and pulled her unconscious body out of her seat with one hand, dropping her unceremoniously on the deck. He took her seat and started punching commands into her workstation, scrolling through various screens as he searched for something.

Josh shook his head, dazed by the blow that nearly derailed his gunship. Regaining his wits, he quickly scanned his primary systems. Jump drive, auto-launch sequencer, propulsion...everything was still in order, except... *A hull breach!*

"*Cobra Three,*" Nathan called. "*Talk to me, Josh!*"

Josh tapped his comm-set as he unfastened his restraints and quickly climbed out of his seat, running aft. "I'm here!" he replied as he jumped through the open hatchway into the airlock compartment and turned right. The view took him aback for a moment.

"*Can you still jump?*" Nathan asked.

"Yeah!" he replied over the roar of the air rushing in through the torn-open starboard side. "Auto-sequencer is running! All primary flight systems are…"

At the end of the access tunnel to the starboard gun turret, the entire side had been torn away by the impact. The turret was gone, and the hull and supports were torn and twisted. The air rushed in through the breach, howling in through the access tunnel. "Yanni," Josh said solemnly, realizing that he was gone. He was about to close the inner hatch, when he saw a hand reaching up onto the floor of the access tunnel…*from outside the ship.*

Josh's eyes widened. He glanced forward, seeing that they were starting up the launch ramp. He only had seconds. Josh jumped into the tunnel and crawled quickly to the end. "I gotcha!" he yelled over the roar of rushing air as he grabbed Yanni's hand. He twisted himself around and placed both his feet against the bent, twisted metal and pulled as hard as he could, dragging Yanni's bloodied body up into the access tunnel. "Come on!" he yelled as he felt the ship's pitch change, realizing they were heading up the launch ramp. "We gotta move!"

Josh grabbed Yanni by the back of his jacket collar, half dragging him as both men clumsily crawled back toward the airlock compartment at the inboard end of the access tunnel. Josh fell through the hatch, into the airlock compartment, just as the motion of the ship stopped.

We're airborne.

There was a metallic clunk, followed by several simultaneous explosions outside. Josh spun around and grabbed Yanni, just as the access tunnel filled with brilliant blue-white light.

The blue-white light disappeared a split second later, and the compartment began to explosively decompress, the outboard end of the access tunnel open to space. Josh pulled on Yanni with all his might, determined not to allow either of them to get sucked out into the void, but the suction was too great, and the best he could do was maintain their position and not slide out any further.

Josh breathed out slowly, trying to get as much pressure out of his lungs as possible as the pressure inside the compartment approached zero. Yanni was limp, most likely unconscious either from his injuries, lack of oxygen, or both. But Josh refused to let go, not even to save himself.

Finally, just as he feared he would lose hold, the pressure reached zero, and the suction faded away. His breath now completely expelled from his lungs, Josh pulled Yanni the rest of the way into the airlock compartment, his friend's body falling in a limp pile on the deck. Josh could feel the cold encircling his entire body, his fingers rapidly becoming numb. Barely able to maintain consciousness, Josh stumbled over to the hatch and swung it closed. He twisted the handle to lock it, then slapped his hand clumsily on the pressurization control pad next to the hatch, collapsing to the floor himself as precious oxygen began to return to the compartment.

"*Three Eight Three, Cobra Two!*" Nathan called over comms. "*Did Cobra Three make it?*"

"I've got them," Sergeant Dagata reported. "They just jumped in, but they're not accelerating. They haven't lit their mains yet. They're drifting! They're already losing altitude! They'll hit the atmosphere in a few minutes, at the most!"

"We have Cobra Three!" Aiden replied over comms. "But they're adrift and losing altitude fast!"

"I've got a pair of bandits coming over, Ali!" Ledge reported as he and Ali continued to ward off the attacking Super Eagles.

"I'm coming around to cover them," Aiden decided. "Char, you get your jump drive overridden yet?"

"*We just got it online!*" she replied. "*We're good to go!*"

"Then get the hell out of here!"

"*To where?*"

"Corporal Anson will know," Corporal Chesen told Aiden.

"Your Ghatazhak dude should know," Aiden told Charnelle. "For now, just jump anywhere! Anywhere but here!"

"*Copy that,*" Charnelle replied. "*We'll see you there!*"

"I've almost got the safeties on your point-defenses overridden," Corporal Chesen announced.

"My what?"

"The safeties that prevent your automated weapons from targeting friendly ships," the corporal explained.

"You can do that?" Sergeant Dagata asked.

"Of course," the corporal replied. "I am Ghatazhak."

Cobra Four's windows cleared as they completed their launch jump from the surface of Kohara into low orbit. Alarms immediately sounded, and Loki yanked the flight control stick, putting the gunship into a roll to avoid a collision with Cobra Three, which was tumbling end over end in front of him.

"Oh, my God!" Deliza exclaimed, watching the out-of-control gunship that her husband was on.

"Josh!" Loki yelled. "You still with us?" Loki

waited for a response as he fired up his engines to accelerate in order to hold orbit.

"*Cobra Four, Cobra Three Eight Three!*" Aiden called over comms. "*We're coming in over the top of you to fly cover. There are at least six Super Eagles inbound, and we have full weapons capability, including point-defenses. Get your jump drive working and get the hell out of here! We'll cover Cobra Three!*"

"Copy that, Three Eight Three." Loki looked at Deliza. "Do as he says."

Deliza wiped the tears from her eyes as she started typing in the long code string to override the jump drive lockout that prevented their escape.

"*Cobra Three is firing thrusters!*" Aiden announced over comms. "*They're coming out of their roll.*"

"Please tell me it isn't designed to do that automatically!" Loki replied.

"*I fucking hate auto-flight, and you know it,*" Josh declared over comms.

"Josh! You're alive!" Loki yelled.

"*No shit.*"

"Is Yanni alive?" Deliza asked, almost afraid of what the answer might be.

"*He's still breathin', princess,*" Josh replied. "*He's gonna need a whopping dose of nanites as soon as we get to the Tavi, though. So am I, for that matter.*"

"Get your engines burning, Josh," Loki advised. "You're only ninety seconds from atmospheric interface."

"*I'm on it,*" Josh replied.

"*I've got them, Four,*" Aiden insisted. "*Get the hell out of here!*"

"Copy that," Loki replied. "See you at the Tavi, Josh."

"*Four is down! Raker Four is down hard, no chute!*"

"Damn it!" Commander Jarso cursed to himself. He had just lost his third pilot, and in only five minutes time. Now there were only three of them left, and there were still six more gunships to launch.

"All Rakers, jump to rally point Echo Two and form up on me. We're going to attack as a three-ship element from now on."

Gil watched Martin's gunship roll down the tracks as his own ship moved sideways to line up with the launch rails.

"*Four more bandits, inbound from the south,*" Lieutenant Latfee reported from Combat One, which was jumping about, acting as an aerial surveillance platform, while providing air support.

"Port gunner, swing south," Gil ordered.

"*On it,*" the Ghatazhak soldier in Cobra Six's port gun turret replied.

The tracks moved into the center of the windows, and the gunship's sideways motion stopped. Gil scanned his displays one last time, then pressed the launch button on his console. The motors in the dolly that carried his gunship applied power one last time. The nose of his gunship came down as they rolled over the lip of the launch deck. The dolly's motors disengaged, and they began to free-roll down the hill. "Cobra Six is rolling," he announced over comms.

"*Cobra Five! New bandits! Four just jumped in from the east! Dead ahead! One click! On the horizon!*" Lieutenant Latfee warned from Combat One.

"I see them," Sergeant Notoni said, pointing out the forward windows.

Commander Ellison glanced up, barely able to make out the approaching fighters against the lightening pre-dawn sky. "We're coming to transition."

"Torken, Deplaz! You got'em?" the sergeant asked.

Sergeant Torken swung his plasma cannon turret around to face forward, adjusting the weapons pitch to lock onto the approaching fighters as they opened fire. He pressed his trigger and held it down, sending a barrage of red-orange plasma bolts skyward toward the targets. The enemy fire walked along the ground of the level transition area right up to the gunship, pounding her shields and causing them to flash red-orange as they absorbed the incoming energy. Sparks began to fly from shield emitters along the hull in front of the sergeant's gun turret, and the shield in front of him disappeared.

All the sergeant saw was red and orange, and finally black.

"Port shields are gone!" Sergeant Notoni reported. Red-orange plasma continued to vault skyward from their starboard side as the Super Eagles ahead of them continued with their diving barrage. The ship shook as their shields took a pounding under the bombardment from all four attacking fighters. "We're losing dorsal shields, as well!"

"We're losing speed!" Commander Ellison warned. "I'm going to try to override and fire maneuvering thrusters to give us a..."

A deafening blast drowned everything out, and a blast of air slammed into his face. Pain everywhere... Face, eyes, arms, chest... So much pain he couldn't focus... His vision was blurry, and the noise and the wind were overpowering.

"*Marty!*" a voice called.

Martin struggled to open his eyes, but the wind and the blood made it difficult. From what little he could see, the entire cockpit was open to the outside, all the way back to the airlock compartment. Twisted metal surrounded him. Warning lights were flashing on what was left of his consoles. He looked at Sergeant Notoni. His head and the right half of his torso were gone, the remainder of his armored body limp and lifeless.

"*Marty! Are you there?*"

Martin looked forward again, his eyes squinting against the wind in his face. They were starting up the ramp, but they were slowing down...*rapidly.*

"Marty! Are you there?" Gil called over comms as his gunship continued picking up speed down the launch rails.

"They're not going to make it," Sergeant Ayers warned from the copilot's seat. "They're losing speed too quickly."

The same barrage of red-orange plasma that had devoured Cobra Five was walking its way up the hill toward Gil's gunship. His gunners were tracking the attacking Super Eagles, firing away with everything they had.

An explosion appeared at the opposite end of the barrage. "*I got one!*" Sergeant Morano exclaimed.

"Marty! Can you jump?" Gil called in desperation.

"*Strike Leader, Cobra Seven is holding!*"

"*Negative!*" General Telles insisted. "*Start your roll!*"

"*Gil,*" a weak voice called over his comm-set.

"*Cobra Seven is rolling.*"

"Marty!" Gil yelled. "Can you jump?"

"Oh, my God," Sergeant Ayers exclaimed. "They're coming to a stop, and they're not even at the top."

"Marty! You have to jump, now!"

The overhead shields continued to flash red-orange as enemy plasma bolts pounded them relentlessly. Three blue-white flashes appeared to their right, without warning.

"*Rakers! Fire at will!*"

Plasma bolts fired by the Rakers diving in from the south slammed into the fighters directly ahead of Cobra Five, tearing them apart, sending burning hunks of debris spreading down and forward along the targets' path of flight.

"*Cobra Five, Strike Actual,*" General Telles called, his voice calm as usual. "*Charge torpedo cannons and prepare to take the shot.*"

"Marty!" Gil cried out, his voice becoming more desperate.

"*Gil!*" Nathan urged. "*You have to take the shot!*"

"NO!"

"*Don't let me be the one who causes everyone's death, Gil,*" Martin's weak voice begged. "*Take the shot.*"

Gil was silent. Chunks of destroyed Super Eagles rained down upon them, bouncing off their shields.

"Charging plasma torpedo cannons," Sergeant Ayers said, his tone solemn.

Gil looked out the forward windows as their gunship entered the transition stretch and leveled off. At the other end of the level run, the burning hulk of Cobra Five was rolling toward them.

"Plasma torpedo cannons are charged and ready," the sergeant reported. He looked at Gil. "I can take the shot, sir. You don't have to."

Gil closed his eyes and swallowed. "No. I'll do it,"

he said, his voice trembling as he reached for the flight controls. He opened his eyes again, looking straight ahead at the burning wreckage rolling toward them. "Goodbye, Marty," he whispered, pushing the fire button.

As their gunship rolled in line toward the launch deck, their shields flashing with each incoming blast from the Alliance Marines, Robert and Jessica witnessed the destruction of Cobra Five, more than a kilometer away. Neither of them said a word, both of them feeling the pain that Gil Roselle had to be experiencing at that moment.

Gil and Sergeant Ayers kept their eyes straight ahead, holding on tight as they slammed through the fireball and wreckage they had just created. The ship shook violently, pieces of the destroyed gunship that had carried his friend bouncing off their shields. Burning propellant and plasma energy spilled across their shields, illuminating them in brilliant reds, oranges, and yellows. Their ship bucked, pitching to starboard as if they were about to come off the rails, but then settled back down with a thud a second later.

They broke through into the clear and started up the ramp. Sergeant Ayers looked down at his displays. "We lost some speed," he warned. "We'll make it to the top, but if we jump short of orbit..."

"We'll make it," Gil stated calmly. He reached down and tapped several items on his display, then fired his forward translation thrusters, accelerating them up the ramp.

A few seconds later, the shaking stopped as their gunship ran off the end of the ramp, becoming airborne. A metallic clunk from underneath and the concussion of the separation thrusters announced their dolly dropping away, headed toward the recovery lake below.

Gil glanced down at the auto-launch sequencer as it read zero, and their windows turned opaque.

"*Cobra Six is in orbit!*" Sergeant Ayer's voice reported over comms.

"Yes!" Vladimir exclaimed from the copilot's seat of Cobra Two.

"*Mains are burning!*" the sergeant added.

"*Cobra Eight is rolling,*" Commander Kellen reported.

"*I'm hit!*" one of the Raker pilots cried out.

"*Two is hit!*" another voice reported. "*Raker Two is hit!*"

"*Two! Punch out!*" Commander Jarso ordered.

"*I...*"

"*Two is down hard!*"

Nathan looked up, his attention drawn by a massive explosion as Raker Two plowed into a parked propellant truck. "How much propellant do we have?" he asked, an idea coming to him.

"We're fully loaded," Vladimir assured him.

"Cobra One, Cobra Two," Nathan called over comms. "How much propellant are you carrying?"

"*We're topped off, why?*" Jessica asked.

"Cobra Nine, propellant status?" Nathan continued.

"*All tanks are full,*" Lieutenant Commander Lazo replied.

"Cobra Ten?"

"*Also topped off,*" General Telles, the last crewed gunship in the line, answered.

"Vlad, if one gunship stops moving, what happens to the one up track?" Nathan asked.

"It stops, as well," Vladimir replied.

"General, have your starboard gunner shoot the dolly on gunship thirteen, the one next to you. We need it, and the gunship beyond it, to stop moving," Nathan explained as a blue-white jump flash appeared in the distance just beyond the ramp nearly two kilometers away.

"*Those gunships are acting as barriers between us and those marines,*" the general argued.

"It's not the marines that are killing us, General. Our shields can handle anything they can throw at us. It's those Super Eagles! We're down to two Rakers! If any more Alliance fighters show up, the rest of us won't make it out of here!"

"*Cobra Seven is in orbit!*" Lieutenant Jessup reported over comms.

"I'm receiving the weapons safeties override code from Corporal Chesen," Sergeant Ayers told Gil. "I can have our point-defenses up in less than a minute."

"Good," Gil replied, turning his ship around to help defend the others.

"*Cobra Seven, Three Eight Three,*" Kenji called over comms. "*You've got three Super Eagles on your six!*"

"*Cobra Seven, I can't maneuver yet! I don't have enough speed!*"

"Use your thrusters and spin around to bring your plasma cannons on them!" Gil instructed. "You damned Ghatazhak may be able to fight, but you sure can't fly!" he grumbled to Sergeant Ayers.

"*Cobra Seven is taking fire!*" Lieutenant Jessup reported. "*We're taking...*"

"*Cobra Seven's aft shields are down!*" Kenji reported.

"*Three Eight Three is turning toward you, Seven, we'll be in firing range in one minute!*" Aiden assured them.

"They don't have one minute!" Gil yelled to no one in particular.

"Seven is breaking up," Sergeant Ayers reported solemnly.

"Goddamn it!" Gil burst out. "Three Eight Three! Fly that thing like a jump fighter, not a gunship!"

The Ghatazhak corporal in Cobra Ten's starboard gun turret swung his plasma cannon around to starboard, lowering it until he was lined up directly with the base of the motorized dolly that was carrying the next gunship in line. He pressed the trigger, firing several shots into the dolly. The entire gunship shook, coming to an abrupt stop as its dolly shutdown.

"Gunship thirteen is stopped," the Ghatazhak sergeant reported.

"*The last two gunships are no longer moving,*" General Telles reported, looking out his starboard window and seeing the distance between his gunship and gunship thirteen increasing.

"*Strike Actual, Cobra Six,*" Gil called over comms. "*Six gunships just arrived. They're going to try to ambush you once you reach orbit. Three Eight Three and myself will try to keep them busy while you enter the jump drive override codes and make your escape.*"

"*Cobra Nine is rolling,*" Lieutenant Commander Lazo announced.

"That means more fighters will be headed our way," the general realized. "Strike Actual to all gunners, more fighters will be arriving any moment. Stand ready to defend."

"More?" Jessica quipped from her position in the copilot's seat of Cobra One. "When did they *stop* coming?"

Robert just shook his head. Things weren't going as well as they'd hoped.

"Why can't we enter the override codes now?" Jessica asked.

"We can't take the chance," Robert explained. "It might screw up the auto-launch program."

"Can't we launch manually?"

"Gil and I could," Robert said, "but the others don't have the training. Not in gunships, anyway. It's too risky."

"Riskier than getting ambushed by Alliance gunships as we come out of the launch jump?" Jessica shook her head. "We *really* didn't think this through well enough."

"It's the best we could come up with on short notice," Robert defended.

"*Cobra Eight is in orbit!*" Commander Kellen reported.

"Four more to go, and we can all head home," Robert added, trying to ease the tension.

"How the hell are we supposed to take on six gunships?" Kenji asked over comms. "We've barely finished basic flight!"

"*Those gunships will be using auto-swarm!*" Gil

told him. "*You studied the auto-swarm patterns, didn't you?*"

"Only how to initiate them," Aiden argued as he pulled his gunship into another tight turn and rolled it to port, avoiding incoming fire from the last of the Super Eagles flying cover, while the rest of the fighters departed.

"*But you know the patterns, right?*" Gil said.

"Well, yeah, but..."

"*Then just anticipate! When you recognize one of their swarm patterns, get yourself one step ahead and ambush them as they come out of post-attack escape jumps to make their turn!*"

Aiden looked at Kenji. "I can do that," he realized. He keyed his comm-set. "I can do that!" he assured Gil.

Gil looked at Sergeant Ayers. "Jesus, I'd fucking hope so." He looked at the threat display. "Okay kid, your last fighter just jumped away. Your six is clear. Join up on me so those gunships will make a run at us. When they do, be quick on the jump and get the hell out. You won't be able to survive more than two, maybe three, rounds from their plasma torpedo cannons before your shields collapse, so you've only got maybe five seconds to recognize their attack pattern and jump out. As soon as you do, change course and jump to their turning point. Each ship will be alone at that point, so they'll be more vulnerable. And screw that rapid-fire stuff. One shot from each cannon, full power, simultaneously. Wait to see if their shields fail, and if they do, make the kill shot. If not, jump the hell out and join up back at the rally point for another try. We can probably sucker them through this three, maybe four, times if we're lucky. After that, they're going to be on to us. But with any luck, everyone will be in orbit by then, and we can hightail it out of this fucking system! Understood?"

There was a pause.

"*Uh, yeah,*" Aiden replied. "*Just one thing though. Where's the rally point?*"

"Right fucking here, kid," Gil replied.

"*I've got six more jump flashes to the north!*" Lieutenant Latfee reported. "*Two clicks! Moving fast!*"

"Come on, come on," Robert pleaded as their gunship moved slowly into launch position at the head of the launch track.

"*Raker Six, take them from the south!*" Commander Jarso instructed. "*I'll come in from the west, a little high!*"

"*Got it, One,*" Ensign Dakus replied.

Jessica glanced out her window, noticing something. In the distance, she could see a squad of Alliance Marines running down the hill from the landing pad near the security building, toward the launch track...and they were carrying something. "Strike Actual, Cobra One Bravo. Marines moving down the hill from the security building, toward the launch tracks. I think they mean to blow the tracks!"

"*I thought these tracks were designed to be indestructible,*" Nathan said over comms.

"They're shielded against plasma blasts, but not against demolitions," Robert replied. "If they're carrying compound one five seven, or HV twenty-eight, we're fucked!"

"*Combat One, Strike Actual,*" General Telles called. "*Engage the marines on the hill moving from point sierra one toward the launch track. Do not let them reach the launch tracks.*"

"*Combat One, moving in,*" Lieutenant Latfee replied.

The tracks came into position at the center of their windows, just as the combat jump shuttle jumped in low to their left and began strafing the marines on the hill to their right. Their gunship stopped moving, and a second later, Robert pressed the auto-launch button.

Jessica looked out her window again as Combat One's side-mounted plasma cannons tore the marines apart as the shuttle passed in front of them.

"Cobra One is rolling," Robert announced. He turned to Jessica. "Finally."

"Jump flashes, high left," Aiden said, noticing them out his window.

"Two high right," Kenji added. "Delta Seven or Delta Seven Bravo."

Aiden's mind raced. If they were using swarm-pattern Delta Seven, then the next two would jump in from directly ahead and slightly below their flight path, expecting him to pass over them and get a clear shot at his ventral side. But if they were using Delta Seven Bravo, the next two would jump in directly ahead of him, forcing him to either pitch up or pitch down. Either way, they'd be shooting at his weaker ventral or dorsal shields, instead of his stronger forward shields.

"Torpedo cannons from either side, high," Sergeant Dagata warned.

Seconds later, their shields flashed red-orange as the Alliance gunships' plasma torpedoes struck their shields.

"Port and starboard shields at fifty percent!" Corporal Chesen reported, having assumed the engineer's station in lieu of the still unconscious Chief Benetti.

Aiden was betting on Bravo.

He pushed the translation thrusters, firing the ones on top of his ship, pushing the gunship downward. The thrusters fired for several seconds, pushing them down enough that the next round of plasma torpedoes passed over them from both right and left.

Two more jump flashes appeared directly in front of them as the last two gunships jumped in to complete the swarm maneuver.

"Another contact!" Sergeant Dagata reported excitedly. "Directly overhead! It's Cobra Six!"

"*I've got a bead on the two headed to your three!*" Captain Roselle announced. "*Take the ones in front of you!*"

Fly it like a jump fighter.

The words echoed in Aiden's mind. He glanced at the threat display, noting the range to the two gunships directly in front of him, and selected the same as his jump distance. He tapped the escape jump button as he pulled his flight control stick back, bringing his gunship's nose up and over past vertical as they jumped. He released the stick as they came out of the jump, looking out the forward windows as the two ships passed over him. As his gunship's nose came over onto the fleeing targets, he pushed his stick in the opposite direction to stop his pitching motion and fired his plasma torpedo cannons at full power.

"Left target has lost aft shields!" Sergeant Dagata

reported. "Right target's aft shields are down to twenty percent."

Aiden's next shot was at the left target; four plasma torpedoes in his unshielded stern, taking him apart.

"The right target can't jump!" the sergeant reported. "Cobra Six is in his way!"

Aiden adjusted his ship's attitude as he coasted away from the fleeing gunship to track it while it tried to turn to a clear jump line. He fired again; four torpedoes at full power. Two of them destroyed the target's aft shields; the other two blew the target apart. A split second later, he tapped his escape jump button for a standard escape jump.

Kenji looked at Aiden. "How the hell did you know?"

"They were doing a frontal attack," Aiden replied. "Procedure dictates that forward shields receive most of the power, aft shields receive the least. So, I hit them where they were least protected."

"*You're* quoting *procedure*?" Kenji said, dumbfounded.

Eight Super Eagles jumped in directly in front of Cobra Nine, only half a kilometer away. They opened fire immediately after jumping in, striking the rolling gunship repeatedly as it reached the bottom of the hill. Within seconds, the gunship's shields were overwhelmed and failed, and the front of the ship came apart.

With half its front gone, the gunship's center of gravity was well aft of the dolly, causing it to tip backward. The mortally wounded gunship, and its dolly, continued along the level transition portion of the launch run and up the ramp, the aft end of the gunship dragging on the tracks, sending up a wave of sparks as metal ground against metal.

Ensign Dakus jumped in behind the last two gunships, less than a kilometer away.

"*Combat One is hit!*" Lieutenant Latfee cried out. "*We're going down!*"

The ensign's targeting display lit up with eight targets directly ahead of him, closing extremely fast. He pressed his cannon trigger, holding it down as he yawed slightly left and right. Immediately, two icons disappeared, and another two jumped...but the rest kept coming.

He glanced up just in time to see four Super Eagles directly in front of him. He rolled his fighter onto its side, hoping to pass between two of the ships, but clipped one of them, instead. His ship began to tumble wildly, alarms going off all over his console. "Six is hit!" he called out as he reached for his ejection handles. "I'm going..."

He never got to punch out.

"Get out of the bubble, Sarge!" Lieutenant Latfee ordered as the combat shuttle spun out of control on its way down.

Sergeant Torwell quickly unbuckled himself and hit the release on his seat, allowing himself to slide back down into the main cabin of the combat shuttle. "Hold it together, sir!" he said as he fell onto the cabin floor.

"I'm trying!" Commander Kainan assured them.

Nathan looked out the windows as the spinning combat jump shuttle passed overhead, nearly hitting them, crashing onto the downhill slope on the other side of the launch deck, just as Cobra Two lined up to the launch rails and pulled to a stop. "Oh, my God," he exclaimed. A huge explosion from the right rocked their ship. Both Nathan and Vlad looked to starboard and saw pieces of General Telles's gunship spewing in all directions, and smoke and fire spewing from his opposite side.

"*Bozhe moi*!" Vladimir exclaimed.

Nathan pressed the auto-launch button and their gunship started rolling forward. "Cobra Two is rolling!"

"Cobra Ten! Cobra Two! Are you okay?" Vladimir called over comms.

"*Nine is hit!*" Jessica reported from further down the launch tracks. "*She's dragging! I don't know if they're going to make it off the ramp!*"

"Take the shot!" Nathan insisted.

"*Cobra Ten is still alive!*" General Telles reported.

"Can you still jump?" Vladimir asked. "How are propulsion and maneuvering?"

"*Yes!*" the general replied. "*But our starboard turret is gone! We won't be able to take out the last two gunships to cover our escape!*"

"*Raker One is hit!*" Commander Jarso reported. "*I'm sorry, General. There's too many of them! I'll try to put it into gunships to...*"

"Jesus!" Nathan exclaimed as Raker One plowed into the hillside only fifty meters to their right, just short of gunships thirteen and fourteen.

Alarms sounded inside the battered cockpit of Combat One as it lay on its right side, slightly downhill.

Commander Kainan shook his head several times, trying to get his wits about him. Finally, he came to his senses. "Everyone alright?" he barked. He released his restraints, bracing himself so he wouldn't fall onto his copilot below him, who was just starting to move. "Latfee! You still with me?"

"Yeah, I'm with you."

"Can you move?" the commander asked as he pulled the window eject lever in the overhead console.

The front windows of the combat shuttle popped out, landing a few meters away.

"What kind of a fucked-up landing was that?" Sergeant Torwell asked from the back.

"Sarge! Can you move?" the commander asked.

"Yeah, I can move. It hurts like hell, but I can move."

"Then move your ass out of here. Ten is rolling up to the launch deck right now, and that's the last ride off this rock!"

"Right behind you, sir," the sergeant replied.

"I've got nothing!" Jessica insisted as she studied her displays. "It must have been damaged by one of about a hundred hits we've taken in the last five minutes!" She looked at her brother as they headed up the ramp. "The plasma cannons are dead." She turned and looked forward. Ahead of them, what was left of Cobra Nine was reaching the top of the ramp, barely moving, sparks still flying from its dragging tail. As they grew closer, the ship came to a stop, teetering on the top edge of the ramp. As they approached, it fell flat, its dolly going over the end of the ramp. The weight of the dolly pulled on the wreckage, pulling its stern upward, blocking their view of the sky. Finally, what was left of Cobra Nine went over the end of the ramp, clearing the way for them.

Then it exploded.

Both Robert and Jessica threw up their hands to protect themselves as their doomed ship plowed into the massive fireball erupting before them.

"Oh, no," Nathan said as they rolled down the ramp, headed for the transition section at the bottom of the hill. "They didn't make it."

"Maybe they..." Vladimir started, but then stopped, not wanting to give his friend false hopes.

"I didn't see a jump flash," Nathan said. "Did you?"

"*Nyet,*" Vladimir admitted. His head and eyes dropped. "*Nyet.*"

"*Cobra Two, did you see Cobra One jump?*" General Telles asked anxiously.

"Negative, sir," Nathan replied.

"Gunners," Vladimir called, noticing new contacts on the threat display. "Bandits! *Bozhe moi*! They are everywhere!"

"We're not going to make it, Vlad," Nathan admitted.

"You do not know that, Nathan!"

Nathan just looked at him as the six Super Eagles directly ahead of them opened fire.

"*Cobra Two, did you see Cobra One jump?*" the general asked anxiously.

"*Negative, sir,*" Captain Scott replied.

Aiden looked at Kenji. "Did they make it?"

"It's hard to tell, Aiden. There are so many damned gunships flying around, and not all of them are squawking transponders."

"How bad is it down there, Dags?" Aiden asked his sensor operator behind him.

"They've got Super Eagles everywhere, Aiden, and it looks like another QRT shuttle just landed. They'll get picked off on their launch rolls, just like the others."

Aiden looked at his navigational display. He had just come about to jump back to the rally point, to sucker more gunships into Captain Roselle's trap. Kohara was directly ahead, and Geraleise was just passing over the planet's horizon.

Aiden looked at Kenji and smiled. "I have an idea."

General Telles looked out the forward window as his gunship came to a stop, directly in line with the launch tracks. Ahead of him, Nathan's gunship was taking a beating from Super Eagles coming in from all directions. From the looks of things, he doubted very much that Cobra Two's shields would hold out long enough for them to get away, and their own shields were weak at best. He looked at his copilot. "It's been an honor, Deno."

"The honor has been mine, Lucius."

"Shall we get this over with?" the general said, reaching for the auto-launch button.

"*Cobra on the launch deck!*" Commander Kainan called over the comms, his voice scratchy and broken. "*This is Kainan! We're coming up the hill to your left. Don't leave just yet!*"

General Telles leaned forward, straining to see to his left, spotting three men in flight suits running up the hill toward them. "Move your ass, gentlemen!" the general replied.

"Our shields are down to twenty percent!" Vladimir warned as plasma bolts from the attacking Super Eagles continued to pound their front and dorsal shields as they headed up the launch ramp. "Fifteen percent!" Vladimir looked at the forward camera display. "*Bozhe moi*! The end of the ramp is damaged! We'll derail!"

More plasma bolts slammed into their shields.

"Five percent!"

A blue-white flash appeared behind the Super Eagles bearing down on them. "What, more fighters?" Nathan exclaimed as he brought up the mains.

"Shields are gone!" Vladimir exclaimed. He looked at the threat display as Nathan brought the main engines up. "That is not a fighter..." He looked at Nathan. "It's a gunship!"

Cobra Three Eight Three passed over the recovery lake just as Cobra Two fired her main engines, blasted through the broken end of the ramp tracks, and disappeared in a blue-white flash. The Super Eagles that had been bearing down on the launch complex were forced to break off their attack, turning away to the left and right and jumping to safety.

Four plasma torpedoes leapt from the barrels under the nose of the gunship as it fell toward the surface. They sped ahead of the gunship at incredible speed, slamming into gunships thirteen and fourteen, still sitting on the transfer rails about one hundred meters from the launch deck.

Both gunships exploded, their full propellant tanks igniting into a massive fireball that rose triumphantly skyward, spreading out in all directions.

Tossed about by the shock wave of the explosion, Super Eagles still on their attack runs were forced to either pitch up or turn away, all of them eventually jumping out of the area in order to survive.

The shock wave from the exploding gunships nearly knocked them off their feet but, underneath Cobra Ten, the crew of Combat One still managed to scramble up the ladder into the access tunnel above.

Master Sergeant Anwar quickly scrolled between the underside camera view and the one in the ventral access tunnel, making sure that all three crewmen from Combat One were safely inside. "Now," he finally said.

General Telles pushed the button and initiated the auto-launch sequence. "Cobra Ten is rolling," he reported as he watched Cobra Three Eight Three glide toward the expanding fireball to their right.

Aiden's eyes widened in fear as their forward windows filled with the rising fireball of burning propellant. The ship shook violently as it passed through the expanding fireball.

Aiden reached for the jump button, but when they came out the other side of the fireball, he saw nothing but the ground rushing up at them.

"I'm sorry, guys," Aiden said softly, just before their ship struck the surface of Kohara.

After several seconds with his eyes closed, Nathan realized they were not dead, after all. When he finally opened them, he saw the stars once again.

"*Move your ass, Cobra Two!*" Jessica warned. "*You've got three gunships on your six!*"

"JESS!" Nathan yelled, overjoyed.

"*Get those codes entered, and let's get the hell out of here!*" she added. "*Did Telles make it?*"

Nathan looked at Vladimir.

"I'm on it," Vladimir insisted as he typed in the long override code.

"He should be right behind me!" Nathan answered, pushing his ship into a diving right turn to avoid the plasma torpedoes headed his way.

"*Anyone see Three Eight Three?*" Gil asked.

"They passed over us as we launched," Nathan replied.

"*WHAT?*" Gil said, shocked.

"*Cobra Ten, in orbit,*" General Telles announced, with his usual lack of emotion. "*And we have the crew of Combat One with us.*"

"*Get your jump drives overridden and head for the rally point!*" Gil instructed. "*There are at least twenty damned gunships in the area, and there's no telling which way they'll attack from next!*"

Nathan looked at Vladimir and smiled.

"Jump drive is overridden and ready for use," Vladimir reported.

"Then, let's get the hell out of here," Nathan said.

CHAPTER FIFTEEN

Nathan put the last case of supplies into the storage locker on Cobra Two. It had taken them three hours to complete their evasion algorithms before joining up with the Morsiko-Tavi at the departure rally point.

Once they had arrived, the gunships had docked with the Tavi three at a time, transferring their wounded to the Tavi's sick bay, and accepting provisions needed to get home, should one of them become inadvertently separated from the group.

"Is that it?" he asked Vladimir.

"That is the last one," Vladimir replied.

"I have to get back to Cobra One," Jessica said. "Robert and I have a lot of catching up to do."

"Well, it will take us nearly a week to limp back to the fleet together," Nathan said. "That should give you plenty of time."

"I'll see you guys at the first layover point," she told them, before stepping down into the ventral access hatch tunnel.

Nathan and Vladimir watched her float down the weightless tunnel, disappearing into the Morsiko-Tavi's docking hub joining Cobras One, Two, and Ten to their host.

Vladimir swung the hatch down onto the deck and locked it closed, then followed Nathan forward to the gunship's cockpit. After climbing into his seat, he looked at Nathan and said, "You really didn't think we were going to make it, did you?"

Nathan thought for a moment and then looked at his friend. "You know, for the first time, I didn't. I really didn't." Nathan checked his displays, making sure the ship was ready to separate from the Tavi. "Actually, it was the second time. I didn't think I was going to make it out of that Jung prison cell, either," he corrected. "We ready?"

Vladimir checked his displays. "Outer ventral hatch is secure. We're good to go."

"Morsiko-Tavi, Cobra Two, ready to separate," Nathan called over comms.

"*Cobra Two, Morsiko-Tavi. You are cleared for separation.*"

Nathan reached down and pulled the docking release lever on the side of the center console, releasing the docking clamps that held them to the Morsiko-Tavi's docking port. "Thrusting away," he said as he fired the ventral separation thrusters.

Nathan guided the gunship away from the Morsiko-Tavi, letting his ship slowly drift. They were not due to depart for another hour, as there were still two more gunships that needed to be provisioned, and engineers from the Tavi were still effecting repairs to the hull breaches on Cobras Three and Ten.

Nathan stared at the stars as they drifted clear of the Tavi. "Earth is out there," he sighed. "Someday, I hope I can return... I mean, *really* return."

"I never did ask you how your reunion with your sister and father went," Vladimir said.

"It went well," Nathan said. After a moment, he added, "I have to admit, it was a bit emotional for all of us. I've never seen my father cry. Not even when my mother died." Nathan was silent for a moment. "Honestly, I felt guilty for all that he's been through. Losing two sons, a wife...and everything he's had to deal with since I left. I never realized what an incredibly strong man he was—and *still* is, even at his age."

"You're a lot like him," Vladimir commented.

Nathan smiled. "You know, there was a time when I would have punched someone for saying that."

"It was a compliment, you know."

"I know," Nathan replied. "*Now*, I know."

"I've got a contact," Vladimir said. "It's a jump flash." He suddenly became concerned, studying the contact data more closely. "I think it's a gunship."

"Morsiko-Tavi, Cobra Two," Nathan called over comms. "Can you verify a contact at one five seven, by two five one; three hundred thousand kilometers out? We think we're seeing a gunship. Can you confirm?"

"Should I charge weapons?" Vladimir asked.

"Not a bad idea," Nathan agreed. "Cobra One, are you picking up the contact?"

"*Affirmative,*" Robert replied.

"*Cobra Two, Tavi. Contact confirmed. Unknown gunship. One five seven, by two five one, at three hundred thousand kilometers and closing fast.*"

"*Tavi, Cobra One, requesting immediate separation,*" Jessica called.

"*Cobra One, Tavi, go for sep.*"

Nathan powered up Cobra Two's main drive and started turning toward the unknown gunship. "I'll take him head on, Robert. You jump in from his starboard side and high."

"*If we see him, he sees us,*" Robert advised. "*Jump in to him immediately, beat him to firing.*"

"We haven't even identified this guy, yet," Nathan reminded him.

"*He can't be a friendly, Nathan,*" Jessica warned.

Nathan brought his ship onto an intercept course, checked his systems and weapons, then triggered an intercept jump. A split second later, when his windows cleared, they found themselves looking at a *very* battered gunship. "What the hell?"

"*Don't shoot!*" someone begged over comms.

"Identify yourself, or we will open fire," Nathan warned.

"*This is Cobra Three Eight Three, Captain Aiden Walsh. Is that you, Captain Scott?*"

Nathan looked at Vladimir, his mouth agape. "I don't believe it." He keyed his comms again. "I thought you guys slammed into the ground on Kohara and died. How the *hell* are you still alive?"

"*I'm as surprised as you are, sir,*" Aiden replied. "*Who knew gunships bounced?*"

Nathan started laughing. "Are you guys alright? Is anyone injured?"

"*No sir,*" Aiden replied. "*But we had to restrain Chief Benetti. She's a bit pissed.*"

"Yeah, I'll bet," Nathan laughed.

Thank you for reading this story.
(*A review would be greatly appreciated!*)

COMING SOON

Episode 6
of
The Frontiers Saga:
Rogue Castes

Visit us online at
frontierssaga.com
or on Facebook

Want to be notified when
new episodes are published?
Join our mailing list!
frontierssaga.com/mailinglist

Made in the USA
Las Vegas, NV
26 July 2022

52179266R00268